I0699193

# CORPO AGE

BY
R. B. CAT

# CORPO AGE

Copyright © 2024 R. B. Cat

All rights reserved.

The characters and events portrayed in this book are fictitious. Any similarities to real persons, living or dead, are coincidental and not intended by the author.



979-8-88993-034-1

Written by R. B. Cat
Edited by Joi Massat

Published 2025 by MoonQuill
www.moonquill.com

# TABLE OF CONTENTS

# PROLOGUE

"Start packing your things. I want you out of my office by the end of the day," the obese man in front of me said as he took a swig from his whiskey glass.

He had called me into his office first thing in the morning and dropped this on me all of a sudden.

"Sir? What is this about? You just gave me excellent reviews on my work last week."

The man adjusted his glasses while he whirled his drink around. "The past isn't something you can fix. If our company had known of your history, we would not have hired you."

"What do—"

"Enough. Your gang relationship has come to light. While I have found no problem with your work so far, if it got out that we had someone like you in our company, it would ruin our reputation. The decision is final."

"That's in the past. I don't—"

"Enough. If you could please stop wasting my time, I am busy here."

And that was how I ended up losing my first job within the first three months.

* * *

At first, it was devastating.

All the work I had put in to better myself felt like it was all for nothing because of where I came from. I thought I had escaped from my past, only for it to catch up, and that pained me more.

My dream of getting rich and having an easy life seemed impossible now. No other company in the industry would hire me with my meager experience. They would only hire their former interns for the beginner roles, and they wouldn't touch someone a Fortune 500 company had quickly let go.

I admit, back when I was growing up, I had to do some pretty horrible things. I still remember the moment I was first handed a gun, the moment I first pulled the trigger, and the shock and resignation on my target's face. It was hard to decline when I knew they would simply push the task on the younger kids.

At the very least, doing those dirty jobs had earned me enough cash to get through school and even college. I had thought that after graduating at the age of twenty-three, I could turn my life around for the better, but reality wasn't such a forgiving place.

But I refused to give up. After my termination, I took several part-time jobs in retail, aiming to save up enough to start my own business. The small amounts I could scrounge up into my savings each month were depressing. With rising food prices, rent, and inflation, it seemed like some force was out to get me.

It took three years of diligent saving, but I was finally ready.

"It was nice talking to you today, Mr. Halls. I will have the documents emailed to you soon. Once you have signed them, we should be able to incorporate your business. Hope you have a great rest of the day. See you soon."

As I exited my attorney's office with a hop in my step, I put on my earphones and hummed along as I made my way to the bus stop. From now on, I no longer had to juggle my part-time jobs and could wholeheartedly focus on my business.

I watched the light change before crossing the street. Just when I had made it halfway, car horns rang out all around me. I turned, only to see bright headlights rapidly growing.

I had just enough time to make out the terror on the truck driver's face before everything turned dark.

# CHAPTER I

# THE FIRST STEP

It was hot...

Too hot.

I opened my eyes and found a wall of fire trapping me in the corner of a room. I turned to find a window behind me, my only source of fresh air.

Wherever I was, it seemed like it was well above the ground floor and—

Gunshots rang out from below. I stuck my head out the window, looked down, and found a giant man slowly walking into the courtyard about four stories below, firing his shotgun at people hidden from my view by trees. I knew there were people, as shots were fired back at the man, but he ignored them. The bullets bounced uselessly off him.

*That... isn't a human, is it?*

"Hector, load the EI rounds. I'll disable him!" another voice yelled out from the courtyard. I was too afraid of all the bullets flying around to try to poke my head out any further.

Before long, something was thrown at the man, and a light blinded me for a full second. When my vision returned, I found him frozen stiff as the people below pelted him with more gunfire.

I wanted to shout out for help as the fire continued to rage on behind me, but my vision started to blur and my throat was parched. I felt hazy, and soon I couldn't even hold my eyelids open.

* * *

The morning alarm chimed loudly in greeting for a new day.

The dreaded noise made me regain consciousness instantly, though I refused to open my eyes yet. I took a deep breath as I gathered my thoughts.

*Did I set an alarm last night again? Was there even anything to do today besides sleeping in?*

The alarm continued to ring.

Lazily, I leaned over towards my nightstand to reach for my phone where I had always left it. But my hand made contact with a large glassy surface.

*Glass? But my nightstand is made of wood. What the...*

As the alarm rang once more, I snapped my eyes wide open and looked over to see a completely unfamiliar nightstand. On top of it was a thin translucent screen that seemed to be the source of the noise.

The screen lit up with options to either stop the alarm or put it on snooze. I tapped the Stop button and silence was restored.

I looked around and saw an undecorated room with only a simple desk in the corner and the nightstand that stood beside me.

*Shit... did I get kidnapped or something?*

I got up and quietly opened the door closest to me, finding a washroom. Then I opened two folding doors to find a walk-in closet that had two sets of clothes on the hangers. The last door led to a small living room with an open kitchen off to the side.

*It seems like I'm alone in here, but where in God's name am I? The fact that I don't even know how I got here scares me the most. I don't normally drink, so that rules out a hangover. Did I get drugged?*

With nothing interesting I could find, I moved back to the bedroom and picked up the thin screen. It appeared to be a cell phone, and the instant I started playing around with it, it lit up with the words "Biometric Confirmed" before the display opened to a familiar-looking dashboard. It was similar to but unlike any of the operating systems I knew of, so I turned the phone over and saw the word "Zenitech" engraved on it.

I searched through the apps for any clues, but instead of resolving the mystery, I only got more and more confused. I found a chain of emails that were addressed to *my* name on a phone that I'd never seen before.

| | |
|---|---|
| FROM: | Kyle.Alpin@SocialCorpHR.corp |
| TO: | Rollo.Halls@SocialCorp.corp |
| DATE: | Friday, November 16, 499 |
| SUBJECT: | Resettlement Package |

*Dear Rollo Halls,*

*First, I would like to express my condolences for the loss of your place of residence, Happy Homes, due to a fire caused by hostile parties engaging on the premises. Rest assured, the perpetrators have been accordingly dealt with.*

*Since Happy Homes is a subsidiary of SocialCorp, it is our responsibility to help resettle all the charges who were under Happy Homes, as they can no longer do so. However, we would like to offer you the opportunity to apply for emancipation. If you choose to proceed, we will provide you with a compensation package that exceeds the normal benefit package. I have included the details in the files attached to this email.*

*To apply, please...*

There were dozens more back-and-forth emails down the chain describing what turned out to be a story about an orphan, who had the same name as me, dealing with the aftermath of the destruction of their orphanage.

The orphanage was a subsidiary of some company named SocialCorp. With the old orphanage effectively disabled after being caught up in some fight, it'd fallen to SocialCorp to deal with the surviving orphans.

Instead of rebuilding or moving my namesake to a new orphanage, they'd offered a package that basically said, "Agree that we are no longer responsible for you, and in exchange, we will offer you some money."

My namesake had agreed and received ten thousand credits that'd somehow become five thousand after a bunch of processing fees I didn't bother examining.

*What a sucker he was. He should've at least negotiated and milked them dry!*

I dug around on the phone a little more to find what I could and went on the web as well, but even then, I couldn't access any of the usual websites I frequented.

*Wait a second...*

*This can't be...*

Something clicked for me all of a sudden, and I rushed out to the living room, pushed the blinds aside, and stared out of the window.

What greeted me were giant megabuildings that stretched into the sky. Futuristic vehicles zoomed by between the colossal skyscrapers, but the thing that drew my eyes the most was the giant tower off in the distance that stretched infinitely up into the sky.

*Well, shit... I don't suppose I'm in some foreign country, am I...*

*Wait... That means all the money I'd been saving for the past few years is gone now. NOOOOOOOO!*

* * *

Yeah... so it turned out this wasn't the world I knew, and I was now somehow in a place called Elevate City, one of the largest metropolises and artificial islands in the world. Home of the only space elevator on the planet, and from what I saw on the maps, huge was an understatement. This city alone housed over fifty million registered residents.

How did I know this, you may ask? Well, a full day on the web will fetch you some useful information sooner or later. It also helped me get situated and distracted me from panicking like the lost chick that I was.

Food was running out in the apartment, forcing me to go out. I found a convenience store nearby, where I spent twenty credits for some really shitty-tasting food. I used money from the wallet I found in the apartment. It had a few bills that totaled fifty credits.

Credits was the currency used here, and they used plastic bills as cash, though most transactions were done electronically. The wallet also contained an ID with my name and a photo to match.

*Sigh...*

As I walked back to my apartment, most people who went by completely ignored me, but I spotted a small group scanning everyone from the corner of my eye. They were doing exactly what I had done in the past when I was part of the gang.

*They must be looking for easy marks to rob or something.*

I quickly blended into the crowd, away from their attention, and hurried home.

When I returned, I immediately sat down in my living room, trying to accept the idea that I may have replaced an alternate version of myself. Either that or I had suddenly gone crazy and all these memories from another world were made up by my crazy self.

*Either way, I'll have to keep living here, since I don't know what else I can do. And to continue living, I need a certain something to survive—money.*

I found the banking app on the phone. Luckily, everything was unlocked by my biometrics. I apparently only had around twenty-five hundred credits left, after including my cash. But two thousand credits' worth of rent was waiting for me to pay in twenty days. That wouldn't even leave me with enough to afford three meals a day if I didn't do something.

*I guess things don't change, even in another world. Money makes the world go round. I wish I still had my savings... Time to search for a job.*

* * *

"Hmm... First job, I see," the man at the counter in front of me mumbled.

I subconsciously nodded after a second of delay. Then I stared straight back at him. He didn't react. It took me another second to realize he wasn't even paying attention to me. His eyes gave off a soft blue glossy glow as he stared forward blankly.

While I may have read about them, I couldn't help but feel a little amazed at cybernetic implants like his eyes. In this world, they were just everyday tech seen by the dozen out in the streets. Their price might start from several thousands of credits at the very least, but they were as common as my world's smartphones.

It also wasn't hard to spot metal prosthetic limbs here and there while I went about my daily life. I didn't think those would be anything to worry about, which was fine by me, as those were likely way out of my budget for the foreseeable future.

All the job postings I found required either prior experience in similar roles, degrees from some expensive corporate-certified school, or both, and I had neither.

My alternate self was an orphan who only received the minimum required education, as the orphanage didn't really care unless we showed promise. In that case, we would be whisked away by some corporation.

That brought me to this gig at a convenience store that was only a few blocks away from my building. They offered twenty credits an hour for a dead-end job with no future prospects in sight, but I needed this to survive in the short term.

Why couldn't I have changed places with a version of myself who was rich so I could take it easy?

"Bi-weekly pay and shift changes, twenty creds an hour. You good with that?"

Trying to wipe the frown off my face, I said, "Yes, thank you for having me. When do I start?"

* * *

So it turned out other big things were different in this world: crime and safety.

It was safe to say that throughout the past few weeks, traveling on my route to and from work, I passed at least two shootings a day, from the gunshots I heard. The news hadn't even covered them, as they were too common throughout the city, barring the rich corporate areas.

I looked into getting a weapon, or something defensive, like a bulletproof vest to wear underneath my shirt. There was a gun shop conveniently located in my building, but their prices started from a few hundred credits.

With my current income after taxes, I didn't have much leeway, so I had cheaped out and bought nothing instead, and now I came to regret it.

Why, you ask?

Well, what started as another regular day at the job, working the cash register, ended with two not-so-friendly clients pointing their pistols at me.

I thought the only thing I had to deal with was ringing people up, whether it be by cash, card, or, more commonly, wirelessly through people's cybernetics.

Now, as much as I wanted to look brave and cool, not much gets you shaking with fear as quickly as the thought of being murdered when you least expect it. My panic grew when I realized I had no control over the situation.

"Hey, co, you deaf or what? Give us the damn money already!" the man with the pure-red cybernetic pupils said as he shoved the gun closer.

I blankly stared straight at the unfamiliar gun, then towards him, before I snapped out of it and started to work the cash register. I complied, hoping he wouldn't shoot if I followed his instructions.

*There is still so much money to be made and so much to do. I don't want to die here.*

"Hey, you! You ain't leavin' till you give me all you have."

At his words, I looked up and caught sight of his partner in the back. He was threatening a customer who was trying to leave.

The customer, a man wearing shades and a bomber jacket, looked completely relaxed. He sighed before replying, "You really want to do this?"

"Do I look like I'm jokin' to you?!" the robber yelled, and pointed his gun at his face.

An electric buzz rang with a bright flash that abruptly filled the entire store and blinded me.

Pain flooded my eyes. I could still see flashes behind my eyelids, flares that seemed to mock me with the futility of blocking the light. I then heard rapid gunfire, which made me duck down behind the counter for cover.

*I may have gotten used to hearing gunshots from the daily commute between here and home, but hearing them so close without warning always makes me flinch. Damn shots are loud as hell.*

As I slowly recovered my vision and rose, I saw the robber who had been threatening me lying on the ground by the counter in a pool of blood. He was still breathing and was trying to get up, but it seemed like he could only move his head. It made for a comical sight, as if he was struggling to complete a sit-up.

He soon noticed my gaze, and his red eyes snapped towards me. Then he tried to bring his arm up to point his gun at me, but he was moving as slow as a snail, struggling to make every little bit of progress.

*Goddamn it! Give it a break already. What did I ever do to you?*

I darted around the counter and decisively stepped on the wrist holding the gun.

"Stop that shit! I'll call an ambulance for you, so just lie still already! You don't have a death wish, do you?"

The man tried to speak, but choked on his own blood and coughed instead. Then his hand grabbed onto the ankle of my other leg.

I reflexively raised it to break free from his grasp and succeeded. But with my only other foot on the uneven surface that was his wrist, I lost balance.

As I began to fall, I hastily stepped forward instead to counteract the momentum. This resulted in me stomping right onto the robber's chest.

*+10 EXP*

A notification suddenly appeared in my vision, just above the robber's head.

*What the hell?*

# CHAPTER 2

# BREAKING THE STATUS QUO

I dove headfirst into the bed and burrowed my face into the pillow as I reflected on my day and what to do from now on.

*Well, that sucked.*

Stomping on the injured robber had apparently been enough to kill him. I called the cops right after, and they didn't show up until thirty minutes later. That was enough time for me to snap out of my daze, only to find the store in a mess. I even mindlessly rang up a customer who didn't seem to care one bit about the two dead bodies while they shopped.

When the cops arrived, all they did was ask me a few basic questions and take a few pictures of the crime scene. They didn't even take the bodies away, saying, "Not our job."

Not even five minutes after the police had left, I received a call from my manager. "You imbecile! Why did you call the police? Do you know how much they charge per call?!" He continued yelling profanities at me. In the meantime, I wallowed in the realization of how differently things worked in this world.

"You don't have to show up tomorrow anymore! You're fired! And you better clean up the goddamn mess in that store before the day ends or I'm taking it out of your pay!"

I hadn't even bothered arguing. I had done enough research to know it was expected of every business to screw their employees over just because they could get away with it. If you tried to fight back, it would only waste time and money, with the lawsuits always ending in a battle of attrition.

Once you were rich enough, you could bend any rules to your will or, at the very least, play by an easier rulebook.

I suppressed my simmering anger and got to cleaning.

Before disposing of the bodies, I looted the gun and dagger from each of them. It didn't seem like the cops cared at all about their weapons, so I helped myself. It would save me some credits, as I'd been looking to buy a weapon anyway.

I left the store as soon as the person for the next shift had arrived and power-walked straight home.

Once I'd had enough of self-wallowing, I jumped straight into the shower to clear my head.

Finally I had some time to think back on the floating message I had seen. Did I hallucinate that, or could it be real? If it was real, then did I attain some sort of system?

When that thought came into my mind, I couldn't help but be a little excited. I started testing out my theory. "System!" I called out louder than I had wanted, but luckily the sound of the shower dampened the noise and no one else was here to hear me.

Nothing happened, so I kept trying. "Menu. Status." On my third try, a menu popped up. The third time's the charm, they say.

**Status**
**Level:** 1
**EXP:** 10/100
**Musculoskeletal:** 11
**Neural Reflex:** 15
**Visuomotor Coordination:** 12
**Endurance:** 9
**Sensory Perception:** 12

**Upgrade Points:** 6
**Upgrades:** null
**Enhancements:** null

I instinctively reached out to touch the screen, but my hands went straight through it. I went over what the screen displayed, and when I got to the upgrade points, the screen automatically changed and displayed a list.

Looking through the list, I quickly got the hang of navigating, as it simply moved according to my intentions. What it showed were various skills, from hand-to-hand combat, pistol, and stealth to more knowledge-focused selections, like kinetic weapon technology.

This was just like the status screen of a game. However, the only part of my status I could interact with was the upgrade points, and those could only give me skills. I couldn't upgrade the other stats or anything...

I held back my impulse to test it out and upgrade something right away. I needed a plan first before I randomly upgraded anything, assuming it even worked.

Shelving my thoughts regarding the system, I left the shower and started looking for a job once more. Despite being paid last week, with the amount I had to set aside for rent, I wouldn't be able to build up much of a war chest at all. It would have been so much easier if the money I had been saving came along with me to this world...

*I always used to say, "Money is power." It has never hurt so much to be right. Time to start saving... again.*

***

It wasn't long before I found a new job. Well... old job, but different store. At least this time it was closer to my home, being just down the street.

On my second day of work there, I stopped by the gun store in my building and brought along the two guns and knives I had looted from the bodies.

Upon passing through the first set of doors, I was asked to unload my weapons or store them in a nearby locker. The guard watched me awkwardly pocket the bullets I unloaded, as I had nowhere else to put them.

With the guard's permission, I headed further into the store. Past a second set of doors, I found the store's merchandise on display.

Good thing I had practiced with the guns at home and understood how to handle them safely, with the help of my personal advisor, the web. Otherwise, it would've been even more awkward.

I headed directly to the checkout counter, where a woman wearing an army vest over a tank top waited. She stood on the other side of what I presumed to be bulletproof glass with a bored expression. I placed the pistol and knife into the opening of the glass between us.

"How much can I get for these?"

The woman ignored the knife and picked up the pistol to look it over. She took it apart with practiced ease before she replied.

"Decent-condition Vipera, I'll take it for one fifty creds. The knife is just a hunk of metal. I'll take it for ten creds, a total of one sixty creds."

"C'mon, you can do at least two hundred!"

"No can do. We still have crates full of these sitting around. One sixty is the best I can do, or you can try your luck elsewhere."

Well... it wasn't as bad of a deal as I had expected. From what I'd found online, a brand-new ACN-90, more commonly known as the Amazing Corp Vipera, would cost around three hundred credits.

I made the sale and looked around before I bought a few extra magazines and ammo for the Vipera I kept. Also, I got a small belt holster that had room to fit three additional magazines.

So I came out of the store in the positive, though only by ten credits, but that was better than nothing. Plus, I had some new gear.

Once I got to my workplace, I promptly headed to the back to get changed. I kept my new weapon strapped to my waist underneath my uniform. It was somewhat hidden beneath the shirt, but anyone could spot the bulge if they paid enough attention.

The other employee on duty likely had seen the gun, but they didn't bat an eye.

*That's just how it is in this world, I guess...*

As I started working, my mind inevitably wandered towards the system. I thought about what I should upgrade, and what awaited me if those upgrades were real. I was so excited by the prospect of escaping from these dead-end jobs and becoming filthy rich!

* * *

For the past week, I had settled into a routine of going to work and then heading to the shooting range at the gun store to practice with my new firearm. It also doubled as a test of my system, since I saw the pistol skill available to upgrade. I wanted to see if practice would help me gain a level in that skill without having to spend a point.

There really wasn't an option to add points to any of the other stats, like musculoskeletal and neural reflex, so I only focused on what I could control for now.

So far, I had nothing to show for my efforts, so it was probably one of three scenarios:

One—It would take even more practice to upgrade the skill.

Two—The upgrades provided a fixed amount of knowledge. That meant if I naturally learned the same talent before upgrading it, I wouldn't gain much from boosting the skill, as it would be redundant content.

Three—These would be upgrades on top of what I already had, kind of like a plus-one to my base stats if this were a game. However, that brought the question of whether it would be dynamic; if my natural ability increased, would I suddenly learn more, or would I just build on top of what I already had?

Without more information about the system, I shelved my thoughts and continued practicing my shooting.

On a quiet day at the range, two women approached me and struck up a conversation all of a sudden. "You new at this, co? We could give you a few pointers if you want."

I looked over. They both fit the description of textbook Amazonians to a tee. They were muscular and stood around six feet tall, just around the same as me. However, the one who spoke to me had a distinctive dark-red right arm made of metal and matching cybernetic legs.

"Sure. If it doesn't cost me anything, why not?"

She proceeded to watch me shoot, while her friend began shooting at her own pace in the lane beside me. Once the last of my mag was spent, the target returned, and I embarrassedly examined the results.

"How long you been shooting?" the woman asked without a hint of belittling in her voice, much to my relief.

"Just started up again for a week or so. Previously, I had only shot maybe three or four times in my life," I answered while I reloaded.

"You a corpo or something?" she said with an eyebrow raised.

"What? No, um… orphanage, corpo-sponsored." I quickly made up an excuse and kept my eyes on the target, not wanting to meet her eyes.

"I see. Well, why don't you take a look at how we shoot for a bit, and then we'll give you some pointers? By the way, I'm Flo and this is Erza." She pointed at herself, then at the stoic woman beside her.

Flo then gave me a grin as she drew a large pistol that suited her size. Erza looked over and gave me a quick wave.

I introduced myself before Flo demonstrated her shooting skills. It was evident from her form and stance alone that she knew what she was doing. Once she finished, it was my turn again. She helped correct my stance and coached me as I tried to imitate their form.

As they took turns teaching me, I became more comfortable chatting with them, and my aim became slightly more consistent as well.

"Nice. You're getting at least five outta ten in the inner circle now, much better than before," Flo commented with her arms crossed.

"Better than before, yeah, but how does that even compare to the average?" I asked.

The two of them were hitting seven or eight out of ten shots at a much longer distance than I was shooting from.

"Well, at that distance, the average wasteland raider would probably hit about seven. The average security guard with a few weeks of training would probably hit about six outta ten. And as for mercs who have been in the game for a while like us, if they can't get at least nine outta ten, they should probably consider different careers. This is a stationary target we're talking about, after all."

I soon ran out of the practice ammo I had bought for the day and was relegated to being only a spectator. The pair also didn't continue for long, as they had apparently only been testing out their new iron.

"We're done for the day too. Wanna head out to grab a drink with us?" Flo asked as they stashed away their weapons.

"While that sounds great, I gotta get up early tomorrow, and I don't have much disposable income right now." I gave them a helpless smile.

"Oh, what do ya do?"

"I work at a convenience store."

She instantly furrowed her brows at my answer and exchanged looks with her partner before they both gave me a weird look. "You work at a store and don't know how to work your piece? Are you serious?"

I was a little taken aback by her question. "Yeah... I just work the register most of the time."

"That's even worse. Do you have any idea how often stores get hit up? I swear the casualty rate is higher than being a merc because you're just a sitting duck if anything happens."

"Is it that bad?" I weakly muttered as I thought back to the robbery I had recently experienced.

"You work for a corp, for goodness' sake. You're disposable. Why do you think they employ humans instead of just getting a bot to work the store? Because they know how often their stores get hit and humans are the cheapest to replace. They'd rather just hire the next desperate Joe off the street if you die than replace those fancy bots."

After her words, it began making a lot more sense why convenience store jobs were so readily available.

"Well, you do you," she continued. "But if I were you, I'd brush up on my shooting skills and work as a merc instead. Much higher reward for the risk you're taking."

"Thanks. I'll keep that in mind."

"You improved pretty damn fast in a day. Once you've had some more practice, you can reach out to my QG. His name is Fitel, here." She held out her terminal and passed me the contact details. "Oh, you can save my contact as well, in case you need anything."

As appealing and exciting as mercenary work sounded, I needed to start exploring more alternatives. I would much rather live a long and healthy life where I could enjoy my wealth. If there was one thing I learned throughout my life, it was that good health cost a pretty penny. I would need safety, healthy food, doctors, financial security, and more.

The best way to do that was to start a business. However, I needed startup funds and dependable employees for that. Mercenary work might prove to be a decent way to break free from being a wage slave and attaining those funds, but I had no idea where to start in terms of finding people I could trust.

"QG?" I asked, despite having gotten the gist that it was some fixer guy.

Flo raised an eyebrow. "Seriously? Quest Givers, the people who mercs like us, work with to arrange jobs and guarantee."

As Flo rambled on, I couldn't focus on her words. I was too busy screaming internally.

*I mean... Quest Giver? Really? Who the hell named it that?*

# CHAPTER 2

## QUESTING

A few weeks had passed since I met Flo and Erza. I finally requested a day off. We usually only had one day off every week, and on a random day of the week too, depending on how the shift schedule went.

That morning, I thought a lot about what to do moving forward. While the first thoughts that came to mind about finding myself in another world with a system naturally leaned towards thrilling action, I knew that wasn't what I wanted out of my own life.

Running straight into danger was not the smartest idea. Being a one-man army sounded cool and all, but didn't really appeal to me as much as getting rich did. There was so much more in life to enjoy, but most of it required money and your life being intact to savor.

In the end, I still wanted to live a laid-back life, but it didn't take a genius to foresee it would be a lot harder in this world. On top of that, I was a wage slave, in or near the lowest caste, while the people from the top corporations could do whatever they wanted.

If for some reason I couldn't work at any point, my income would come to a halt, and with no safety net in place, it wouldn't end well for me, to say the least.

This world really lived up to my life motto, "money is power," maybe too much.

That was why I wanted to strike it rich with the power of my system. Once I got rich, I would have to spend more on security to protect my wealth, which would throw me into a cycle of attaining more and more, but that was fine. It was much better than living in fear of being snuffed out on the whims of others, with no control over my life whatsoever.

I created a plan for what I wanted to do with the system during this time, but what troubled me were the consequences of the system. Making use of it meant I would need experience points to level up, and the only known way to gain EXP was to kill.

I had no intention of becoming a bloodthirsty serial killer, but thankfully, I could tell there was no shortage of bad people in this world despite my short time here. It wouldn't change the fact that I would have to kill. Some might deserve it while some might not. I wasn't a saint nor savvy enough to confirm that first without putting myself at serious risk.

If I planned to go down this path, I would have to steel my resolve.

All my enemies would simply have to die for the sake of my wealth and power. Nothing was truly free, after all.

With my determination reaffirmed, I got off my bed and started preparing for the day. I dressed and sat down with my handheld terminal. "Terminal" was what they called the phones here, along with most computer systems. I used mine to call a number I had previously saved.

The call connected after ringing three times. "You have reached Fitel. May I ask who is calling?" a man said, with a calm and measured pace.

"Hi, this is Rollo. Flo said you were the man to call for some jobs."

"I see... How many are on your crew?"

"Just me."

"Depending on the type of job you are looking for, some may have much higher success rates working with a crew. While I may not provide matchmaking services, you may consider asking Flo for a list of establishments where other security freelancers frequently gather."

"No, thank you. I plan to continue working alone."

As much sense as Fitel's words made, my plans did not include working with any others for the foreseeable future. With the rapid improvement I could achieve with the help of the system, it just wasn't smart to involve others, as they would ask questions I wouldn't want to answer. I would only work with someone I could really trust.

"Understood, though that may limit the types of jobs I will be able to entrust you with. The larger jobs will be off the table for now because they require more of a 'heavy' touch. That is, until I can confirm what you are capable of."

"Actually, I was looking for jobs that need a delicate touch. I don't mind starting small first."

"I see. Well, I do happen to have a job that would fit the criteria, though be warned, if you prove inadequate for a smaller job like this, you won't be hearing from me again. I will have the details sent to you shortly. Contact me when you are done. Have a great rest of the day now." The man had spoken at the same measured pace the entire time, and somehow ended the call before I could reply.

I thought he would have wanted to see me in person and test me first, so it was a surprise that he gave me a job right away. While I wouldn't have any second chances if I screwed this one up, I had no intention of failing. It was time to see what the system was made of. I was honestly amazed that I had held back until today.

A text came a few minutes after the call. It was a complete dossier with the details of my objective and the targets involved.

The job was to poison a certain employee of a medium-sized corporation, though poison may have been too strong of a word, as I would use a strong laxative. The target was also a small-time corpo, just another grunt who happened to be a member of their corporate football team.

On paper, the sports teams were simply methods corporations used to let their employees exercise, blow off some steam, and socialize with other corps. It was an open secret that they also served as the basis for a gambling ring that catered to middle management, and a means for the senior management to gain bragging rights.

The dossier included my target's entire history, address, and even salary. I definitely was not jealous that he had that extra digit in his salary despite only having an entry-level job like mine.

I considered applying again to a corporation, but quickly dismissed the idea. All corpo employees had to install their company's software in their implants, which monitored their activity and who they were in contact with. That was certainly not an option for me with my system, unless I wanted to be bagged and caged somewhere the sun would never reach, reduced to a lab rat.

While the job didn't entail killing, meaning I wouldn't gain any experience points, I still wanted to complete it to earn Fitel's trust and open up the way to bigger jobs with larger paychecks. Then I could buy better equipment, and cybernetics, so I could safely target the scum of society for the EXP.

I memorized all the relevant information from the dossier and deleted the files as instructed.

Subvocalizing "Status," I brought up the system. The long-awaited upgrade time had come.

I scrolled past various skills, like pistol, sniper rifle, and melee weapons, and went for the option that I found to be the most effective at killing.

With six points to work with, it might be worthwhile to select two skills. I looked around my room at the shuttered windows, the closed doors, and the devices on the walls that locked them. There were cameras everywhere, but I was certain that none were watching me now. Then I made my decision.

A rush of knowledge flooded my brain. Strangely, I gained muscle memory of the skills I learned as well. All the new know-how made me want to try it out immediately.

*Without further ado, let's go test it out.*

* * *

I stopped in front of a newsstand and looked over the holographic projections of assorted papers laid out in front of the bored-looking owner, who was sipping his morning coffee. I picked out one at random and downloaded the new file onto my terminal before I entered the megabuilding nearby.

Inside, it resembled an enormous mall / office conglomerate. There were only a few people walking around in the lobby this early in the morning. All dressed in suits, they completely ignored me as they rushed about their day. Once I made my way up the elevator, I found a discreet corner in a lounge area, outside the view of any cameras, and used a cord from my terminal to jack into the wall.

It took a few minutes for me to breach its flimsy security and gain access to the cameras, then I found myself a seat on an empty bench next to a vending machine. Though it was off in a corner, it still gave me a clear view of the elevators.

I casually crossed my legs and started reading the news articles off my handheld terminal, with the nearby camera's feed pulled up to keep an eye out as well. The main article covered a huge raid on corporate transports traveling through the New North American wastelands, how much money the corporations lost from it, and how much they condemned the raider activity in the area, although there wasn't much they could do about it.

*What utterly useless threats. As if some raiders living out in the wasteland would even hear about it. Though I guess they needed to do some posturing for their stock prices or whatever.*

No corporation could truly eradicate wastelanders because, true to their name, they lived out in the wastelands, where a furious sandstorm raged on without rest. No planes could go near it, and it jammed all communications inside. It resulted from climate change and nuclear war, a testament to human folly.

I skimmed over the other articles that spanned business news, local incidents, and celebrities. When I checked the time, I found my target was scheduled to leave for work soon and then doubled my attention on the camera feed by the elevators.

My terminal stayed in front of me. From the corner of my eye, I watched group after group of corpos mechanically wait for their elevator from the camera placed right above them. Some of them were staring blankly ahead with glowing irises, likely going through the screens in their optics.

On the fifth batch of people waiting for the elevators, I finally spotted the person from the dossier.

I silently took a deep breath and waited for the elevator doors to close. Then I stood up and waited for the next free elevator so I could head towards my target's apartment. Emerging in a hallway, I used my terminal to turn the cameras away so I could stroll by the blind spots and reach the unit.

Then I repeated what I had done earlier and slotted a cord into the panel by the door, and within a few seconds, the door clicked open.

*I'm glad this building cheaped out on their security and used old software straight from the box.*

Closing the door gently behind me, I took in my surroundings and found a small one-bedroom apartment with a layout similar to mine. I took out the hidden camera I bought, which was the size of a grain, and placed it in a spot that gave me a clear view of both the open kitchen and the door to the bedroom.

I had gotten the camera for a hundred credits while I was out picking up the package that came with this job. It only had enough battery for three days, but barring any accidents, it should be more than enough.

Just when I had finished placing the camera, the mechanical lock of the front door clicked.

*He's back already?*

The door swung open, and I fluidly slipped into cover behind the island of the open kitchen. I moved as if I'd practiced this hundreds of times before, but it was thanks to the system and not my hard work.

Then I started navigating my terminal to connect to the feed of my newly placed camera one-handed, the other hand firmly gripping my pistol.

By listening to the footsteps of the new intruder, I got an idea of where they were. I used that information to keep the island between us, keeping me out of sight.

It didn't take long to connect with my camera, and I soon had the video feed that showed both me and the intruder. I could clearly see myself crouched behind the island, staring at the terminal in hand, while the intruder, whom I recognized as my target, entered his bedroom.

Taking another breath, I relaxed my grip on my gun.

*This guy had to pick today to forget something...*

He soon came back out to the living room and headed to the sofa right beside me. I stayed crouching as he walked around the home until he finally left.

With the door closed once more, I switched the feed to the cameras outside, where I watched him enter the elevator. I didn't relax until the door closed behind him, but when I did, my legs gave out from all the crouching, dropping my butt to the floor.

*Damn, I should've gotten access to the cameras on the ground floor as well... Maybe even programmed something that could recognize and highlight targets, then alert me when they showed up on the cameras I had access to.*

Multiple things that I could've done to avoid that close call flooded my mind, but I promptly forced myself up once my heart rate settled. I double-checked my work, then planted another camera in the bedroom before I left.

On my way back, I reflected on the entire episode. I couldn't deny feeling a little happy at having completed my job undiscovered, but there were definite areas I could improve on.

The battery for the camera lasted three days, so I needed to go back at least once to either swap out the battery or retrieve the camera.

I had to suppress the giddy feeling while I worked at the convenience store that evening, and I was so excited I couldn't fall asleep, as if I had a test the next day.

I daydreamed about the future, knowing I had a working system, until the sky started to brighten and sleep overcame me.

# CHAPTER 4

## MERCENARIES

The day after my seamless infiltration, I returned to the same megabuilding in the early morning. This time, I could effortlessly access the building camera again, and also get a clear view of the inside of the unit, thanks to the camera I had planted yesterday.

From the camera, I watched as my target woke up and brewed coffee in his open kitchen before he retreated to his room. Immediately, I entered the unit the same way as before. Right into his freshly brewed coffee, I poured some of the special laxatives I had received specifically for the job.

The laxatives would have the man trapped in the washroom for the next week. Then they'd drain him of strength, which would take a whole second week to recover from. That time period happened to coincide with his football game. It'd be pretty impressive if he even had enough stamina to play ball, not to talk about performing well.

While I felt a little bad, as the man had done nothing wrong from what I knew, a job was a job.

With my objective complete, I smoothly retrieved the cameras and exited his unit. Moving around silently was so natural now that it felt a little off-putting, but it showed that the points I had spent on Stealth really paid off.

Once I left, I returned to my apartment safely and called Fitel.

"Mr. Halls, congratulations on a job well done. If you would send me the account you would like me to send the payment to, I can have the payment deposited immediately."

"Did I tell you my last name? And don't we need to wait and confirm the laxative worked first?"

"I apologize if I offended you, but in my line of business, it is often wise to know who we are working with. And as for your other question, your target has informed their employer that they will be absent due to illness, and my other sources have also confirmed this, which means the job is complete," Fitel explained in his usual relaxed rhythm.

"I see. Here, I just sent you the account information," I answered.

"Yes, I have received it. You should receive the payment shortly."

I opened my account using my desktop terminal and confirmed my balance had increased by two thousand credits.

It was more than I had made from two weeks of work, all from two days of work. I could see why mercenaries were so common. It was an accessible job to anyone who would take the risks. Otherwise, you would have to settle for a dead-end job like mine.

"One more thing, Mr. Halls. I have found your performance satisfactory and have another job lined up for you. The job will require a lot of your time, as you will be surveilling a target for anywhere from a few days up to a week. You will have to take some time off or quit your current job. In return, you can expect one thousand credits per day with room for bonuses. Do you find this agreeable?"

"Yes, I'll do it. I'll have to start tomorrow, though," I answered without hesitation. *Goodbye, crappy job. I won't miss you.*

"Very well. I will have the job details sent to you. Have a good day, Mr. Halls," Just like last time, Fitel seamlessly ended the call once the business discussions were done.

The moment it ended, a familiar text appeared in my view.

*+10 EXP*

What? Had I ended up killing someone? The guy I poisoned?

No, it could also be for completing the job, or for incapacitating my target.

This was something I would look into more when I had the chance. Right now, it was faster and easier to kill despicable criminals.

I pulled up my status as I reflected. Things had raced by in a blur for the past few days.

**Status**
**Level:** 1
**EXP:** 20/100
**Musculoskeletal:** 11
**Neural Reflex:** 15
**Visuomotor Coordination:** 12
**Endurance:** 9
**Sensory Perception:** 12
**Upgrade Points:** 0
**Upgrades:**
  Stealth +3
  Hacking +3
**Enhancements:** null

Just as I was ready to take a nap, I realized something...

*I still have to call my boss and tell him I'm quitting!*

* * *

I spent a week doing the surveillance job. The only exciting parts were at the start, when I set up the cameras, and at the end, when I retrieved them.

Though it was boring, it paid well, so I didn't have too many complaints except that I had received no experience points for completing the job.

I spent the rest of the week looking for ways to kill time. During that time, I had messaged Flo asking where other mercenaries usually hung out. She sent me what she knew and invited me to where she and Erza went to celebrate completed jobs. It was a bit far away, located in District 10, and my place was in District 8.

Only when I had finished the week-long job did we meet up at the bar, Haven.

Neon lights glowed brightly around the spacious bar, with private rooms surrounding it. Through some glass walls, I could see people sitting and chatting, while other rooms had glass walls that were blacked out.

The place was packed, with many people sporting cybernetic limbs. Several had weird eyes like metal snow goggles that melded into their skulls. I even saw builds that were so unnaturally large I doubted much of their bodies were organic anymore.

Despite the vast array of flashy-looking individuals, it didn't take long before I spotted Flo waving her maroon-colored cyberarm from a table. Erza was stoically sitting beside her as always, along with two others, a man and a woman.

The man was of a medium build with dark-brown hair, and sitting there beside Erza probably made him smaller than he actually was. He sat there hugging a huge rifle in one arm and raising a beer with the other.

The woman and her average build looked even smaller, her light-blue hair tied into a ponytail. Her ample figure sat in the lounge chair low and lazily, looking bored.

I waved and crossed the busy room. Though it was rowdy, it wasn't loud enough that we couldn't hold a conversation.

"Hey, Flo," I said as I took a seat.

"How's it going, co? Finally done that job you were on?"

"Yeah, I've been doing a lot better now that I actually have some savings. Are these people your crew?" I looked over at the two new faces.

"Right, introductions, sorry 'bout that. The guy's Max, our overwatch, and the bitch is Liz. Don't mind her, she's always like that unless she's doing a gig."

I nodded over at the two of them. "Nice to meet you. I'm Rollo."

Liz's eyes dimmed and glazed over. Then the glow of her eyes returned once more, and she resumed staring blankly at the ceiling. Max was more engaged and gave me a return nod before staring daggers into Flo.

"Don't forget 'bout my wife's introduction." Max returned his gaze to me. "Flo and Erza had talked about you. Glad to meetcha. On a more important note, this here is Lucy." He held the rifle up for me to see before pulling it towards him to give it a kiss.

"Buzz off, you're making my drink taste bad," Flo retorted.

"What was that?"

As Flo got into an argument with Max, Erza leaned towards me and whispered, "Sorry about that, don't mind them. This happens all the time. It's just what happens when a bunch of weirdos like them gather."

Flo abruptly paused mid-sentence and turned toward us. "But at least I'm your favorite weirdo."

Erza leaned over, gave Flo a quick kiss, and grinned. "That you are."

As if proud of the fact that her point was proven, Flo flashed me a gloating grin.

"Oh, so you guys were together. I should've known, considering how happy you looked."

"Yep, we've been full time for three years now. Anyway, there are a few other common merc spots, but Haven is the one for the mercs who've been doing well."

At Flo's words, I took another look at the venue, and then at the prices on the menu. Even the cheapest drink would cost an entire day's work at the convenience store.

"Don't worry about it," said Flo. "I got you covered tonight. By the way, this may be a bit sudden, but how 'bout you join us on a little gig tonight?" She gave me a pat on the back that staggered me a little.

"Oh, you have a job tonight? No need to worry about me. I just wanted to have a look now that I'm in the business as well."

"Ha, it's just a small gig we usually wouldn't even bother with, so don't sweat it. I only took it outta habit. Felt weird coming here if we weren't prepping or celebrating a job. As a smaller gig, it won't pay too much, though. Your cut would be about seven thousand creds. You in?"

"What's the job?" With the pay the same as my week-long job, it was hard to resist.

"Just eliminating some targets. Don't worry too much about it, intern. As I said, I got you covered tonight."

I sighed at the thought of how easily I caved. "Okay, I'm in."

* * *

We left Haven and got into Flo's car, which was basically an armored van. It had more than enough room for eight people, and we were only five.

I wasn't even sure what the plan was yet, since Flo only replied that it was a simple job that didn't need much prep, and to just follow her lead.

"So where are we going and who are we eliminating again?" I spoke to the person sitting in front of me, Liz, who was likely just as clueless as I was. Meanwhile, Max seemed preoccupied with checking his rifle.

"Oh, it's just some poser gang that took over some old building slated for demolition. Suckers refused to get out, so we just needa flatline them all. Best part is since the building is scheduled to be destroyed, we won't have to care about collateral damage."

While a frontal assault wasn't something I specialized in or wanted to be part of, with these guys, who seemed to be experienced, it should probably be okay just for tonight...

"So is it just us, against an entire gang?" I couldn't help but confirm.

"Yeah. We usually have one more in our crew, a computer geek, but he isn't really needed here. And you know how them geeks are, always yapping nonstop as if they were still corpos. We're more than enough to snuff out twenty or thirty posers with just us."

"Right... So what's the plan?"

"Ha, as if we'd need one for this. Even just Max boy here could take them out by himself."

I turned over to the person mentioned, but he was already gone. Leaving an empty seat where he once was, and the back door completely open while the car continued to move. I could see the receding road and the city backdrop behind us.

*What the hell?! Did he jump out of a moving car?*

Before I could ask questions, the car violently jerked, joined by the sound of a crash. The seatbelt pressed into me so tightly that I had trouble breathing until it loosened.

"What the hell happened?!" I cried. The front door opened, and Flo and Erza were already standing outside when they turned back to reply.

"We've arrived. Time to do our job."

# CHAPTER 5

## TAG ALONG

Flo rushed away with a massive gun. She wore a heavy-looking vest and matching closed-face helmet, and Erza followed right behind her in a similar getup.

"Ha ha, finally! Time to go shoot up some scumbags. Follow me, intern, and watch the show!" said Liz, whose demeanor took a sudden turn as she exited the vehicle holding a compact SMG.

I followed her into the tree line off the side of the road. It appeared we'd crashed through the metal gate surrounding a worn-down two-story villa just visible in the distance. Trees framed the road to the estate and its unreasonably large yard.

Not long after we started navigating through the foliage, the sound of gunshots echoed, coming from the road we'd left.

I barely kept up with Liz even though I wasn't wearing a heavy-looking backpack like her, but it wasn't long before we made it out of the thicket and got a clear view of the firefight taking place.

To our left was the villa, where several gunmen took turns peeking out from behind sandbags and blocks of concrete to fire potshots. Meanwhile, Flo and Erza were right in the middle of the road, shooting and slowly advancing.

Flo held a heavy-looking metallic tower shield with her cybernetic arm. Her gun poked through an opening made to allow her to lay down suppressive fire. Based on the sound alone, I could tell she had some sort of shotgun, not the rifle that it appeared to be.

Erza, on the other hand, took cover behind Flo's shield, where she fired what seemed to be a grenade launcher.

"Come on. Let's go," Liz said.

She led us closer to the enemy position, where we had a clear view of a dozen of them behind cover. She signaled to me with her eyes before we took aim.

I brought up my pistol and aimed at a woman with a face full of tattoos. She was reloading, which made her a sitting duck from my vantage point. I took a deep breath, and when I heard Liz shoot from beside me, I pulled the trigger.

I watched my target drop, then readjusted my aim before I pulled the trigger again.

*+10 EXP*

Finding my next target, I pointed my Vipera towards him. As I lined up my shot, he reacted and tried to aim his rifle at me, but he was too slow.

*+10 EXP*

This time, it appeared I shot him right in the head, as the Experience notification floated above him instantly.

While I took my time lining up shots one after the other, Liz dumped her entire mag on everyone in sight while laughing maniacally. She got quite a few of them, but her theatrics definitely caught their attention.

Right after I finished my second kill, I ducked back down into the tree line for cover, and Liz followed a moment later. Following her was a hail of bullets that landed where we had just been.

Immediately afterwards, explosions rang out from the enemy positions. The bullets stopped flying our way, so I peeked to see Flo and Erza much closer to the enemy than before, with several new bodies lying in a pool of blood by their feet.

Without saying anything, Liz rushed up to join the fray while our foes were distracted. A few noticed her running out, but before they could do anything, giant bullet holes appeared in their chests. I looked in the direction where I thought the bullets had come from, yet I couldn't spot the shooter. I had a pretty good idea who it was, though.

Our enemies, pressured from two angles, started retreating into the mansion behind them. The only ones left outside were dead or incapacitated, so we gathered by the entrance. When I walked by the carnage, I noticed a few gang members on the ground were unconscious but still breathing.

I took out a knife and plunged it into any bodies that were still breathing. For my efforts, I was rewarded with several experience notifications, though most were duds.

*Hey, if they're going to die anyway, then don't mind me. I'm just helping them avoid prolonged suffering. Never mind that I get something out of it too. Ha-ha-ha, isn't this what they call a win-win situation?*

Once I reunited with the group, Flo and Erza both stared at me. Probably because I took too long, which was kind of embarrassing. At least Liz simply flashed me a smile, which I returned with my own.

The group exchanged glances while I awkwardly stood there. Just before I asked what was going on, Flo spoke up. "You should look into getting some optics and a SAID soon. It'll do you well in group ops like these so you can see Liz's drone feeds and be on comms with us. Okay, we're ready to head in. Stay behind us."

I followed them in, but couldn't see anything from the back with the tower shield in the way. Flo moved surprisingly fast while lugging that thing around. She stood at the forefront, bashing open doors, and unloaded her heavy shotgun into any poor sods we found.

"Rollo, stay on this floor while we clear the next one," Erza said when Flo was halfway up the stairs.

I nodded. I preferred not to be in a straight-up firefight or mess up their teamwork in enclosed spaces.

A few seconds after they went out of sight, gunshots roared from upstairs. Carefully, I made my way towards a window. Right outside, a body lay motionless in a pool of blood.

Then a thunderous impact rang out from the floor above. A window shattered, and a figure came crashing down onto the ground and quickly rolled to their feet.

I stared at the large man, whose entire body was metal except for his face. He was missing an arm, and his shoulder socket gave off electric sparks. He took a moment to get his bearings, but then stared straight at me through the window.

The cyborg man aimed his remaining arm at me, and his hand snapped to the side to reveal a barrel. I stood frozen as he braced himself for the shot when suddenly, another figure leaped down from the second floor onto him.

It only took me a split second to recognize the figure to be Erza, the stoic mercenary, and she came down like a meteor, slashing her sword down as she landed on top of the cyborg. As her blade was about to make contact with his metal torso, I couldn't help but wonder if it could cut through the steel.

But my worries were unneeded, as the blade met no resistance and smoothly bisected him from shoulder to hip. The cyborg's upper body hit the ground first before the lower half began to fall back.

With the enemy dealt with and the sound of fighting gone, the entire place suddenly sounded eerily quiet. I walked outside and stood near the dead cyborg while Erza took the body apart.

"Think we got all of 'em that were here," Flo said. "Though no vehicles were around, so a few probably weren't home. But I don't think we need to worry about them coming back here. Those corpos will probably have their demolition team here within the hour as soon as we let them know the job is complete."

"Corpos?" I asked.

"Construction jobs like these are all usually for corps. Not that hard to guess, though I doubt Fitel would confirm it if you asked. C'mon, let's gather up any loot and jet."

I headed back and looted any guns or cybernetics that were still functional from the corpses. Everyone else did the same.

Before I left the estate, I went over to what remained of the dead cyborg and stabbed his skull. It shattered like a jar as fluids came gushing out.

*+20 EXP*

It seemed like I was right: his brain had been kept alive. I wasn't sure what exactly the system counted as a kill, especially when I still got experience messages right away when I hit the torso. The brain couldn't have possibly died so fast, yet I still got the experience points.

I also got double the EXP, for some reason...

We then returned to the car, where Max was already waiting, and rode off together. The moment Liz sat down, it was like her switch flipped. Her energy disappeared, reverting her back to her listless self.

"So what do you say? Wanna join our crew?" Flo said as she stared at me through the rearview mirror. Thankfully, the car was on auto drive, because she was at the wheel.

"You guys were great and all, but I'm not really looking to join a crew. I'd rather be solo and doing jobs that involve less fighting for my life."

"Ha, no need to mince your words. Suit yourself."

We parked near Haven and sorted out the loot while Flo made calls to report the successful job.

With the sun coming up soon, she paid me my cut. Instead of getting any loot myself, I received some extra credits for my share, which I was glad to accept rather than have to carry the parts back and sell them.

With business settled, the group quickly split up to get some much-needed rest. It felt a little awkward to be the only one who didn't have their own vehicle. I declined Flo's offer for a ride, as I was sure they were more tired than I was. They'd done the heavy lifting.

A car... Well, that was one more thing to add to my shopping list.

I seriously needed to take a few days off. I hadn't had the chance to really rest since I started doing mercenary work. It didn't help that I got more excitement than I was looking for today.

Luckily, my trip back home went smoothly, as I called a cab. Better yet, it was self-driving, so I didn't need to interact with a driver while I was exhausted.

Like a drone, I mechanically went through my nighttime routine and threw myself into my bed.

"Status," I muttered.

The stat window displayed that I now had 90 out of 100 experience. Ten more to go, but I wasn't in any rush. It would become a lot easier once I had more practice, and with the upgrade points, it would snowball sooner or later.

I had to start investing in better gear and cybernetics as well, but for now, it was time for some rest. With that as my last thought, I fell asleep as soon as I relaxed.

* * *

I slept until late afternoon, and by the time I left my apartment, it was already evening.

Typically I shopped in my megabuilding or in the area nearby, but this time I decided to go somewhere new. This shopping mall I had looked up online had a comprehensive variety of products and was classier than what I was used to.

The first thing I looked for was food!

All the stuff I had been eating was honestly terrible. It was all synthetic food, insect protein, and stuff that was no different from flavored animal feed.

Now that I had a little more money, I wanted to splurge for once! I mean, there was absolutely no point in money if I didn't use it. This would surely motivate me, as good food was one of the reasons I wanted to be rich anyway!

I went through many menus, but to my disappointment, I found nothing I was looking for at all.

*How hard can it be to have some real meat like chicken or beef?*

I picked the place with the most traffic and ordered a few recommended dishes, but it was hard to be excited about "Authentic Locust Stir-Fry" when I didn't even know what the unauthentic version was like.

Unfortunately, it was about as expected, but it at least seemed like food suitable for human consumption. The one saving grace of this restaurant was the dessert menu. The artificial sweeteners or whatever crap they used actually tasted good. I would have been so pissed if they somehow managed to make ice cream bad.

Finally having found something that tasted familiar, I couldn't help but get a milkshake to go as well.

With my appetite sated, I was ready to start shopping.

# CHAPTER 6

## SHOPPING TIME

Leisurely strolling around the mall, enjoying my milkshake, I observed the different stores and the people who patronized them.

I made my way across floors selling clothes, cosmetics, and home electronics. Though I had noted the store I wanted to check out, I also wanted to do a little bit of window-shopping first.

From the money I made recently, I had set aside how much I would spend today. I needed to leave some leeway for food, rent, and an emergency fund, so that brought my budget for the day to ten thousand credits.

Each floor sold a single category of products. They tended to be more expensive the higher up you went.

I eventually made my way to the floor that sold what was at the top of my shopping list—cybernetics. With a dazzling array of brands, each store showcased a variety of metallic prosthetics in their flashy displays.

When I came to this world, cybernetics were some of the first things I noticed when I found the courage to step out of my apartment. Now that I had also seen them in action, it was hard to resist the allure of a quick path to power.

There wasn't a need to train for years, simply a need to spend credits. Cybernetic parts were sorely needed if I wanted to survive the fights awaiting me as I leveled up my system.

That was why I was fully prepared to replace my organic parts with cybernetic ones. Besides, even if I regretted it, I heard it was possible to regrow your limbs or organs.

I went into a store that had a decent flow of traffic called Nova Tech and started browsing their catalog on a store terminal. It included detailed specifications and videos of the products in action, with one showcasing a prosthetic hand bending a bar of metal.

Choices ranged from minor enhancements, such as tendon replacements, to major ones that replaced your entire legs and spine.

For some reason, only a few products had their prices listed in the catalog. They all had one thing in common—they were all really pricey, and entirely over my budget.

I found an employee who seemed free. "Excuse me, where can I find the prices for some of the products in the catalog?"

The lady gave me a quick once-over before replying, "Apologies, sir. The products with no price listed are models we have phased out, and we no longer carry them. Though you may still find them quite easily in the open market, especially the arm prosthetics, as our company is a leader in the field."

"The open market?"

"The cybernetic clinics that are the main retailers of cybernetic products. I can recommend a few that are Nova Tech-affiliated, if you would like."

I thanked the lady for her time and declined her offer before taking one last look around. I'd rather do my own research about these clinics than take their word for it. Surely they didn't have my best interest in mind with their offers, just their own benefit.

All the other cybernetic stores, too, only had the current latest generation stocked, so I headed off to another floor to shop for something else.

The next thing I wanted to buy was equipment. The job last night highlighted how unprepared I was, though an open firefight wasn't something I planned to do often. I wanted to be equipped enough to handle myself and really start leveling up, and the best way to do that was to make sure my targets didn't see me coming.

The floor that sold combat equipment differed greatly from all the others, where each brand had its own shop. All the brands here shared a single floor-wide store, each having its own space. It was like a department store split into sections.

This equipment was located in the basement levels, where security didn't allow customers to carry their firearms around loaded. Heavy security was apparent throughout this floor, but unlike the store in my building, it was obvious they catered to a more affluent clientele.

First, I wanted to buy a new weapon. If stealth was my theme, then I had to stick to it.

The Vipera was nice and all, but it was a bit too loud for my purposes. I could get a suppressor for it, but according to my research, a regular weapon with specialized attachments would still be inferior to a purpose-built weapon with covertness in mind.

The stealth skill had given me knowledge and muscle memory for how to move quietly. It also taught me how to track the perception of people and cameras, but I would still need weapons to deliver the blow.

For each brand, I had a salesperson assist me in looking for the silenced weapons they had in stock. It seemed like the only things they weren't selling were silenced sniper rifles, unless you had a permit issued by the government or a corporation.

I went through many models, from pistols to SMGs to rifles. In the end, I found pistols were more to my liking, as they were easier to sneak around with.

The weapons weren't completely silent like in the movies, but quiet enough that they would be hard to notice if you were having a conversation.

So many of the options I saw were just okay. Nothing stuck out to me until I came across the weapons made by Premier Arms. The company specialized not in traditional firearms but in electrically propelled weapons.

"Sir, our company has just what you are looking for! The ECG-704, more commonly referred to as the Suri, is one of our latest releases and has been thoroughly field-tested! As a coilgun with almost no moving parts, it carries twenty rounds per magazine and is even more durable than traditional firearms. It is also as quiet as you specified. It shoo—"

"Can I test it out first?" I interjected, as I had quickly learned that it was faster experiencing it in person than listening to these salesmen babble on.

"Yes, right this way, sir!" The man put down the show model and snapped up a metallic case from the cupboard below.

I followed the salesperson to one end of the main floor. There was the typical changing room there, but beside it was the entrance to a shooting range as well.

The man nimbly opened the case and started loading the gun.

"So just like a traditional firearm, the safety, magazine, and release mechanism are all the same. The rounds are of course different, so be sure not to load it with regular ammo. There is also one new part here that replaces the hammer with the battery. The battery is good for two hundred rounds when fully charged and takes five minutes to recharge. Another way to reload it is to purchase a magazine like this."

He squeezed the release mechanism on both sides, then slid out the cubic battery and showed it to me.

"Does that thing explode?" I couldn't help but ask.

"Ha, rest assured, the battery is proudly produced by Premier Arms using our proprietary technology. We have field-tested it extensively, and it is not flammable, nor will it explode!"

The gun felt heavier than the Vipera, but was still easy enough for even a child to hold, although it had a slightly longer barrel than what I was used to.

As the sales agent looked at me expectantly, I lined up a shot and pulled the trigger.

Instead of the loud bang that you heard with traditional firearms, the Suri emitted a short and quiet electric buzz. The most dramatic difference was the much lower recoil that lured me into firing several more rounds consecutively to confirm.

Once I was out of ammo, the salesperson took the chance to give me another pitch.

"The Suri was designed to be as quiet as possible, as you may already have noticed. As it is a coilgun with no moving parts, it is only audible if you are standing within five meters in most environments. Another advantage of an electrically propelled weapon is that there are no gasses either. It would be very hard to spot the weapon even after firing."

"Are there any other types of rounds as well?" I said, as he packed it back into the case.

"Yes, of course. The Suri fires standard coilgun pistol rounds. The most common rounds are the solid alloy ones you have just fired, but our company offers a selection of rounds that pack a larger punch, which can compensate for the subsonic nature of the bullets that allow it to be as quiet as it is. The most popular ones are explosive rounds, incendiary rounds, and EI rounds."

"EI rounds?" I furrowed my brows at him.

"Electronic intrusion rounds, more commonly referred to as hacker rounds. They are loaded with nanite transceivers that help you invade the closed-off networks of the target shot, usually to open a connection to your target's cybernetics for hacking."

"That sounds kind of fancily redundant."

"It is quite useful as a nonlethal option or against heavily armored cyborgs, as long as you have an individual who can perform the hacking once the connection is established."

We continued discussing the specifications as we made our way back towards his section of the store. Once we were there, I took another look at the price of the Suri: a good twelve hundred credits.

"How much for the magazines and battery?"

Instead of answering, the sales attendant smiled and pointed towards two nearby price tags.

The magazine price was comparable to the price of the Vipera's, but the battery was almost as expensive as the Vipera itself!

I looked back at the salesperson and grimaced.

"I can throw in a free holster for you if you purchase today."

Sigh... I could only tell myself that it was a necessary investment, as I felt my wallet lighten.

* * *

On my way out after purchasing my new gun, I dropped another two thousand credits on a compact backpack, first aid supplies, some combat-rated clothes and boots, and jet-black body armor that didn't constrict my movement much. A small vibro-bladed dagger took up a good chunk of the credits.

I had asked Erza about the short sword she had used to cut through the cyborg. She said it was a vibro-blade, not just an old-fashioned hunk of metal. It could get through most armor like butter, though it had a limited battery life and was pretty dangerous for an untrained wielder. That was why I stuck with a small dagger instead.

As stealth was my theme, I thought an extra-sharp blade could come in handy when I wanted to be really quiet.

Soon my day at the shopping mall came to an end. I then looked up reputable clinics and made a next-day appointment to purchase the cybernetics I wanted.

* * *

I made my way to the highly rated Roseland Clinic downtown. Behind a set of glass doors stood a fancy lobby.

After checking in, I was led to a spacious room with a desk off to the side and an operating table in the center. I sat at the desk, where a man in a traditional lab coat soon arrived.

"Mr. Halls, I presume this is your first time here, correct?" the doctor asked as he shook my hand.

"That's right."

"Pleasure to meet you. You may call me Dr. Keyes. Do you have a file of your medical history?"

"No, will that be a problem?"

"Hmm... No, not really, but we will have to take some scans before we can operate on you. The scans will not take long, but will cost a thousand credits."

"Then let's go over the cybernetics you have in stock first, and do the scan after," I replied, wanting to ensure I was actually going to be buying something here first.

"Very well. Please browse our available products in the terminal here." He pushed one to me.

It was like what I had seen at the mall yesterday, only with a mix of brands. I first filtered the products by type and set it to show only secretarial assistant implant devices, or SAIDs, as Flo had called them.

The SAID was the mandatory foundation for most other cybernetics, as it acted as a hub and bridged your other cybernetics with your brain.

Prices varied greatly, starting from a few thousand to hundreds of thousands. The more expensive models, of course, had more functions and better specs. A standout feature I saw was the ability to download knowledge to the implant, which would help your brain absorb it while you slept.

That model was way out of my price range, so I picked a more suitable one before proceeding to the optics category that would use up the rest of my budget.

"Are there any options for stealth or camouflage? I can't seem to find any."

A flicker of annoyance crossed Dr. Keyes' face, but he hid it before replying.

"Unfortunately, Mr. Halls, while stealth cybernetics are not explicitly restricted products, companies do not tend to sell them to the general market. This keeps their proprietary technology a secret and prevents targeted countermeasures from being developed. So the answer is no."

"I see... Well, I'm ready to proceed with my selection here, then."

"Great. Please move over there to the table and we can get the scans started. We can start administering some anesthetics first as well. It is just a small operation, so it shouldn't take too long."

I lay down on the table, wore the mask the doctor handed to me, and inhaled the anesthetics. Before long, my vision darkened, and I lost consciousness.

# CHAPTER 7

## NIGHT OWL

The first things that hit me when I woke up were the dull throbbing pain in my head and how dry my eye sockets felt.

*I guess that's what happens when you plug a chip into the brain and replace your eyes...*

Thankfully, I could see and my vision was much better than before, as if I had switched a video from 480p to 1440p. There was also something else in my vision, a HUD. Off in the corner was the word "Settings," and when I focused on it, a new menu appeared.

"Mr. Halls, I am glad to see you awake. Please wait here while I notify Dr. Keyes."

I glanced over at the woman. She was dressed impeccably in a light-gray suit jacket and skirt. Before I could reply to her, she exited the room.

Massaging my temples in an attempt to treat my headache, I looked around. They had moved me to what looked like a small eye examination room.

After five minutes, Dr. Keyes returned holding a small paper bag.

"Mr. Halls, how are you feeling?"

"Like a hangover, and could also really use some eyedrops."

"No need to worry. This is normal for your first time installing optics. You should make a full recovery in a week. Here are some painkillers while you recover. I included the dosage instructions inside."

Inside the bag was a small bottle of green pills. I immediately took one, desperate to relieve the pain.

Then we tested the implants. The doctor made me do various exercises and try out the features of my new eyes, including night vision and thermal vision.

Better models would have better definition from greater distances. Some could highlight hostiles and potential weapon systems as well.

"Good, now open up your secretarial assistant program. You should see your Nova Tech Stars Mk.4 and the Zenitech Hoth Mk.3 itself listed there."

I confirmed it, which didn't take too long because the SAID allowed me to navigate its menus with just a thought.

Just a few more exercises remained. It was quite strange having my intentions read by an inner secretary and texting with my mind.

Then I was finally free to leave. After I had made my payment, of course.

Once I got home, I stuffed myself with food and jumped into my bed before opening my status screen.

**Status**
**Level:** 1
**EXP:** 20/100
**Musculoskeletal:** 11
**Neural Reflex:** 15
**Visuomotor Coordination:** 12
**Endurance:** 9
**Sensory Perception:** 37
**Upgrade Points:** 0
**Upgrades:**
    Stealth +3
    Hacking +3

**Enhancements:**
　　　SAID: Zenitech Hoth Mk.3
　　　Optics: Nova Tech Stars Mk.4

*Hmm... My sensory perception went up and my new cybernetics are listed under enhancements now. I guess it makes sense that getting better eyes means better perception.*

I couldn't dwell on my status screen much longer. The pain and fatigue prevented me from focusing and my eyelids struggled to stay open.

Hopefully, I could sleep this off.

* * *

I spent the next five days resting at home and taking walks around the neighborhood. I also tried out the milkshakes throughout the area, as they were among the few things that tasted like they were meant for human consumption. The soothing coldness helped numb my dull headache.

On the sixth day, I took public transit to the south end of the city.

"Good evening, everybodyyyyy! Tonight, we are going to go crazy! It will soon be five hundred years since we restarted civilization, from living in the toxic wastelands to building a space elevator... twice! Out in space, we—"

The sound from the radio died as the subway doors opened and I exited. I followed along the GPS route displayed in the corner of my vision.

The roads grew more and more crowded as I got closer to the seaside. In the distance, the enormous space elevator lit up the middle of the ocean as it loomed far above. It was like a giant glow stick.

The mood was festive as people drank and partied out on the streets along the waterfront.

I arrived a little early for the real celebration, so I found a cafe and passed some time by working out how businesses were started here. I had gradually grown accustomed to my new implants and, with them, the convenience of a computer on standby in my head.

The SAID was super useful even aside from communication, as I could use it as a digital wallet, allowing me to pay fast like some of my convenience store customers.

When it was almost midnight, I headed out and patrolled the area.

I made my way into the alley of a building, one of a handful I had picked out earlier. There I found a suitable place to jack into the security system with my worn-out terminal. I really needed to look into getting a specialized hacking terminal or a cybernetic version of one once I could afford it.

Within a minute, I could tell the building's security wasn't something I could breach with my current skills—not in a short time, at least—so I did the sensible thing and gave up. I repeated the same thing with several other buildings until I found one that had an older security system, something that I could bypass.

Once I had access to the building, I made my way to the roof.

With my new optics, there was no need for binoculars, as I could directly zoom in on my surroundings, though they didn't have the best clarity.

A stark contrast existed between the waterfront, where a boisterous crowd gathered, and the other streets in the opposite direction, where it was deserted and quiet.

The crowd grew louder when party boats came into view, along with several vehicles hovering above.

Not long after, midnight arrived. Everyone counted down together for the last ten seconds. Once it was over, fireworks shot up around the space elevator, in the shape of a giant 500.

For a few seconds, I took some comfort in how similar the celebrations were to my old world before I shook off the sentimental thoughts and turned on the night vision mode on my optics.

* * *

For hours, I had looked around from the roof of the building. If I still had my organic eyes, I surely would have felt the strain by now. While I didn't miss them, I wondered if I would feel the same when I started replacing other parts of my body.

I planned to get an implant to address my weak stamina, which was critical when I worked alone and had to do everything myself.

My thoughts were interrupted when I finally spotted what I was looking for. Two figures exited their van and approached a drunk couple making out in a dark alleyway.

As it was now a race against time, I sprinted down the building and made my way towards the van.

Quietly, I followed them, trying to control my breathing. I spotted one of the two figures crouched over the couple, who were now unconscious. One of the figures had connected two terminal cables to the couple. It was hard to see from here, but the cables must have been plugged into their implants. Meanwhile, the other figure, who appeared to be a rough-looking woman, stood guard against the wall with a metal baton in hand.

"—longer till the damn jammer is up? We could probably snatch half a dozen more tonight if you could hurry your ass up." The woman turned in my direction and spat on the ground.

I got closer by moving as her field of view turned the other way, hiding behind a nearby dumpster. Once I was close enough to feel confident in my aim, I double-checked the safety on my new pistol.

"Yeah, yeah… Easy for you to say," a man's voice said. "Our clients this time want healthy adults, and these two have some decent corpo hardware. It'll just take a little longer to jam the signal."

With a clear view of both my targets in the alleyway, I took my time aiming and pulled the trigger. Before the first bullet reached her, I gently squeezed it again. Two soft electric buzzes hissed out.

*+10 EXP*

Immediately, I aimed at the crouched figure and shot out another two bullets from my coilgun as he tried to turn around. I rushed forward down the alley, carefully keeping the Suri trained on the prone man.

Once I was right above him, I placed another careful shot in the back of his head.

*+10 EXP*

After examining the bodies, I knew that the couple was still breathing, so I disconnected the cables from their necks.

I looted any guns and valuables off of my kills and found the unconscious couple's wallets with their corpo IDs in them. They were low-level employees who worked at Amazing Corp, one of the largest corps that dealt in military equipment.

Then I checked my aim with the first target, noting the woman had two gunshot wounds in the chest.

The guy I had shot also had a Nova Tech-branded cyberarm, but a really old model. I thought about taking it so I could sell it, but it sounded like a lot of work, lugging around an arm and finding someone to buy it when the returns on it weren't that great. I decided to leave it and continued on.

I found four pistols and the baton, so I left two of the pistols with the couple, assuming they were theirs, along with enough credits for them to get home, just in case they couldn't access their SAIDs.

Once I was done, I calmly walked out of the area and returned to the roof.

Although the space elevator gave Elevate City a great concentration of wealth, it also brought along its own issues of crime and wealth disparity.

There were tons of kidnappers looking to make some quick cash through ransoming, harvesting organs and cybernetics, and selling people for corporate experiments, which had probably been happening to the couple.

I settled in my spot on the rooftop and opened up my status while I continued to keep a lookout over the surrounding area.

**Status**
**Level:** 2
**EXP:** 10/200
**Musculoskeletal:** 11
**Neural Reflex:** 15
**Visuomotor Coordination:** 12
**Endurance:** 9
**Sensory Perception:** 37
**Upgrade Points:** 2

**Upgrades:**
  Stealth +3
  Hacking +3
**Enhancements:**
  SAID: Zenitech Hoth Mk.3
  Optics: Nova Tech Stars Mk.4

It was reassuring to see that I had finally leveled up, and I got two upgrade points from it as well. I thought I would only get one, which made it a pleasant surprise. It also confirmed that none of my other stats went up from leveling up, which was a shame. Good thing I wasn't planning on becoming a superman.

As much as I wanted to invest my new points into something that would help me safely make money, I knew that increasing my ability to level up as safely as possible came first. Taking that into consideration, I dumped both points into stealth.

Once again, a wealth of knowledge entered my mind, as if someone uploaded textbooks directly into my brain. Gaining the new muscle reflexes made my body feel like a puppet on strings, though that uneasiness went away as fast as it came.

Not long after I returned to the rooftop, I noticed a police cruiser and an armored vehicle marked with Amazing Corp's logo pulling up by the alley where the couple was. It seemed like the jammer thing the guy was talking about was undone. Lucky them.

With the presence of the police vehicle nearby, I decided to roam around the other desolate parts of town to try my luck elsewhere.

Not even fifteen minutes had passed when I spotted some guy stun-gunning a drunk who was puking his guts out.

*Hopefully it'll stay this easy to find them for the rest of the night.*

# CHAPTER 2

## BACK TO THE GRIND

When I woke up, it was already late afternoon, not long before sunset. I had stayed out until sunrise yesterday, but only found a grand total of three encounters.

Maybe I should start tracking these people back to their hideouts, because what I was currently doing didn't seem efficient at all. I could also try asking Fitel, though I doubted he would hand out information for free.

With no obvious answers coming to me, I headed out to visit the weapon store downstairs. Remembering my last visit, I unloaded my firearm with practiced ease and headed further into the store.

I headed straight to the counter to sell the loot I had gotten last night. It was a different clerk this time, a gruff man sporting scars on his face. We completed our transaction quickly, and my HUD notified me of the new funds.

My next errand brought me to a place I had never visited before. It was three blocks down from where I lived, at the edge of the downtown area.

Honestly, I was surprised this place was open. My common sense told me a bank wouldn't be open on New Year's Day, let alone past five p.m., but I had checked online, and here it was. I guessed there weren't any unions in this world and corporations didn't have their employees' working conditions in mind.

Now that I thought about it, I didn't think there were even public holidays, ever.

Fortunately, I didn't need a teller, so I headed for the much shorter line to use the ATM. Then I deposited the cash from my new gains.

As I navigated the machine, my thoughts couldn't help but stray towards leveling up my Hacking skill until I could hack the bank.

There was so much I could do with that money, though their security seemed tough. I was confident I could do it as long as I invested enough points into the skill.

It was only a thought, though, as I doubted I would get away with it without an entire corporation or two hunting me down. I was just one man. I'd rather not take on an entire organization alone.

While getting rich was my goal, there was no point if I couldn't enjoy my wealth.

Putting away any tempting thoughts about robbing banks and corporations, I returned home.

I had rested enough, so it was time to take on another job. Immediately, I made a call to my QG through my SAID.

"You have reached Fitel. What can I do for you today, Rollo?"

I minimized the empty profile picture with the Sound Only option to the corner of my vision.

"Fitel, got any jobs that suit me?"

"I hope that means you have fully recovered?"

"Yeah, I'm fine now."

"I see. There is a job that I have been waiting for someone like you to handle, though it's more of a lead in finding an item, so it may not pay if the lead is wrong."

"What's the missing item?"

"A SAID from one of their presumed-deceased middle executives. Raiders wiped out a Nova Tech caravan in the New

North American wasteland and they want the SAID retrieved, or proof of its destruction."

"New North America... You think it's here in Elevate City, a few thousand kilometers across the sea? And a big corporation like Nova Tech didn't have some fancy self-destruct function on their important equipment?"

"That is correct, and they did, but it seemed to have malfunctioned when their caravan got hit with an EMP. That is why we were hired. You'll be paid thirty thousand credits if you can retrieve the item, but nothing otherwise. They want this to be done quietly before any rival corporation catches wind of anything." Fitel emphasized the last part.

"Okay, I'll take the job, but you better find me something else if this lead doesn't work out. I'm not trying to waste time looking for a needle in a haystack or anything, not for long, at least."

Fitel uncharacteristically paused. "Excellent. I will have the information sent to you soon." He got his last line in and hung up as usual.

I lay flat on the couch as I browsed through the intel he sent over. It helped that I didn't need to hold anything as I read, since the screen was literally in my eyes.

The lead was kind of a stretch. To be honest, it was just some guy selling some military-grade weapons that matched the ones the raided caravan used.

Even if these were the same weapons, there was a possibility they'd come from a different band of raiders who'd been killed and looted. Still, even that meant I could learn more about the raiders by tracking the looter down.

I first had to find the person, and the only clues I had were pictures of him and his car taken from a street camera in the Neon

District. The two sets of pictures were practically identical, though taken on two separate Sunday mornings.

* * *

I moved along with the flow of the crowd, passing by clubs and bars with huge lines. Many had pink neon lights outside, with windows where you could look in and see the people dancing, in their birthday suits.

There was a mixed bag of individuals around here, from gang members to average-wage drones, to wealthy-looking guys who were let in as soon as they stepped out of their rides.

I kept my eyes open as I watched a valet driving the car, recently put into his care, towards a nearby parking complex.

My GPS guided me to my destination. I pulled up the photo on my optics so I could compare the faces of anyone I came across.

Before long, I arrived and, thankfully, found the same car from the photos. I saw no one nearby, so I approached the vehicle and attached a small chip.

With that done, now I could take it easy. I made my way to a bar that had outdoor seats and a good view of the car, where I then sat back and ordered a drink. The cheap alcohol I had drunk in this world was frankly nasty, but it was better than nothing.

Another server, different from the one who took my order, brought my drink, but then sat down instead of leaving.

"You seem lonely. Mind if I join you?"

Not wanting to cause a scene, I nodded and resumed watching the people walking along or lining up for the venues.

"So you looking for anything tonight, hun?" The woman moved her seat closer and grabbed onto my arm.

"No, I'm just having a drink." I spotted people flirting.

The woman had been staring at me. I realized what she was getting at, so I ordered her a drink.

"Hun, no one comes to the Neon District desiring nothing. Here, anything can be bought. At the right price, of course." She took a sip and leaned in closer.

While she was attractive, I would never part with my money for anything she could offer.

The lady leaned in close and whispered into my ear. "I can help you look for the person you're searching for."

"What do you mean? I'm not looking for any—"

"Hun," she said, her voice still quiet, "you don't have to pretend. I've been here long enough to tell what a man is looking for. I don't care if you're some detective looking into adultery or some hitman. You give me the creds and I can get you the information."

"I don't need your help. Maybe next time."

I paid the bill, left her a tip, and moved to where I would meet my cab.

The tracker I had put on the car started to move. It seemed like my target had gotten in while I was distracted, but that didn't matter. I wasn't going to follow too closely.

My automated taxi arrived in three minutes. I guided it towards my target, taking a slightly different route.

After twenty minutes of driving, the target seemed to have stopped at a secluded area that had nothing but storage buildings, so I had the cab stop a distance away.

With night as my ally, I stayed in the darker parts of the street and made my way closer. It didn't take long before I spotted a pair of old warehouses. They faced a shared outdoor parking lot with concrete broken apart by overgrown grass. The buildings were gated off with flimsy chains, nearly surrounded by a thicket of eerie-looking trees.

The area was quiet, but with the thermal vision of my optics, I spotted figures at both entrances.

I moved around to an unmonitored section of the fence. Then I pulled out my dagger and flipped the switch. It produced a dull buzzing noise as it was brought to life. Slowly pushing the blade toward the fence, I parted the obstacle with little resistance.

I moved cautiously, mindful about making any noise, and got to the other side of the fence. The car I was tracking was in front of the warehouse closest to my position.

As I had done to infiltrate buildings previously, I moved towards the side door, but to my surprise, it didn't have any electronics to hack into. It was a mechanical lock.

*Why can't these people use half-decent facilities?*

I hugged the building's walls and made my way around until I noticed an open window on the second floor.

Luckily, there were also dumpsters nearby, so I slowly pushed one toward the opened window. When I was halfway there, the dumpster screeched.

*Damn it! Right underneath the grass where I pushed it was a hidden patch of worn-out pavement.*

I quickly jumped into a dark patch of tall grass and aimed my firearm at the nearby back door.

I waited for five minutes, but there didn't seem to be any movement.

After another minute, I got back up and started moving the dumpster again, while trying my best not to screw up again. Before long, I managed to push it right under the window and climb up. I reached for the window when I suddenly heard the metal door just around the corner swung open.

It caught me off guard. I froze awkwardly atop the dumpster with my gun pointed at the corner of the building, hoping no one would come my way.

The soft click of a lighter rang out, accompanied by footsteps that only grew louder as they headed my way.

A bald man entered my vision with a cigarette in hand. He took a puff before looking up, and found me frozen atop the dumpster.

Our gazes met for a full second before he reached for the gun on his hip, but he was too slow. I pulled the trigger repeatedly in a slight panic.

The Suri hissed out multiple times, and the man soon collapsed.

*+10 EXP*

I jumped off the dumpster and took cover behind it, keeping my gun aimed towards that corner. It took a full minute before I realized there wasn't anyone else and released the breath I had been holding.

Okay, while I had to admit that wasn't the most elegant, it did the job. The previously locked door was now opened, and I also had the window as another potential point of entry.

*Let's hope the rest of the night goes more smoothly than that did...*

# CHAPTER 9

## SNEAKY BEAKY LIKE

Once I realized there were no other threats, I collected myself and inspected the person I had shot.

From the experience notification, I knew he was dead. The body didn't have keys or anything similar, so I threw it into the dumpster along with any equipment, opting to go over it later. With that set aside, I entered the building from the door that the man had opened.

I tried to stay as silent as possible as I passed through the hallway, checking each room I came across. Most of them looked abandoned and were filled with piles of trash or dusty boxes.

At the end of the hallway was a door that led to the main warehouse floor, where tall empty shelves loomed overhead.

Off to one side was an open area with stacks of metal shipping containers half surrounding it. This area was well lit, and I spotted a person sitting below a set of stairs that led atop the containers, leisurely reading an actual book.

It seemed like there weren't many people active at this time. I couldn't really blame them, either, as it was around four in the morning.

With the place so lightly guarded, I moved off to the side away from the lone man reading, where I climbed up the tightly packed shipping containers. They were being used as makeshift rooms. I slowly opened the door to one and found a man in a sleeping bag snoring away. When his face didn't match with the image of the target in my optics, I moved on.

Then I repeated the same steps for all the container rooms on this floor. Some of them were empty, but most weren't. Still without my target, I made my way back down to the first floor, taking a staircase several feet away from where the man was still reading.

I dropped down as lightly as possible, but I couldn't entirely kill the sound. Hastily moving to another spot, I kept watch for any reaction. The man looked up from his book for a second, but didn't bother investigating and returned to the story.

After allowing the man some time to be absorbed in his book, I resumed investigating the ground floor.

It wasn't until the third one that I found someone awake.

"Would it kill you to knock—" The man froze as he turned toward the barrel of my gun.

I gestured for him to stay silent while I kept my Suri trained on him and closed the door behind me.

"Adam, I'm just here to ask a few questions. Now, answer them quietly, and we all can go our separate ways. Do you understand?"

He nodded before I gave him permission to speak.

"Who are you? Why are you looking for me?" Adam kept alternating glances between me and the barrel pointed at him.

"No, Adam, I am the one asking questions here. Tell me, where did you get those weapons you sold a few weeks earlier?"

"Weapons? What weapons?"

"Come on now, Adam, we both know you're lying. Let's not make this difficult."

"Look, I do a lot of errands for our group, so I probably sold off many packages, but that doesn't mean I know what they were," he said as he wiped the sweat building around his temples.

I stared at him unflinchingly.

"Okay, look. It wasn't my idea. I'm just a grunt. I didn't know we were raiding your corp. I'll do anything you tell me. Just let me go!" he pleaded.

*So his group was responsible for the raid? I thought wastelanders did it... Was this guy a raider? No way. I thought they didn't stay in cities.*

"So what did you do with the things you stole from us?" I asked, playing into the role of the corpo that he had assigned me.

*Might as well go along with it, right?*

"It's all here with us. I even have the keys to the stash. They're right there in the drawer." He slowly placed his hand on it, then looked towards me for permission to continue.

I nodded and took a step back.

Adam gradually opened it, but then abruptly jerked. The drawer flew out, and he snatched something from within it.

Two soft *pfft* noises filled the small shipping container, followed by two *clink*s of bullets hitting the walls.

*+10 EXP*

*I should have known this was how it was going to end...*

As I inspected the room and his body, I found nothing in particular besides the gun he tried to pull on me.

I was getting ready to leave when a knock came from the door.

"You okay in there, Adam?" a man's voice said, and when no one responded, he continued knocking.

*Shit. My gun may be quiet, but the sound of the bullets hitting the metal walls wasn't.*

I stalked closer to the door, pushed it slightly open, aimed my gun at the gap, and waited.

"You mute now or what?" His head peered through the gap. "The fuck you doi—"

I opened fire from almost point-blank range, right at his forehead. I dashed back into the warehouse, away from the shipping containers.

Five minutes passed. It didn't seem like anyone else had noticed the commotion.

Now that their group was deemed hostile in my book, it was time to earn some experience points. I already killed three of them, and the last thing I wanted was to be a potential target of revenge.

I retraced my previous path, then slipped into the shipping container rooms one by one to silently dispatch the occupants with my dagger. I didn't even need to turn on the vibro-blade function, as I could take my time aiming for the vitals.

After I went through every container, I secured the area. I combed through to go over any loot they had and piled it all up near where I dispatched the man who had been reading by the stairs. Most of them were guns, and not all that interesting.

Just as I was bringing the last few hauls out, someone called out. I had my hands full and was in the middle of descending the stairs. Turning, I saw a man walking my way.

"Hey, Baron! When the fuck are you coming to relieve my shift? I've been—" He stared at me once he got close enough to make out my masked face and dark attire.

He raised his rifle toward me. "Who the fuck are you?"

I dropped everything in my hands, jumped off the side of the stairs, and took cover behind the metal staircase.

Several loud shots echoed throughout the warehouse. The man had started shooting as soon as I'd moved.

Now that I was in cover, I could take the time to prepare for a fair gunfight... Okay, maybe not a talent I was confident in, but thankfully I had some aces up my sleeve.

As I swapped the mag in my gun, I fumbled it, as my left hand didn't respond like I was used to.

*Shit!*

I looked down and saw my blood trickling out of a hole in my upper arm.

Deeming the imminent threat more important, I peeked out to scan for my opponent's location. In response, I was sent several more shots that forced me to duck back into cover. At least now I had a rough idea of where he was: behind an old forklift.

I swapped the ammo in the gun with my one good arm and blind-fired several times in his direction.

*Boom.*

*Boom.*

*Boom.*

Three explosions rang out. He didn't shoot back this time.

"Haha!" I couldn't help but laugh. Firing off explosives sure was fun. If only I wasn't starting to feel the pain from my wound...

Those explosive rounds had better be effective, too. They were quite expensive! At least the cost would keep me from getting addicted to them.

I took another peek out, and bullets once again came at me.

I responded with my own shots, exploding ones at that. But this time, I started pushing forward by diving behind a crate while laying down suppressive fire.

*Let's see if you can fight back when pelted by a rain of explosive rounds! I'll show you that money is power!*

When I jumped out of cover again, no more shots were fired. I made my way to the forklift where I last saw him.

There, I spotted the man holding onto his bloodied chest while panting heavily. His rifle was lying on the ground nearby.

I pulled the trigger to finish the man off.

*+10 EXP*

With the system having confirmed the kill, I took a closer look at my left arm, as I felt warm blood continuing to drip out.

*Shit, I sure fucked up.*

I should've known there still was a guard out front. This wasn't a video game where enemies stayed in place and patrolled on fixed routes.

*Wait... There's still an entire building next door that I haven't checked out yet, and there's a guard posted out in front there too.*

After I realized the threat I was under, I retrieved a syringe from my med kit, stabbed it right beside the wound to stop the bleeding, and double-timed out of the building the same way I entered.

By the time I was outside, I heard car engines starting up and lots of yelling. I made my way out of the fenced area and back into the thicket.

"Over there!" a voice shouted out behind me.

*Damn it.*

I headed further in where the foliage was thicker, covering my tracks. I made my way around a hill to ensure I broke my pursuers' line of sight before I found a nice hiding spot atop a large tree.

In a minute or so, I spotted several lights moving nearby. I waited until it was a distance away before dressing my wound and collected my thoughts.

*Well, at least I now know that I hit the right target. But if I left now, who knows if they would relocate or not? In the first place, could I even get away?*

They had cars on standby, and people searching for me on foot. I would need to call for a pickup to extract me, but that was probably something they would expect.

In that case, I should play to my strengths.

"Status," I said.

**Status**
**Level:** 3
**EXP:** 20/300
**Musculoskeletal:** 11
**Neural Reflex:** 15
**Visuomotor Coordination:** 12
**Endurance:** 9
**Sensory Perception:** 37
**Upgrade Points:** 2
**Upgrades:**
>Stealth +5
>Hacking +3
**Enhancements:**
>SAID: Zenitech Hoth Mk.3
>Optics: Nova Tech Stars Mk.4

*You know, I planned to start spending my points on technology skills that could help me start earning credits, but I guess the saying "No plan survives contact with the enemy" is too true.*

I took a deep breath, mentally preparing myself for the direct knowledge dump into my brain that came when I used my points, and double-checked my equipment.

*I really need to be more careful and avoid falling into situations like this from now on. Let's hope this will be the last time.*

# CHAPTER 10

# SNEAKY BEAKY LIKE PT. 2

**Yuri Kasakov—Outland Marauders**

"What the fuck is going on, Yuri?" The six-foot-five man walked towards Yuri with anxiety in his voice. His face was stoic as always, though. All his augments likely meant he could no longer display any facial expressions.

"It seems someone attacked the other warehouse. Everyone there is dead. We spotted a person running from the scene, and a team is chasing them right now."

"Everyone is dead?! How many of them are there? We better get ready to evacuate this shithole."

"Yes... Most of our people were killed in their sleep, and we only spotted one of the enemies so far. Our cars are all on standby, but we don't even have twenty men left now..."

"Idiots! The lot of them! Go recall everyone. We're packing up and leaving."

"We're just going to let them go?"

"Do I have to repeat myself?"

"No, sir. I'll go call the team back myself," Yuri said, and speed-walked out of the boss' room.

"That fucker is probably happy now that there are fewer of us to share our latest score with," a beautiful red-haired woman said from behind him.

"Now is not the time for this, Kat."

At his words, Kat pouted, to which he could only ruefully shake his head.

He used his SAID to place a call to Jarvin, the leader of the pursuit team, and was answered on the second ring.

"Jarvin, it's time to leave. Get your men back here right away."

After a few seconds of waiting, he still had no response, but he knew he was on the line, as he could hear heaving and breathing on the other end.

"Hey, Jarvin. Answer me!"

"Can't talk, we're pinned down, send reinforcements," the man whispered before the call disconnected.

*Damn it! Did they get led into a trap?*

"Kat, darling, I'm going to pick up Jarvin and his team. I need you to stay here to coordinate."

"What?! I'm coming with you!"

"No, we don't have any men to spare. I need you here. Don't worry, I'll have Roman with me."

She sighed. "Fine."

He walked out of the building and found his brother leaning against his car.

"Roman, let's go. Jarvin and his boys are calling for help."

He nodded back at Yuri before grabbing his shotgun from the trunk.

Yuri led the way out of the compound, towards where he had sent the team earlier.

They headed into the thicket fast, without needing to use any lighting equipment. Both of them could see perfectly fine in the dark with their optics.

Occasionally, the two heard shots in the distance, so they had no confusion about the direction they needed to go. Once the gunshots grew louder, they readied their weapons, kept low, and moved from cover to cover.

In fifteen minutes, they were close enough to start worrying about friendly fire. He called Jarvin again as they inched closer to receive updates on their position.

The two made their way to a small space surrounded by thick trees and a steep hill. They spotted their man peeking out and rushed towards him.

"What's the sitch, Jarvin? Where's the rest of your team?" Yuri said as he looked him over, along with the only other person with him. She was named Sandra, he recalled, someone he had spoken little to. Both were wounded, but not down.

"We're the only two left. Someone's out there hunting us. They keep shooting us from every direction and we can't find them, so we took cover here."

Yuri took out a mirror and used it to look around from the safety of cover.

"How long has it been since you were last under fire?" he said. He threw the mirror over to his brother to see if he could find anything that he hadn't.

"I don't know... Maybe like five minutes ago."

His brother finished scanning the area and shook his head.

"That means they could've been gone by now. We didn't see anything or get shot at on our way here," Yuri said as he rose to his full height, making sure his gun covered the gaps in his armor. Before he could step out, a hand landed on his shoulder.

"Or maybe they're waiting for us to get out of cover to start picking us off again," Jarvin warned.

"Boss wants us out of here ASAP. We don't have time for this." He brushed Jarvin's hand off and started jogging back in a zigzag path, just in case there really was someone out there.

Several minutes of jogging later, the group arrived at the edge of the compound, where he stopped them.

"Something's wrong... I don't see any movement up ahead, and they're supposed to be packing up right now."

He made a call to his boss, but it just kept ringing. He then tried Kat, but got the same result.

"Hey, you guys. See if you can reach anyone. The boss ain't answering."

After everyone had tried every number they had, they still couldn't get in contact with anyone.

"This ain't right, man..." Jarvin said nervously. "I knew it! It's probably some corpo's hit squad. They found out after all. I don't want none of this shit, man." He started backing away.

"Come on, Jarvin. Boss won't enjoy hearing about you going off with that shit again. Let's carefully check things out. We still have a huge fortune sitting back in there," Yuri pleaded. He wanted as much help as he could get to go save Kat.

"I don't know, man..." Jarvin gave a troubled look to his partner Sandra, who simply returned a shrug.

"We'll be quick," Yuri said. "I mean, if you leave and the boss is still kicking, he ain't going to take kindly to traitors."

"Fine, fine. We're in. Let's go quickly. We needed a car anyway."

Yuri gave Roman a quick glance. He nodded back.

*Guess I don't have to ask if he's in too.*

They moved in a diamond-shaped formation as they had been trained to do, with Yuri at the front.

Seeing as everything was quiet, they opted to go into the warehouse swiftly as opposed to quietly. They weren't that good at being quiet anyway.

The group got close enough to the parking area to make out a few bodies spread around.

As they approached, Yuri briefly noted who the bodies were, ensuring Kat wasn't one of them. He led the team towards the boss' room, which was right next to where the gang had stashed their loot.

Inside the warehouse, it was completely dark beside the flashlight attachments Jarvin and Sandra had on their rifles. Night vision wasn't perfect. In total darkness like this, their optics couldn't see far ahead. Their lights shined on the floor, showing a few trails of blood, but no bodies since they entered the building. It was so quiet Yuri could hear Jarvin swallow and adjust the grip on his weapon.

Soon the four of them arrived at the shipping container that was the boss' room. The door was already open, and they saw him with his head planted on his desk, face down. It almost seemed like he had fallen asleep, but the gaping hole in the back of his head told a different story.

They next went to check the room with the loot. It was locked, but the second-in-command had a key.

Just as Yuri was about to insert it, he heard something dropping, followed by a few dull thuds. He turned around and saw Sandra sprawled out on the ground while Roman crouched down and fired his shotgun repeatedly into the darkness.

Even with night vision, he couldn't spot anything in the direction Roman was shooting.

"Back to back—now!" Yuri yelled out louder than he intended.

He ran up, setting his shoulders against Jarvin's, and covered a different angle. After a moment, he didn't feel Jarvin anymore, and turned around.

"Fuck! I told you this was a bad idea!" Jarvin yelled, running towards the exit.

*That goddamn coward.*

"Brother, we should get out of here," Roman whispered.

"But what about Kat—"

"She probably already escaped if… the worst hadn't already happened. We need to stay alive to find her."

"Fine." He gritted his teeth. He knew Roman was right, and he wasn't thinking straight right now.

The brothers set their backs against each other, but were startled by the sound of automatic gunfire followed by explosions coming from the parking lot.

Spying out a window, they noted a new flaming vehicle by the main entrance.

That settled it: it wasn't worth it to go towards the parking lot. The duo continued towards the back door.

When they were about halfway there, something punched into Yuri's chest with a dull thud.

He could tell from experience that he had been shot, but luckily, it hadn't penetrated his body armor. Laying down suppressive fire, he briskly scanned for what shot him.

He caught a glimpse of a shadow just as it ducked back behind a nearby shipping container. Roman followed closely behind, but both of them had been caught, and the figure was herding them to the front again.

The two dashed away from the enemy while staying alert. Yuri felt bullets hitting body armor once more, but this time from a completely different direction.

Roman started firing back to no avail, as they could only catch glimpses of the enemy before they disappeared.

"We can't stay any longer," Yuri said. "There's too much cover in here. Their weapons may be silent, but they can't penetrate our armor. Run out together now!"

They sprinted back toward the main entrance. When they were just around the corner, an explosion boomed right next to him. It threw him straight onto the ground and left his ears ringing.

His body heat left him, carried away by the warm liquid flowing out from his wounds.

*Fuck, is this the end?*

After what felt like an eternity, the ringing in his head eased up. He tried to get up, but only made it halfway when he saw a figure standing over him. It pointed something blurry in his direction... no; he realized it was his vision that was blurry, and that something pointed at him was obviously a gun.

*So I guess this is the end...*

He always knew it was coming. He had killed enough to know it would one day be his turn, especially with all the misdeeds he had done.

But he didn't regret it. You did what was needed to survive in this world.

He mustered every bit of air he had left in his lungs and muttered out his last words.

"Do it."

Then everything faded to black.

# CHAPTER II

## RAIDERS

Once I finished what looked like the last enemy, I immediately went to examine the rooms near the big, dangerous cyborg I had taken out first.

Unfortunately, with one arm injured, I hadn't had any leeway to leave anyone alive to question, but judging from the reactions of the last group I dealt with, it seemed like he was someone important. I found the key my last target had dropped earlier and unlocked the container.

Inside were neat stacks of crates with Nova Tech logos on them. Upon opening one, I found several hands, prosthetic ones. The other crates were all filled with similar cybernetics: various limbs, tendons, and muscle replacements.

This was a fortune. It was worth way more than the thirty thousand credits from this job. It was a flat-out jackpot.

The models in the crates were all current-gen ones, worth a pretty penny. This was a huge payday! I couldn't wait to be able to afford better food, buy bots to do cleaning and cooking, and maybe even move to a better place... though that would require a more stable income.

I could also use this as a startup fund to bring forth my business. I just needed to level up more and upgrade a suitable skill to base my business around.

While taking in the mountain of expensive tech packed in front of me, I spotted a box in the corner that didn't have any markings on it. Within it lay limbs and other smaller cybernetics in a disorganized fashion. As I rummaged through the box, I set aside the smaller ones and examined what make and model they were.

It wasn't long before I found the SAID I was originally looking for. I guessed the box contained all the chrome looted from the bodies of the caravan's personnel.

With my newfound fortune came the problem of how to move it.

Now that the mission objective was secured, I walked out to the parking lot to find a means of transport. It was about time I got my own ride. I wondered how the ownership and insurance stuff would work. I was not looking forward to that one bit.

Inspecting the vehicles, I found they were all pretty worn, and some of them had bullet holes all over. Only two didn't: a sedan and an SUV. After spending some time searching the bodies, I found the corresponding keys and started packing away all my loot into the cars.

It took over half an hour to load them with all the crates from the shipping container. With some room left, I went to search all the other locked areas I had ignored when I was busy taking out the surrounding hostiles.

The shipping containers I searched in the first warehouse I snuck into were simply bedrooms. When I went back now to comb through what remained in the second warehouse where the boss was, my search came up empty until I opened up the one furthest from the exit.

The moment I opened the last container, a pungent stench rushed out, and within, I could make out the two slim figures in the corner, huddled together. Most notable about the silhouettes were the chains tied around their arms and feet, attached to the railing welded to the wall.

As I wasn't able to make out much detail even with night vision, I took out a flashlight and shined it towards them. With color restored to the world, I spotted a girl with long brown hair around my age holding onto a boy around eight, who looked like her brother.

"Who are you two?" I asked as I made my way closer.

The girl snapped, "You're not with them, are you? Why don't you introduce yourself first?" She placed herself between me and the boy.

"I'm Rollo. I had some business with your captors, but they aren't around anymore. Now I can leave you alone and be on my way if you want, or I could do some charity work and bust you out of there, up to you."

Helping them wasn't profitable in a financial sense. In fact, depending on who they really were, it could be a big risk. But I hoped it would pay off. Whoever ran the warehouses had locked them up for a reason. Maybe they wanted to jam their cybernetics like the couple in the alley and loot them for parts.

What I really hoped, though, was that these children had intel or connections I could use for my business.

Right now, they weren't hostile like the others in these warehouses. They were innocent until they proved themselves guilty. I couldn't stomach the thought of killing them.

Saving them wasn't that steep of an investment for me. I wouldn't even mind giving them food and shelter, as long as I stayed wary and kept my own cards close to my chest.

"Yes, remove these chains... please."

"Sure thing. Stay still." I pulled out my handy vibro-dagger to cut the chains loose.

The two of them followed me out. I had everything packed and looted the place clean, so I was ready to leave. They didn't speak until the moment they had stepped outside.

"Where are we?" the girl said as she looked around.

"We're in… the outskirts of District 12." I read off the map in my optics.

"Is that in the north part of NLA?"

"NLA?"

"New Los Angeles." The girl stared at me as if I was dumb.

*Okay, maybe they aren't the local connection I was looking to make.*

"I'm just going to go ahead and let you know we're in Elevate City, over thirty-five hundred kilometers off the coast of New North America."

"How many miles is that?"

"Um, over two thousand."

She froze for a second as the boy held her closer.

"You guys want to stay at my place for now?"

* * *

"Excellent work, Mr. Halls. Send me a message once you have dropped off the package at the designated spot."

"About that loot I mentioned. Are you sure Nova Tech won't be wanting it back?" I asked while I kept my eyes on the stoplight, waiting for it to turn green.

"The chances are very low, as they've likely written it off and claimed their insurance policy already. Unless you retrieved a sizable part of the shipment and flaunted it around, there should be no one looking for it," Fitel replied at his usual measured pace.

That was useful to know. I had only told him I found a few cybernetics instead of the dozens of crates that I actually had.

"I see... Thank you. I'll text you once I drop off the package."

"Understood. And one more thing, Mr. Halls, I would recommend keeping minimal contact with people affiliated with raiders, regardless of age."

"Thank you. I have it under control."

"Very well. Until we speak again," Fitel said before he hung up.

His last words gave me the impression that harboring these two was a greater risk than expected. But as before, I liked to do my own research.

I turned to look back at the other two people in the car and gave them a smile.

They had opened up a little, and we managed to hold a conversion while the auto-drive of this car and the one behind it did its work. It seemed they were children of a tribe living out in the wastelands of New North America, what most people called wastelanders or raiders. Apparently, they had been held hostage, and their tribe was forced to work for the group.

I guessed that wasn't a half-bad plan for a motley crew, as corporations rarely cared much about raider attacks. They were considered cockroaches that kept coming back no matter how many times they were put down, and it was an unprofitable business trying to wipe them out, considering the harsh terrain they lived on.

The group was using the information they gathered in the city to force raiders to do the actual work, and would have gotten away with it too, if only they hadn't happened to get a hold of some sensitive item the corp wanted back.

I took some time to message my building's management office through my SAID and attained two guest parking passes. It seemed I would have to go in person if I wanted to rent one.

Once that was done, I spent some time surfing the web, looking for ways to send these two to NLA, the closest city to their tribe.

Plane tickets were way more expensive than I had thought, easily in the five digits, and these two didn't have any IDs in the first place either.

"And we're here. How about we grab some food first for you guys before going up to my place?" I turned to ask as we pulled up to the colossal megabuilding.

"Woah... You live in this giant tower?" the little boy asked.

"Just renting a small place here. It's almost two hundred floors, housing hundreds of thousands of people."

"That's like a lot," the boy replied, counting on his fingers.

I grabbed a crate with my one good arm, dreading the fact that I had to move them all to the apartment now.

"Here, let me give you a hand." The girl quickly took a crate, wincing at my poor one-armed display.

"No, it's fine. I'm sure you're both tired. Let's go get something for you guys to eat first."

"I insist. It would shame my clan to eat without having worked for it." She glared at me with determined eyes.

"I'll help too!" the boy said brightly, and carefully picked up a crate.

"By the way, my name is Sarah of the Wells Clan, and my brother is Caleb," the girl muttered, carefully watching her brother.

"Well, nice to meet you, Sarah, and Caleb. Now, follow me. I don't know about you, but I'm starving."

We arrived without incident and picked up some food along the way. The siblings did not enjoy the cheap food here, but still ravenously ate it all.

*Can't believe even raider clans probably eat better than the garbage sold around here. How far have we fallen...?*

Once we finished eating, I discovered that I could rent a cart from the building to move things in and out, and transported all the crates into my unit. I had the two accompany me, both to keep an eye on them and to make it seem like they were moving in to help keep curious eyes off my cargo.

With all the moving around done and the excitement dying down, Caleb fell asleep soon after. I let the two of them rest while I headed out.

I ensured the cameras placed in my apartment were in order. Now I could hack into them, if need be, to make sure the kids didn't do anything suspicious.

After that, I headed to drop off the SAID at a lockbox and messaged Fitel. Then I went to the cybernetic clinic I had previously used. Fortunately, I only had to wait twenty minutes even without an appointment, though it had to be very early in the morning.

"Dr. Keyes, we meet again. How are you doing?"

"I'm fine, but you have seen better days." He paused and stared at my bandaged-up arm. "You know, you should go to a normal clinic to get your wounds looked at. We mainly perform installation or removal of cybernetics here."

While I could have gone to the hospital instead, my arm would still have taken some time to heal. Not to talk about the rehabilitation period. I had been planning on installing cybernetics, and this just accelerated that decision.

"Yes, I am aware. I'm looking to have my arm replaced with this." I placed a package on the desk between us.

I had gone over the cybernetics from my loot and picked the best one that suited me: a Nova Tech Mudra. It retailed for twenty thousand credits and was considered among the better middle-tier cyberarms.

Dr. Keyes took a few minutes to take the arm out from its factory-new packaging and inspect it.

"I can do that. There doesn't seem to be any problem with it. The fee for installing a cyberarm for the first time will be five thousand credits. Is that acceptable?"

"Yes. Do you guys accept cybernetics as payment, or would you like to buy some? I happen to be in possession of a few pieces you may be interested in." I immediately took the chance to hawk my new wares. The loot wasn't useful to me until I converted it to credits, after all.

"No, Mr. Halls, it is against our company policy and procurement contracts."

*Damn it.* Well, even though the payment for the job hadn't come through yet, meaning I'd be using almost all I had left, I had plenty of stuff to sell elsewhere if I needed, so I wasn't too worried. It was better to get the cyberarm now than to wait weeks for my wounds to recover naturally. Plus, there'd be all the new functions that came along with it.

"Understood. Please go ahead with the installation."

"Perfect. As a licensed cybernetic surgeon, I do need you to sign here to confirm that you would like to remove your current arm. I will not be able to reattach it after the operation if you change your mind."

"Ha, I can always get a new one grown if I come to regret my choice," I said as I read over the waiver.

"Well, if you had a couple hundred thousand credits to spare, you could do that. The procedure won't be too different from last time. Please lay down on the table and inhale from this."

*I guess that means it's time for lights out. Hopefully, Fitel will come through with the payment by the time this is done.*

# CHAPTER 12

## PLANNING

After having my new Nova Tech cyberarm installed and running a few errands, I returned home by early evening. When I stepped into the apartment, both Sarah and Caleb were sitting on the couch, watching TV.

"You guys all good?" I asked as I set down several bags.

"Yes, we're fine," Sarah said. "What did you bring back?" The two walked over to sate their curiosity.

"Woah! Is that a new arm there?" Caleb's eyes sparkled as he stared at my cybernetic.

"Yeah, the old one wasn't in the best condition anymore." I gave Caleb a wink.

"Woah, can I get an arm like that too, sis?" Caleb pleaded with puppy eyes.

In response, Sarah crossed her arms and made her displeasure apparent. "You know you can't. Don't make me tell Dad."

"Aww..."

"Here, both of you, I got you guys some stuff. See if the clothes are the right size." I pushed two bags towards them.

Since all they had were the dirty clothes they had been wearing, I'd bought some daily necessities, clothes, and blankets.

The two went ahead and tore open the bags, and inspected the items within.

"I guess this will do," Sarah muttered while Caleb continued going through everything with excitement.

"Hey, I can't say I'm well-versed in fashion, let alone for teenage girls."

She glared at me, took a bundle of clothes, and walked away towards the bathroom.

Once they'd both cleaned themselves and changed into new clothes, we sat down and ate.

"So, do either of you remember anything about how you got here?"

"We don't really know... Once they captured us, they kept us in that container the entire time until you came."

"I see... How long were you guys in there for?"

"I don't know. It's not easy to keep track after the first few days trapped in a box."

"Thanks for telling me about it, even though you may not want to. I'll try to figure a way to get you back to your tribe."

"It's 'clan,' Clan Wells, and we can take care of our—" Sarah paused and looked at Caleb, who had pulled at her sleeve. "If you get us back to NLA, we can make it back from there. In return, I'll handle cleaning and laundry for you." She looked around at the unit as if to emphasize how valuable her service would be.

*I mean, it isn't that bad. Presentable, at least. The priority of a cleaning robot on my wish list might need to be bumped up a little...*

"Sure thing. I'll see what we can do. Let's eat before the food gets cold."

If they were in the shipping container the entire time, that meant they probably didn't get here by plane. The more likely method was by cargo ship. That made sense, as that was the best way to smuggle wasteland humans, considering they didn't have IDs.

Now I had a lead to look into.

* * *

With Fitel not wanting to get involved, I had to go find a cargo ship to smuggle Sarah and Caleb out myself. I doubted Flo and her team were experts at that, and I'd rather not bother them for this.

The next morning, after having failed to find any information regarding the ship routes online, I went to District 20, where the biggest commercial port in Elevate City was.

Everywhere, crowds of workers were rushing about their day. I managed to enter the port management building uncontested. Signs said that port customs was on the third floor, but I didn't need to head all the way there.

I went directly to an automated terminal that dealt with all the ships that docked here and jacked into it, using the cable from my new cyberarm. Actually, the arm itself wasn't jacked in. It had a slot to hold a tiny portable terminal, making it more convenient for me to perform the hacking that I had been doing with my old one.

To be honest, the three points in Hacking weren't enough to make me into a super hacker. If one point gave me beginner knowledge, three points only made me a little better than an amateur. Judging by my stealth upgrades, five points would make me average in the relevant industry, enough to be a professional, and seven would be around the veteran level.

Luckily, the shipping routes submitted to the port authorities were stored in this outdated security terminal that even an amateur like me could handle. Plus, it was easy to idle around in front of the thing and still look like I was deep in thought or doing work. I got through after several minutes and downloaded everything into my terminal, then exited the port by merging with the crowd.

With my new data in hand, I headed to a fast-food chain and got to work, looking over the data while enjoying a refreshing milkshake.

Dozens of vessels arrived in Elevate City every day, so the files I downloaded were quite a pain to go through, even with a search function. Still, I narrowed down the dozen ships that would leave within the week.

I crossed out the ships that had their cargo noted as classified or were obviously managing stuff from large corporations, which left me with four options.

Then I checked the shipping company for each one and investigated how much their employee pay was. To nobody's surprise, workers were paid like crap unless they were higher up on the totem pole or had valuable skill sets as captains did.

I looked up the file for the chief stewards and examined it.

Within two hours, I found everything I needed. I headed to the closest hostel, where one of the chief stewards was staying.

Waiting outside, I soon found a tall woman walking out with several others who matched the profiles I had. I followed them, heading into a diner, where they ordered their lunch. My patience paid off as she left the table and headed to the washroom.

"Chief Stewardess Ava, can I have a moment of your time?" I asked, as she almost passed me by.

Her body snapped towards me. She had a hand on her holster, eyeing me warily.

"Ambushing a lady on her way to the washroom isn't very gentlemanlike. Why don't you introduce yourself first?"

"You can call me... User. I don't mean any harm, just wanted to propose to you a business opportunity."

"Really?" she said as she raised an eyebrow at me.

"Your ship is heading to NLA next, right?"

"Yeah, I ain't doing anything that would harm our ship. The crews are like family to me." She glared at me and tightened her grip on her pistol.

"Relax, I just want you to bring some people with you and ensure their safety. How does five thousand credits sound? That's almost your entire monthly wage."

"Smuggling? They wanted or something?"

"No, just no IDs. They're fine otherwise."

"Five K per person, up-front payment."

"I'm only paying you half up front, then the other half once I confirm you got the job done."

"You look here, boy, I'm the one taking the risks here. Up-front payment or no deal." The chief stewardess made a show of slowly walking away.

"Six thousand per person, if you can accept half now, half after the job."

I didn't mind paying more, as long as she accepted my condition. People worked harder if they still had something on the line. Up-front payment would incur a higher risk of her screwing over Sarah and Caleb if anything went wrong.

"Fine, but they bring their own supplies. The trip's going to take a week or two."

"Deal," I replied, and held out my hand.

* * *

While the siblings and I ate lunch, I informed them of the ride back I secured for them. The ship was scheduled to leave in two days' time.

With their situation settled, what remained was for me to begin serious planning for my business.

I had a ton of valuable cybernetics that hadn't been liquidated yet. It wouldn't be easy to do in a short time without tipping people off about the amount I had.

To start my business, I, of course, had to decide on which industry I would go into. The system would definitely be an integral part of this, as it served as the basis of the business. Therefore, I opened up my status page and went through all the potential upgrades that would fit what I was looking for.

**Status**
**Level:** 3
**EXP:** 210/300
**Musculoskeletal:** 51
**Neural Reflex:** 15
**Visuomotor Coordination:** 12
**Endurance:** 9
**Sensory Perception:** 37
**Upgrade Points:** 0
**Upgrades:**
      Stealth +7
      Hacking +3
**Enhancements:**
      SAID: Zenitech Hoth Mk.3
      Optics: Nova Tech Stars Mk.4
      Cyberarm (Left): Nova Tech Mudra Mk.6

After installing my cyberarm, my musculoskeletal stat had shot straight up. This definitely tempted me to install more implants to raise the scores, but I was wary of the augments that dealt with how my brain worked, especially the cheaper models.

I selected Upgrade and went over the vast collection of things I could spend points on. What could I use to establish my business?

While some options like energy weapons popped, I doubted I could enjoy my wealth for long with all the attention that they would draw. Some corp was bound to violently take over my business if I proceeded recklessly like that. I also didn't want any tech in markets that would make me compete against big corporations for the same reason.

The more mundane everyday products weren't anything I wanted to go into either, as the system's technological aid wouldn't be as helpful, and those industries required brand recognition more than quality assurance.

I remembered a line I had heard before: "Third-class businesses sell products, second-class businesses sell brands, and first-class businesses sell markets." I would have to start from the bottom with a great product first.

Still, I would need to level up a lot more in order to attain enough upgrade points for my selected field. Gaining experience points would only get harder and harder, so maybe I should select something that synergized with me gaining the experience points as well. In other words, killing.

It was possible to level stealth technologies, but all the best stealth products I knew were, for good reason, cybernetics. They simply blended in better when they were literally hidden within you. But cybernetic engineering was a separate category in the system.

There currently weren't many stealth-oriented cybernetics out in the market, as corporations kept that technology to themselves, but a solid target market for them was there too. Mercenaries like Flo had sufficient disposable income and were willing to spend big, since they could always die on their next job.

That meant I should focus on cybernetics first. I probably needed points in both cybernetic tech and stealth tech to create any half-decent implants, but I happen to be sitting on a pile of cybernetics right now.

This field was something incredible that only this world had, and it was exciting, too.

*It's decided. I'll focus on cybernetics first and then go into stealth technologies to create my own implants.*

* * *

In the afternoon, I finished up the last of my errands, dealing with my two new cars. They may have seen better days, but they were still new in my book.

I tried to rent one parking spot to keep the SUV, but apparently, car registration was required, so I headed to a secondhand dealership first.

The place had a wide selection of vehicles out front, and they all looked to be in much better condition than my two rust buckets. For now, I would be satisfied just to have something practical; I'd rather not waste unnecessary credits in my current situation.

The moment I came in, a man in a suit immediately came to greet me.

"Hey there," I said before he could start. "I wanted to sell my sedan out there and fix the registration information on the SUV."

"Welcome to Don's Auto. We can definitely do that for you. Why don't we get a closer look at the vehicle you would like to sell?"

To no one's surprise, the sedan wasn't worth much, but it could cover the cost of the SUV's registration. It didn't sound very legal, but I guessed no one cared, especially not for an old car.

Once I sorted out the insurance, I was on the road, enjoying my first actual trip without the auto drive this time. Just as I got out of the dealer's parking lot, I received a call.

"Hey, Mr. Rollo. This is Caleb. Can you buy some ice cream when you come back?" a voice chirped.

"Sure thing, kid."

"Thank you!"

"I'll be back in half an hour." I hung up, only to realize I forgot to ask what flavors they liked.

As I was about to call back, another call came in, and I quickly picked it up as I accelerated onto the freeway.

"What flavor did you—"

A different voice than the one I expected interrupted. "Rollo, are you free right now? We could really use your help."

It took a second for me to realize it was Flo on the line. Well, unfortunately for Caleb, it seemed like ice cream was going to be delayed.

# CHAPTER 12

## THE WAY IN

"Rollo, are you free right now? We could really use your help."

"Flo? What's going on?" I put the car back into auto drive to focus on the call.

"An idiot on my team got picked up a few days ago, and we finally located him. The problem is that he's being held in some corp facility, so we can't just go in guns blazing this time."

"I'd love to help, Flo, but I don't think I can go against some corporation. Even *you* are hesitant to antagonize…"

"Look, they aren't some big untouchable corp. They're just some fucked-up startup specializing in human experimentation that other corps outsource to. If we went in guns blazing, they would activate fail-safes that would dispose of all their 'subjects' for some bullshit confidentiality contract. Can you take a shot at sneaking in to disable it?"

"Fine. I'll try, but no promises. You guys already have a plan?"

"Great, we'll owe you one. Come on over to Haven and we'll go over the details."

* * *

They filled me in on the plan in one of Haven's private rooms. There were glass windows that looked out to the rest of the bar, but we set them to opaque.

By the time we finished, the sun was just setting.

We sped out, driving circles around a small but normal-looking office building with only a dozen floors and a loading area in the back.

I ensured I had everything I needed before getting out of the car.

A woman's voice rang out in my head thanks to my SAID. "Test, test. Can you hear me all right?"

"Yeah, loud and clear."

"Okay, you can respond by text once you're in, but our connection will break up once you pass into the jammed area and you'll be cut off. Once you get in, you should be able to disable it."

"Yeah, yeah. We just went over it."

"Just wanted to remind you that once you're in, you're on your own. You better do exactly as I instructed, because your shitty intern-level hacking skills ain't going to do shit in their system."

I sent a thumbs-up emoji through my SAID and observed the people going in and out of the building.

The girl was a hacker they brought on for the rescue called Lana. She was apparently the one who had tracked down our target: her friend, Leo, who was normally the hacker for Flo's team.

I waited until the loading area was clear and casually walked as close as I could without entering the camera's view. Once I was in position, I aimed my Suri and shot right at the base of the camera.

I texted, *You should get a connection soon.*

"Okay, I'm in, but as we expected, their security systems are air-gapped from the cameras. I'm looping the camera feeds now. You should be good to go," Lana responded almost instantly, with a symphony of clicking and clacking noises in her background. I couldn't believe someone still used mechanical keyboards when she could do it through her SAID.

I walked up to the door and pried open the panel covering the jack for technicians. Once I plugged in, I didn't have to do my usual hacking and could sit back while Lana did the job for me.

Before long, the door's lock clicked open, and I made my way into the building. I headed for the staircase, where my call connection with Lana started breaking up as I descended.

I went as far as I could until I reached a floor that required an ID card to access. Then I backtracked up to the previous floor and moved through the mechanical rooms, searching for the one that was responsible for this building's HVAC.

According to the info we had, the lab where they were holding Leo was on the bottommost floor, and the security control room was on the topmost restricted basement level, so I somehow had to gain access to that floor.

Eventually, I found the mechanical room I was looking for and brought out a grenade that looked more like a toy. I pressed the button and threw it at the control panel. After a second, a loud fizzing echoed throughout the room.

Within seconds, I heard the machines around me slowing down, everything making a whining noise that it definitely wasn't supposed to make.

I picked up the spent grenade, then concealed myself in a corner of the room, and started praying the plan would work. If no one came, then we would have to abort the mission and go back to the drawing board.

With no connection to the outside world, I spent my time playing around with the settings of my cybernetics and ensuring they were in optimal condition. Right now, I relied on official patches to their firmware, but I was also going through those patches carefully, using them as references for the time when I would design my own cybernetics.

After fifteen minutes, I finally heard someone approach. Watching the door intently, I tried to calm my nerves and stay quiet. A man in a dirty technician outfit and a hard hat opened the door and walked straight towards the control panel.

I gave it a second, but once I was sure there was no one behind him, I made my move. In one swift motion, I covered his face with a cloth I had gotten from Flo and put him in a chokehold. I felt his surprised struggling, but my cyberarm had him tightly locked in place, and soon his struggle weakened until his body fell completely limp.

After quickly dragging his body to the corner, I then swapped outfits and packed my old clothes into a bag. Checking that I had his security card and all my gear, I headed back down the stairs.

With the card, I could pass through. I strolled through the empty hallway while searching for the security control room. The entire floor looped around in a circle, so I eventually spotted the room.

I walked up to the door and pressed the button on the intercom.

"What do you want, techy? You better have good news about the cooling, cuz it's getting really hot in here with all the equipment running."

"Yes, sir. It should be fixed now, but I need to manually reset each control panel until we get the replacement parts."

"All right, hurry up and reset ours." The door automatically opened.

I walked in slowly, my eyes scouring the room: not that large and had only two guards in total. One guard watched me, and the other had his attention on wall-mounted screens while he fanned himself with a terminal.

"That's the panel for the AC." The first guard pointed and then crossed his arms, eyes still on me. He didn't seem like he was going to go away, so I guessed it was time to pull one of the oldest tricks in the book.

I placed my bag down beside the panel and then pretended to rummage through it as I grabbed my Suri within. Looking back, I locked eyes with the man who still had his full attention on me.

"If this is the AC panel, then what is that one for?" I put on a show of looking as confused as I could and pointed at the one on the other side of the room.

The moment the man turned, I brought my gun up and placed a well-aimed shot right in his head, then unloaded the rest of the twenty-round mag into the remaining guard still in his seat until I saw the experience notification.

*+10 EXP*

*+10 EXP*

I raced over to the security terminal, pushed the body out of the way, and searched for the jack. After fumbling for a bit, I found it and inserted the chip the hacker Lana had given me.

After I executed the program as instructed, the chip automatically took over with no further need for my input. While I let the program do its thing, I started looking over the screens and the layout of the floors that we didn't have information on.

I could see a set of rooms that looked like a group living space, holding about half a dozen people, all wearing simple white gowns. Some rooms also had surgical tables, like the one found in Dr. Keyes' clinic.

Outside in the corridors were a few people in lab coats walking around and a few armed guards.

Before I could find and rescue Leo, the console in front of me made a *ding* noise. The program was complete. A familiar voice then spoke to me in my head.

"Can you hear me, Rollo?"

"Yeah, loud and clear."

"I've got full control of their system now, but I can't disable the fail-safes remotely. You've got to go to the head researcher's room and do it from his terminal. I'll send you the floor layout with real-time information on where everyone in the facility is."

"Okay, got it, but you do see how many people are in there, right? Do we even have enough transportation to get them all out?"

"No, we're only here for Leo. The rest of them are going to have to find their own way once they're out."

"Really? At least half of them are going to die or get caught again." I took a deep breath and sighed.

"We aren't charity workers. They can stay there if they want, but if they do, they're guaranteed to be dead within a year or two. A slow and painful death, too. We're already giving them a chance to escape. Come on, focus on what we came here for."

She was right. There was no profit to it even if I could save them all. I could only do so much.

I placed the real-time layout in a corner of my vision like a minimap. Then, after swapping into the guard's uniform, I made my way to the head researcher's room.

Using the minimap was practically cheating. I effortlessly hid in the blind spots or avoided anyone in my way. It was really annoying how each set of stairs only went down a single floor and they were located at opposite ends of the building, but I eventually managed to arrive at the door to the head researcher's office.

*I hate whoever designed this place, security be damned. It must suck having to go through this maze every day to get to work.*

I scanned my security card, but the scanner turned red, denying me access.

Seeing no one to catch me, I texted my helper. *Hey, I need help getting into the researcher's room, plugging you in now.*

"Where's the 'please'?" She sighed. "Give me a second... and you're in."

Entering the room, I found the terminal at the head researcher's desk. I repeated the same steps as in the security room, plugging in the chip and then waiting for the program to do its job.

"Okay, the program is done. Can you deactivate it now?"

"That terminal doesn't respond to remote commands, so you will have to be the one to deactivate it."

Following Lana's instructions, I eventually found the command to disable the fail-safe. Even so, once the test subjects escaped, they would still need to visit a cybernetic clinic to remove the physical chips that were forcibly installed in their heads...

I then searched the files on the subjects within this facility and downloaded what they had into my SAID. The information included a file on Leo and where they kept him.

"Okay, I found him, and the fail-safes are off. It's time for you guys to do the heavy lifting."

"Gotcha. Flo's team is coming in hot now. Go secure Leo before the chaos spreads down to you."

Within ten seconds of her words, the entire place violently shook, almost throwing me off my feet.

# CHAPTER 14

## THE WAY OUT

Once I regained my balance after the quake, I quickly went back to the hallway. The way was clear as researchers scrambled back into rooms and the guards congregated by the entry points.

I carefully approached a group of guards from behind. They were fortifying their position against the staircase I had entered from. Six, divided into two groups to form a crossfire.

Once their sergeant finished giving out commands, their attention was entirely on the entry point. I took the opportunity to close in with two new toys in hand.

I grasped the tops of the toys and twisted them open like childproof bottles, then threw the first one at the trio furthest away from me. Next, I gently lobbed the second one at the other group before taking cover behind the contours of the corridor.

As soon as I had gotten into cover, an explosion rang out, swiftly followed by another.

From behind the cover, I saw the six experience prompts.

*+10 EXP*

*+10 EXP*

*+10 EXP*

*+10 EXP*

*+10 EXP*

*+10 EXP*

*That was a lot easier than I thought. I should definitely stock up on a few more explosives just in case, even if it doesn't go well with stealth.*

Searching the bodies, I found two usable submachine guns and strapped them to my back, along with the chest rigs that carried several spare mags. I booked it back to the head researcher's office and issued the command to unlock all the rooms that held the test subjects.

Then I raced towards the room where Leo was. On the way, I saw several doors slightly opened. The people peeking out quickly hid when our eyes met.

My reception was the same at the door to Leo, though they thankfully didn't slam the door on me.

The person at the door, a red-haired teenage girl, retreated further in and chatted with the residents of the room while I entered.

"—one's coming," she said.

"Calm down, Claire," a voice from the back replied.

The room was only furnished with six beds, three on each side of the room. There were four other people standing around the girl, children and teenagers, and the last man in the back was in bed. He turned to face me as I came closer.

"So Flo did call in another team for this shithole." He scanned me from top to bottom.

"I'm not much of a team by myself, but yes, Flo did send me. I'm Rollo." I offered my hand.

"The new guy she met?" He gave me a doubting gaze, though he still shook my hand. "I'm Leo, as I'm sure you already know. What's the plan?"

"Flo and your team are upstairs—"

"Heh, so I've heard... Go on."

"They are upstairs fighting their way down, so we're going to make our way up to meet them. You know how to use one of these?" I said, throwing a submachine gun to him.

"As if anyone in this city doesn't. Proficiency, on the other hand... I'm more of a computer guy than a fighter."

"Well, they shouldn't be expecting us from behind, so just point and shoot."

Leo fiddled with his new gun as I looked over at the other five eavesdroppers.

"You guys, go gather up everyone else on this floor. We're all leaving... unless you want to stay."

One of the older boys, who was about sixteen with short curly brown hair, nodded immediately and dashed out of the room.

In the meantime, I connected a call with Lana.

"I'm with Leo. What's the situation up there?"

"Little busy here. They're past the control room." Her mechanical keyboard kept clacking at a rapid pace.

"Okay, we're heading up from here."

"Roger. Stay on the call. I'll keep you updated."

Seeing that Leo was ready, we exited the room and headed towards the stairs, where we found a crowd of people wearing white gowns gathered.

I spotted the one who was in Leo's room earlier and walked up to him.

"Is everyone here and ready to go?"

"Well, almost everyone. Thorne and Claire are still in there." He pointed to a nearby room that was visible through the glass walls.

At the center of the room was an operating table, and a few moveable hospital beds stood off to the side. Standing still by one of the beds were the teenage boy and girl from earlier. The boy's lively expression was completely gone and the color of his face had been drained.

As I approached him, he stayed motionless.

With a better view of what he was looking down at, I grimaced. It was an unzipped body bag with the face of a middle-aged woman poking out. Her features resembled the boy's, though I couldn't say if their eyes were similar, as the body was missing eyes.

"Thorne and Claire, right? I'm sorry for your loss, but we need to get out of here. Now." I placed my hand on his shoulder.

Without looking back, Thorne replied, "I don't have anywhere to be... I'll stay here."

"You think that's what your mom would've wanted, staying here with no future?" the girl cried out.

It seemed like the one called Claire had the same objective as me: to convince Thorne to leave.

"I have no future even if I leave. I wouldn't survive alone, not without Mom. I'd become a beggar at best... and I have nothing to live for." Thorne's voice grew quieter as he went on.

"Idiot! You won't be alone. I'll stick with you, and we'll make it work somehow. As long as we are alive and free, we'll have a chance. Come on, do it for me. Let's go," Claire said as she started dragging Thorne.

I knew we didn't have time for this drama unfolding before me, but I also couldn't bear forcefully removing the young man when he was grieving.

*I've seen those dead eyes before when people gave up hope. There isn't much I can do... or is there...?*

I had planned on starting my business once I gathered enough funds. However, I was missing a crucial part of every business. The people.

It was hard to find people you could trust back in my world, and it was only harder here. Still, I would need to hire people for my business plan to take off. There was only so much you could do alone.

As much as it felt wrong to take advantage of others' moments of weakness, if I reached out a helping hand right now, I could gain a reliable helper I could trust. This job would allow him to earn his keep and give him a reason to continue on. It was practically a win-win proposition for both parties.

I took a deep breath and approached the two teenagers.

"Well, I just happen to be starting a business. Come work for me. As my employee, I'll make sure you live a life that will make her proud." I offered my hand to him as he glanced over.

The two looked over at me in unison. Thorne's face went through a host of changes before he closed his eyes and took a deep breath. His eyes then snapped open and stared straight into mine for a brief moment before he reciprocated my handshake.

* * *

"This floor is clear too. I'll go check out the next one now. Shouldn't be long before we rendezvous with Flo."

"Okay! No worries, I can protect everyone!" the red-haired girl replied while lifting the submachine gun in one hand.

I was talking to Leo, but I decided not to bother with it and proceeded to the next floor. I gave Thorne and Leo one last look before I moved on.

All the cameras were destroyed by now. The guards had done it themselves, realizing someone had breached their security. I made my way up the stairs to the next level and found two guards posted up on the other side of the door.

Lana the hacker had informed me that Flo's team had just made it to this floor, so it made sense that they had guards stationed here in case the intruders tried to sneak by. Too bad their communications were a mess and they never found out about the intruders from below. We had them sandwiched now.

From where I was, I could hear the ongoing fighting. Wasting no more time, I slammed the door open, right into one guard, and immediately shot another. Just as the dazzled guard turned to face me, I sent another bullet right into his eye.

*+10 EXP*

*+10 EXP*

As I peeled my eyes away from the experience text, a sword poked out around the corner down the hallway. I'd brought my Suri up and aimed at it when a seven-foot-tall man came into view. From all the visible cybernetics on every limb, it was safe to say the man was a genuine cyborg.

I reflexively unloaded my entire clip at him, only to see it deflect off his armor and synthetic skin.

He grinned and dashed straight at me with inhuman speed. I threw myself back into the stairwell and closed the door behind me, then retreated down to create more space between us.

Just as I made it down the first flight of stairs, a loud impact rang out, and the walls around the door I just closed cracked.

Changing ammo as I made my way out of the stairwell, I spotted Leo and Claire down the corridor with their guns at the ready. I double-checked that my connection with Lana was still good.

"Lana, I'm going to need your help really soon. Get ready for a new connection that'll open up in a second. And you two, stay back!"

"What's going on?" Claire said, while Leo glared behind me cautiously.

I ignored them and continued, "Lana, you hear me?"

"Yeah, yeah. Just busy getting the corpo nerds outta the security system, but sure, I definitely can help you out even with my hands full. I'll just have to use my third hand."

Standing at one end of the corridor, I aimed at the door to the stairwell on the other side. Leo and Claire hadn't listened to me. They hadn't retreated at all, staying by my side and looking ready to fight, but I didn't have time to care or rebuke them right now.

As I expected, the cyborg showed up before me, ramming the entire door towards me as he came into view. He once again dashed forward as soon as he saw us, and the three of us unleashed a hail of bullets in response.

This time, he zigzagged around despite our bullets simply dinging off his body even when they struck. Maybe he knew what I knew: all I needed was for one of my bullets to get in.

Once he was halfway to us, I stopped shooting and tapped on both my allies' shoulders.

"Move back. We need to buy some time."

Then we sprinted away from the incoming cyborg while I sent a text to my hacker. *Lana! Did you get the connection?*

We dashed into an empty room. If he'd continued any further down the hallway, we would've led the threat to the rest of the group.

The cyborg followed right behind us, ripping the door from the hinges and holding it in one hand like a makeshift shield.

"I'm working on it. It should just take a second. You're lucky this baby corporation's security sucks."

Right when the cyborg started his dash, he suddenly lost steam before he tripped over himself and fell face-first into the ground.

"I locked his chrome. Hurry, before he restarts his soft," Lana's voice cried out.

Pushing down instincts that told me to stay away from the menacing cyborg, I quickly unsheathed my dagger and plunged it into the back of his head.

There was some resistance when the vibro-blade made contact with him, but it couldn't stop it from piercing through.

*+20 EXP*

We collectively released a sigh of relief as we stepped over his body and exited the room.

Leo spat at the body as he walked by. "Cyborg fucker. Lucky I don't have any of my gear on me right now."

Thank the heavens I bought the EI rounds and had a hacker on the hotline, because I definitely didn't have the skills or equipment to do any hacking in the middle of a fight.

I swapped my ammo back to my regular rounds and split off from the group again to check on the floor above, but as I was halfway up the stairs, Lana said to me, "Flo's team cleared the floor, I let her know you're on the way."

That was the kind of good news I liked to hear.

*Now, let's hope the rest of this outing will be smooth sailing.*

# CHAPTER 15

## STARTING A BUSINESS

Having met up with our reinforcements—Flo's team, who frankly looked like they needed more saving than us—we all returned to the surface level without incident.

I witnessed the results of what shook the entire building earlier. There was an enormous hole in the wall, next to the back door I entered from.

Once we were outside, the place became a lot more chaotic as the former test subjects went their own way and scattered.

It may have caused a mess, but it also served as a good distraction for us.

Our group immediately went back to our cars.

"Did you really have to release everyone?" Flo asked as we reached their vehicles.

"Better to have a chance at survival than be lab rats for the rest of their lives. Besides, it gave us a nice distraction for our getaway, right?" I pointed to the chaos behind us.

"Right... We should be good now. The mission was a success, and we got Leo back, so you can head on home. Thanks for your help, and sorry for complaining. We owe you one," Flo told me, energetic despite how worn out she looked.

"No problem, I'll take you up on that favor. Are you sure everything is okay now, though? No corpo hit squad chasing after us?"

"Neuro Nexus is a startup corp at best. We'll be fine."

"What about the police?"

"Ha, good one. The ECPD only shows up after incidents to do cleanup. All right, we're set. Let's hang out at Haven sometime once Leo gets his shit fixed," Flo said as she stepped into the back of her armored van.

I waved as I got in the driver's seat of my car. Thorne, who had been following me, got into the passenger seat.

Watching the former test subjects disperse into the streets, I started up the car and was about to leave when the back door clicked open.

"All right, boss, I'm ready for a new adventure. Let's get going!" a cheerful red-haired teenager declared from the backseat.

"I don't remember offering to hire you or to give you a ride, Claire..." I said as I turned on the auto drive.

"Come on, you heard me when I said I'll be sticking with Thorne. An offer to him equals an offer to me."

"Claire..." Thorne looked back and sighed before turning to me. "Can I ask you to hire her as well?"

"Sure, that's what I intended. But it's not like I have a company or anything yet, so don't expect much."

We drove aimlessly for a while until I decided to bring the two to a motel near my place first. Sarah and Caleb were still in my place, so it would be too crowded to have them all stay over. Not to mention the trackers still embedded in the teens.

*Speaking of Caleb... Oh, right. I still have to buy him ice cream. They're probably asleep by now, so I guess he'll have ice cream for breakfast.*

* * *

After a night of well-deserved rest, I was fully charged. I quickly got ready instead of lazing around, as I was expecting guests later.

Yesterday, I left Thorne and Claire at the motel with some money to pay for their rooms, food, and clinic fees for removing their trackers. We decided to meet up this morning at my place to plan things out.

As I basked in the hot water during my morning shower, I brought out my status sheet and deliberated on my next steps. With two people under my care now, I had to start earning more so I could pay them. Overall, it wasn't a terrible trade for two employees that I could trust. Well... trust more than the average employee I would find off the streets.

Following my plan, I went ahead and dumped my new points into cybernetic engineering.

**Status**
**Level:** 4
**EXP:** 50/400
**Musculoskeletal:** 51
**Neural Reflex:** 15
**Visuomotor Coordination:** 12
**Endurance:** 9
**Sensory Perception:** 37
**Upgrade Points:** 2
**Upgrades:**
    Stealth +7
    Hacking +3
    Cybernetic Engineering +2
**Enhancements:**
    SAID: Zenitech Hoth Mk.3
    Optics: Nova Tech Stars Mk.4
    Cyberarm (Left): Nova Tech Mudra Mk.6

A familiar rush of knowledge entered my brain. I felt like I had gone to college studying the subject, only that studying was condensed into an instant instead of a few years.

I knew the material requirements, which metals were and were not compatible with the human body, the procedures to install them, and the tools required. Though I doubted I could create anything nearly as good as any of the cybernetics I'd seen, not without more upgrade points.

Upon walking into the living room, I noticed an argument between Sarah and Caleb. It seemed like Caleb wanted to have the ice cream for breakfast while Sarah forbade it until lunch. The argument had nothing to do with me, so I proceeded to make my food.

I spent the time after breakfast looking up the procedure for starting a business in this city. There were different classifications, with a clear distinction between the local run-of-the-mill businesses—which I would have to start with—and the corporations that were further divided into several levels.

If a business did well, it could then apply for membership to join the Elevate City Consortium, which would mark the transformation of a business into a corporation. It would enjoy an assortment of benefits, being in a higher social class from all the riffraff. However, it would need to pay an annual membership fee that varied depending on the tier. In return, the Consortium would reduce tax rates and offer conveniences related to importing and exporting.

By the time I finished arranging for a law firm to complete the paperwork for establishing my business, the doorbell rang. Thorne and Claire had arrived, so I introduced them to the raider siblings and we all got comfortable before beginning our discussion.

"To start things off, I plan to open a cybernetic clinic, and I will be hiring you as my assistants for now, as there isn't really a fixed set of duties for you guys yet."

"Okay, cool with me as long as you're paying," Claire replied with a smile while Thorne solemnly nodded.

"I'll be paying you both five thousand credits a month for now. I'll also cover all your expenses within reason until your first paycheck."

They both nodded and, seeing as they had no comment, I continued, "I'll be dealing with the bureaucracy side of it for now, so I want one of you to deal with our current inventory and the other to search for potential properties for the clinic itself."

"Oooh, real estate shopping, I always wanted to buy my own place. I'll do it!" Claire enthusiastically raised her hand.

"I'll do the inventory, then."

"Sounds good. I look forward to working with both of you." I smiled and shook their hands.

*Great, bureaucracy time. Woohoo. So exciting... Hopefully, this won't take too long.*

* * *

It turns out starting a local business wasn't too hard, but starting a cybernetic clinic attached to that business was, simply because I had no credentials to operate, and the alternative methods weren't anything I could afford right now.

Seeing how I was mainly targeting mercenaries, I decided to simply start an underground clinic.

The major disadvantages were having no access to licensed suppliers, being unable to advertise via legitimate avenues, and being unable to do business with most companies, like insurance providers, without a hefty surcharge.

The major advantage was simply no taxes. With an unregistered business, I wouldn't be paying any money to the corporate overlords.

This also meant that I didn't have much to do, now that there was no bureaucracy to manage for the next week, so I looked for suitable locations with Claire during the day and continued hunting for experience during the evening.

In the middle of the week, Sarah and Caleb left. I saw them off with the chief steward I had hired. She gave me regular updates, as half of her payment was still with me.

Claire was finishing up her talks with the owners of all the places she'd found, and wanted to go over the options with me to finalize our choice soon, but before that, I had other business to attend to. I barely had enough money to cover all the fees and rent.

Which was why today, I headed to a clandestine clinic recommended by Flo to sell off some of my wares.

I drove to the Neon District and found a dark stairway in between a bar and a nightclub. It led down to a large metal door that looked like it could withstand a small bomb. There were no signs or anything the entire way down. I was sure if I hadn't been told its location, I would have thought it was just some random back door.

After pressing on the intercom, I backed away from the door and stared straight at the peephole.

"What do you want?" a feminine voice said rapidly.

"Dr. Rad? Flo told me about this place. I have some business with you."

The door clicked open automatically. Inside was an identical door with turrets hanging from the ceiling beside it. I walked in and the first door closed behind me.

After a few seconds, the second one opened, leading me to a brightly lit area with a few empty chairs neatly lined up. A large glowing sign stood in my path, reading, "Wait here and don't wander or you're dead!"It seemed like coming at noon meant I was a little earlier than the rest of her clientele.

Before I had a chance to sit down, a thin girl with purple hair walked out from the back. Her most distinct features were all the tattoos she had.

She froze and snapped her head towards me. "Follow me, you looking for a checkup, new chrome, or what?" she asked while she started walking away all jittery, as if she'd had too much caffeine.

I rushed to keep up with her. "Actually, I had some cybernetics to sell, brand new." I held up the bag I was holding to emphasize my point, though she didn't turn my way.

"Let's have a look."

We moved into her operating room and proceeded to lay out all the cybernetics I brought on the table.

While she examined them, I took the time to check out her setup, which consisted of a simple terminal by the operating table that listed her products. I couldn't match the variety she had at the moment, and needed to pay extra to a corporate salesperson because I didn't have a proper license.

Soon, Dr. Rad finished inspecting the cybernetics and quoted me a price for everything. She offered about half of what it all retailed for, which was pretty good. She would at least have to sell below the retail price. Otherwise, people would simply go to the legit clinics, unless they really didn't want any records of their hardware.

"I still have more of the same kind, if you want. I can get it here within the hour." I continued to hawk, as I'd only brought a few of each model I had.

"No thanks, maybe next time, no reason to hold too much stock. If that's all, you know the way out." She started to ignore me, picking at some half-completed cyberarm.

"Do you happen to know any other places that may be interested in buying?"

She paused for a second and put a finger to her chin. "Hmm, there may be a few, not sure. I don't really contact them that often. Here, I sent their info to your SAID."

With the transaction complete, the balance displayed on my optics was much higher than before. I exited and restocked before I made my way to the locations she sent me to rinse and repeat the sale.

Some contacts I visited completely ignored me and shooed me away, while others only bought limited quantities.

*Now I know how those salesmen pestering me feel. Maybe I should've cut them some slack.*

As evening approached, I made my way to the last contact I had gotten, in some warehouse on the outskirts of the city. By the looks of the heaps of shredded cars I passed, there wasn't much here besides a couple of chop shops.

Just as I exited my car, I heard a thunderous noise coming from just around the corner. I instantly jumped back in with my gun unholstered, ready to sneak out at a moment's notice.

I sighed. "Come on... I just wanted to sell my stuff in peace today!"

# CHAPTER 16

## PROPERTY

The thunderous noise rang out again, though it was quieter now that I was inside my car. Seeing nothing but the junkyard around, I left it and moved to a better vantage point to assess the situation.

Cautiously hugging the warehouse, I peeked around the corner to find two men wearing eye-catching red plate carriers and maroon uniforms underneath. They were both facing away from the warehouse, towards the scrap cars piled up. One of them had a hand raised, pointing it towards the rusty vehicles. The hand wasn't a regular one, but a prosthetic that looked more like a gigantic gun barrel than a human limb.

Before I could get closer, the thunder came back, much louder this time, as I had a direct line of sight to the source. I watched the hand cannon fire, decimating the scrap metal in its way.

Assuming they were only doing target practice, I proceeded towards the clinic, albeit discreetly, trying not to draw their attention just in case.

The door was completely open, and I could see a small lobby. There were a few people waiting inside, all seeming to be the rough-looking mercenary type, with a couple dressed in the same red uniform as the two outside.

Walking in, I spotted a lady behind a counter smiling at me.

"Hi, I'm here to see Dr. Bennett." I put an arm on the counter and leaned forward.

"Yes, take this, and please take a seat." The lady ripped a queue ticket in a practiced motion and handed it to me.

I sat down and saw a screen displaying the queue. Patiently, I waited for my number to come up, spending the time surfing the web through my optics.

After almost an hour of waiting, I could finally see the doctor, an older man with a hunched back, wearing a monocle.

I repeated my sales pitch, which had been well practiced by now, and handed him some samples for examination.

"Ahh, these are brand new. Very good. How many of these do you have?" the doctor asked as he looked them over.

"How much can you offer for these models?" I fired back. This was my last sale for now. I didn't want to sell everything right away, and I only needed a few more credits to hit my goal.

"Hmm... How about this price?" He sent over a small spreadsheet file with the models and offered prices directly to my SAID.

The prices were a lot lower than what I'd seen all day, which was around 35–50 percent of the retail price. He offered a measly 25 percent.

"Twenty-five percent is pretty low. I'll need at least 40 percent or I'd rather try elsewhere."

"Now, now. I'm willing to buy in bulk, which I'm sure my colleagues wouldn't. How about this? I can raise it to 30 percent at most."

We spent another few minutes bargaining back and forth, but the doctor wouldn't budge any further. Being so close to my goal, I decided to take the hit and sell just enough to reach my goal.

With the transaction complete, I headed back home just as the sun started to set and texted my two employees.

Once I was home, I took in the now slightly more spacious living room, having sold off a few bulky crates. I barely sold more than a tenth, but should now have enough credits to get the equipment I needed and pay for the lease, considering I wasn't looking for any prime locations.

Before long, Thorne arrived with Claire. We sat down, and Claire began going over the results of her hard work.

"So, as you said, I went to look for the best potential spots for your clinic. Further narrowing down the options to the neighborhoods near District 10, there are three main types of properties listed here."

She set a terminal down on the table between us. Examining its files, I secretly looked up the address for each and left markers on the minimap in my eyes. Once everything was settled, I really had to install proper SAIDs and optics for these two.

"The first type is the street-level retail locations like these. Since we don't have a license yet, we may not be able to openly operate, so this may not be the best option. The second one is these units inside various megabuildings and apartments. The third option is leasing properties from complexes and plazas."

Considering my primary target market for the foreseeable future was mercenaries, the best general location was District 10, where Haven was located. All these options had their own pros and cons, but now that I had sufficient funds, I could go for the one that best fit my preferences. Which would be the most private one.

"Let's go for the commercial properties, something with privacy," I said while tapping my finger on the table.

"Okay, in that case, these are the remaining options." Claire started filtering them.

There were five options left, all buildings in a huge plaza, though two stood out to me. They were larger units set a distance away from other buildings, being at the plaza's corner. The road surrounded each one on two sides, with a parking lot on the other two.

Having made my decision, I met the siblings' eyes and stated, "Let's go take a closer look at these two. Set up meetings so we can go take a tour."

* * *

While I sat at a red light, I watched the ECPD carry body bags into a van while some old lady wearing a badge leaned against the van and smoked. It was awkward when the lady made eye contact with me, but thankfully, the light turned green.

Fighting the urge to steal a glance back at her, I received a timely call. The display showed the caller ID, Flo.

"Hey Rollo, you wanted to talk?"

"Yeah, I had a job for you guys to do. When do you think you guys are available?"

"Leo's been recovering, so we haven't taken any jobs recently, which means we're free. What kind of job did you have in mind?"

"There's some medical equipment I need. Was hoping you could pull off a heist," I said as I watched a group of ruffians, all armed and wearing matching green uniforms, march down the streets like they owned them.

"I thought stealing shit was more your thing. You expecting company?"

"The equipment I want is gonna take up a whole truck. I'd rather not sneak in a forklift."

Honestly, I'd rather buy the equipment properly and save myself the trouble, but without a license to operate a clinic, I was having a hard time with the sales staff and how much they were increasing their prices. I could've gotten a surrogate to buy parts, but I didn't know anyone I trusted enough with the money. This heist definitely had nothing to do with me wanting to get back at the sales staff.

"Hah, I'd love to see that."

"I'll be tagging along. Of course, I'll need you guys to do the heavy lifting. Sending the details to your SAID now."

It only took a minute before Flo replied, "That's some hardware, all right. What do you need this for?"

"For my clinic. Didn't I tell you? I'm starting a business."

"Oh, is that why Fitel's been bugging me about when you're coming off hiatus?"

"I'll get back to him once everything settles down. Anyway, I gotta go. Let me know if your team has any issues with the plan. See you," I said as the car pulled up and I gazed at the building in front of me.

"They'll be good. Catch you later."

Exiting the car, I spotted Claire waiting at the door with a woman in a dull gray suit and skirt.

"Hey there, Mr. Halls," Claire said. She emphasized "mister" with a wink.

"Nice to meet you, sir. I am Lea. Please feel free to ask me anything about the property," the lady said. She held the door open, gesturing for me to enter.

We toured the entire building. It wasn't furnished at all, but was quite spacious and had two floors. The place seemed to be set up as more of an open retail space, though, so I would need to have walls built or add dividers. It had enough space to divide the first floor into six rooms and a lobby area, and the second floor could be where I lived for now until everything was running smoothly.

As the tour wound down, I made sure I had asked everything I needed regarding the work to be done on the property and the details for the lease.

"Sir, we can definitely accommodate your needs. You only need to sign a one-year lease with us."

"I see. I'll look over the details and get back to you. Thank you for your time." I quickly departed before she had a chance to continue talking.

Claire rode with me this time to another location quite a ways away. This place was even larger, though with the caveat that it was only one floor. The price was similar, and it also fulfilled all my requirements. However, the young man who led our tour wanted a lease term of at least two years.

Once we finished the tours, I brought us to a nearby coffee shop. I frequented this chain, as I was a fan of their milkshakes, or chills, as they called it.

"So, what do you think?" I asked the girl in front of me while sipping on my drink.

"I like the location of the second one more, but the first one seemed to be better space-wise for a clinic. Both could work, honestly." Unlike me with my sweet tooth, she was chatting while enjoying a latte.

"Sounds about right. Let's see what Thorne thinks before we finalize the decision."

"Sure thing, Mr. Halls. You're the boss!" she said mischievously.

I glared at her. She sounded like she really enjoyed calling me Mr. Halls, though she used to just call me boss. Thorne was more rigid and wouldn't stop calling me sir. Not sure which one I preferred; they all made me sound old.

"Well, I sure hope you like doing logistics, because you'll be responsible for all of that after I pick out all the furniture we'll need."

"What?! At least let me participate in the shopping too! That's the fun part."

"I have a feeling our tastes wouldn't match. I'll have Thorne shop with me this time."

"No way! You guys are going to pick something so boring."

"Boring is safe, and safe is good. Go decorate your own room."

She stared daggers at me for a moment before replying, "Maybe after I get my first paycheck. Speaking of the first paycheck, that is worthy of commemoration, right? I think you should commemorate it with a big bonus!"

"I'll see what I can do after we're done spending and start earning. For now, let's head out. Thorne's still waiting for us."

"Right behind you, Mr. Halls!"

*Okay, maybe I should look into some auditory implants.*

# CHAPTER 17

## SOURCING EQUIPMENT

"How may I help you, sir?" asked the well-dressed salesman with the Premier Arms pin on his collar.

"I wanted to browse your handguns with greater armor-piercing capabilities."

"Of course, sir. Please let me show you some options that meet your specifications," the salesperson said with a glint in his eyes.

While the man fetched various firearms to show me, I kept an eye on Thorne, who was browsing a distance away in a section for a different arms company. He had asked for an advance on his pay; when confronted, he said he wanted to buy weapons and learn how to fight so he could run security for the company.

It seemed he thought himself to be unproductive. He had finished doing an inventory of all the cybernetics at my place within a few days and had nothing else to do. Thorne was very helpful, according to Claire, in helping her out when she was going over the properties, but he thought otherwise.

Of course, I refused to give him the advance, as it would set a bad precedent for our professional bond and the company in general. Purchasing equipment for the security of the company was a different story. It was definitely something I could justify as a necessary company expense.

"—and this here is the latest model."

"Thank you. I'll take some time to think it over myself first."

The sales attendant tactfully went to help the next customer while I examined the guns. As expected from Premier Arms, their products consisted mainly of coilguns and railguns.

They were a lot more expensive than conventional arms, yet had lower durability and stopping power. In return, they also had much higher penetration power, which was certainly nice to have handy, especially after that run-in with the cyborg.

Although I wasn't planning on fighting cyborgs often, at least not fair and square, I wanted something handy, just in case.

Searching online, there were several reviews for all the models that the salesperson had presented to me. I went through them, searching for the highest-star reviews and the lowest ones to try to gauge which one would fit me.

In the end, I decided on a well-tested model from the Electra Force line, the EF-012. There was a newer model, but it's better stopping power wasn't worth the cost, considering I was looking for a secondary weapon—especially since not only the gun, but also the battery reloads would be more expensive too.

The EF-012 could shoot eight rounds before needing a new magazine, which also included the battery. It was definitely convenient to have it all reloaded together as one. They designed it that way because the railgun required considerably more energy, and considerably more of my funds for the special mags.

After an uneventful test fire, I went away to see what Thorne had been up to.

I found him waiting beside the Premier Arms area, carrying a large gun case. He was decked out in rugged clothing and body armor, a combination I normally saw mercenaries wearing.

"You sure look like you had a large haul."

Thorne could only sheepishly smile. "Thanks to you, sir. I've been doing some research online and signed up for a training course. It had a comprehensive list of items I would need."

"Well, I'm glad you're taking it seriously, and I'm sure Claire would love to see you in this getup."

He looked much more mature. I commanded my optics to take a picture and sent it to the person in question.

"Please don't. She'll make me model for her in this."

"Might be a little too late for that. Wanna go grab something to drink before we head back? I've been to this mall before." I gestured for him to follow and headed towards the food court floor.

"No way..." his voice echoed behind me.

* * *

"You in yet?" I whispered over the call. It was nighttime, after closing, and the mall towered above me.

"Give me another few minutes," Leo said. "This isn't some off-the-rack security they're running here. Fancy places like these hire actual security specialists to tailor their systems. You're lucky to even have someone skilled enough to breach undetected."

"Yeah, yeah. You're awesome, I get it."

"Unlike regular gun-for-hire mercenaries, hackers require a high level of education and training. There's a reason why almost all of us are ex-corpos, you know. Ones that could hack into a mall like this are rare. You should show us a little more appreciation."

"Okay, let me know once you're done, mister genius hacker Leo."

I put the call on hold and switched over to another channel. "How are you holding up, Thorne?"

"I'm fine, sir. Can't say I'm not nervous, but rest assured, I've trained enough this past week to at least not be a liability."

"If this all goes smoothly, you'll only need to be carrying stuff back and forth, so relax. We've also got a lot of professionals here to cover our backs."

After I checked in with the rest of the team, Leo finally breached the cameras using the connection we established earlier when the mall was still open.

I rushed towards the wall and shot a grapple gun to secure a way onto the roof. After a quick climb up, I entered through the roof entrance unchallenged and started making my way to the objective by following the building layout Leo sent.

Though this mall was considered on the upper-middle tier, their security was less stringent than I had expected. I assumed it wasn't worth it for the mall to invest too much into protection, as it was suicide for criminals to piss off several corporations at once.

This was why we carefully planned our route and only targeted the medical equipment reseller. While it was a medium-sized corporation that had its hands in several different pies, Leo was confident he could cover our tracks well enough for it to give up and just claim insurance instead. Besides, what we took would likely just be chump change to the company.

With every terminal I came across, I opened up a connection to Leo. That way, he could do the hard part, gaining control of the cameras to spot any patrols and loop the feed that was being sent back to the security room.

With the security cameras on our side, I avoided patrols entirely or had ample time to find places to hide.

Eventually I gained access to the medical equipment store and found their security terminal.

It took only a few minutes before Leo disabled all the in-store security measures, and we then called the rest of the team in.

While I waited, I browsed around the storage room, examining the collection of medical equipment and supplies from various brands.

It was a pity that we couldn't take too much. If their whole store got hit, the entire corporation would surely respond, but a few missing items could go under the radar, as it could be embezzlement or inventory error.

The team soon arrived. I pointed out what to take and everyone got to work. It took three round trips to carry everything we were here for. Fortunately, we didn't encounter any trouble and packed everything into a truck we parked in the loading area.

There was a different type of satisfaction in pulling off a heist quietly, with no hiccups along the way. It felt... professional and badass.

After off-loading everything onto the first floor of my new and very empty office, we gathered together.

"I'll be sending over the promised payment now. Should I send it to each of you individually?"

The mercenaries exchanged glances for a second before Erza playfully shoved Flo forward.

"Look, we owe you with the Leo thing, so we decided to not take any payment for the job this time, since we didn't do much. It's not enough to pay you back for the risk you took, so we'll still owe you."

"No, this definitely returned the favor. Let's call it even. I don't like keeping favors from friends."

"If that's what you want... But still, call me if you need anything." Flo patted me on the back and exited the building, followed by Erza, who gave me a quick nod.

Liz left next, looking as if she would pass out at any time, but Max stopped in front of me.

"I'll come by with a few friends once your clinic opens." He winked as he walked by.

Then Leo came straight up to me and was about to speak, but stopped himself and chose to leave with the rest of his team instead.

With them gone, I looked over at the only other remaining person.

"While I'm glad that went smoothly, it seems like there's a lot of work ahead of us."

Thorne nodded and alternated looks between the pile of boxed-up equipment we just received and the emptiness of the rest of the future clinic.

"Well," I said, "We'll deal with it tomorrow. Let's go get some rest."

We made our way up the stairs to our rooms. We'd leased the building with two floors and contracted a construction team to renovate it, but the work hadn't started yet. I kept the designs simple, so the bulk of the work was simply putting up several walls, along with the wiring and plumbing that the new rooms required.

At least we'd gotten our bedrooms furnished, as that was our priority. Now that I had some extra cash from the money I set aside to pay Flo's team, I figured it was time for additional investments.

I set a reminder to browse through the security options for the building tomorrow before I fell asleep.

* * *

**Status**
**Level:** 5
**EXP:** 350/500
**Musculoskeletal:** 51
**Neural Reflex:** 15

**Visuomotor Coordination:** 12
**Endurance:** 9
**Sensory Perception:** 37
**Upgrade Points:** 0
**Upgrades:**
    Stealth +7
    Hacking +3
    Cybernetic Engineering +4
**Enhancements:**
    SAID: Zenitech Hoth Mk.3
    Optics: Nova Tech Stars Mk.4
    Cyberarm (Left): Nova Tech Mudra Mk.6

With surgical tools sprawled out across four tables before me, I got busy organizing and inspecting the equipment's conditions. By putting points into cybernetic engineering, I'd learned how to use related tools. I even knew the entire process of installing cybernetics from start to finish, though that didn't change the fact I had zero experience doing it.

I was nervous about my future first operation, so I was taking the time this morning to sort out all my equipment and set up an operating room on the first floor. Before opening, I really should put a few more points in cybernetics first.

Unfortunately, the net in this world didn't have any useful academic knowledge for me to consult. It seemed like all the useful knowledge was being kept exclusive or behind paywalls.

"Whatcha doing?" A voice from over my shoulder startled me.

"Have you heard of knocking?" I glared at the red-haired girl behind me.

"I did. You just didn't answer." She brushed off my glare and brought her face closer to examine the equipment spread around the room. "This stuff seems expensive."

"Yeah, which is why I set up a meeting with a representative from Amazing Corp about security installations in the afternoon."

"Sounds boring. I'm more interested in all this stuff here. Teach me!" Claire turned and gave me the classic puppy eyes.

"Maybe when we have the time later."

"What do you have to do now?"

"Me and Thorne are going to the range. Wanna join?"

"Nah, sounds boring. You boys have fun." As swiftly as she had entered, she took her leave.

*Hmm, maybe I should start teaching her some cybernetics. Wouldn't hurt to have some help. But how long would it take to teach her the knowledge in my head...? It's not like she can just download it into her brain like I did.*

*Wait...*

Some of the high-end SAIDs interfaced with your brain while you slept to promote learning. I would definitely look into it once I raised my cybernetic engineering level up some more.

# CHAPTER 12

## SETTING UP SHOP

**Thorne—Rollo Halls' Associate**

"Stay there and watch. Don't do anything unless I say so or you're spotted."

"Yes, sir, I'll do my best. I think I'm getting the hang of staying out of sight."

For the past month, he had followed his new employer out during the night to hunt down society's miscreants. He had been taught how to stay away from them his entire life, so it was strange to be searching for them instead.

His employer nodded and quickly melded into the shadows of night. If he weren't used to it, he would definitely have lost sight of him. Luckily, he knew where his boss was going.

He watched him slip a tracker with practiced ease onto the target's vehicle and return to Thorne's location in the dark alley.

They then both monitored the car with the help of the night vision mode on their optics.

Thankfully, his new employer had offered him the set of optics along with a SAID, and allowed him to pay it back in installments deducted from his pay.

It was the norm for companies to force employees to use their standard cybernetics that they retained ownership of. If you left the job, they would recover them whether you agreed or not. You wouldn't even be able to run away with them, as the company cybernetics had software that monitored their employees twenty-four seven.

After a few more minutes, the criminals they were tracking returned to their car, carrying a person over their shoulder. They tossed the unconscious girl into the back, where several other victims lay, and started their car up.

The two gave chase in a car of their own, following them from a distance. Even though it wasn't their first time doing this, Thorne couldn't help but feel excited. It was every kid's dream to be a superhero who lurked in the dark and stopped the villains.

That is, until he learned that only worked in fiction, and that in reality, the best way to survive was to live with your head down and avoid drawing any attention. His family had done just that, but his mom had still suffered a tragic ending.

So his new goal was to attain strength. He needed it to protect himself and his friends, to never let what happened to his mom be repeated ever again.

"Thorne, you there?"

"Yes, sir. Sorry, I spaced out."

"Are you sure you're okay? You don't have to come with me if you're tired."

"Yes, I'm fine, sir. Let's finish this before the sun rises, or Claire is going to talk our ears off again."

"Yeah... you have a point. It looks like we found one of the bigger hideouts this time, too. Let's hurry. Same old rules—follow my lead."

The car they had been tracking had stopped in the back alley of some desolate stores. Parking their ride a distance away, Thorne and his boss approached the tracker.

The duo spotted their targets: two men carrying the bodies, one at a time, down into a store's basement.

Making sure he kept up with Mr. Halls, Thorne made his way behind the other car. Then he received a text.

*We'll each take one down the next time they come back.*

Not long after, the door squeaked open and the two targets returned to their victims. As they were pulling out another from the back, Thorne struck out with his combat knife, slitting the man's throat as he cupped another hand over his mouth, like he had trained to do. He held the man, preventing his body from dropping, and gently lay it on the ground.

Once he was done, he saw Mr. Halls standing above the other body. He came over to Thorne's kill and plunged his combat knife into the back of the head. Thorne didn't question it, as this wasn't the first time it happened and his employer didn't seem to want to talk about it.

He had thought Mr. Halls didn't trust he had done a proper job at first, but he kept reassuring him, so he decided to just stop overthinking it.

The two then entered the basement. The entire time, he was focused on Mr. Hall's movement, as while he had picked up a few things, he was still far from moving so quietly with such agility.

They soon spotted the room where they kept their victims. It was a small holding cell, with a few tables where they could strap victims down, cybernetic parts lying sprawled across the room, and clear containers holding organs.

*So these guys were a bunch of harvesters, sickos who stole people's chrome and organs and resold them.*

He gripped his weapon tighter, secretly thankful that he hadn't been kidnapped by these people instead of the research corp.

At the far end of the room, a white light shined on a table. Through the curtains, they could make out a silhouette standing by the table, holding sharp tools.

"AAAAAH! STOP!" a voice yelled out from the table, followed by laughter tinted with insanity.

Thorne had aimed his pistol at the laughing man when a hand touched his shoulder. He turned to see Mr. Halls giving him a look, and soon found another incoming text.

*Calm down, gather information about our surroundings first. We'll take that guy out all right, but we need to play it smart.*

Taking a deep breath, he nodded back and followed.

There was an open door behind the gruesome scene, leading to a room with several couches, each with a person resting on it. From their glowing irises, it was obvious they were focused on what was displayed in their optics.

Having scouted out the entire place, Thorne and Mr. Halls meticulously ended the lives of all the preoccupied harvesters. They then made their way back to the other room, where Thorne let out all of his frustrations on the man still operating on the poor man on the table.

While he dealt with the last disgusting harvester, Mr. Halls skillfully prepared to operate on the victim. He rummaged through the room and found some prosthetic organs and limbs that he used to put his mangled body back together.

It took over half an hour. Thorne used the time to check in on the other victims who were still alive, and pack away all the ill-gotten chrome the harvesters had.

By the time the two finished up in that basement and ensured all the victims would be okay, the darkness of the night sky started to brighten.

* * *

"Seriously, you two, do you always need to go out until morning?"

"But Claire, we had to…"

Checking out my progress from last night, I ate my first meal of the day while Claire gave us an earful. Well, more like giving Thorne an earful, so I let him handle it.

After all, I was busy studying my status sheet, where I found that my endurance had gone up by one. I hadn't installed new augments or anything, but it went up.

But I hadn't had the chance to go on any gigs, as I had to supervise the clinic renovations. There were expensive cybernetics and equipment lying around, after all.

That left only nighttime for doing community cleanup, which Thorne had started tagging along for. I wasn't sure if I was lucky or not, but the area around my clinic had quite a few harvesters. Maybe that was why they were eager to lease this place out, even if it was only for a one-year contract.

Maybe the exercise from all the outings was what increased my endurance. If so, it was a lot slower than simply installing a new cybernetic instead.

It was convenient that I was able to find a few wrongdoers every night, and that helped me make good progress on leveling up. I'd been holding off on upgrading for a while, and now that I had four upgrade points available, I wasn't sure how best to use them. Of course, I could invest them all into cybernetic engineering, but that might draw unwanted attention if someone who had no prior record of studying the field was suddenly able to create sophisticated implants.

Perhaps I was paranoid, but I was sure someone would find out what was going on eventually, just from my handiwork.

I also wondered how low the skill ceiling was for cybernetic engineering. Each time I upgraded it, I learned a little more about how to configure cybernetics to help them fit more seamlessly with the intended users. However, I was starting to feel the diminishing returns.

There was a definite allure to spending the points elsewhere. Having learned this much about cybernetics, I realized that seriously moving forward would require putting some upgrade points into software engineering. That would allow me to design and create unique software for the new cybernetics, making them function exactly the way I wanted them to.

I also had to spend points on stealth technology. With leveling up being harder and harder, I didn't need to dump everything into fields I didn't have a use for right now.

Maybe I should see how things went with my clinic first and do more market research on the types of cybernetics I wanted to create. The upgrade points didn't expire, so there was no need to make a decision right away.

"—oss? Hey, boss, you hear me?"

Glancing over, I found both Claire and Thorne staring at me.

"Sorry, what's up?"

"The foreman said they'll be done by tonight," Claire said. "Is it okay if I have the furniture delivered tomorrow morning?"

*Finish by tonight? That is pretty fast by my old world's standards. Thank you, whatever technology sped it up.*

"Sure, I'll try to have all the medical equipment set up before then so we can move the new stuff around freely."

"Are you sure you're going to be awake tomorrow morning? You're not going off all night again, are you?" Claire scowled back and forth between me and Thorne.

"Yeah, don't plan to tonight. Let's have the clinic open tomorrow. It's time to get the revenue to start rolling in. Actually, let's all go out for drinks tonight." Sensing Claire's eyes boring into me, I quickly added, "We're going to Haven to start marketing to our potential clients!"

* * *

Out in Haven's main lobby, I had Thorne and Claire sit beside me while on the couch were Max, Liz, Leo, and Lana.

"So you're finally opening soon, eh?" said the brown-haired man across from me. He was embracing his rifle as usual. "Flo and Erza couldn't make it tonight, but I'll get the word out to them and a few other acquaintances."

"Hmph. I guess I could try reaching out to my acquaintances as well," said the girl holding onto Leo's arm, "but I doubt they'll check out some unlicensed back-alley clinic."

Leo said, "Hey, come on, don't be like that. Sorry, Rollo, she may have worded that badly, but our circle comprises mostly ex-corpo like us, so they aren't exactly anti-corpo and would rather go to official clinics."

From what I'd heard, most hackers and their ilk were ex-corpos who were down on their luck but looking to get hired again by another corporation. In the meantime, they were eager to show off their skills.

"No worries," I said. "Just spread the word if you can. No need to force it." Leo nodded in response.

I looked over at Liz, whose eyes never lost the distinct glow of optics. She leaned back lazily into the couch, occasionally grabbing snacks off the table.

*Yeah, I'll leave her alone.*

We then drank and made merry. My two employees familiarized themselves with the rest of the group. The mercs brought us around to some other groups they knew, and overall, it was a fun night.

*Hopefully, I'll see some familiar faces tomorrow as customers on my first day.*

# CHAPTER 19

## THE CLINIC

"Wake up!"

I opened my eyes to the words everyone definitely wanted to hear first thing in the morning.

I doubted I could ever be a morning riser. Especially not today, after I'd stayed up late setting up my whole clinic with the proper equipment and surgical tables.

Hounded by Claire, I was dragged downstairs for breakfast, then forced to help her direct the delivery of the new furniture along with Thorne, who looked far more energetic than me.

Good thing we already knew where to place the larger pieces, as they were made to order. The only furniture we had to move around was armchairs and small sofas for the lobby and the break room.

By the time we finished furnishing the place, it was well past lunchtime. Seeing as we planned to start business hours at three p.m. today, we ordered delivery and splurged a little to celebrate.

While we waited, we paced around the first floor, making sure everything was in order. It was frankly cute to see the siblings so nervous, considering this was my company, and not theirs.

When the time came, we didn't do anything special. As an unlicensed clinician, I would not have any signs outside or grand opening florals. That was why we had instead focused on word-of-mouth marketing amongst mercenaries.

Back in operating room one, I closed my eyes and started reviewing the steps of a few common procedures. I didn't think any other cybernetic professional had experienced what I was feeling right now, having all the knowledge of what to do in my head but absolutely zero hands-on experience.

Once I had my fill of practice, I made my way to Thorne. He was in the security room, where he monitored all the cameras watching the inside and outside of the building and the controls to the turrets installed all over the premises.

They were surprisingly cheap and had a pretty advanced targeting system. The turrets could retaliate automatically against hostiles, including anyone pointing guns at the employees in its system. But as a programmed system, the whole thing wasn't perfect, so the seller recommended having someone manning the controls.

Tapping my security card, I entered the cool room filled with screens. "Everything all right in here?"

"Yes, sir—Rollo."

I smirked at him as he fumbled his words; I had been trying to get him to be more casual with me, but he always reverted to sir, especially when we were in the heat of it.

Looking at the main screen, I watched the cameras pointed towards the parking lot and the one showing the lobby. I could see Claire sitting at the reception counter behind a glass panel. It went without saying that it was bulletproof because it was actually harder to find non-bulletproof glass in this city, apparently. What a world I lived in...

"So, how's it going with your training classes?"

"A lot of the same drills over and over again, but I'm hanging on. Can't complain when I'm only there in the mornings a few times a week."

"Well, keep it up. Were you planning on moving out like Claire as well?"

"Hmm... I think—There's someone approaching, sir."

The parking lot feeds displayed three guys walking towards the front of the building. It wasn't hard for both of us to recognize one of them, especially when he carried his signature sniper rifle. I buzzed them in through the front door and made my way out to greet them.

As I approached a hall corner, I noted the turret mounted on the ceiling jerking around, searching for its targets.

Huh... I should definitely fine-tune the settings. It wasn't very welcoming, to say the least.

Going down the hallway, I found the three men standing in front of Claire's counter.

"—seeing you again."

"Yeah, you too, and look who we have here. If it isn't Dr. Halls!" One of them grinned widely as he turned my way.

"Hey, thank you for showing up. You can call me Rollo. Are these your friends here?" I glanced over at the two men beside Max. Now that I got a closer look, I could see that their arms were all prosthetics from the slivers of exposed alloys between their gloves and sleeves.

"That's Rick and Will. They're my buddies from back when we fought down in Texas."

The two nodded at me and looked me over before one of them spoke up. "You the chrome doc we can trust?"

"I respect all my clients' privacy. If that doesn't reassure you, I was hoping you could give me a chance to earn your trust. I wouldn't want to let down Max or any of his friends."

"Okay, that's what we're here for. We're looking to get a checkup that's long overdue. We don't trust any of the corpo scum this island is infested with and we haven't had a chance to go back to NNA for a while now."

"Sounds good. Follow me, let's see what we can do for you." I led them into the closest room and prepared for the task.

*This will be a good warmup.*

* * *

"Your synaptic nerve connectors are ancient and require a replacement," I explained as I brought the terminal over to him to illustrate what I was talking about. "That's why you're feeling the disconnect with your arm. Other than that, the internal of the arm just needs some cleaning done. Though... you can get a much better-performing model in a decent price range nowadays. If you want, I can—"

"No thank you, doc. I'm used to this old arm and will stick with it until it breaks. Just fix what you can within my budget of two thousand credits."

"Understood. The nerve connectors are common enough. Those are well within your budget."

I pushed the terminal off to the side and went to grab the parts. His arm was still disassembled on the table beside me, and I got to work on it. Working on the cyberarm was the easy part; the hard part was replacing the connectors that were still attached to his nerves.

"Here, I'll need you to take a whiff of this. It'll put you to sleep for a bit so it doesn't hurt while I work on the nerve connectors."

Once he was out cold, the surgical suite brought me the various screwdrivers and scalpels I needed to open up the port that connected his cybernetic bits to his organic ones.

*It's a little nerve-wracking knowing that a mistake could damage the nerves in his shoulders permanently. Having that regrown is not cheap in the slightest.*

I successfully kept my hands steady throughout and completed the operation.

My patient woke up after half an hour, as the dosage given to him wasn't too high to begin with.

"How are you feeling? Ready to do some calibrations?"

"Yeah... I've been worse. Got to say, my entire shoulders feel a lot lighter already. My hand feels as responsive as my real one!"

"Happy to hear that."

Max and his friends left once I finished some fine-tuning. We didn't have another client until the sun had set.

We never expected any significant traffic today. Having just started out, making a few hundred credits from checkups was pretty cool, though I was looking forward to installing actual cybernetics. The checkup only consisted of adjusting the fit, checking diagnostics, and renewing lubrication.

When it was completely dark out, Thorne sent me a text that someone I knew had come, so I once again ventured out to the lobby.

Turning the corner, this time I spotted two women, one with familiar light-blue hair while the other had short brown hair.

"Liz, thank you for coming."

She lethargically raised a hand. Then she simply continued to stare at me blankly, so I turned to her friend. "And this here is?"

The girl with short brown hair jumped forward to explain. "Hi, I'm Serene. I'm Liz's guildie."

I didn't believe they were mercenary guilds or anything here. Was she talking about games?

"Nice to meet you. What can we do you for today?"

"Umm, I was thinking about upgrading my right arm."

"We can go over some options. Follow me," I said as I watched Liz make herself comfortable on a chair in the lobby.

Upon leading Serene to an open room, I let her browse her options with the room's terminal as I proceeded with a pre-installation checkup. She didn't take long to finalize her decision, though frankly, my catalog wasn't that extensive.

This was it. I really was going to perform an operation today. Once the checkup was complete and everything was ready, I put Serene to sleep and began.

As this was her first cyberarm, I would need to perform an additional procedure to remove the original and install the nodes where the new one would connect with the nerves.

The cybernetic engineering knowledge I received from the system had detailed information on how to go about the entire process. It even included how to account for compatibility when designing any cybernetics, as compatibility was its core focus.

I isolated the knowledge I didn't need at the moment and focused on the surgery.

With the blood flow to the arm halted, I removed the arm with various tools, including a scalpel, surgical scissors, and a bone saw. The step I was most nervous about was the final connection between the cybernetics and the human body, as it was the most delicate part.

While everything proceeded smoothly, I had to take it slow, as I was performing the installation for the first time. I definitely did not have the muscle memory to do it efficiently. It felt like writing really slowly in order to keep my letters neat and legible.

After over an hour, I finally slotted in the arm and completed the installation. Plugging a cable into the arm, I let the computer take care of the real-time diagnostics. I left the room, as the last step could only happen once the patient was awake again.

I found Liz in the same chair with glowing eyes.

"Hey, your friend should be up in another half hour. Did you want anything?"

She looked up at me briefly before her eyes flickered back to whatever was on her optics. "I'm good."

Seeing how she didn't want to talk further, I shrugged, turned back, and found Claire smirking at me. "Got turned down too, huh?"

Opting to ignore her, I returned to my patient and prepared for the testing and calibrations.

* * *

Throughout the week, I had visits from acquaintances as well as new clients. Hopefully, that meant word about my clinic was spreading around.

Every cybernetic installation was a huge sale for me, as I didn't have to pay the cost of my inventory. It was all either from the initial gang hideout where I found Sarah and Caleb, or looted from the local harvesters.

Though that meant the cybernetics weren't brand new, from a technical standpoint it made no difference, as long as I recalibrated them, replaced the connection nodes, and customized them to increase the affinity with the users.

With a routine settling in, I decided to reach out to the Quest Giver I had been neglecting.

"Hey, Fitel, it's been a while. How's it going?"

"Mr. Halls, I was starting to think I would not hear back from you." After a slight pause, Fitel responded at his usual measured pace. "I take it that you calling me means you are ready for some work again."

"Yeah, I'm looking for work that will give me info on harvesters, gangs, whatever criminals."

"Yes... that can be arranged. May I also offer you other work in other areas? While in return, I provide information on what you want from my network?"

"Sure, and also, could you maybe recommend my clinic if anyone's looking?"

"I will consider it after looking into it. Anything else?"

"No, thank you."

"Good day to you, then. You will receive the information for the job soon."

After the call disconnected, I received the mission dossier swiftly, as usual. The gig was taking out one of the hideouts of a small gang, and quietly at that, to send a "message" to the targets on behalf of the client.

This was something I could do, but it would be difficult if I wanted to bring Thorne along. He wouldn't be able to keep up with me, at least not quietly. And I doubted he would agree to being left behind.

Well, thankfully, there wasn't a pressing timeline. There was something I wanted to test out as well.

Upon checking my status, I saw that I had 260 experience and 4 upgrade points.

Since the clinic had been operational for a while, I felt I didn't need to spend any more points on cybernetic engineering at the moment. But I had another idea about how to use them.

I hadn't been able to focus on leveling this past while, but I was sure that with the jobs and information from Fitel, the pace should start picking up again.

Going on the web through my SAID, I could see if the items I needed were available. I made my way to an empty room on the second floor of my clinic for some tinkering.

*Hmm... This seems like it'll work. It definitely will be an excellent learning experience, regardless of the ultimate results.*

# CHAPTER 20

## TESTING

First thing in the morning, I ventured to an electronics store I found online with positive reviews. It was on an entire street dedicated to electronics with only pedestrian access, and was crowded even this early in the day.

Disembarking from the car, I watched it drive off to auto park itself in a nearby parking lot.

Taking in all the people, I couldn't help but note the cybernetics they had. Now that it was my field of work, I had to pay them much closer attention.

I slid past the crowd while following the GPS. I soon arrived at my destination: a store that spanned ten floors of an entire building.

I made my way to the floor for the components that were on my shopping list and marked down everything I wanted to buy. When I was ready to leave, I'd submit the list to checkout and they would prepare the products for me.

The last item I wanted to buy was on the top floor, where there were much fewer people. This one was enormous and felt a little empty compared to the other levels. There were even more staff than customers here.

With the signs clearly labeled, I found my section and saw rows of metal boxes that ranged from the size of a microwave to the size of a bedroom.

I compared the descriptions of the first few that caught my eye. It was easy to get lost, as there were many specifications, and technical jargon, that made no sense to me.

"Hello, sir. How may I help you today?" I looked up to see a young woman's smile.

"I'm looking for a 3D printer for some personal tinkering. Can you go over some models and their differences?"

"Why, certainly. Please follow me to the demo terminal."

The woman walked with an exaggerated sway in her hips, bringing me to a corner of the floor where a large terminal lay. With a few commands from the woman, a hologram shot out from the terminal and displayed another boxy printer.

A few different models soon popped up beside the first one, and then each one began printing a similar figurine. There was a featureless hologram person next to each printer, showcasing how it was operated, that also served as a benchmark to determine their sizes.

"Sir, these models here are suitable for beginners and experienced people alike, and have the versatility to print with most materials. These should satisfy most personal workshops unless you have something specific in mind."

"I'm mainly looking to work with electronic parts and apparel."

"Hmm..." The woman took a moment to go through the terminal. "I do have a few that specialize in those areas, but do note that complex and sophisticated electronic parts like CPUs cannot be printed unless you use a specialized industrial model we do not carry here."

The previous models disappeared and were replaced with new ones a few sizes larger.

"That's fine. Explain to me the differences between these models you have here."

"Of course. All the models here have various systems that allow for electroforming, chemical etching, electrochemical machining, and laser cutting, on top of all the usual features of a standard 3D printer. You should be able to work on the vast majority of electronic parts and apparel as you requested. The main differences between these models and the previous ones would be the speed of printing, build volume, and resolution. Please feel free to filter the options on the terminal as you please."

Taking a closer look at the specifications shown below each model, I saw that the prices and sizes of the printers varied quite a bit.

I filtered out every size except the smallest possible that still efficiently printed human-sized apparel. That was all I needed, working with cybernetics and equipment. Any larger would be overkill, and I didn't have too much cash remaining, since I invested it all into the clinic.

In the end, I decided on one that cost just over ten thousand credits and finalized the order, before returning home to assemble it before the clinic opened in the afternoon.

* * *

"I got all the cameras set up around the perimeter. How's it looking on your end?"

"All clear, sir."

"Good. Let's rendezvous by the car."

Since he was all the way on the roof, I made it to our meeting spot first, allowing me to watch as Thorne approached with unnaturally quiet steps.

"How is it? Everyone working fine?"

"Yes, it feels fine. I tried jumping and running while I waited, too, and it still worked."

"Okay, but if anything goes wrong, I want you to sit it out and just stay out of sight."

"Understood."

After confirming that there wasn't anything unexpected on the cameras, we made our way to a back alley. We headed straight for the door between two dumpsters. There was a camera looking down from right above the door, though I had already breached it earlier when I was setting up surveillance to keep a lookout for any unexpected guests.

The door had similarly outdated security, which meant we easily bypassed it as well.

The lights were still on inside, giving us a clear view of the kitchen area that the back door had led us into. No one was here, so we made our way through towards the dining area. There, we spotted a man and a woman sitting at the bar. With their eyes glued to the screen on the wall, they enjoyed a drink.

My optics zoomed in on the man's neck and identified the distinct tattoo of a spider, the same as the one in the dossier I received from Fitel.

Noticing a third drink on the seat beside them, we waited a little longer and soon spotted three people coming out from the corridor adjacent to us.

"Only managed to convince these two shitheads to join us. So who's dealing?"

The two seated people got up and followed the others to a larger table. The women then whipped out a deck of cards and started dealing.

I looked over to Thorne and whispered, "We're dashing behind the bar to where those new guys came from. Match my timing.

We're going when they have their attention on their cards, when the round starts."

Thorne nodded back in acknowledgment, and we waited patiently for the gangsters to start their game.

Once the cards were dealt, we silently opened the door and dove behind the bar. The corridor we were aiming for was at the other end, so we ducked behind the counter and smoothly made our way over.

Then we waited for the next round before we dashed out from behind the counter, down the corridor.

We passed by the washrooms and storage room before we found a door that led to the cellar.

Down there, we found an open area set up like a communal living room with an open kitchen. There was no one in sight, so we confidently strode down the hallway that led further in.

Silently entering the first room, we found a bunk bed with a lump visible on each mattress. Exchanging nods, we each headed towards a target, with me going for the upper bunk. With our targets fast asleep, we effortlessly disposed of them. On my way back down, I plunged my knife into Thorne's prey as well to get the extra experience points.

*+10 EXP*

*+10 EXP*

Thankfully, he stopped asking about my strange behavior after the first few weeks we worked together.

We continued clearing out the entire hideout, but with Thorne holding the hallway in case someone left their rooms or the people upstairs came back down.

In one room, a bright lamp showed a man sitting by a desk cleaning what seemed to be a disassembled gun. He was completely focused on his work, allowing me to sneak behind him.

*+10 EXP*

Just as I was exiting the room, I heard metal clanging, followed by a soft hiss from the hallway. Rushing out, I spotted Thorne staring down at a body with his gun aimed at it, and his knife on the ground.

"Sorry, sir. The guy reacted better than I thought and caught me off guard. I had to shoot him." Thorne glanced downwards and retrieved his knife.

His pistol wasn't a coilgun like mine. It was a more economical traditional firearm with a clunky suppressor. Even then it was louder than my Suri, though still enough to remain quiet in an enclosed space.

"Don't sweat it. Treat it as a learning experience."

I continued going from room to room, and soon we managed to clear the entire basement.

This time we left all the valuables and cybernetics intact as requested, to send the message that they were targeted. In the living room area, we brought out a can of spray paint and drew a symbol the client requested onto the wall.

"I think we're all done here, and I don't think we forgot anything. Just have to go up and finish off the last stragglers, right?" Thorne said as he cleaned up.

"No, we lure them down here first. The client is looking to take this bar back, so we don't want to risk damaging anything."

"With all due respect, sir, what a pain in the ass."

He had a point. It would be much simpler to just sneak up and shoot them. What could even lure them all over?

"You take this chance to try luring them. I'll wait behind them upstairs to prevent any from getting away."

*What a great opportunity we have here for Thorne to gain some experience! Definitely not because I can't come up with any good ideas.*

I snuck my way back upstairs and took shelter in the washroom. A few minutes later, I heard a door slamming open, followed by something dropping down the stairs.

With my ear against the door, I soon heard a set of footsteps coming from the bar that walked past the washroom towards the basement.

"You okay?" A female voice yelled out, "Bloody hell! Hey, you boys, one of you come give me a hand, this idiot fell down the stairs."

Another set of footsteps approached and passed me again, so I informed Thorne of the situation via SAID.

*Just two are headed your way.*

Within a minute he responded, *They're taken care of. Are the other three budging?*

I took a peek out of the restroom door and listened intently.

"Let's call it a night, boys. They're taking their sweet time, so let's go see what's going on."

*Yeah, they're coming. I'll follow them down.*

Once I counted three sets of footsteps going by me, I softly opened the door and followed behind the trio. Just as they were starting to get confused here at the top of the stairs, as they looked down at the three sprawled bodies below, I lifted my foot and stomped as hard as I could onto the back of the person in front of me.

The man instantly tumbled down the stairs, bringing the other two with him. Before they could recover, Thorne came into view and finished them off.

Once he was done, he made his way up the stairs, and I grimaced at the creaking noises as he ran.

*I guess the boots aren't perfect yet after all.*

"Okay, good job. You can write the review for the shoes tomorrow, after some rest."

# CHAPTER 31

## A DAY OUT

One day, when the clinic had just opened and there weren't any clients yet, I tinkered around in my new workshop.

I placed a pair of boots on the workbench and disassembled them for maintenance. There was barely any wear and tear, which was good news, but they weren't flexible enough yet. I needed to expand the programming so that it could account for different surfaces and conditions.

My current skills in software engineering were barely enough to do more than ensure its ongoing functionality and fix the on-off button.

Right now, the boots allowed users to move noiselessly most of the time, but had issues with obstacles like glass shards.

There were superior models on the market that performed better, but nothing too advanced. The top-of-the-line stuff, tech that shared similar working principles, was kept off the market for corporate operator use only. They implemented various reverse engineering countermeasures to strictly guard them against their rival corporations.

I was sure the world of corporate espionage was going full throttle in this world, fueling an R&D war between stealth and detection tools, just like with offensive and defensive armaments.

Once I finished examining the boots, I had my SAID put a call through.

"Thorne, how did it go this morning with testing the boots?"

"It no longer feels like the shoes are clamping onto the ground and they're definitely more natural, but I still can't tell what type of surface I'm stepping on from feeling alone. I'll send you the detailed review form once I finish it."

There was a limit to how much I could enhance my work with my current knowledge, as I had to rely on trial and error.

Previously, I had gotten started and upgraded Stealth Technology and Software Engineering. With only a few points invested, I couldn't produce anything amazing yet, but it was a start.

*Now that I have more points, I should be able to comprehensively improve my old work and open up new options. There are a few things not available on the market that I could start developing.*

I spent the points and took a moment to sort out the new knowledge that rushed into my head.

**Status**
**Level:** 9
**EXP:** 60/900
**Musculoskeletal:** 51
**Neural Reflex:** 15
**Visuomotor Coordination:** 12
**Endurance:** 9
**Sensory Perception:** 37
**Upgrade Points:** 0
**Upgrades:**
> Stealth +7
> Hacking +3
> Cybernetic Engineering +6
> Stealth Technology +4
> Software Engineering +2

**Enhancements:**
>SAID: Zenitech Hoth Mk.3
>Optics: Nova Tech Stars Mk.4
>Cyberarm (Left): Nova Tech Mudra Mk.6

With the new information dumped into my brain, the way I looked at my earlier creation instantly changed. Various mistakes and inefficiencies stood out to me. It wasn't like I suddenly had a better design, but my application of theories and scientific principles had been rough and I now knew I could do a lot better.

I got to work and started tweaking the boots on hand until the lack of components held me back. Since I also wanted to start another project, I definitely had to go stock up on parts.

Adding shopping to my to-do list for tomorrow, I exited the workshop and went to greet the first customer of the day.

* * *

The next morning, I left the clinic at the same time as the other two residents. Thorne headed off to training while Claire decided to tag along with me, as she was free.

Returning to the same electronic store where I had bought my 3D printer, I quickly found the high-tech components I was looking for and the additional resin for the printer.

"Hey, boss, can I take a look around before you check out?" Claire said without even turning to me, as she was enamored with a small processing chip in front of her.

I double-checked I had ordered everything I needed before replying, "Sure, why not? We have some time before lunch."

Thankfully, the items were only brought to me once I had paid by the exit, so I didn't have to lug anything around.

We went from floor to floor, browsing through electronics that ranged from home appliances to niche specialty equipment, and even to gaming terminals that gave me the urge to check out what the gaming community of this world had to offer.

It wasn't like I was struggling as I had been in the early days when I would worry about how to spend every little credit. I could afford to have a hobby now.

*Maybe when everything can run smoothly without my intervention.*

My stock of cybernetics was dwindling day by day, as the harvesters seemed to have gone underground, getting ridiculously difficult to find. My initial stash of Nova Tech cybernetics was close to being gone, but I had a plan on how to restock.

"I was thinking, boss... I wanted to get a good terminal as well, so I've been saving up for one. Did you want one too?"

Claire's voice drew me away from the gaming terminal I had been eyeing. "Hmm... Yeah, I might want one to play around with. Why did you want one?"

"Thorne has been working so hard, training in the morning and going out with you at night. I wanted to do something useful myself."

"You're plenty useful already. I need you here to help me hire more people soon too, and the HR management that comes along with it. You won't have to worry about having too much free time for long."

"It's just... I wanted to do more than that. Lana said she would help me get started on learning how to code and stuff."

"When did you manage to get so close to Lana?"

She smirked. "Us girls have our ways of bonding. Don't worry about it."

*If she's going to get free lessons from someone who knows what they're doing, then maybe I should encourage it.*

Unlike in my previous world, knowledge and skills were closely guarded, or behind paywalls. To attain a similar level of expertise to Lana in hacking, I would need to invest quite a few points or pay a sum I couldn't afford to some educational institution that I probably wouldn't even trust to begin with.

"If you're serious about learning from Lana, why don't we buy one to share for now? I don't plan on using it too much."

"Really?!" She turned towards me with a sparkle in her eyes.

"Yeah, let's call it a company expense."

"In that case, let's go over there. I want one that's more lightweight so I can carry it around with me anywhere I go." She dragged me over without waiting for my response.

*Carrying it with her wherever she goes? Did she not just hear what I said about sharing it?*

* * *

"Come on, doc, can you give me a discount on this? Ten K for the arm is way too much."

"That Nova Tech model goes for fifteen thousand credits normally. It is already discounted," I explained. I had been getting more and more new clients, which inevitably came in a mixed bag.

"Yeah, but that's because this is used or stolen, right?"

"All our cybernetics here are in prime condition, I assure you. If this is too pricey, maybe you can check out these other ones here." I filtered the prices for cyberarms and pushed the terminal over for the client to see.

He took a quick glance at it, disinterested, "So where do you even stock these models? Some of these are older than me, I think."

"No comment, but the prices are justified. You get what you pay for."

"I'm going to save this list and think it over first, then, doc."

"Understood. I look forward to your visit."

I walked the man out to the lobby and looked over at Claire, who was completely in the zone with the terminal we had bought the other day.

"There's a client waiting in both rooms two and three," she noted without even looking up.

*I should start considering hiring more people... I'll need the clinic to go legit first, though.*

We closed the clinic at the usual time and decided to go out for dinner for once. We hadn't really gone out much during nighttime, as we had each been busy with our own matters.

Driving through the city, I enjoyed the view of the colossal megabuildings, and how they towered over the smaller buildings surrounding them.

The restaurant we went to was at the edge of the island, with a clear view of the water. Sitting on the patio, I could spot a few ships out in the distance, their lights shining. Elevate City was one of the few free trade zones, owing to the joint corporate control plus the space elevator. It was inevitable that tons of ships came and went every day.

Instead of human servers, the staff that greeted us were robots. They weren't AI-controlled, as AI was banned, so they could only speak and perform pre-programmed tasks.

For this meal, we splurged a little bit. I wasn't sure if the food was actually good or if it was just a sharp contrast to all the junk I had gotten used to eating, but it was definitely a few steps up.

After finishing our meal, we leisurely took in the scenery and watched the musicians perform.

"So are you guys planning to go out again tonight too?" Claire said as she set down her cup of tea.

"Yeah, don't have any jobs from my QG, but he did have some information on potential hideouts."

"I don't get it. Why are you still doing dangerous things like this? You make more than enough in the clinic, and we could source the chrome from somewhere else. Even if we have to pay for it, it would be much safer." Claire frowned, looking at the table, while Thorne alternated glances between us and decided to sip on his drink and not get involved.

From Claire's perspective, I guessed it didn't make any sense to put myself and Thorne in danger so often. I needed to keep doing so to continue leveling up, but that wasn't something they could even fathom. While I wanted to come clean, the system was a secret I didn't plan on sharing lightly.

"Look, I can't explain or go into detail, but this is something I need to do to continue making progress with myself and the company."

"Fine, do what you want. You're the boss."

Having sensed Claire's deteriorating mood, Thorne quickly injected, "So what are you planning with the business? I know you've been working on something in your workshop. Do you plan to sell those?"

"Hmm, yeah, I'm still just testing out the tech, but something along those lines. Will have to figure out the profitability, manufacturing, and market viability of it first, though."

We moved to more benign topics before we paid and went on our way back home to the clinic.

Going back into the city this time, it was hard not to notice the stark transition from the more well-off districts to the regular ones. As we drove by, I couldn't take my eyes off the homeless, gangsters, and lifeless corporate drones who went about their evening.

It reinforced how important money was to me, and that my desire to get rich wasn't wrong. However, it also highlighted how truly horrible the society in this world was compared to my old one. An urge to do something about it welled up inside me, but I knew it wasn't something one person could tackle. This was something that would have to be shelved until the time was right.

We pulled into the clinic parking lot.

"Hey, boss, sorry about earlier. You don't have to tell me anything you don't want to. You have a right to your own secrets. I just somehow took it as you not trusting me, but I know that's not the case, right?"

Before I could reply, engine noises roared from the main road, rapidly heading closer. When I looked over, I saw a car racing towards us and someone's upper body popping up from the front. Without a word, I opened the door and hurried behind the car, taking cover on instinct. Claire and Thorne did the same. A thunderous noise resonated through the parking lot.

The two turrets installed at the front door of our clinic came online and locked onto the threats. Only one managed to get a shot off at the car, as enemy gunfire disabled the other one. It seemed to be a targeted attack. They knew what they were doing.

We heard another car closing in as well, but taking the opportunity while the attackers were occupied with the remaining turret, Thorne and I laid down covering fire while we swiftly shepherded Claire with us into the clinic.

*Okay, what the fuck? Who is attacking us? I don't remember pissing anyone off.*

# CHAPTER 22

# ATTACK ON CLINIC

The first thing we did when we went inside the clinic was head straight for the security control room. From the cameras within, we saw about a dozen masked men outside, all armed and wearing ballistic vests, who were trying to enter our building. They were only waiting for their vanguard to finish prying open the front doors with a crowbar.

Meanwhile, at the back entrance, there were also two men, but it seemed they weren't planning on entering.

Claire and I ensured the turrets were ready for them as soon as they entered while Thorne got geared up.

"Thorne, buy some time up front. I'll go flank them," I said before leaving the room.

Instead of rushing out, I headed to my workshop and retrieved the bodysuit I had been working on. I changed into it as fast as I could. Once I finished dressing, I heard multiple gunshots coming from the lobby.

Running over to one of the operating rooms, I then popped open the window, activated my new suit, and climbed out into the parking lot. There wasn't any cover, but I boldly strode around the building, heading towards the front.

I arrived and watched as the masked men took cover nearby, engaging Thorne and the turrets inside. In fact, I walked straight by them towards their cars behind them. There were only two SUVs, though each had a driver and a gunner manning a light machine gun on the roof.

It was time to test my new creation, so I opted to move in at a slightly different angle from where their guns were pointed, just in case.

I couldn't help but wave at them as I got closer, to see if they would notice, and they didn't react. They were still focused on the building and its surroundings.

Though I looked down at my hands, I only spotted them when they were moving and I really focused on them. There were still some kinks to work out, as this was still a prototype, more of a test of the applications of some new tech.

*At least it's good enough right now for them not to notice. It would be really awkward if they saw me...*

Moving to their blind spots, I pulled out my trusty Suri and examined it. It seemed like it was working properly and the camouflage tech was projected onto it correctly, which meant it was invisible, like the rest of my body.

With the two cars right beside me, I lined up the shot at the driver and pulled the trigger, then rapidly switched to the next targets.

The shattered glass drew the attention of the men in front of the clinic. They quickly took cover, either ducking behind cars or forcefully pushing into the clinic, where they had a foothold.

I flanked them, moving where I could freely fire into several of them, but midway to my destination, I noticed that the camouflage from my suit began to flicker.

Damn it, the battery and the projectors needed some time to cool off. I really had to get around to linking the display of its remaining duration to the SAID so it could be displayed on my HUD, and an alert for when it was about to turn off.

Thankfully, the men in their cover hadn't spotted me. I had quite some experience sneaking around without the crutch of active camouflage, so I wasn't too worried. I returned to old habits and quietly moved when I knew their attention was directed elsewhere.

The few who had stayed outside were lined up around the corner of the vehicle I was behind. I drew my other pistol this time, the Electra Force railgun that had much better penetration than the Suri. It wasn't suppressed. There was no need for that this time.

Releasing a deep breath, I carefully lined up as many targets as I could and fired the shot.

*+10 EXP*

*+10 EXP*

*+10 EXP*

The kick I got from the railgun was much stronger than the Suri's, and it felt satisfying. The blaring sound of the projectile breaking the sound barrier was almost unbearable. I really needed to get some auditory implants.

Of the five that I saw outside, three dropped down from my shot. The other two further away turned their gaze towards me as I pulled the trigger a second time.

*+10 EXP*

*+10 EXP*

With the experience prompts confirming that the threats were neutralized, I took a peek at the camera feeds connected to my optics to see how the situation was. As expected, Thorne was holding them off inside with the help of our defensive emplacements. The enemies couldn't push in without heavy weapons to deal with the turrets.

With the last of them trapped like fish in a barrel, I notified Thorne that I was in position. I watched as he pulled the pin to a grenade and lobbed it over towards the entrance where the men were pinned down.

I propped my gun on top of a car by the entrance and watched as the masked men tried to retreat away from the grenade, straight towards my line of fire.

*+10 EXP*

*+10 EXP*

*+10 EXP*

After three new experience prompts, the grenade exploded. The camera feed confirmed they were all out of commission. I checked in on the two who were posted out back and found that they were gone already.

The suit had recharged by now, with the integral parts having cooled down, so I swept the area in search of the two stragglers. They seemed to have escaped, so I gave up, as I didn't have any clues to search with.

Instead, there was a whole mess waiting for me to clean up now... just great...

Whoever these guys were, they were so on my list.

* * *

The ECPD did show up, but only took brief statements and collected the bodies for "evidence."

The unfortunate thing was that as an unlicensed business, my clinic didn't have insurance, so all the damages I had to pay out of pocket. The attackers' loot that we secured before the police arrived covered it, though, especially the loot from the two cars they left. Though the police claimed a part of the loot, it was overall nice that losses were minimal.

One thing I learned from this incident was how fast the construction industry in Elevate City worked. When we called for someone to repair the clinic, they sent someone over to inspect the damage, and the next morning, they had everything repaired within a few hours.

Now, I couldn't say all the constant violence throughout the city had no benefit. It certainly gave the construction industry plenty of practice. The help of nanomachines may have played a vital part, but nevertheless, the speed at which the walls and doors were repaired and replaced with the exact same look as before was quite something to behold.

Once everything settled down the next day, I commanded my SAID to place a call.

"Mr. Halls, are you calling about the unfortunate attack on your clinic?" the man on the other side of the call said in his rhythmic tone.

"You're already informed, I see. Yes, I wanted to hire you to learn more about the attackers." I was glad he already knew what I wanted before I said anything. A well-informed person was exactly who I needed right now.

"While I would be happy to oblige, the jurisdiction of your clinic lies with the fixer for District 10. It would be better for you to reach out to her. The attackers are likely from around the area as well, based on what I know."

"Okay, send me the contact info." I knew each Quest Giver had their own jurisdiction. Talking to another one might be a good chance to connect with someone new, especially since they definitely had some influence with the mercenaries in my district.

"Very well. Now, if that is all, I will contact you again once I have a job or the information you seek. Best of luck with your endeavors."

The contact was sent a short moment after the call ended, and I immediately had my SAID dial it.

"Hello, who is this?" a plain-sounding woman answered.

"Hi, is this Oli? Fitel gave me your contact. I have a job that you may be able to help me with," I said as I made my way to the lobby to pick up a food delivery.

"Meet me in Haven in thirty minutes, booth number two."

The call hung up before I could say anything else. I looked at the food in my hands and scarfed it down.

Coming to Haven in the late morning was a first for me. The main area felt unusually empty, while the rooms at the edge of the place had their glass windows tinted or only displayed vague silhouettes. I made my way to booth number two as directed and found a buff cyborg at the door.

"Hi, I'm here to see Oli."

He stared at me for a second before he pointed the way with his head.

Once inside, I spotted a middle-aged lady seated casually on the couch, with an elbow on the shoulder of a well-built man. Upon a closer look, my experience with cybernetics told me he was definitely as much of a cyborg as the guy at the door, though he had some quality synth skin to cover it all up.

"You're Rollo Halls, from the new chrome shop. I can't say I'm a fan of that corpo wannabe QG you associate with. You should've reached out to me sooner instead. Is this about the recent attack?" she said before reaching for her drink.

"Yes, can you help me look into the attackers?"

"Of course, as long as you have the credits. I already have preliminary profiles for a few of the people that were on the scene. I'll need a day or two to dig into the others and uncover the details."

"Okay, please do so. I'll take what info you have right now as well."

A quick transaction of credits and information took place through our implants. "I'll contact you once I learn more. You're also available to do jobs for me, right?" I nodded. "Great, talk to you soon."

Taking the hint, I took my leave for the clinic, as we were due to open soon. I browsed through the info she sent me on the drive back.

There were profiles for three of the people I had shot, all with various petty and violent crimes. Only one had a more complete profile: Mark "Screwer" Layton, a known harvester in the ECPD database who was released due to lack of evidence and likely some bribing.

He operated out in this district as well, and his profile came with an address that led to one of the megabuildings in the area.

I quickly took the opportunity to send out a text.

*Thorne, we got a lead to pursue tonight. Bring along something to disable someone, nonlethal.*

A reply soon came. *This is Claire, I'm coming too.*

Why... or how did Claire reply instead?

*No, that's too dangerous.*

*I'll stay a distance away. I've learned a few things from Lana and Leo that can help.*

I could tell that Claire would be stubborn about this. *Fine... remember to listen to us and stay far away from any action.* Allowing her to tag along would let us keep an eye on her.

It seemed like now that we had a lead, we were all looking forward to the counter-attack.

*Let's see where this goes. Hopefully, it'll lead me to the mastermind of the attack so we don't have to worry about them too much longer.*

# CHAPTER 32

## TRACKING

A few hours later, I picked up Thorne and Claire and we drove off to one of the megabuildings in our district.

"Boss, plug this into the network for a bit and I'll be able to get access to the cameras." Claire handed me a small lipstick-shaped device.

"Got it. Remember, don't leave the car."

Having warned her, I strode confidently into the building with Thorne and went up to the elevator. We emerged in a lounge leading to a hallway of apartments. There were a few people just hanging out, but they didn't pay us much attention despite Thorne's armor and the deactivated stealth suit I was wearing.

I went and plugged in the device Claire gave me when the opportunity presented itself.

Claire's voice resonated from my implants. "I'm in. I don't see anything unusual on that level."

"Rollo, I'll go knock on the door," Thorne said. "You hang out of sight in case anything goes wrong."

"Go ahead." I agreed without hesitation, as Thorne was the one wearing proper armor while my suit's defensive properties were questionable at best.

My eagerness had nothing to do with being happy that he was finally getting used to calling me by my name at all, though it was a welcome change.

I shadowed Thorne as he went towards the address we had received from the QG, Oli. The hallway was narrow with no cover, so I engaged the camouflage function as soon as he knocked on the door.

After a brief moment, the door opened slightly, and an older woman peeked out from behind the chain lock. "What do you want?"

Thorne visibly relaxed his grip on his weapon. "Hi, we're looking for acquaintances of Mark Layton, we—"

The woman's face soured at the mention of the name. "What do you want from my son? Are you some of those 'friends' of his? I want nothing to do with you people. Leave my son alone."

"Um, no. We're here for his friends, actually."

Thankfully, Thorne was the one to speak with this lady. I didn't think I could talk to her face-to-face considering I was likely the one who killed her son, regardless of whether he deserved it or not.

"I don't know anything about them. Go away!" The door slammed shut with a bang.

I tapped Thorne on the shoulder and signaled for us to retreat. It wasn't likely the lady was lying and there wasn't much for us to do. We could try more forceful methods and plant hidden cameras around her house, but I didn't think we would have any luck. I'd rather wait and see if Oli dug anything up first.

We returned to the car and made our way back.

"So, what do we do now?" Thorne asked pensively, breaking the silence.

"There isn't much we can do but wait for Oli to turn up with some info. We don't have a network comparable to QGs like her."

"I could try to dig around as well. If I can't handle it, I can ask Lana or Leo," Claire noted.

"Don't, you're still new at this. Let's leave it to the professionals. And don't bother Lana or Leo either. They do this for a living, so they deserve to be paid for it, but I already paid Oli and her team to do the job."

She looked like she wanted to say something back, but decided against it and started playing around with the terminal in her hand.

"Cheer up, guys, learning to delegate is something you'll have to do sooner or later. Shall we grab some desserts before we head back?"

Having worked in an office of one of the biggest companies in the previous world, it had been common for me to wait around for the other departments to finish their part before I could start mine.

*This will be a good experience for these two.*

* * *

Late afternoon the next day, a call came from Oli, sooner than I expected.

"I'll be right back with you. Please feel free to browse our wares on the terminal. The prices are listed there as well."

I left the client to browse at their leisure while I went into an empty room and closed the door behind me.

"Hey, Oli, you found something?"

"Yeah, identified most of the bodies of those who attacked you, and we found out that half of 'em are small-time harvesters in the area and the other half are from a gang called the Rust Scrappers. I'll send you the details. We even have the location of the base the harvesters operate out of."

"Thank you," I replied as I sent out a text to my two employees with the good news.

"Well, that's all for now. See ya later." Then Oli hung up.

Later in the evening, when the clinic closed, the three of us headed to the new location. The alleged harvester base was in a worn-down apartment made of adjacent units connected together.

We repeated what we had done the previous day, gaining control of the surrounding cameras before we approached. Unlike before, the entire apartment was sparsely populated. It may just have been because it was late, but we didn't see a single person around.

When I connected Claire to the floor of the suspected units, she called me after a few minutes. "I can't get past the security anytime soon. They actually have some decent up-to-date shit."

"Forget it, then. Don't risk exposing yourself and go back to the clinic first."

"What w—"

"We'll be fine. We can still keep in touch while you head back. There's no reason for you to be so close to danger anymore."

With the likelihood of this place being a real harvester base skyrocketing, there was no point in Claire being here any longer if she couldn't breach their systems.

This time we didn't just stroll to their front door, we went to the floor above and climbed down onto their balcony. I went first with my active camouflage activated, followed by Thorne once I deemed it safe.

Thorne was hugging the wall while I, with my camouflage system still engaged, scouted out the apartment through the windows. As the info had indicated, I saw the unit in front of me connected with the adjacent unit, separated by a crude half-broken wall.

The living room area was empty as well, so we proceeded to enter. The balcony sliding doors were unlocked.

*With how easy this is, did I walk into a trap?*

Cautioning Thorne, I stealthily led him into one of the rooms. Inside was a familiar sight to us in recent times, an operating room with various sharp tools and organ containers messily sprawled around. For some reason, the containers were empty and there were no cybernetics in sight, as opposed to what we typically saw in a harvester den.

We quickly moved elsewhere and found a bedroom with three actual people inside, snoring away.

"Don't kill them, bind them up," I told Thorne, who returned a nod before pulling out several bracelets from his pack and handing me a couple. He then moved towards one of the unsuspecting harvesters and slapped the bracelets onto the ankles and wrists. They instantly activated with a soft hiss and bound their limbs together.

Following his lead, I swiftly did the same before they had a chance to wake up. We continued clearing out the place and found only one other bedroom, having captured only a total of five people in this base that spanned three apartments.

It was honestly strange to me to see so few people in a base of this size. Usually, if there were only half a dozen of them, their base would be the size of one unit, instead of this one the size of three.

They were all wide-awake now, as it was hard to stay asleep when your limbs were restrained. We took each one to a different room, separating them. Once we thoroughly searched the place, we started the interrogation.

"So, you are the leader here? Were you the one who decided to attack my clinic?" I glared at the bound man sitting on the toilet, being mindful of any changes in his expression.

"What? No, they just forced me to work for them. I had no idea they attacked you, I swear!" he pleaded.

"Oh, then I have no need for you." I drew my weapon and aimed it at his head.

"WAIT! WAIT! I've been in this group for a long time. I can tell you anything you want to know! Please, just let me go after."

"I'm listening." I steadied my gun and kept it pointed at him. He started spewing his entire history with the harvester group, going into the minute details.

"Stop, give me only the relevant information about your leader and why you attacked me."

"Sir, I—"

His face twisted like he was coming up with an excuse, so I interjected, "We'll be asking this of your friends, by the way. If yours doesn't match, I won't mind pulling the trigger."

"Of course, I speak only the truth, I assure you! Sir, the reason we attacked should be obvious, shouldn't it?" He stared up at me with disgusting puppy eyes.

"Spit it out." I slowly placed my finger on the trigger and ensured he saw it.

"Okay, okay... It's because someone's been sacking all the other harvester groups. That made the higher-ups worry, and we wanted to end the threat so we can do our business with peace of mind."

"And why do you think it was me?" Though he didn't explicitly say it, it was obvious he was referring to me.

"Someone noticed a lot of the chrome you have in stock matched what some groups were holding onto. Competitors keep a close eye on each other, after all."

Well, shit, with all the harvesters I had been hunting, I thought everything would be fine as long as there were no survivors. I guessed the harvesters were smarter than they looked. I needed to think things through more...

"So one of you guys saw what I was selling and came to that conclusion. You guys are a lot more aware than I had thought."

"Well, someone else noticed and approached us about it, so we teamed up..."

Oli did mention there was some gang involved as well.

"You sure know a lot for someone who swore they had no idea about the attack on me."

"Haha, I learned a lot of things, since we had nothing to do but gossip for the past while after the boss disappeared."

"Disappeared?" I frowned.

"Yeah, after the attack failed, our boss and a few others went out and haven't come back."

"Did they say where they were going?"

"Yeah, yeah... They went to meet with the Scrappers to discuss the failed attack." I gave him a questioning look. "They're a large gang... so we didn't dare to bother them. We've just been waiting here ever since."

"Send me the location of where you usually meet them."

"Of course, of course... Will you let me go, please? I swear I won't bother you or anyone again. I'll leave the city!"

"I'll see what your friends have to say first."

There was no way I was going to let him go. Harvesters like him were like cockroaches that always sprung back up, but even if he really quit doing any crimes, he'd have to pay for all the people they had brutalized until now. While personally, I would have wanted to have him spend the rest of his days doing hard labor and creating profits for me, the value of experience points was hard to argue against.

All the corroborating stories our prisoners provided gave us a clearer picture of what was happening. The location they provided was some bar they met at, so it wasn't too useful, but still worth checking out.

Once I finished dealing with the harvesters, I received a group call that included me, Thorne, and Claire. Sharing a look with Thorne, I immediately knew who initiated the call.

"Guys, some people just came after me. I got away and I'm tracking them down right now. I'll ping you my location."

# CHAPTER 24

## PURSUIT

**Claire—Rollo Halls' Associate**

"Forget it, then. Don't risk exposing yourself and go back to the clinic first," Rollo, her current boss, dryly commanded.

"What w—"

Before she could voice her complaint, he cut her off. "We'll be fine. We can still keep in touch while you head back. There's no reason for you to be so close to danger anymore." Then he hung up.

"Damn it!" She slammed her hand onto the dashboard.

She couldn't believe this. She thought she could finally be useful and help him and Thorne out. That was why she had been working so hard to learn cybersecurity.

Taking a deep breath, she started sorting out her thoughts. She knew it wasn't Rollo or anyone else's fault, and she blamed herself for being inadequate. She knew she was only a beginner, so she shouldn't even find this surprising, but she couldn't help but feel frustrated. She wanted to contribute and make it safer for those two, and the current her wasn't able to do that.

After searching through her contact list, she placed a call while the car drove her back.

"Hey, Clairy, what's up?"

She sighed before responding, "Lana, are you free? I could really go for a drink right now."

"Woah, I thought you were a law-abiding citizen who wouldn't drink until you're past twenty."

"Yeah? Who's going to enforce the drinking age, the corpos?"

"Ha, they'd probably encourage you to drink more instead, to up their sales. I would know, I've worked for them. Anyway, sorry, I can't come out tonight. We can do it tomorrow when you come over for lessons."

"Okay..."

"So what happened, girl? Want to talk about it?"

She let out another sigh. "I got told to sit out because I couldn't breach some dumb network."

"Girl, you've been learning about cy-sec for how long? It'll take a lot more learning before you'll be able to consistently breach most up-to-date civilian networks."

A text came in from Thorne with an update, confirming the hideout was a harvester den and they got in safely.

Claire groaned. "How did scum like harvesters even get up-to-date security patches? Don't tell me they pay for it like normal people."

"You'd be surprised. Most groups past a certain size have a cy-sec specialist on hand. It takes a lot more brains than you think to run their shit. It's not as simple as just randomly picking people up and chopping out their chrome and organs."

"So I won't be able to breach any harvester network anytime soon... just great. Please tell me you have some way to help me learn faster. I can't stand this."

"Not unless you've got a high-end SAID model with a hypnopaedia feature. Then you'll need the cassettes with the right knowledge on them, which are even harder to get. There's a reason why most skilled cy-sec specialists are corpo or former corpo."

She sighed for the third time. "We can talk more when I come over tomorrow. Thank you for listening to me vent." She watched as the car pulled into the clinic parking lot.

"Sounds good. See you."

With the call ended, she exited the car and set its course to go back to the boys using the auto drive.

Instead of returning to the clinic right away, she started walking down the street. She needed something sweet to cheer herself up first.

Just as she made her way out of the plaza, she noticed from the corner of her eye a couple standing around, both staring daggers at her from across the street. When she turned towards them, they both looked around, avoiding eye contact. They were holding hands, but otherwise seemed to ignore each other.

She continued onwards to Rollo's favorite milkshake place while she kept an eye out. Not her actual eye, but the street-facing security cameras that she could breach. She plugged her terminal into her neural port discreetly and continued walking down the street.

Once she was down the street, the camera feed she had pulled up on her optics showed the two suspect individuals walking in her direction. It was late at night, so there weren't that many pedestrians, which made it easy to keep track of them.

Trusting her gut instinct, she made a few turns to confirm if they were tailing her.

And they were.

*Are these guys related to the people who attacked us? Now, I can call for help and be a damsel in distress, or... I can deal with it myself.*

Deciding she wanted a safety net just in case, she started moving towards the street with all the clubs and bars. These places weren't like Haven. They were cheaper, and catered to the more casual folks instead of mercenaries. This meant that the security policy was different, and they didn't allow weapons to be brought inside.

The old weapon detectors in the lobby worked via automated scans and had an open connection for her to invade from. Claire used the programs she received from Lana and breached it like she was taught. She wasn't experienced enough to know exactly how these machines worked and could only use her pre-made programs to alter them slightly, but the old detectors still had known exploits.

She passed the detectors while still keeping possession of her pistol and entered further inside. A moment later, one of the two people stalking her followed her in. The woman was forced to leave her firearms in the weapon locker.

Little did she know that even though she stowed her guns away, Claire could still trigger the detectors the moment she tried to walk through. Immediately, the bouncers nearby moved to intercept and tackled the woman onto the floor.

Taking advantage of the commotion, Claire swiftly made her way to the weapon lockers and hacked into the one her pursuer had used. As fast as she could, she unloaded the magazine and attached a tracker to it before loading it back in.

Looking at the cameras pointing outside, it appeared the male stalker was covering the back door, which meant the woman, who was now having an interesting conversation with the bouncers, was responsible for watching the main entrance.

Claire briskly made her way towards her original destination while her SAID called a cab to wait for her there. Once she bought the sweets she had been craving, she entered the cab and observed the location of the new tracker she had placed. It was on the move, so she made the group call to Thorne and Rollo.

"Guys, some people just came after me. I got away and I'm tracking them down right now. I'll ping you my location."

They were going after them. And she was too.

* * *

Thorne and I rushed out of the harvester den, and thankfully, my car had made its way back and was already waiting in the same spot.

We set the car's auto drive to follow after Claire. Thorne checked his equipment beside me while Claire was on the line with us, retelling a more detailed version of what happened.

"So they're pulling up to a gated mansion," she said. "Let me see if I can find a way—"

A shout suddenly rang out. "Stop! Wait for us first!"

I looked over at Thorne, taken off guard, and listened quietly as he continued, "You've done enough already! Why didn't you call us in the first place when you noticed you were being followed?! It could've gone so much worse."

"Come on, you want me to just sit here doing nothing? I'm not some kid that needs babysitting. I can handle myself."

"That's not what I meant. You should've given us a heads-up, so we could back you up if anything went wrong! You can't be taking needless risks like this, Claire. Not when your life is on the line. Promise me you won't do that again."

"Okay... I might've acted too impulsively. Sorry..."

That was the first time I heard Thorne lash out, but his anger was understandable.

I needed to start upping our security after this. Right now it was just street gangs, but if more organized groups or mercenaries set their sights on us, we were grossly unprepared, to say nothing of corporations.

We arrived and met up with Claire on the main street closest to the mansion she had tracked her pursuers to.

Claire wore a bashful smile as we approached. "Hey, guys, here's the receiver for the tracker. Take this as well. You guys haven't eaten or drunk anything for some time, right?" She handed us each a burger and a drink.

"Thank you." I took a sip of the drink, my usual milkshake. It was slightly melted, but the sugar helped energize my mind. "I'll head in first to scout it out. You two stay here and wait."

Thorne waited until he finished chewing to respond. "Okay, you really need to get me one of those suits soon."

"The suit's really just to test the tech out. I'll definitely get you one once the cybernetic version is done."

I moved out as soon as I finished snacking. The entire estate was fenced off with metal gates. There were cameras spaced out as well, but with my suit's stealth system on, I could climb over and approach the distant building undetected.

There was a limit to how fast I could move, as the camouflage system became wonkier the faster I moved. It was something I planned to work on further before moving on to the implant version. This suit was destined to only be a prototype, plainly inferior to a cybernetic version. Especially when the stealth system wasn't active. It screamed out "suspicious activity" to anyone who saw you wearing one.

The three-story mansion soon came into view and had even more security around the premises, but thankfully, someone left a window open on the second floor.

Once I climbed up, I hugged the walls to stay out of sight, allowing the suit to rest while I tracked down a camera to breach.

The security in place here was notches above everything I'd tried to breach before. I knew Claire wasn't better than me at hacking yet, so I had to be mindful of cameras from here on.

Moving cautiously, I cleared each corner and noted down more spots to hide when the suit needed a break. The rooms I had entered so far appeared to be simple bedrooms, storages, and bathrooms. Only several minutes in did I hear the sound of people.

"—back?"

"Yeah, I led him to the boss, and he seemed pissed. Better to stay out of sight tonight lest he take it out on you."

"If Larry can't do a proper job, then the boss should use us. I don't get why we're being kept in the dark."

"Shhh! Stop complaining. Larry is his wife's cousin, so of course, he trusts him and his group more. We don't need to snoop where we shouldn't."

The two who were conversing soon came into view. They both had combat vests and rifles, decked out in matching red clothes, and stood by staircases that led further up.

They changed the topic to the girls they'd seen lately and other mundane things. I slowly moved past them with the camouflage activated while their conversation distracted them.

On the third floor, my search for important people bore fruit when I spotted a pair of sentries who stood guard by a set of fancy double doors. With the doors shut, it wasn't feasible for me to walk by even if they couldn't see me. Instead, I went into one of the adjacent secluded rooms and climbed out the window.

My boots clamped onto the outer wall as I made my way towards the guarded room. For some reason, the people in the mansion really liked their open windows, allowing me to peer into the study, where two men sat on a sofa, having a conversation over a drink. In front of the two were a man and a woman who kneeled before them, staring straight into the ground.

# CHAPTER 25

## A NIGHT AT THE MANSION

I held onto the ledge as I peered through the open window. On one side were two men facing away from me. On the other, a man and a woman were kneeling before them.

"Doctor, are you certain that this clinic is worth further investment?" one of the men on the sofa said. "I lost a squad already, and this is proving to be quite a hassle. I won't be able to cover up further damages, and if the higher-ups find out, there'll be hell to pay." He took a puff from some tube connected to the walls.

"Don't worry," said the other one, "I'm confident in my assessment of the value of our target. We should be able to get quite a paycheck from it. All for ourselves, too, the higher-ups wouldn't have a clue. We can easily recruit replacements. Let us wear them down using various harvester groups. They should all be looking forward to putting down their bogeyman once and for all."

For some reason, the man who was called Doctor sounded strangely familiar.

"Fine, but it's up to you to convince the harvesters. Jim and his lackeys are still downstairs."

"Understood."

I pulled myself up into the room as they continued their conversation. I'd heard enough to confirm that these were the perpetrators of the attack, and not some other random thugs looking to kidnap Claire.

Unholstering my Suri, I walked closer and lined up a shot. By the time I dropped the two on the couch, the remaining two kneeling were halfway up as the bullets struck them.

*+10 EXP*

*+10 EXP*

*+10 EXP*

*+10 EXP*

Seeing how there were no cameras in the room, I came out of stealth. The suit would've needed a break soon anyway. Then I turned over the body of the man who sounded familiar. He was an old man wearing a monocle, the one whom I sold some cybernetics to before...

I checked the other bodies for anything useful, then took pictures using my optics and sent them to Claire.

*These the two that were following you?*

Almost instantly, she responded. *Yep, that's them.*

Before I could inspect the last body, the door slammed open.

"Sir, are you okay?!" The two guards I saw outside came rushing in, with two people behind them carrying first aid kits.

The guards saw me, and we all froze for a second before they brought their rifles up. I ducked straight behind the couch, knocking over the whiskey glasses in the process.

Immediately, I reactivated the active camouflage and started crawling on all fours as the bullets came ripping through the couch.

The men stopped shooting and approached from both sides of the couch in sync.

"Where'd he go?"

"There's something moving behind you!"

Unfortunately, the stealth suit was still somewhat visible when people paid attention while I was moving. There was a lot of room for improvement, but that would have to wait.

The man tried to make a one-eighty turn, but was interrupted by the roar of my railgun successfully punching a hole straight through him. Not waiting to see the results, I continued pulling the trigger to ensure I got his partner behind him as well.

*+10 EXP*

*+10 EXP*

Once I saw the experience notifications appear above their heads, I turned to the door, where the remaining duo with first aid kits had been, but found them gone.

An obnoxiously loud alarm started resonating throughout the mansion, so I didn't bother to look for them.

With my element of surprise gone, I stayed in the empty room and let my suit rest while I peered down from the window to scout out any movement. There wasn't anything outside the building yet, so I called Thorne.

"Thorne, prepare the car. We're leaving as soon as I get back."

"Got it. Are you okay?"

"Yeah, but they know there's an intruder."

"Their security detected you?!"

"The boss I zeroed probably had some health monitoring system or something... I should've known. Though there aren't that many people here, from what I can tell. I'll come as soon as my suit has cooled down."

"What?" Thorne seemed to be talking to someone else, and the line went quiet for a while. "There's cars rolling in fast to your location! Get out of there quick!"

I glanced over to the main gate of the mansion, which was being slowly opened by the two guards there. A moment later, the roar of engines rang out as three cars sped their way onto the estate.

They immediately split off to surround the mansion. I had a clear view of the one that came to a stop near my side of the building. Several fully armed men in their red uniforms disembarked from the car, each looking ready for war. With my experience as a cybernetic surgeon, I could tell they all had quality cybernetics just from a glance. The way they carried themselves showed they had proper training as well.

The group then split into two teams of three, with one team entering the building while the other set up defensively around their vehicle. I was sure the same thing was happening where the other two vehicles were. I had to get out soon.

The gauge on the suit showed that it should be good for a little under two minutes before it needed to rest again. I should be able to escape if I hurried.

With the camouflage's assistance, I climbed down the building and started making my way out of the estate. I tried to keep my distance from the group keeping watch outside and moved straight for the fence I had jumped over previously.

On my way past their vehicle, carefully watching the men as I went, I heard something that made me pause.

"Witness reports say the intruder was last seen using optical camo," one of a pair of guards blurted out. "Derek, you switch to thermal!"

The man next to him began panning around. Soon he'd see the entire area. Including the man in the stealth suit behind him.

I hesitated for a moment to decide on which gun to draw, but seeing their armor, I opted for the safer option. I drew my railgun, as I wasn't confident enough in my aim to target the gaps.

*Please don't look behind you. Focus on the mansion.*

He didn't focus on it for long, but that was long enough. Just a moment before I entered his vision, I pulled the trigger.

*+10 EXP*

The projectile broke the sound barrier with a boom, alerting everyone, especially the other two armed men beside me.

Swinging towards the one who had spoken earlier, I fired. By the time I turned to the last person, I was staring down the barrel of his gun. Two gunshots rang out at the same time.

*+10 EXP*

I watched the experience notification fade from above his head as he dropped.

Phew, that could've gone a lot worse... Now I had to book it before their backup arrived. Fortunately, there happened to be a perfect getaway car right here.

Several resident and visitor cars were parked not far from the gate. Racing down the row, it took me only moments to look at the dashboards and find one with a key still in the ignition.

Every car I'd seen in this world used a traditional key. Electronic keys were rare, as you had to keep the security on digitally locked cars up to date, or else they could easily get hacked.

I ran for the door, but after taking my first step, my body screamed out in searing pain. I looked down to see blood flowing out of a small hole from my torso.

*Not this shit again...*

There was no time. I didn't want to be here for a second longer, so I gritted my teeth and rushed into the car as fast as I could.

With the pedal to the metal, I accelerated at full speed towards the gate. I watched as the two gate guards in the booth turned towards the noise of my approaching vehicle. They came out and motioned for the car to slow down, but their expressions changed when they noticed it had sped up instead.

There had been no time for me to inspect the car. They could've had an anti-theft tracker on it, so I chose to take no chances. I pulled the pin to a grenade I had been carrying and dropped it on the dashboard before diving out.

I made sure my prosthetic arm took the brunt of the impact and rolled to disperse the damage as best as I could.

A moment later, a tremendous boom almost deafened me, along with the residual shockwaves. I forced my groaning body to get up and found the two guards lying on the ground, writhing around in agony. I quickly put them out of their misery and inspected the gate, which was now a scene of flaming, deformed metal entangled together.

*+10 EXP*

*+10 EXP*

There were engine noises coming from the mansion, but with the gate wrecked, the security would have trouble following me in their vehicles. I leaped over the fence and dashed back into the city.

It was painful to take every step, but I found my car after a short jog.

"Go! Start driving!" I called out upon throwing myself into the backseat.

"Holy shit, you're bleeding!" Claire exclaimed beside me. "Where's the first aid kit?"

"There's one in the back!" Thorne cried, gripping the wheel tightly despite it being on auto drive.

"Calm down! I have one on me here. Claire, do you see an exit wound?" I turned my back towards her.

She held my sides and leaned down. "Umm... there's a hole about the same size as the one in the front."

"Perfect." The poor defensive properties of the suit turned out to be a boon somehow. The round they shot me with cleanly overpenetrated my flimsy defenses.

I stabbed myself with the first aid stim to stop the bleeding and started applying the combat gauze to my wound.

"Rollo, should I take us to a hospital?"

Taking a quick glance around, I saw no one pursuing. "No, bring us back to the clinic."

Although a cybernetic clinic definitely wasn't the first place to go when injured, it still was stocked with equipment and nanomachine injections that helped close wounds and heal holes in the body.

The hospital might be watched now if they were still pursuing, and honestly, the medical fees in this world counted as horror stories in themselves, from what I heard.

It felt like it took no time at all to arrive at the clinic, and my two employees helped me into one of the operating rooms.

The scan began once I was seated, and I started calibrating the room's terminal for the small operation my nanomachine would have to do. The two of them just stood by and watched, as they didn't know how to help.

It was a little sketchy to have to direct an operation on myself. Still, I preferred it to relying on computers for this. There was a reason why they were called incredibly fast, accurate, and stupid, while humans were incredibly slow, inaccurate, and brilliant. Despite the size of the operation, it would not have been reassuring at all to leave it all to a terminal. If only I had an AI to control this or something.

As if able to read my worried expression, Claire stepped forward and placed a hand on my shoulder. "Is everything okay? Can we help somehow?"

I took another look at the damage the scans showed; nothing hit any important organs, and what was damaged could be put back together by the nanomachines. The wound should heal fine, with no aftereffects.

Simulating the steps I would normally do and potential incidents, I compiled a quick tutorial using my SAID and sent it over.

"Here. Although the machine should do everything, follow these instructions in case anything happens," I muttered as I struggled to keep my eyes open.

Claire stilled for a moment with a serious look in her eyes before nodding. "Got it. You can rely on me!"

I weakly nodded before I grabbed the mask and breathed in the anesthetic.

*Lights out.*

# CHAPTER 26

# BUSINESS DEVELOPMENT

When I woke up, it felt like only a few minutes had passed. Claire was focused on the medical terminal while Thorne was still standing there in the same spot facing me. He quickly noticed I was up and tapped Claire on the shoulder.

"You're awake!" she said. "How are you feeling?"

I sat myself up. "Like every morning, tired. How long was I out for?"

"Just a bit over an hour!"

That wasn't too much longer than expected. According to the logs on the terminal, everything went fairly smoothly. Claire only needed to make some minor adjustments, and she did well.

"Isn't it almost morning? Let's all go get some rest." I stood up and stretched. The area around where I was shot felt a little sore, but should be fine in a few days.

"Umm, is it okay to do so?" Thorne said, sounding awkward. "The guys that shot you are still looking for you, right? They must suspect it was retaliation for the clinic attack."

"Should be fine. From what I learned, the only people who targeted us are already dead. The rest of the whatever-you-call-it gang shouldn't know about us, but we should keep our guard up for the time being."

"You mean the Rust Scrappers. They're a pretty big gang, so I guess it makes sense that they aren't too centralized," Thorne muttered.

"Right, Rust Scrappers... Maybe it's time for us to hasten our plan to recruit more people. A security team sounds like something we could use. A receptionist and another couple surgeons too, but I'll need to get a license for the clinic first to hire any proper medical professionals."

Claire hesitated before clearing her throat. "About that... I think I want to learn about chrome as well. That was pretty cool what I just did." She smiled towards the medical terminal.

"I thought you were learning about cybersecurity? Are you switching over, or are you planning on juggling both?" I raised an eyebrow.

"I'll do both! Come on, don't look at me like that. There's a limit to how long I can throw myself on one subject until my brain explodes!" Claire exclaimed. "Oh, and can we look into getting those fancy SAID models that have the sleep learning feature? That would make me learn a lot faster!"

"Hypnopaedia models shouldn't be an issue, but the cassettes with the relevant knowledge on them aren't cheap, and only SocialCorp sells them, as far as I know. And they aren't sold to just anyone."

*With six points in cybernetics engineering, I can probably design a working hypnopaedia model, but how the so-called cassettes inject knowledge into the brain in a safe and effective fashion is beyond me. I'll need more points in software, and even then, I'll still have to do a lot of testing on live subjects, so that isn't really an option.*

"Tsk, okay, I'll study the old-fashioned way..."

"You also were going to do the interviewing, right?" Thorne ruthlessly delivered another blow.

"Yeah... I'll manage."

* * *

There was a flood of ads whenever I tried to watch any videos online. I could command my optics to shut off while they played, but the interruptions made me want to stop watching entirely.

Sitting in a chair inside an empty office lobby, I spotted the distracted receptionist busy with whatever was playing on her cybernetic eyes. I got up and stretched when the door opened.

"Mr. Halls, I presume?"

I shook the man's outstretched hand. "That's right."

"Nice to meet you. I am Luis Torres."

"A pleasure as well, Mr. Torres."

"Please, call me Luis." I nodded amiably, and he continued. "About what we previously discussed on the phone, preparations are complete. Once you have the funds transferred over, we can go ahead to the examination room."

My SAID wired over the funds, and I proceeded to follow Luis out of the office into the maze-like hallways of the campus. We passed by crowds of students either rushing about to their classes or simply socializing in the hallways.

We took an elevator to a more secluded floor and passed through the type of security check you would typically see at concerts or sports games in my previous world.

After crossing through a large open area, we entered a small classroom with a couple dozen desks and a terminal attached to each one.

"Well, Mr. Halls, feel free to pick any seat here and we can begin. If you need anything, please notify me or any of the other proctors that may periodically replace me." Luis sat down at the front of the room and his eyes then took on an unnatural glow.

I picked a random seat and before long, a woman entered and tapped her security card on the terminal in front of me.

The console unlocked and I found several test subjects to choose from. Not wanting to worry about remembering which ones I had completed, I started from the top.

Skimming the test, I found it boringly similar to the ones I had taken in my old world. It mainly consisted of multiple-choice questions with a few short answers at the end. I guessed, in a way, they took prospective corporate employees' training seriously.

After a long and grueling amount of time, I was finally done, but it wasn't entirely over yet. Next, they led me to an adjacent room with several stations and a test proctor manning each of them. I had to diagnose or perform specific procedures to get a passing grade for each one.

Though it was tedious, thanks to my experience at the clinic and the knowledge from the system, I breezed through everything without being stumped.

Despite my results, there weren't scholarships or anything to soften the blow on my wallet.

* * *

After wasting a whole day and a whole lot of credits, I returned to my clinic with a new medical degree. The clinic was closed today, so it was not surprising I didn't find Claire in the lobby. As I walked towards my workshop, I heard noises in the break room luring me in to investigate.

"—you for your time today. We'll contact you as soon as we have made a decision." I watched as Claire shook hands with an older woman.

They noticed me as the woman was gathering her things. She smiled and nodded at me as she walked by, and I returned the gesture as I watched her close the door behind her.

"Interview? How'd it go?"

"Super tedious. I need something sweet after this. Wanna order ice cream or something?"

"Sure, get me the same milkshake as usual, then," I replied, and took a seat next to her. I stole a glance at the profiles displayed on her terminal. "Any interesting candidates?"

"What do you call interesting? They were all qualified for the position they applied for on paper. I didn't ask for their life stories, but I got the basic gist of it from their education and work history, and from speaking with them."

"Well, okay. I let you handle it, so you do that."

"How about you? Everything went okay?"

I sent her a copy of my new credentials. "Yep, it was expensive and tedious, and I still have to spend another boatload of credits for a forged residency record."

"It's that easy to get certified? That's a scary thought."

"I doubt the doctors you've seen had bribed their way through to get their medical licenses. Any corporation or medical facility could figure it out with a little digging during the hiring process. People usually only bribe their way to a license to just brag or collect it like a trophy."

People who bribed their way through wouldn't be hired unless their employers were oblivious to a ridiculous degree. They could start their own practice like I was doing, though.

"I see... Let's pick up where we left off yesterday in our lesson! I can't handle staring at people's resumes any longer."

"Okay, sure." I could spare some time before resuming my project at the workshop.

* * *

**Thorne—Rollo Halls' Associate**

As he pulled up to the parking lot, he received a call.

"Thorne, can you get some food for us when you guys come back?" Claire blurted.

"Sure. The usual?"

"Yeah, gotta go now. See you."

"All right, everyone, let's go," he said to the rest of the car, and started making his way into the enormous low-rise they had parked in front of.

He spared a glance back at the four other people lagging behind before walking up to the reception.

"Hi, I made a reservation for Thorne."

"Yes, we've been expecting you, sir. Please sign here."

Once the paperwork was complete, they were taken to a locker room to get changed. He grimaced. They appeared to be a ragtag group, all wearing different equipment with no uniformity whatsoever.

They then went into a lobby before a set of metal doors with a terminal beside it. The door opened once he keyed the specifications into the terminal. Inside was a tactical training facility that made extensive use of projection technology to allow anyone to quickly customize the course.

However, instead of training on how to assault a facility, they were doing the opposite, focusing on defensive tactics, as defense was the job guards were hired for.

"Get ready. Training begins as soon as we step inside."

* * *

The numbers in my account grew smaller and smaller. I still had a decent income from the clinic, but the expenditure was greater than the income. I was on the last few crates of cybernetics I had available for sale too, so I had to find a new supplier.

The harvesters in my district went to ground recently, so I switched to targeting other scum and expanded my area of operation to other districts. I tried not to target any one group in particular, which resulted in my experience gain slowing down as I had to carefully pick my marks.

I opened my status as I waited.

**Status**
**Level:** 10
**EXP:** 270/1000
**Musculoskeletal:** 51
**Neural Reflex:** 15
**Visuomotor Coordination:** 12
**Endurance:** 24
**Sensory Perception:** 52
**Upgrade Points:** 0
**Upgrades:**
      Stealth +7
      Hacking +3
      Cybernetic Engineering +6

Stealth Technology +5
Software Engineering +3
**Enhancements:**
SAID: Zenitech Hoth Mk.3
Optics: Nova Tech Stars Mk.4
Cyberarm (Left): Nova Tech Mudra Mk.6
Auditory: Amazing Corp FieldTac Gen 2
Cardiovascular: BioGen Labs Marathon 4

After the previous incident, I had gone ahead and installed a combat-rated auditory implant and an implant for cardio. As a result, my sensory perception and endurance went up.

The cardiovascular implant was like a pacemaker, but housed nanomachines instead, which enhanced my stamina. I was a little too hesitant to replace an entire organ as important as my heart with an entirely cybernetic one (not with my budget, at least), so I opted for this one. For the same reason, I shelved the idea of getting cybernetics that improved my visuomotor coordination and neural reflexes. After all, the brain wasn't to be casually messed around with.

A man's voice drew me from the status screen. "Thank you for waiting, Mr. Halls. We are ready to receive you now. Please follow me."

"Yes, of course." I got up, buttoned my suit, and followed the man into a place that was reminiscent of a small courtroom. I took a seat in the middle while a panel of three sat at the judges' bench, looking down at me.

The man who led me had a seat amongst the panel before he continued. "Well, we have reviewed your documents and completed your background check. We believe we have enough information on hand, based on your evaluations and requirements, to skip the tedious interview process and grant you your Cybernetic Surgeon License. Congratulations, you are now officially recognized as a licensed medical professional in the field of cybernetics."

Well, I might've spent a lot on the bribes, but at least I got what I paid for. I listened to each member of the panel recite some iteration of congratulations and excitement for embarking on a new journey in my life.

"We look forward to seeing the positive impact you'll make with your practice."

Great—with my license finally obtained, my clinic could now operate legitimately, meaning I could get proper supplier channels that weren't as overpriced, and hire professionals to increase the number of surgeons so I wouldn't be the only one at the clinic.

Being over the moon, I immediately set out to purchase my favorite milkshake before I made some calls with cybernetic suppliers. I then sent a message to Claire, asking her to start hiring cybernetic surgeons and filing the bureaucratic forms to legitimize the clinic.

Having pushed all such responsibilities to Claire and her team of newly hired clerks, I couldn't wait to finish the latest creation that I had been cooking up in my workshop.

*"Time is money."* *If only I could buy more time. It feels like I never have enough of it.*

# CHAPTER 27

## STARTING PRODUCTION

"All right, deploy the security team," I told Thorne, who was beside me with the new security guards we hired behind him.

"You guys, set up position." He watched the team file through the door. A minute or so later, he nodded at me. "They're in position now."

I issued a command for my SAID to double-check my new implant and ensure the settings were all correct.

"Sounds good. I'm heading in now. No need to notify them."

Passing through the metal door, I made sure to move as stealthily as I could while I made my way towards the center of the room, where a small house was. It looked quite real, and I wouldn't have doubted it if I didn't know projection technology was at play beforehand.

*I wonder what the actual material is beneath the projections.*

Moving towards a window, I soon found the security guys all set up in one room, carefully guarding the only entrance and window.

A quick command through my SAID booted up my new implant. My hands blurred from view until I could no longer see them. My limbs and body were now see-through. I unholstered my pistol by touch alone, as the active camouflage prevented me from seeing the weapon at all.

I switched to thermal on my optics and could see the outlines of my limbs again. I knew it was possible to create a version that could mask my heat and IR signature, and there were other detection methods that involved the surrounding airflow as well, but it would cost more points in stealth tech, time, and money for those materials. Those versions also wouldn't be suitable for mass production for the same reasons.

The front door and one window were opened for this exercise, since they knew I was coming. Their attention was glued to the two entry points. While my instincts from the stealth skill screamed at me to only move in their blind spots during a lapse in their attention, I slowly strode into the room.

Walking around them, I picked up the small bag placed in the middle of the room. On my way out, I took the opportunity to place a sticker on each guard.

Once they were no longer in sight, I swiftly toggled the stealth mode off and made my way back to Thorne.

"You can recall them. Tell them to check the back of their boots, too."

A moment later, the guards returned grumbling to each other.

"Thanks, guys. We'll do a few more tests and we can finish up."

We repeated the test several times. Each time, I entered the house a different way, with a few surprising results. Usually the guards couldn't find me, but going through the window when they were paying attention was a no-go, as the wind blowing through the window coming to an abrupt stop easily gave me away. That was definitely something to improve on with later iterations, but this current one worked well enough for a mass-market model.

We grabbed some food at the company's expense and then returned to the clinic in time for our operating hours.

Now that we had one other surgeon, I could spend some time in my workshop fine-tuning my latest work and going over production plans.

* * *

"Hello, you have reached Airo Tech. How may I help you?" A woman's voice rang directly in my ears, thanks to my auditory implants.

"Hi, I wanted to place a bulk order for some electronic parts."

"Of course, sir. What is your corporation's ID number?"

I gave her the number.

"Apologies, sir. Our company only sells to corporations that are members of Elevate City Consortium and have trade agreements with us. Thank you for calling us. Have a good day."

The call quickly disconnected.

This wasn't the first one to hang up on me, though; I had several other failures. Whether they dealt in electronic parts or raw materials, as soon as they heard I wasn't from a corporation, they hung up.

With no alternative in sight, I called up my resourceful Quest Giver.

"Mr. Halls, how may I help you?"

I'd still been doing jobs for him now and then, but there were fewer leads recently that suited my criteria and were on his turf.

"Hey, Fitel. Do you know a way to source electronic parts or raw materials in bulk?"

"Apologies. Based on what I know, that isn't possible on a consistent basis. We can arrange a heist to target a shipment, but that isn't something you will get away with if done repeatedly."

"I see. Thank you for your time."

Before I could hang up, Fitel continued. "If you plan to continue your search, I would advise against it. The sellers for the items you are looking for have the initiative, and they only sell in bulk to other corporations."

Over the next few days, I did some research and confirmed most of what Fitel said. Most small corporations couldn't even source enough raw materials for their needs and would have to either mine it themselves or establish teams to go into the wastelands and scavenge the junk there. Either of those options required significant investment and real estate off the island, so neither was viable.

Instead, I had to make do with the retail-priced products, which meant I had to dial back my production plans. The cost was higher, and I'd be selling fewer units, lowering my profits. The margins were going to suck if I didn't raise the prices.

* * *

"Here's the program you guys wanted." Leo placed a storage drive on my workshop table, in a corner that wasn't crowded with parts.

"Thank you. Hey, Cla—" I glanced away from my project and found Claire busy talking with Lana a short distance away. "Here, Thorne, can you start uploading it to the server?"

"Sure, I'll have everyone install it tomorrow as well." He took the drive and walked out of the room.

"So you're becoming more and more of a corpo, huh?" Leo said.

"It wasn't my idea, if that's what you're asking. Those two were super stubborn about it; wouldn't stop going on about how easy it was for our employees to steal, get threatened, or be bribed to screw us over."

Leo shrugged. "Doesn't change the fact you're going to be monitoring them twenty-four seven. I'm not criticizing you. Though, any corpo would understand the necessity of it."

"Well, here's your pay. Want to get some new cybernetics while you're here?" My SAID sent the credits at my command.

"Received. Not much of a fan of chrome. I'd rather invest in better terminals. By the way, what are you working on? Can't say I've seen that implant before." He leaned over my shoulder.

I continued with my work and reinstalled a cover with an engraving. HSU-002. "It's the new camouflage implant we've been working on. Doing last checks on this batch, then we're having a volunteer test it out."

"This small thing? Where does it even go?" He moved his face closer to examine the thin metal board in my hand.

"It goes under the skin, and can be anywhere, but I tuned it for the mid-torso section."

It was basically a nanomachine housing unit. The nanomachines had video and projection capabilities that enabled the camouflage. It worked similarly to the suit I had worn before, but was much more compact, so people wouldn't notice anything while it wasn't active. After all, anyone who saw you wearing an entire suit with that function would expect something was up.

"I see. Well, good luck with that. We got a job to do tonight, so see ya. Lana, let's go!" After the two had a little back-and-forth, Claire walked them out while I continued my work.

I took breaks and worked on a few clients until it was almost closing time.

"Hey there, did I come too early?" a girl with short brown hair said. She came just as I was getting resettled in the operating room. Behind her was a sleepwalking Liz.

"No, no. You guys are right on time, please sit. We'll need to do a short surgery to install the new implant, but it shouldn't take long at all." I directed Serene into the chair and started my usual scans to prepare for the installation.

"Sure thing. As long as I get the new chrome for free, I'm happy." She winked at me before taking a seat.

Glancing over, I saw Liz already seated in the corner, as if she teleported there.

After Serene was knocked out by the anesthetics, I finished the operation in twenty minutes without incident.

She soon woke up. After some checks and calibrations, we exited the clinic to test out the new implant. For this test, I would tail her to monitor its performance.

I pointed to a megabuilding. "So the test will be to sneak into a unit in there, search every room, and then get out."

"Do you have any idea of who is even there? Might not be such a great idea testing this in a harvester den..." Serene said.

"Don't worry, it's just some kids posing as a gang. They just hang out there, play, drink, and do drugs. Nothing dangerous. I'll be right behind you."

Liz rested her hand on Serene's shoulder and gave her a thumbs-up. Both Liz and Thorne were staying in the car nearby, acting as our backup in case anything went wrong.

Serene calmed herself and started the infiltration with me hot on her heels.

Apparently, she acted as her mercenary team's scout and flanker in combat. So she was used to sneaking up to assess situations, which was also where her desire for stealth tech came from.

Normally, she forwent stealth suits, as they had flimsy defenses and were hard to get a hold of. But with my new cybernetic, she could wear her usual combat gear without any obstruction.

She went straight up towards the target unit. Once she was on the right floor, she maneuvered out of sight and spotted a bunch of teenagers hanging out near the den.

Loud music blasted out of the open door. She took a deep breath and exhaled before activating her new implant and fading out from my vision.

I switched to thermal optics and turned on my active camouflage as well, then followed her in. The unit wasn't very large, with three rooms including the living room we entered from.

There were teenagers dancing, making out, or just sprawled on the couch or floor. I watched Serene carefully move around, ensuring she wouldn't bump into anyone as she inspected each room. One messy room had drugs everywhere while the other had a couple getting intimate.

Once we toured the place, we swiftly returned to the front of the megabuilding. The brief trip had barely drained a fourth of the uptime of the implant, which would be recharged within the minute.

"Good job. I got a lot of useful data from the test. Do you have any feedback?" I asked Serene, who was busy gulping down a bottle of water.

"That was absolute zero! I felt like a ninja in those anime I watched as a kid. They had no idea I was there! Fuck, is this what corpo spy teams use? That sounds scary as fuck!"

I noted that down as "no complaints." "Careful, it's not perfect, as indicated in the manuals. This is a cheap beginner version of what large corporations have, so you better not let it get to your head."

She nodded. "I won't. Anyway, I don't see anything wrong with it. The gauge connected to my optics that lets me know how much longer I can use it is cool, but maybe longer operation time?"

"Right, that's something I'm always working to improve. Anything else?"

"Errrr... Nope, all good to me. I'll let you know if anything comes up."

"Sounds good. In that case, you can go for tonight, as promised, and you can keep that as payment. Please let your friends know about it as well. I currently only sell it in my clinic, but I'm planning on changing that soon, too."

"Got it. I will definitely let them know. They're going to be so jealous when they see this shit!"

*Great, now to solve my production problem...*

# CHAPTER 28

## EXPANSION

**James—???**

"James, I want you to handle this incident review here."

"Yes, sir. Consider it done." He received the dossier from his boss stiffly, with both hands.

His boss clasped a hand to his shoulder. "You may be new, but I'm expecting good things from you. Don't let the director down."

James had to force himself not to wince at the mention of his dad. He tightened his facade and escaped from the office after some small talk.

Turning on auto-drive, he reviewed the dossier as the car drove him to the place of the incident. This case was a typical theft from their corporation's stores, so it wasn't anything too important. A case that was hard to screw up on, which was likely why his boss had given it to him, knowing who his father was.

A quick check in the company's database showed this wasn't an isolated incident, either. Theft was on the rise in various retail stores that sold medium- to low-value goods, and whoever was behind it was targeting the ones with the lowest security.

The camera footage from the incidents hadn't shown much, just some products up and disappearing by themselves.

He soon arrived at the store in question.

As soon as he got out of the car, a man greeted him from the door. "Sir, we've been expecting you. My name is Nathan. Please allow me to be your guide."

"Take me to your security room. I want to review all the footage you have."

"Of course, sir. Follow me."

He followed Nathan into the elevators, up through several floors, and past high-security scanners before they arrived in the monitoring room.

*If we had the equipment on this floor pointed at our goods, we would have caught the perpetrators right on the spot.*

Looking over the monitors, James watched as the feeds cycled through hundreds of cameras across the dozen floors of retail space. Several people in reclining chairs were hooked up to the security terminal, scrolling through the camera feeds in real time. Even with this setup, they still somehow hadn't noticed the incident until five minutes after the theft.

*Talk about incompetence.*

Upon noticing him, a woman left the monitors and closed the distance. "Identify yourself, only authorized personnel can—"

"Stand down, Debra, this is an esteemed guest from headquarters' security team," Nathan said. "I apologize for her rudeness, sir. Please feel free to review the footage you wanted here." The man brushed aside and pulled a chair back for James.

He took up his offer and plugged a cord from the security terminal into the port in his hand. The company-provided SAID instantly keyed in his corporate credentials and he soon gained administrative access.

With the help of his cybernetics, he reviewed all the footage from the day of the incident at a rapid pace. He looked for all the common theft tells he was trained to recognize, including camera tampering, tricks people placed on the product beforehand, and changes to the internal employees' logs from the same time.

The most common options were ruled out, so he reexamined the footage of the products disappearing. He placed the footage on the room's biggest screen and zoomed in.

"Nathan, you guys reviewed all the footage yourselves, right? Did you cross-check the position of every customer and employee in the store at the time of the incident from other cameras?"

"Yes, sir. They were all accounted for."

It could be internal tampering with evidence, but he was sure their division's cy-sec specialists would have caught that by now. Unless the thief was someone really skilled, maybe from another corp.

*But why would another corp resort to petty theft?*

"Sir?"

A voice pulled him out of his musing. "Yes, what is it? I'm thinking."

"Apologies, sir, but doesn't this look like the stealth tech your department's operatives typically use?"

James' gaze shifted upwards to the screen again and replayed it in slow motion. The way the product disappeared did remind him of the stealth tech he had used in training...

A few days later, he reported his findings back at headquarters.

"James, my boy, what was the result of your investigation?" The man in front of him poured two cups of whiskey and handed one over.

Following protocol, he placed all of his printed findings on the table.

"We found the method of theft and captured the suspect. It seems like stealth tech had leaked out somewhere and some kid was using it to lift our products."

His boss raised an eyebrow. "Stealth tech? You run it by R&D yet?"

"Yes. It isn't any tech that any known corporation uses, but it is simple in design and function. Just basic camouflage features, so no new information could be extracted. It is either a new player or dead gear."

From the lack of distinctive features and the homemade feel of the chrome, he thought it was more likely to be dead gear, disposable chrome for some black ops team, but that left the question of where it leaked from.

"Countermeasures?"

"It is a basic camouflage unit, so any IR or acoustic units could detect it. There's no need for any specialized detection equipment. I recommend installing an IR camera at the entrance of each store. We'll be able to identify future suspects by cross-checking the locations of everyone in the store if they choose to enter normally."

"Excellent low-cost solution. I'll submit the recommendation to all our retail stores as it is. Good work, James! Just make sure R&D gets a more detailed pass with the retrieved tech. We may be able to figure out how the more advanced version of this stealth tech works by exploring its application."

"Yes, sir."

*This small investigation earned me a lot more points than I had thought. Give me another few cases like these and my promotion will be guaranteed, even without my dad's help.*

*Thank you, whoever leaked the stealth tech to some dumbasses.*

* * *

"Hello, sir. What would you like to drink?" a pretty brunette asked as she leaned down to my eye level.

"Just water, please."

She took a cup from her tray and handed it over to me, then asked the person in the next seat over.

I continued the in-flight movie in my optics. At the same time, I had the camera feeds from the clinic pulled up in the corner of my vision. Everything seemed to be operating smoothly with the new hires, with Thorne and Claire at the helm.

Other people on the plane were moving to the bar, but I stayed to enjoy my business-class seats. It was only a four-hour flight, so I wasn't desperate to stretch my legs.

When I finished the movie and only had less than an hour to landing, I reviewed all the information Max had given me. He had a contact waiting for me in the city before I began hiring and planning for the outpost in the wasteland. Once we had that settled, I should have a stable supply of materials from scavenging to kick-start the production of my cybernetics.

Then I could meet the rising demand of the mercenary community. I would start selling not just in my clinic, but across the entire city, and I could rake in the profits.

I looked out the window at the landmass we were flying past. A giant sandstorm engulfed everything further inland while the area we flew in was eerily calm. Whatever war happened many years ago threw the ecosystem to hell.

*No wonder the elites prefer to live in space now.*

Inside the sandstorms of the wasteland lay countless valuable hunks of salvage and natural resources that the big corporations ignored due to the rising cost-effectiveness of space mining. They were also the key to expanding my business.

The signal to sit and buckle up for landing turned on as I watched everyone slowly scramble back to their seats. The flight attendant returned to check on everyone and soon disappeared into the back of the plane.

A moment later, more flight crew walked by in the same direction, and the sounds of a commotion grew louder until people started to crane their heads back in curiosity.

It was too far away for me to see anything from here, so I used this time going over my status instead.

**Status**
**Level:** 11
**EXP:** 70/1100
**Musculoskeletal:** 76
**Neural Reflex:** 15
**Visuomotor Coordination:** 27
**Endurance:** 24
**Sensory Perception:** 52
**Upgrade Points:** 0
**Upgrades:**
>Stealth +7
>Hacking +3
>Cybernetic Engineering +6
>Stealth Technology +5
>Software Engineering +3

**Enhancements:**
>SAID: Zenitech Hoth Mk.3
>Optics: Nova Tech Stars Mk.4
>Cyberarm (Left): Nova Tech Mudra Mk.6
>Cyberarm (Right): Nova Tech Shiva Mk.5
>Auditory: Amazing Corp FieldTac Gen 2
>Cardiovascular: BioGen Labs Marathon 4
>Miscellaneous: HSU Custom Shade

As I took a sip of water, the commotion suddenly grew louder and the source got closer. I joined the majority and peeked out; a large man with cybernetic limbs was walking straight up the aisle while several crew members tried to hold him back.

"Sir, please return to your seat! The plane will be landing momentarily," one of them desperately cried out.

"Get out of my way if you don't want to get hurt. I'm just going to take a seat where the chairs actually fit me."

"Sir, all the seats at the front are full. Please, it won't take long before we land."

"I'll go to the cockpit and sit with the captain, then."

I couldn't tell if the man barging his way through was on drugs or plain stupid, but it seemed like there was no reasoning with him.

Maybe this was why corpos had exclusive flights: to not have to deal with the riffraff. The prices were high, though, and I wasn't even eligible for them, so no point in crying about it now.

"Sir, do not approach the cockpit. We will have to abort the landing if you disturb the pilots."

The man ignored the cries around him and continued on his way, passing my seat.

Ugh... I really didn't want to have a delay on my first trip abroad in this world, but I guessed I had to do something...

I climbed over to the other aisle and got ahead of the commotion, waiting for the man to come through. Once he moved the blinds aside and moved into my vision, I sprung my ambush and thrust a hand at his throat. I didn't relent, following up with elbows and punches to his chin and temples.

The new surgeon at the clinic had helped me install a second arm more geared towards precision movements, such as aiming my guns or surgery, but that didn't mean it couldn't pack a punch in a melee.

Surprised by the storm of blows from my metal limbs, the man slumped over as I swung, dodging my attack—as he collapsed.

The flight attendants quickly closed in and restrained the man in a shocking display of unity. They weren't even fazed by the violence.

After I returned to my seat, the plane landed safely as scheduled at the NLA International Airport.

I couldn't wait to recover my weapons from the checked bags. Never on Earth would I have believed I would think this way one day, but it didn't feel safe or right to walk around unarmed.

Security barged onto the plane soon after we landed, but skipped me and went straight towards the back where the man was held. Without even being questioned, I successfully retrieved my bags, cleared customs, and was on my way out of the airport.

What I didn't expect when I landed was someone in the arrival hall holding up a sign with my name on it. A buff guy with cybernetic arms like the man who almost delayed my flight.

*I really hope there isn't going to be more trouble.*

# CHAPTER 29

# NEW LOS ANGELES

I tried to walk past the man holding a sign with my name on it, but he recognized me the moment we made eye contact.

"Mr. Halls!" he exclaimed. "I hope you had a great flight. I've been waiting for you. My name is Vincent, but you can call me Vin." He approached and shook my hand with both his cybernetic ones.

"Vin...? You're Max's friend, right?" It turned out he was the contact Max had told me about before I left Elevate City.

"That's right, we fought together back in Texas many years ago. History now, but we still keep in touch."

"Nice to meet you, Vin. You can just call me Rollo. I didn't expect to see you so soon."

He laughed. "Max let me know you were on your way, so on a whim, I decided to come. Follow me, my car's this way." He picked up some of my luggage.

We navigated through the airport halls and out into the glaring sun until we reached a spacious parking lot. A few more minutes of walking led us to his bright red pickup truck, which must've been ancient by this world's standards.

"So, where are you headed?" he asked once we both got in the car after throwing my luggage in the back.

"Downtown Summit Hotel." I sent him the nav data to his SAID.

"Yes, sir." He started the car, one with a combustion engine, the only one I'd seen in this world. "Did Max get a chance to tell you about my request?"

"Request? He just told me you're the guy I should talk to to get situated, find potential people I could hire, and find real estate." I tried to enjoy the view and not worry about the occasional rattling noises that came from the engine.

"Figures. Anything that guy could do properly, it's all related to his gun. He says you're hiring security for wasteland salvage operations, right?"

He looked over at me, taking his eyes off the road, so I quickly answered. "Yes, yes, that's right. Watch out!"

He swerved around the vehicle in front of him and overtook it before he continued as if nothing happened. "Great! You see, I'm actually looking for stabler work in security. Do you think I would be a good fit for the job?"

He placed a hand on my shoulder and pointed at himself with the other, smiling brightly.

"I don't see why not, since you have Max's trust—" He once again swerved the car around, this time past traffic as we ran a red light. "Are you sure you're good to drive, though?"

His eyes were still off the road, on me. I really missed auto drive right about now.

"Hmm? Of course! Everyone always insisted I be the driver since forever. I've never crashed before and always got out us of trouble. Just ask Max, I drove him and the boys out of more shitstorms than I could count, while under fire, too."

*No matter what he says, it doesn't reassure me about his driving skills at all...*

"Why did you want a new job all of a sudden?"

"I've been thinking about it for a while. All the new fancy space mining tech in the last few years has made the wasteland less profitable, so in turn, the corps have been reducing my paycheck."

"You work for a corp?"

"Nah, contract security for their transports across the wasteland. The wastelanders have also been acting up all around the place recently, so it's the perfect time to transition away. With you, we would be limiting our activity to fewer areas, where we can actually monitor the local situation in real time."

"I see... Do you have any leads on who else to hire? I'm looking to start off with a small outpost, so we only need about a dozen personnel, including noncombatants."

"Out in the wasteland, everyone is a combatant whether they want to be or not, but yeah, I know a few people I could call up. Give me a few days."

The car finally slowed down as he entered the more urban area. With business out of the way, there was a brief awkward silence as we continued our drive.

"So Rollo, how was the flight? Tired?"

"Yeah, a little. I had to subdue some guy who was making a commotion and was about to delay the flight. I thought there'd be more security on the plane or something, but I guess not."

"Haha, fat chance, that shit happens more often than you think and the corps running the airlines will never care. They did some study where they found the people on the flight would more often than not step in to resolve most issues because if the plane is screwed, then so is everyone else on it."

"Then they can cheap out on security, if that premise holds true. They really aren't afraid of any accidents, are they?"

Vin shrugged. "Guess not. It's just another insurance write-off to them, just like with the convoys I protect."

After a grand total of thirty minutes, we arrived at the hotel. I declined to go out with Vin for the rest of the day, as I wanted to settle in and do some preliminary research. We exchanged contacts and agreed to meet up in a few days once he had a chance to reach out to some people.

Once I had secured my luggage in my room, I decided to take a walk around the area to get a feel for the city of New Los Angeles.

I checked my pistols and holstered them before I left the hotel. The people that walked by didn't seem too different from those I'd seen in Elevate City so far. The restaurants around had less variety, but the moment I spotted a place with my favorite milkshake, I had to try it out.

Then I continued down the sidewalk until I heard sirens and watched as a convoy of cars drove by, each marked with some corporation logo I had never seen before. The people on the street seemed used to it and ignored them as they blared past.

As the sky dimmed, I wandered my way into a decently busy pub to sit down, relax, and listen in on the surrounding conversations. My auditory implants helped me filter out the background noise and the mundane chatter.

"—been rough lately?"

"You could say that again. Those goddamn wastelanders have been popping up everywhere. Can't even hit them back properly when they run so damn fast under the cover of the storms."

"Ha, at least you've got away safely. I heard half of Peter's crew is either dead or maimed."

"He's always been an asshole. Karma finally got his ass. Cheers!"

"Quiet down. They're right over there." The woman pointed towards a corner of the room.

"Ha, whatever. Did you see the Holly Corp convoy rolling into the city again? They've been at it non-stop for a while now. Think they found a mine or something?"

"I'd say most definitely. They stopped hiring contractors for salvage operations, too. Must be trying to keep avenues of information leakage to a minimum."

I searched online for more information. It seemed like these small corporations sometimes found deposits to mine out in the wasteland. The bigger corps weren't really interested, though, with space mining being more reliable and efficient, and they had enough capital to try their hands at it. After all, there was a huge market for resources in space to maintain or expand habitats and ships, which all required various types of minerals.

I filtered through a few more conversations, but they weren't any more than gossip and rumors, so I decided to call it a night and returned to the hotel.

Unlike Elevate City, the city wasn't lit up in its entirety, only in certain sections. I couldn't help but notice that stark contrast as I walked away from the commercial streets into the more residential ones.

As the hotel came into view, the glass of a window across the street shattered without warning and a woman tumbled out of it.

"You wastelanders seriously think you can just strut into the city as you please?" A skinny man with pale skin climbed out of the window.

I tried to avoid drawing attention and silently continued walking by. The man slowly approached the woman, who was still dazed from the rough landing.

"Heh, don't worry, I'll show you a good time before I sell you to the harvesters."

*Harvesters harvesters harvesters. They're all on my list after their attack on my clinic. Now that I'm in a new city, I could really use some info on where to gain some experience points.*

The man stomped down on the woman's back and was fiddling around in his pockets for something. With him distracted, I took the opportunity to power up my stealth implant and close the distance. I got behind him and placed him in a chokehold. He struggled as hard as he could, but it meant nothing in the face of my cybernetic arms.

Once the man fell unconscious, I pulled out the binding bracelets and restrained his limbs.

*Now, where do I even bring him to interrogate? It's not like I can just carry him back to the hotel...*

"Who are you?"

I glanced over to see the woman warily looking up at me from the ground.

"Don't mind me, I just have business with harvesters," I said as I lifted the man over my shoulders.

"I—thank you. My name is Jane. Can I know who saved me?"

There was no reason for me to get involved with a supposed wastelander. I really didn't want to answer, but I also couldn't just leave her hanging. "I am... Max—well," I replied as I walked away from her.

Continuing down the street while I pretended not to hear her, I carried the heavy package around, unsure if I was getting weird looks or not. I was too embarrassed to meet anyone's eyes, so I eventually decided to stop in a secluded alley a good distance away from the main road.

The man wouldn't wake up even when I slapped him, until I pinched his nose together and covered his mouth.

"Wake up! I wanted to ask you a few questions about your harvester friends, and then you can go." I tried to deliver the best customer service smile I could.

"Who the fuck are you? Do you have any idea who you're messing with?"

I took a step back, unholstered my Suri, and aimed the gun at him.

"I can ask someone else if you don't know."

His glare at me softened as his expression of fear was mixed with thoughtfulness. "Okay, fine..."

He began to spill the information I was looking for, such as the locations of harvester dens, but there wasn't any way to know if he was telling the truth or not. Once he was done and I was sure I wouldn't get anything more out of him, I placed a bullet between his brows.

*+10 EXP*

I'd had enough of taking chances. The last thing I needed in a new city was someone working against me.

On the final stretch back to the hotel, I received a text from Vin about being ready to meet. He had several people who were interested in taking the job lined up. After a bit of back-and-forth texting, we finished planning the interviews; they would take place in my hotel meeting rooms.

Until then, I had some harvesting to do. I had a feeling I wouldn't get many opportunities once we got too busy with the wastelands.

# CHAPTER 20

## WASTELAND

"Thank you for taking the time to meet with me today. Did you have any questions for me before you go?"

"Umm, yes, how long is the position for?"

"It is a permanent position. We may not be a big corporation or anything, but we plan to stick around."

"Thank you." The woman stood up and exited the room.

Several tabs on my optics showed various information sheets, resumes, and other miscellaneous administrative documents, creating a mess in my vision. At least it seemed like that was the last interview for the day.

As I was finishing up the paperwork, Vin entered the meeting room.

"Your lawyer says to call once you're free. We can also leave whenever you're ready. The car is already out front."

Releasing a deep breath, I looked up at the man. "Okay, just give me a few minutes."

Soon we got back into Vin's old car. I called the lawyer while he drove, using the conversation to distract myself from Vin's driving as best as I could.

Too bad the call didn't last me the entire ride...

As we drove, the surrounding landscape quickly went from the city to an empty desert, with the road conditions growing dramatically worse.

"We're going to be heading into the wasteland soon. Get ready for a bumpy ride," Vin announced.

*I'm not sure if I should be afraid or very afraid when I hear that from him...*

Not long after his warning, a natural disaster came into sight. The entire view before me was filled with a wall of sand. It was strangely ominous that a raging sandstorm was straight ahead while the area behind us was entirely calm, as if there was an invisible wall blocking the sandstorm.

It was one thing to read about the wasteland and another to witness it yourself. No wonder the corporations gave up on this mess and focused on developing space instead.

"Quite something to see for the first time, right?" Vin noted.

"Is it always like this? That's safe to drive into?"

"Yep, though communications are limited to short-range in there. There's a reason why even corps can't do anything about the wastelanders living there, after all."

"I swear I just saw a streak of electricity flash by."

"It's fine. It only happens high in the sky. It may fry some unshielded electronics if it's too close, but it's mostly harmless."

Not long after, our car slowed down and entered into the storm. The sound of sand rattling against the car rang out unrelentingly, but other than that, we were able to continue moving. I watched while Vin navigated through the storm using the GPS, as the storm blocked almost all visibility.

"I thought long-range communications were blocked. Is that saved nav data?"

"That's right. I have a good chunk of this area mapped out from my jobs. The place we're going to is over here, not too far."

We soon arrived at what the map showed as the foot of a small mountain.

"A lot of corps have outposts in valleys around the area, since it's a good place to salvage materials from the ruins of the old civilization. I happen to know a spot here that I use as a meeting point during my travels. It's pretty small, though, so we'll have to look around for a better spot for an outpost."

The car pulled up in a small valley surrounded on three sides by elevated terrain. It was a spot the storm barely reached.

We only stopped here for a moment before we started searching for potential outpost locations. There weren't a lot of unclaimed natural areas where the sandstorms died down, so we looked for spots to dig into instead.

"I think that's enough for now. We should head back," I said as I reviewed the new nav data I'd gained.

"Sure. Want to go by the ruins as well to check it out? It's not far. Might as well make this trip worth it."

*There are still a few hours until sunset. So why not?*

"Okay, let's check it out."

True to his word, it barely took fifteen minutes to arrive at the ruins. It was obvious when we were there, as the storm weakened, shielded by the many stores and skyscrapers in the surroundings.

Vin handed me a mask as we disembarked from the car. I took in the view of the ruined city that surely once stood tall. Just the materials from the alloys used in the construction of these old buildings alone should be enough for my current purpose.

"Careful, this area is well-scavenged, but mutant wildlife still roams around. They make these old buildings their homes."

We didn't plan to go into any dangerous areas today, so we stuck to a short walk around where we parked. We entered what seemed to be an old apartment building and found the place mostly empty.

Climbing up the stairs and combing through, we found some old furniture, but all the electronics and other objects of value were missing. It wasn't until we climbed up to the floors higher up, in the double digits, that we found more junk in each apartment.

"While most corporations claim an entire town or city for themselves, this one here is unclaimed and anyone can come, including the riffraff who are looking to make some quick creds. But I think all this junk left behind will fulfill your needs."

He was right. To transport it in bulk, though, I would have to invest in some trucks, and that was exactly what I was planning to do. The profits from transforming the raw materials into cybernetics would cover the expenses.

The two of us, with our augmented limbs, carried a fridge back down the stairs. Vin had filled it with a bunch of other junk, like metal pipes. The short walk brought us within sight of the car just as a sudden growl came from its direction.

We stopped in place, and before we could place the refrigerator down, a sand-colored lizard the size of a go-kart leaped over the vehicle, straight towards us. The moment its legs touched the ground, it dashed so fast its limbs blurred.

As if we were telepathic, we dropped the fridge at the same time and pulled out our weapons. We didn't have a chance to point them at the lizard as we both dove out of the way of the charge. I got up and found myself against a wall, only to duck from pure reflex when I caught a glimpse of something lashing out at me.

Concrete crumbled as little chips of debris rained down around me. I brought my gun up to search for the target, only to hear a gunshot a few meters away. Glancing up, I was just in time to see Vin firing another shot of his pistol grip shotgun at the lizard, which was bleeding dull green blood through the holes in its rear leg.

The second shot landed on its front leg, further restricting its movement, so I took the opportunity to line up a shot with my railgun from behind the lizard, mindful of Vin's positioning. The familiar sound of the projectile breaking the sound barrier resonated in my ears as I pulled the trigger again. The third time, the lizard slumped down on its stomach.

*+10 EXP*

The familiar experience notification appeared above its body. I instantly opened my status to confirm, and saw that I had gained 110 EXP since last checking my stats.

*So these mutants really do give me experience points...*

A voice from right beside me startled me. "Sandcrawlers. Could've been worse, but let's get out of here before anything else smells the blood."

I nodded, and we double-timed out of there with our salvage. Looking towards the back of the truck, it seemed much smaller now with the fridge taking up space.

*We'll need big trucks or something to make every trip worth it.*

From the ruins, we headed straight back to the city. I couldn't help but be on the lookout for more lizards crawling about.

I let out a mental sigh of relief once our car exited the sandstorm. "Let's take a day break tomorrow. Then we'll rent equipment and build a preliminary outpost before we work out how we'll operate with the team."

"Sure thing," Vin answered.

With us being out of the wasteland, we could actually see out of the windshield again. Things were quiet without the wind battering against the car constantly. Watching the sandstorm behind me, I caught sight of a small convoy exiting it a distance away.

These were expensive-looking armored vehicles for escorts, with larger transports in the middle of their convoy. They all seemed to be worn out, with small dents and burn marks all over them.

"We're taking a small detour. Those corpos don't like anyone straying too close," Vin noted.

"Those are the transports that you used to escort?"

"Yeah, that's a Holly Corp convoy. They've stopped hiring contractors and gone full in-house only. They're probably coming from further inland, Firebird or something."

"Is it expensive transporting things around here?"

"Depends on the season. It affects the area the wasteland encompasses. Planes can't fly through it, so they have to go on a really long detour that makes it no longer financially worth it."

We safely made it back to the city, though the trip took longer than planned, as we had to take the scenic route. Vin dropped me off at my hotel, ending our first adventure out into the wasteland.

* * *

"You sure we should lease these?" I was staring at a car with a rusted frame that looked like it was on its last legs.

"Trust me, this is the best thing for the job within your budget. It'll just take a little work to fix these up, and then they'll be stellar. Too bad they don't use good ol' combustion engines. Those are less prone to failure when exposed to the magnetic storms in the wasteland."

"All right, I'll leave it up to you to decide."

That took the last thing off the checklist. The production site was ready, and we just needed to go fetch our rental equipment. With the shopping done, we went to rendezvous with our new hires at a small warehouse we rented.

I'd spent all of yesterday confirming the paperwork to receive the keys to the warehouse, where we'd be processing the salvage and turning it into cybernetics.

The zoning was strict here, so all the other buildings around were manufacturing-related. In return, this warehouse had ample space, unlike in Elevate City, where skyscrapers dominated the island with little area allowed for factories. We didn't need a lot of space for all of our productions, so it was possible to do some manufacturing back there as well, but it was simply more efficient to have everything done within the same building.

When we entered, the people inside abruptly stopped their conversation and swiftly assembled in front of us. All their gear and equipment was mismatched except for the blue armband they each wore.

Vin stepped forward. "So everyone here has been briefed? Any questions?" After a short moment of silence, he continued. "Okay, then you all know what to do. We're heading out with the heavy equipment."

We split off into two trucks and two Amazing Corp Vanguards Vin had refurbished. We had a dozen people between the four vehicles.

Our vehicles were of an older generation than the sleek high-tech ones that I saw in the corpo convoys, but they weren't anything to sneeze at either. The Vanguards were each equipped with a proper turret and were quite similar to the Humvees from my old world.

Not long after we entered the sandstorm known as the wasteland, our detection equipment picked up several cars nearby traveling at high speeds and launching suspected gunfire.

The voice of Vin, our head of security, sounded in everyone's comms. "Everyone, check your weapons. We have guests."

# CHAPTER 31

# DESERT ENCOUNTER

**Claire—Rollo Halls' Associate**

Just as she finished changing to be ready for another day, the door to her room suddenly swung open.

"Claire! The harvesters are on the move again!"

"Are they outside?!" she cried, scrambling for her gun and ammo.

"What? No, they've been lurking around recently and now they've attacked our patients."

Claire found the holstered gun still attached to her outfit from yesterday. She transferred it over to today's attire, unholstered the gun, and threw it as hard as she could at Thorne.

"Then don't rush in here like it's an imminent emergency. Have some delicacy, would you?"

"Sorry." Thorne rubbed his forehead. "I panicked for a moment and wanted you to know as soon as possible... Don't give me that look. I'm okay! I'll keep it cool."

"Thorne..." She took a deep breath. "Just because you're technically in charge of security now doesn't mean you have to do everything. Did you talk to the other guys yet? You know, the ones we hired for security?"

"No..." Right after he said that, he retreated from her room.

She double-checked if she had everything again and picked up her gun as she headed out to start a new day.

After a quick breakfast, she found Thorne and the security team all in the control room together.

"We need to widen the area we're monitoring. We can't have our clients being attacked left and right, team—"

Not wanting to disturb them, she retreated to the home office she had set up upstairs, where there was still a free room. They had a new receptionist, so she spent the majority of her time learning more about cybersecurity and how to install cybernetics instead.

She opened the terminal Rollo had bought for her and started reviewing the camera footage they had on their server. The coverage they had outside of the clinic definitely wasn't great, so they didn't have a recording of the attack.

*Not having footage doesn't mean there was no footage at all, though.*

She started breaching the cameras around the block. She'd played around with them previously, so she knew which ones she could gain access to.

The harvesters were far from professional groups, and the various captured clips had their shadows everywhere. It took a while to sift through the sheer number of recordings, but after an hour or so of digging around, she found the footage she wanted.

Thorne couldn't be found in the clinic, so she called him.

"Claire, what is it?"

"Sending you some footage I found. Check it out."

"Okay... I'll spread the guy's image around. It'll make it easier to search, thanks."

"No, I didn't find the footage for that. Did you watch the whole thing? It shows the vehicle they ran away in too."

"Yeah. It's some getaway car they lifted off the streets, right?"

"Yes, but I traced it back to the ECPD database on the report for the stolen vehicle and found the security footage when they stole that car as well, which led to another vehicle they used for the car theft."

"You can just do that?"

"Well, we're not dealing with humanity's brightest here. They at least removed the plates from their car, but following them around on the cameras, I found a fast-food place they visit every day. Sending you the location now, go check it out, and turn on your body cam."

"Yes, ma'am."

A moment later, her terminal received the connection to Thorne's body cam, allowing her to watch. He contacted the rest of the security team, and they made their way to the location she had sent them.

Upon coming close, the cars split up and went around the area. She linked the feed to her optics as she went about studying cybernetics at the clinic.

For hours, nothing happened, but by the time the last scheduled surgery for the day commenced, Thorne's voice drew her attention back to the body cam.

"All units, we have spotted the target vehicle. It is entering the drive-through now."

Staying a comfortable distance away, their entire team started tailing them. They circled around the block a few times to switch out the car right behind them. Then they moved to the downtown commercial area, where Claire would've never been able to access their security footage without alerting corporations.

By the time the last client left the clinic and they were preparing to close, Thorne's team finally came to a stop as the vehicle parked at the edge of the island, by the ocean.

They followed the men to a small harbor, where the footage went dark as Thorne and his team turned on their active camouflage.

When the camera resumed, they were already in the interior of a boat with several bodies sprawled around.

She texted to avoid distracting Thorne too much. *Everything okay over there?*

*Yeah, it's clear, we're just investigating now. This isn't their headquarters, but there should be clues here. I'll plug you in, in a moment, so see if you can find anything from their systems.*

*Sure enough,* she received a new connection a moment later.

*I guess I won't be sleeping anytime soon tonight.*

* * *

"Everyone, check your weapons. We have guests."

Right after Vin called out in our comms, our small convoy slightly shifted direction to stay away from the approaching vehicles.

"They don't seem to be chasing us, but there's continuous gunfire... I think there are two separate parties fighting," Vin noted from the driver's seat. He continued to study the information our detection equipment provided.

"So we've just stumbled upon their fight?" I asked.

"Hopefully..." His gaze stayed glued to the terminal.

A tense few minutes passed, but the screen showed that the vehicles continued without change.

"We're in the clear! Detour a little further before we head to our destination." Everyone relaxed at Vin's words.

We took a long detour and changed direction several times before we arrived at the location we selected to build our outpost. It was at the foot of a cliff that stood tall even against the unrelenting sandstorm.

Our plan was simple. We would simply be using the fastest and cheapest method, which meant we brought rentals: a specialized excavator and tunneling equipment.

The construction specialists got to work deploying their sensors on the cliff and rapidly adjusted the blueprint to account for the terrain. The excavation was much faster than I expected. Within a few hours, a spacious lobby area was dug out, enough for us to unload what we brought.

"How long will the construction take?" I asked the specialist when he was slightly less busy.

"Sir, it'll take a few weeks in total at the very least, but the residential units should be ready in a week once we finish setting up power, water, and ventilation," he noted as he reviewed his handheld terminal.

With the cargo emptied, we split off into two teams. One remained here with the construction crew while the other one prepared to head out into the ruins for salvage.

Following the salvage team, Vin and I repeated the trip to the ruins. The difference this time was that we had to find a spot to park the trucks, so we drove further in. We soon spotted a clearing between the buildings that would work.

As we pulled up to the spot, a low howl roared out. Following it were dozens of wolves, each as tall as a person, rushing out from behind the surrounding buildings.

"Contact! Fire at will!"

Without needing my input, the turret of the Vanguard roared to life and filled the area with the sound of gunfire. The larger-caliber bullets ripped into the wolves, who soon recognized the great threat we posed to them, their disadvantageous position, or both. They collectively made the decision to retreat just as fast as they came.

"You two," Vin barked at part of the salvage team as we left the vehicle, "man the turrets and defend the cars. The rest of us will head into that building over there. Let us know through the comms if you hear anything."

We headed straight into the large office building nearby. The windows were all shattered, but it was in decent condition.

The moment the salvage team leader stepped into the stairway, a figure leaped out at him from the corner. He was instantly pinned to the ground, but as the mutant wolf tried to bite down on him, he held his attacker back with his metal arms, which he had wedged tightly into its jaws.

We quickly fired into the immobilized wolf. "Be alert for more!" Vin rushed into the stairwell, guns pointed up the flight of stairs.

*10 EXP*

I offered the man a hand. "Are you all right?"

"Yes, I'm fine, sir," he answered as he hopped to his feet.

The rest of the trip was uneventful. We successfully loaded the truck with salvage while the wolves seemed to have learned to keep away from us.

We headed back to the construction site, and by then, it was almost time for us to return to the city. We planned to have a rotating team stay here while the rest of us brought our loot back to the city. Then we'd return with more materials for the construction efforts on the next run.

On our way out of the wasteland towards the border, our sensors pinged several vehicles coming at us from an angle again, with more gunfire.

*Not this again... Are these the same ones we found before?*

We repeated our previous strategy and altered our trajectory to avoid the vehicles.

Drivers spoke over the comms. "Look! There's one breaking off from their group and heading straight towards us!"

"Sir, they're going to catch up to us soon. The trucks can't keep up!"

"Head back to the ruins," Vin said. "The buildings there should interfere with their tracking systems. We'll lose them there!" Being a veteran, he adeptly shouted out commands to the drivers as we sped away, but the vehicle continued to chase us down.

Not long after, the dilapidated concrete jungle came into view again. Vin commanded the team to go over some rough terrain, making it harder for our pursuer to take advantage of their faster vehicle.

"They're onto us. We can't lose them, sir!" a driver shouted back.

"I can see that. We need to find a good spot to ambush them..." Vin furrowed his brow.

"I'll get off and disable their car. Drive us somewhere they have to go slow!" I said as I opened the rear door.

A firm hand rested on my shoulder. "It's too dangerous to go alone."

"Don't worry, Vin. I'll make use of my active camouflage to get the jump on them or retreat if it fails. That's why I should go. I'm the only one with the implant to do so. Just rush in to back me up once I disable their vehicle."

He didn't respond, but feeling his grip loosen, I rolled out of the car once it was slow enough.

The car chasing us then made a turn a short distance away, so I readied myself. It didn't take long before a large four-seater dune buggy approached. It slowed down on the uneven terrain, and with my camouflage activated, I patiently waited as they closed the distance.

As they went into the turn, slowing further, I shot my railgun at the wheels until my clip emptied. I repositioned and reloaded my gun, then surveyed the aftermath. The vehicle was at a standstill in the middle of the road.

The two doors at the front violently swung open. Two figures popped out with their firearms at the ready, aimed in the direction I had shot from.

They wore heavy-looking vests, so I edged closer for better accuracy.

After a few steps, I noticed one of the figures was a girl with long brown hair.

*She looks awfully familiar...*

I angled around to get a better look at her face.

"Sarah?"

# CHAPTER 22

# THE WASTELANDERS

"Sarah?" I muttered.

The man and girl instantly snapped their heads towards me. I noticed how agitated the man beside her was, with sweat dripping from his brow and his finger on the trigger. Meanwhile, Sarah had a bewildered look.

"Tell your friend to relax, Sarah. It's me, Rollo."

She turned and gave the man a look. After a brief stare-down between the two, the man yielded. He pointed his gun down, but still kept it at the ready.

"Rollo? Where are you?"

"Right here," I said as I turned off the active camouflage.

"Woah! You scared the shit out of me. Is that what you used to sneak around?"

"Ha, sorry about that, but you guys were following my group." I stole a glance at the inconspicuous turrets mounted on their oversized dune buggy.

"Things have been hectic since I got back. My dad ordered the clan to retaliate against the corpos who kidnapped us. Are you on a job... protecting convoys?" Her face dimmed as she asked, while the man beside her visibly tensed.

"Nah, this is for my business. Needed some raw materials the corporations wouldn't sell."

"Really?" she exclaimed. "That's cool. Wait a second... Take these and bring one with you when you're out here. That way, our clansmen will know you're friendly and won't attack you guys." She handed me several devices, each with a button on it. They looked like car key fobs from my world.

"Princess, *no!* You can't give outsiders those!"

"Okay..." I alternated looks between the two.

"Shut up! Rollo is me and my brother's benefactor." She gave the man the cold shoulder and turned to me. "Don't mind him. You should come to visit us. Caleb would be happy to see you again, and my dad would like to thank you as well."

Before I could respond, the sounds of footsteps closed in. Both Sarah and the man instantly reverted to combat mode, looking serious.

*That's right, that must be my backup.*

"Hold on. They're probably my people," I said as I held a placating hand out.

I moved around a skyscraper's corner and stole glances at the newcomers. Vin was jogging at the forefront of the team. I stepped out into the open where they could easily see me.

"Sir, are you fine? Did you finish them off?"

"I'm fine. I found some acquaintances—they're friendly. Everyone hold your fire." Thankfully, they followed my order without complaint despite the skeptical looks they had.

At my words, Sarah and the man ran in, closing the distance. She stopped beside me and gave Vin a look-over.

"Hmm... Are you the one directing the team? Not bad for a city person."

As Sarah scrutinized Vin, he stood there confused and glanced over at me for answers.

*It's quite enjoyable seeing Vin at a loss for words for once.*

"So Rollo, want to come visit?" Sarah continued.

"Sure. I'm a little busy for the next while, but I will when I have time. How do I contact you out here?"

"You won't be able to while we're in the wasteland, but some of us sometimes go out to the city to buy stuff, so you can reach out then. Take this." She pulled a small chip out from a port in her wrist. "It'll have live updates on where our camp is, so you'll be able to find us even if we relocate."

I awkwardly received it. The man beside her grimaced and held his head in his hands, having given up.

"Thanks... Are you sure you should give this to me?"

"Yep, we still have Andrew's to guide us home. Just be sure to take care of it and don't let anyone else get a hold of it."

*Not exactly what I meant. I tried, Andrew. Forgive me.*

"I'll take good care of it. Anyway, it's going to get dark soon. I think we'd better head out now if we are to make it out of the wasteland while we still have sunlight. Follow us, we'll give you a lift back to your people," I offered as I sheepishly looked over at their ride.

It was only fair, seeing how I totaled their car.

"Sure, you can drop us off by the border too. We've got people there on the lookout for any corporate convoys right now."

"I'm sorry about your car, by the way..."

"Don't worry about it. We really were aggressively approaching you guys. It wasn't entirely your fault. We've got some really great mechanics, so we can fix it up!"

Seeing how Andrew didn't react, I guessed that was true.

We then returned to our vehicles and headed back to where we encountered Sarah and her people at the border of the wasteland.

"So you guys were in the middle of a fight? Why did you decide to chase after us, then?"

Andrew answered in Sarah's stead. "To chase you guys off. We can't be having any spectators who may potentially join the fray or relay information to set ambushes."

"I see..."

Sarah and I then updated each other on what we'd been up to while we made our way across the wasteland. This time, when our sensors detected vehicles nearby, they were able to establish a private line of communication with her people.

After a brief conversation with them, a large car cautiously approached. It had guns messily strewn across its frame, but Sarah happily waved towards it. The people from her clan weren't interested in chatting, so they departed soon after we said our goodbyes.

With their fleet of cars headed back towards the depths of the wasteland, we safely managed to leave it.

* * *

I found the optimal way to go over the electronic paperwork. I could directly display my files on my optics instead of my terminal, so I could go over them while being in any position I wanted. That was why every time someone came into my office, they would find me sprawled on the couch.

Expenses had been racking up from equipment, the large amount of personnel for the wasteland base, and the production facility we had in the suburbs of NLA, where I was currently located. At least the outpost had been shaping up, with the residential unit built. No longer would the teams staying there have to camp out in a cave with no water or power.

The production facilities here were also making progress extracting materials from the salvage. We brought back any random metallic junk and turned it into the precious metals that we needed to create our cybernetics. We were doing so well that the common metals we also extracted were starting to overflow, so we transported them back to our wasteland outpost to be used as construction material.

The only annoying things I had to deal with were the business taxes. Unlike Elevate City, NLA wasn't run by corporations and had an actual government. A corrupt one, but still a government that set taxes much higher than the Elevate City conglomerate did.

While I reviewed our finances, the door to my office opened after a quick knock.

"Rollo, we're ready to head out. Are you sure we shouldn't bring more people?" Vin gave me a look that screamed, "Can we really trust those wastelanders?"

"We'll be fine. Bringing more people will only agitate them. I'm ready, let's go." I stood up and grabbed my stuff.

Following the navigation data I received from Sarah, we headed out early, because the location marked was quite deep into the wasteland.

The entire trip was mostly just staring at the sand and wind, but when we were close to the coordinates, we detected half a dozen vehicles approaching us. Quickly I pressed the button on the device Sarah gave me.

It rang like it was connecting to a call before it suddenly projected a hologram screen right above itself. The figure of a rugged man appeared.

"Identify yourselves," he succinctly commanded.

"I am Rollo. Sarah invited me over to visit."

"Wait." The projection disappeared for a few minutes before returning. "Follow us. Do not stray."

The wastelander cars had come to a stop. Now only one began to move. Taking the hint, Vin drove the Vanguard after it.

As we headed further in, we passed through a short ravine where the storm abruptly abated, restoring visibility. We could see a flat clearing of undisturbed sand with a settlement off in the distance. Glancing back, I saw the sandstorm behind us rage on, making a harsh contrast.

The settlement was filled with short structures the same color as the sand. It would've been hard to spot from the distance if it wasn't for all the little dots that were likely people moving about around it.

We were led to a clearing on the outskirts, where we dismounted. I didn't even have a chance to find my footing before a loud voice called out to me.

"Rollo! You're here!" The familiar figure of Sarah approached with a shorter boy slightly behind her.

"Hey, Sarah, Caleb. How's it going?"

"It really is Rollo! Welcome!" the little boy greeted.

"I can't wait to show you around!" Sarah said, but then Andrew, who was shadowing behind, cleared his throat. "But first, let's go see our dad. He's expecting you. Follow me." Sarah started walking off, Caleb in hand, without delay.

"Sounds good. You guys can wait by the car," I said to the three others who came with me.

"I'm coming along too," Vin said. "Come on, I want to get a closer look at this place. It's not every day you get to tour a wastelander clan." He followed after Sarah without waiting for my reply.

As we passed by the people of their clan, they gave us looks, but continued to go about their day like anyone in the city would. Only this place was much smaller, and people walked around with herds of cows... mutant cows. They were bulkier than the ones I knew, and looked a little menacing.

Having a closer look at the structures, I noticed they were all made of thin alloys.

I'd heard wastelanders were nomadic. I thought they would be in tents or something similar, but it made sense for them to use alloys, since those could be lighter and stronger than most materials.

All the buildings were quite short, but we soon stopped in front of one that was much wider than the rest. At the entrance stood two guards, who looked like they meant business. They sized us up and then gestured for us to go in with their heads.

Inside was a simple, spacious room, with carpets of various patterns overlaid on top of each other. At the center was a fit middle-aged man with a full beard who sat atop a stack of carpets with his legs crossed. He was smoking a wooden pipe that seemed antique even to me.

Sarah and Caleb rushed to his side and took a seat on the carpeted floor next to him.

He wore loose robes and sat casually with his eyes closed while he lit the pipe. He deeply inhaled and held it in his lungs for a moment before blowing ring-shaped smoke back out.

"So you are Rollo?"

"Yes, that's right."

"I'm Eugene, though folk 'round here call me Gene. I welcome my children's savior to the Wells Clan," he said as he spread his arms out.

"Pleasure meeting you." I stepped forward and offered a handshake.

He wiped his hand on his clothes and accepted. "Please enjoy your stay with us... is what I'd like to say, but there's something I wanted your assistance with, pertaining to the city."

*The city? I'm going to have to decline if it has anything to do with getting involved in his fight against the corporations.*

"Do not worry." He smiled as if he could read my mind. "We simply want you to help us look for one of us who has been missing for the past week. Several people from our clan have tried searching for them, but to no avail."

"So you want someone from the city to give it a try instead?"

"It's good that you are fast on the uptake. Jane, enter," At his words, a familiar-looking woman stepped in from behind me. She froze for a second as we locked eyes.

"You will accompany Rollo here and provide information so you may find Perry."

"Understood," the woman replied, her eyes glued to me. "So we meet again, Maxwell."

# CHAPTER 22

## LOOKING AROUND

"So, your real name is Rollo? I didn't have a chance to say thank you the other day."

I stared at the woman for a second. My memory failed to remind me who she was.

"You don't remember me? You helped me the other night in NLA."

*Oh, the one I tried to ignore and walked out on.*

"Right, glad to see you're okay."

"Our leader told me to brief you on Perry. Follow me."

"We'll meet you outside when you're done, Rollo." Sarah broke off her conversation with her father to inform me.

The woman named Jane led me out of the room, leaving Sarah and her family behind. We went to a small office nearby filled with a mess of real paper documents.

Jane dug through several folders, chucking a few in a growing pile until she found what she was looking for. "Here, everything we found in the city. Last seen in the entertainment area, here's the photo captured from a nearby security camera."

The actual printed-out image showed a red-haired teenager: Perry, the missing wastelander from Clan Wells.

I recorded everything with my implants before returning the files to Jane.

"Please try your best to find her. Her parents haven't been doing so well since she's gone missing."

"Understood. We'll start looking tonight when I get back. I'll do my best, but I can't make any promises."

"Did she have any friends or enemies in the city?" Vin stepped forward and broke his silence.

"Of course not. We don't have much contact with outsiders. It was her first time in the city..."

Vin asked a few more questions but didn't uncover anything new, so we made our way back while Jane stayed to pack, getting ready to accompany us.

"Chances are, some corpos got her for who knows what," Vin mumbled as soon as we were out of earshot. Nothing good for sure, with the escalation they have with wastelanders. It's a waste of time looking for her."

"We never know. It's worth a try for sure, though. I'd like to take this opportunity to improve my relationship with the wastelanders, too."

"You're the boss. I'll let you know when you're about to do something dumb."

Despite his words, it was obvious Vin wanted to help, but didn't want to get anyone's hopes up.

"Sure thing. I'm counting on you to do so."

We met up with Sarah's group, who were chatting with the two guards just outside the building where I met Eugene.

"Welcome back. Done with all the business?"

"Yeah, going to be my tour guide now?"

"You betcha! First stop, the mootant stables!"

Following the high-spirited siblings, we passed through the small town and headed towards the outskirts. We passed by more people than I had expected. It wouldn't have surprised me if there were a thousand people there.

We continued until we reached a tent-like building and the air started to smell like a farm. Inside, the smell intensified, hovering around dozens and dozens of mutant cows neatly lined up in their own stalls.

"That's a lot of cows... Where do you even get enough grass to feed them?"

"They're mootants. They don't eat grass like normal cows. They just need lots of water, sunlight, and whatever food scraps we have," Sarah said as she petted a nearby cow.

"Do they produce milk?" Vin asked.

"Yep. Want to try some later?"

"Sure."

Closer to the town, we got a look at their garages, which were more like warehouses that housed dozens of cars plus space for their mechanics to do maintenance. We also saw a giant wagon that was attached to several trucks. It wasn't surprising, considering their need for transport while they were on the move.

Our final stop was their medical facility before we settled for lunch. They didn't have that much in terms of medical equipment and supplies, which I guessed was one reason they bothered to head into the city at all. There were some things that simply couldn't be accessed anywhere else.

Lunch was served in a communal dining hall where we took our trays and lined up for food. Everyone received the same thing.

For once, the food actually appeared to be real, and not the vat-grown proteins with flavoring added. When I bit into the steak, my eyes couldn't help but tear up a little. I just missed good food so much. I'd had enough of all the shit I'd been eating since coming to this world.

"Is that a new model arm you got?"

I glanced over to see little Caleb staring at my arm fervently.

My new cyberarm looked similar to the old one: same build, same steel color. You would have to get a closer look to spot the differences in the model.

"Yeah, how's it look?"

"So cool! I wish I could get one... but I don't think Dad would allow it." He shrunk back.

*From what I've seen, there aren't many wastelanders with cybernetics. They didn't have much equipment for them either, in their medical facility.*

"Caleb, you know better than to ask for prosthetics when you have a perfectly working body!" Sarah reprimanded.

He didn't respond and continued to eat his food, looking down.

It wasn't my place to get involved in something so personal and everyone seemed to agree, so we moved on to other topics as we ate.

* * *

After our visit to Sarah's home, we started our journey back to the city with an additional person on board.

Thankfully, the new place we had in town had ample space, so Jane could stay in one of the spare rooms. Once we got back, we introduced her to the security, then dropped her off while I returned to my hotel.

We regrouped for dinner, which also served as a strategy briefing before we started our search for the missing girl. Dinner was so synthetic it was completely unappetizing after the lunch I had, so I just quickly stuffed myself to fuel my body.

Vin, however, didn't have any obvious preference, which could only mean either his taste buds had gone bad or corporate propaganda had brainwashed him and he was a lost cause, or maybe a bit of both.

"So let's split up for tonight and ask around," I laid out as I sipped on a milkshake. "Tomorrow, we'll hire a cy-specialist through a Quest Giver to do some digging."

"You know," Vin said, "the fastest way is to reach out to as many QGs as possible and enlist their help directly." He struggled to cut through the fake steak he ordered.

"But that'll also notify everyone we're looking for her, and if anyone looks further into it, they'll know she's a wastelander. And I'm not even getting started on how their relationship with the corporations in this city is right now."

"Right, even most city folks don't take kindly to us," Jane chimed in.

"Let's see how it goes tonight first. We'll rendezvous in a few hours."

Splitting off from the two of them, I began my search. I was familiar with stalking the streets at night, as it was my main method of gaining experience points with the system. I could've gotten my other security guys to do it, but I never saw myself sitting back and letting others do my dirty work, not with the system to level.

The difference this time was my goal. I was trying to look for information, not zero some vile criminals.

I spotted a few guys I had seen on my previous nights in town standing around on the streets. They sold drugs and contraband that I had ignored, but this time, I chose to approach one.

"What do you want, co?" a paranoid-looking man asked as he continued to peer left and right.

"Looking for someone. I'll give you a hundred credits for any verifiable info."

The man aggressively shooed me off. "Fuck off! I ain't no snitch."

The other dealers had similar reactions, albeit some more politely. I wasn't getting anywhere. So I changed up the strategy and asked around stores and street vendors. They all made me buy something and gave me vague descriptions that I was ninety percent sure were made up.

Just as I was about to have my SAID hail a cab to move to another area, I heard someone screaming out in pain.

I turned up my auditory implant and moved towards the source. In a nearby alleyway, I found two drunk men, corporate workers judging from their attire. They repeatedly kicked an old homeless man who was still in his sleeping bag.

The pair laughed as they took turns slamming their feet into the torso of the poor man. He groaned in pain at every hit, but otherwise just lay there and took the beating.

"Haha! How do you like that? This is what you get for stinking up the streets. Go get a job, you lazy fucker."

"Watch it, Kevin. You're bloodying him up and it's getting on my shoes."

I wasn't a saint who donated to homeless people at every chance. Maybe when I was younger and more naïve. But as I'd grown up and dealt with the pressure of my bills building up, I simply ignored them, and that was that.

Whatever these two were doing right now, though, was simply too far out of line.

I didn't even bother with my active camouflage, as they were distracted by their senseless violence, so I managed to stroll right behind them. I didn't plan on killing them for this, though. It wasn't worth alarming their corporate security team.

Even with my own business, I had software installed on all my employees to monitor them, so I knew for sure corporations had more advanced versions than the homemade product from Leo and

Lana. A death would definitely alert them, so I grabbed some broken broom nearby as I closed the distance.

With them distracted, I swiped the end of my broom right on the temple of one while I swept the feet of the other, toppling him. I quickly winded up an overhead swing and brought it down on the person on the ground.

The two were knocked out easily, as they likely never had any training whatsoever and lived lives that didn't require any fighting.

My old habit of looting took over, and I emptied their pockets. After all, they deserved it.

"You okay?" I offered a hand to the homeless man.

"Yeh, thank you, but you don't have to worry 'bout me." He avoided my hand and pushed off from the ground for leverage instead, with the other hand tightly hugging his belongings close to his chest.

"Here, take this. It's the least they owe you." I split the credits I got from the two and gave the man half.

He hesitated for a short moment and snapped it up.

"Thanks." He then quickly got up and packed everything he could into his sleeping bag before walking past me, leaning on the wall for support.

*Well, back to asking around. Should I try to interrogate these two once they wake up? Nah, too much trouble. Wait, might as well ask everyone I can.*

"Hey, wait! I'm looking for this person in the photo here. There's some reward money if you provide verifiable info." I showed one of Jane's pictures of Perry once he turned around.

"Yeah, I've seen her before. Doesn't carry herself like most folks, so I remember. She walked into the club two streets down two days ago."

# CHAPTER 24

## THE GLOVE

"The disheveled homeless man told me he'd seen Perry two days ago."

"Are you sure?"

He held his stare for a second before he continued. "I don't have time to fool around with you. I've said my piece, goodbye."

"Wait, give me your contact information. If your info is right, I'll pay you for it."

"No need. I don't need your charity," he said as he kept walking away.

He didn't give me a chance to continue, so I texted Jane and Vin the new info I got and proceeded to the club mentioned.

The NLA night scene wasn't much worse than in Elevate City. The streets were getting more crowded as I approached the clubs and bars. The people had weird getups and came in a wide variety, as they made use of their chrome to customize their eye and hair colors.

It took me a while to find the Glove, the club the old man told me about. It only had a small sign on the main road while its actual entrance was on a side street with much less traffic.

There were still quite a few people inside the spacious, high-ceilinged open area. They were all crowded around a boxing ring, cheering and drinking. Off to the side was a bar, but it wasn't the main attraction.

I walked by a small betting booth and approached the bar. The bartender was busy serving others, so I waited patiently and took a look around.

"Thank you all for waiting, folks." Speakers rang out with the voice of the announcer. "The next fight is about to start. You have one minute to place your bets if you haven't already!"

There was an immediate rush to the booth. A timer was displayed on a giant screen on the wall, and while the timer counted down, the ringing of a gong echoed throughout the venue.

"Time is up, folks. Get ready for our second round of fighters! Give it up for Rabid Jab Joe, and his opponent, Dempasy Rio!" The announcer introduced two walking hunks of cybernetics and muscle, who both sported dangerous-looking cyberarms.

People cheered for their favorite fighters as they entered the ring. I waited until the noise died down a little before I approached the bartender, who now stood idle, and ordered a drink.

"Hey, have you seen this person?" I held up the photo as he set down my drink.

He gave it a brief look. "No, she's not a regular around here."

"I have a friend who saw her come here two days ago. Are you sure?"

"Could have come before or after my shift. I don't know anything. Ask someone else."

"Do you have a manager or something around?"

He pointed over to the betting booth and went back to doing his own thing, ignoring me. I walked over to the gambling counter, which was now free as everyone paid attention to the fight. The attendant there was sitting leaned back with a glow to his eyes that indicated he was watching something on his optics.

"Hey." I lightly tapped the table. "Are you the manager around here?"

The lights in his eyes faded, and he looked up. "What do you want? Bets are closed until the next round."

"I just wanted to ask a question. I'll pay credits for your time." I slipped him some credits.

"One second." His eyes unfocused for a moment before returning to normal. "He's over there near the front, watching the fight. He said you can go over to him."

The fight climbed towards the climax as I made my way to the front. Instantly I'd known where to go, as this area stood out with fancier chairs than the rest. Here, a fit bald man cheered as the fight went on.

Four bodyguards surrounded him, and they watched me carefully as I approached. As I tried to speak with the man, one guard held up a hand, signaling for me to wait.

Looking over at the fight, I watched one of the men, completely on the defensive, being pummeled into the corner. The attacker landed a strong body blow that dropped the defender's hand for a second, then took the opportunity to continue his assault. From there, a downward spiral began as a barrage of punches slowed the defender's reaction time. The attacker soon found another gap and landed a decisive blow, knocking him to the ground.

The crowd cheered in unison for a full minute.

I gave the guard who stopped me a look, and she gestured for me to approach her charge.

"Hey, the bartender told me to speak with you about helping me find someone. Can you check if you or your staff have seen this person?" I held up the photo.

He took a swig from his glass and inspected me. "No, we're not in the business of searching for people or selling info."

"I can pay you—"

He held up a hand to stop me. "Do I look like I need some pocket change? I bought this place for my enjoyment, not to be bothered by random people. But you don't seem so bad. How about I'll help you out if you take part in a bout tonight?" He pointed towards the ring.

Fighting head-to-head was never my forte... Should I give it a go? Fighting augmented people was never safe, but whatever safety features they had here—maybe the gloves the boxers wore—seemed to tone it down. Otherwise, that fight wouldn't have lasted so long with metal cyberarms bashing into each other.

"I'm not much of a fighter, but my friend who's on the way may be interested."

"No, I want you to do it or no deal. We recently got an opening tonight and you fit the weight class. This is a yes or no question." I'd never known how much pressure being glared at from all directions produced, but the surrounding bodyguards helped me gain this valuable wisdom.

"Your opponent isn't any established fighter either. I'll cut you some slack, make it a good show, and I'll help you even if you lose."

*Would it be rude if I sighed in his face? At this point, I guess I'll agree. From my experience with the medical equipment I normally deal with, I can clear most damage sustained from a fistfight within the night with the help of nanomachines. It's just going to hurt...*

"Fine, I'll do it."

With my agreement, the manager and the guards took me to the back. They outfitted me and briefed me on the rules, which consisted of various restrictions that limited you to your hands.

Whatever happened next felt like a blur, because it was my turn in no time.

"Good evening, folks. For our next fight, we have a slight change to the contestants. Fighting in the stead of Roger Guns, we have Seeker versus the Rush! In light of this change, previous bets on this match will be refunded. You have fifteen minutes to place new bets now!"

Since I hadn't bothered giving my name or creating one, I guessed Seeker was what they chose for me. I awkwardly walked towards the ring and waited right below as people hurried to place their bets.

The crowd stared my way with judging eyes, so it was a little uncomfortable. My opponent seemed completely relaxed, though. He was shorter than me, and young, so he couldn't be that experienced, but he certainly knew what he was doing more than me.

Unfortunately, things got worse as I spotted people who did know me approaching.

"What in the world happened for you to get roped into this?" Jane said, befuddled.

Behind her, Vin was holding his stomach, laughing his heart out.

"HAHAHA, do you even know how to throw fists, Rollo?"

I gave him an unamused look, but he didn't stop, so I ignored him. "I'll explain later, but I needed to do this to get our next lead."

The time quickly passed and the lines to place bets thinned.

"Ladies and gentlemen, without further ado, let the fight begin!"

The ref summoned me and my opponent into the ring. We wore thick gloves and activated software sent by the management that caused our cybernetics to turn their power down.

The ref then brought us close and talked loudly so we could hear over the crowd. "You two know the rules?" We both nodded at him at the same time.

"Okay, start!" He pointed to his nearby partner, who rang the gong on the screen in response.

Almost immediately, my opponent closed the distance and threw a wide swing that I instinctively backed away from.

*Calm down, me. I may have only played around, imitating what I saw on TV, but I've seen enough to know the basics. Keep moving, weave, and throw compact punches.*

Just as I was starting to realize how bad of an idea this was, he threw another swing at me and I barely dodged by stepping left. I instantly followed up by throwing a basic one-two at his head and jumped back.

Wanting to continue my offense, I attacked while circling him, making full use of his blind spots thanks to my stealth skills. I landed a few good combos, but the tactic proved to be a big mistake as he started anticipating my movements.

I tried to imitate the most orthodox stance I've seen from most boxers, with my hands up to defend, but I didn't have much time to think as the man in front of me unleashed an unrelenting barrage.

As I continued backing away, his swings started to miss. But what I didn't anticipate was my back making contact with the ropes at the edge of the ring. With nowhere else to run, the blows landed on my guard.

Desperate to defend, I held both arms up and went entirely on the defensive.

*I can't let this continue. I need to get some distance or hit him back.*

Luckily, he started to slow down. I decided to drop my guard, take the hits with my forehead, and fight back. I tucked my head down and threw punches back, caring more about quantity and power than precision.

I felt my fist make contact several times; suddenly I realized he had stopped attacking.

"And he's down! The fight is over and the Seeker wins!" the announcer declared, followed by the cheers and jeers from the crowd.

Feeling awkward, I let them guide me off the ring, and I got changed before one of the previous bodyguards led me back to her boss.

I found the bald man sitting in the same place as before, smirking at me. "Congratulations!" He slowly clapped. "Here, have a drink."

"No thank you. Now, if you'll help me search for my friend as promised."

"Straight to business, I like that. Leandro, go ask the staff about the person our friend is looking for and check the camera footage too. You said your friend came here two days ago, correct?"

I nodded at his question and watched one of the guards head off towards the back.

"Take a seat. It'll take some time."

Accepting his offer, I sat there in silence as he continued to drink. The next fight soon started and captured his full attention. I wasn't too interested in the fight, so I surveyed the venue and found Vin and Jane nearby, occasionally stealing glances my way.

It wasn't until a few minutes after the fight that Leandro returned and whispered into his boss' ear.

"Good news and bad news. Which one do you want first?"

"Bad one."

"Okay, the bad news is none of our staff remember seeing her. Can't blame them, really, we get pretty high traffic around here so you can't expect them to recognize every new face."

"And the good news?"

"We got footage of her time here. The recording is right here." He held a small storage chip out to me.

# CHAPTER 25

## FOLLOWING THE LEAD

"We got footage of her time here. The recording is right here." He offered me a small storage chip that I immediately plugged into the port in my wrist.

I played the video file inside the chip and saw Perry entering the club from the front entrance along with three others, a woman and two men around her age. She was dragged into the club by the woman, but the footage inside showed they were merrily drinking together as they watched the fights.

"Thank you. I've got what I came for, so I will be leaving now. Goodbye."

Just as I turned around, the owner said, "You're welcome back if you want to fight again. Watch yourself tonight, though, a lot of people lost some good credits betting against you." He grinned.

Ignoring him, I made my way out of the club and headed back towards the main street, where I met up with Vin and Jane, who'd followed after me.

Vin had a huge smirk on his face while Jane said, "So what was going on back there?"

"The boss back there wouldn't help with finding Perry unless I fought. Here, check this out." I handed the chip over.

She pulled out a terminal to play the chip. A moment later, she handed it over to Vin, and his eyes took on a glow.

"So what now? All we got was a few new faces to search for..." Jane frowned.

"Use the timestamp to track her from the nearby cameras?" I suggested.

"Won't work. Places like these would have wiped their footage by now," Vin answered.

We stood silent for a moment. No new ideas came up.

"Let's retire for the night. We'll plan things out first before we search again. No use wearing ourselves out," I concluded.

* * *

The next morning, I repeated my office routine and checked out some job applications we received for the few remaining positions.

A college student had applied, seeking an internship that I wasn't planning on accepting, but my curiosity won out, so I viewed her submitted profile. Her resume was filled with extracurricular activities on top of the usual educational background.

Like clockwork, Vin entered my office.

"We're ready to depart, whatcha looking at?" He stared down at the terminal in my hand. "You looking for a 'personal assistant' or something?"

"It's not like that. I just wanted to take a look."

"Hmm, she is pretty, and goes to a good school too."

"Not like that... Whatever."

*So it's a good school, huh? It would probably be too embarrassing to admit I barely know if the school is reputable or not, especially these ones from New North America.*

I took another hard look at the school in the background of her picture and compared it to the ones I found online. They all looked the same to me, though.

*Wait a second...*

"Vin, go get Jane."

"What? I don't think you need to get her opinion of your personal assistant candidates, no matter how pretty you think she is."

"No! Get her to search the schools for their records while we're in the wasteland."

* * *

Upon returning from our trip to the wasteland, my restored connection immediately picked up a text message from Jane.

*Message me once you're back. We should meet up.*

I replied with a meeting location and time and returned to the city to finish off the miscellaneous tasks for the day.

When Vin and I showed up at the designated bar, we found Jane arguing with a man twice her size.

"Say that again, bitch."

"I said to get your fat ugly ass away from me. Your stench is making my drink taste like shit."

The two were right in each other's faces. If we didn't know any better, they could've easily been mistaken for a bickering couple from afar.

The man couldn't hold it any longer and took a swing at Jane, but she dodged it as if she anticipated it. As the man brought his arm back, Jane bashed her drink into his head. Angered, he tried to lash out once again. However, Jane was too quick for him to catch.

The two continued their cat-and-mouse fight for a full minute before one of the man's friends seemed to tire of it and tried to get behind the wastelander.

I intervened, sprinted towards him before he could get close, and shoulder-bashed him back. He regained his balance swiftly and shifted his target, opting to charge straight at me.

I was still in boxing mode from the fight yesterday, so after I sidestepped him, I handed out a one-two combo and began circling him.

"Gentlemen, that's enough. Any more and we won't be able to afford to pay for the damages." Vin's voice boomed throughout the establishment.

Everyone stilled for a moment and turned to Vin before exchanging looks with their friends.

"Fuck this! It's not over yet, bitch! Let's go." The first man lashed out one final time before his friend pulled him out of the bar.

It was perfectly understandable that the incident got us kicked out of the bar too, so instead, we headed to one of the fast-food chains I had been patronizing lately.

"What was that about?" I asked Jane immediately after we sat down with our order.

"Nothing... Sorry, I was just agitated, and that scumbag picked the wrong time to approach me."

I shared a look with Vin, and we both came to the conclusion that we should leave it at that.

"So, did you find anything today?"

She sat back in her seat and sipped on her drink. "Yeah, I found the kids from the University of Holly Corp that were with Perry."

"And?" Vin urged.

"Got their address and everything, but I couldn't get in. They're all in the same gated community."

"Send the info. I'll go take a look."

She looked up at me in surprise. "I said a gated community. With good security, too."

"I still want to give it a try. Send it over."

* * *

Unlike Elevate City, NLA, located on the mainland of the North American continent, had a lot of space, so the city wasn't entirely a concrete jungle.

Vin dropped me off near the location I received from Jane. I approached from the cover of the surrounding thickets.

I carefully approached the metal gates and surveyed for entry opportunities. The gates appeared to be the electric type that would sting and alert the guards, so I snuck around them instead.

There were two guards sitting in the booths that controlled the gates. I watched as they pressed some buttons on the terminal in front of them before the gate opened for a car to exit.

*Okay, so they don't have military-level security as I feared. I should've expected as much from civilian homes.*

Having found no security measures around that could threaten me, I simply engaged my active camouflage and sprinted through the gate when it opened again. It didn't even matter that the camouflage wasn't perfect when I did intense movements, as there were no attentive guards on the lookout, all of them staying in their cozy little booths.

Once I got in, I found a dark secluded thicket to allow my stealth implant to rest. I put together my geographic information and mentally mapped out a route to reach the houses where my targets lived.

I opted to track down one of the men who had accompanied Perry into the Glove for my first visitation, simply due to his house being the closest to my current location. As it was nighttime, there weren't a lot of people outside besides the few who were going on a run or walking their pets.

As I stuck to the shadows, the house soon came into view. The lights were on, so it was likely someone was home.

Cautiously circling the house, I found most of the doors and windows were properly secured, but a window upstairs on the second floor was opened. I warily climbed up and hung from the window with my camouflage on.

Music could be heard streaming from it, and a quick peek revealed a man sitting on his bed, jamming out.

I carefully climbed in and got a better look at the man.

*So it is the guy I saw on the security footage back at the Glove.*

He wasn't paying attention to anything but his music, so I walked up to the terminal on his desk and plugged into it. There was a lot of junk data and porn, but nothing criminal or related to the missing girl.

Quietly exiting his room, I then surveyed the entire house and came to the same conclusion that this place was clean.

With no reason to show myself yet, I left the way I came in and began making my way to the next house.

This one was twice the size of the previous one, belonging to the only female companion Perry had been in contact with in the footage.

It was a lot easier to sneak into, as there were several workers who came in and out of the building to throw away trash, get some air, or smoke.

I repeated my old tactic and followed one of them back into the residence with the help of my active camouflage.

It was hard to miss the dining room the servants went in and out of, so I took a break in an empty room to let my stealth unit charge before I headed over.

In the room, I spotted five people sitting around a dining table: an older couple, a young man, and two girls. One of the girls had led the missing wastelander into the Glove, while the other one was Perry, the missing girl herself, in the flesh.

"Claudia, I hope you've been keeping up with your studies despite your... distractions." The older woman glared at Perry.

"Yes, Mom, I've been studying with Perry."

"Very well. I will be retiring for the night. Good night to you all."

As the woman exited, I watched the older man giving his daughter a defeated smile and shrugging.

They chatted for a little while more before they disbanded. I watched as Perry and her friend left hand in hand.

I tailed the two up to the second floor. They headed into two rooms that were adjacent to each other.

A few seconds later, I knocked on the door Perry went into.

"Claudia? Did you forget something?" The door opened, but she found no one there, so she peeked further into the hallway. "Did I imagine it...?"

After inspecting the hallway, she closed the door and returned to her seat at the desk.

"Perry? From the Wells clan?"

She twitched at my voice and scanned the room. "Who's there?!"

"Calm down. Your clan leader, Eugene, sent me," I answered as I disabled my camouflage.

Her eyes widened as I came into view.

"What, our clan has dealings with corpo black ops teams now?"

"No, I'm just a friend. They're all worried about you. From what I can see, you aren't being confined or treated badly. Why didn't you contact anyone?"

"I messed up... and didn't want to face them until I corrected my mistakes."

"Look, they're really worried about you. You should go back and explain your situation to them. I'm sure they'll help you."

"That'll prove that I'm incompetent!"

*I remember seeing this throughout all the places I've worked at. People who made mistakes and tried to cover it up or had others take the blame.*

"No, being too afraid to ask for help and letting problems grow or persist is what really shows you're incompetent!"

She looked like she wanted to retort, but couldn't say anything and only pouted.

I took a deep breath before I continued. "Look, this isn't any of my business. Do you have a phone?" She nodded. "Give me your number and I'll have someone from your clan call you. Promise me you'll talk it out with them."

"Fine."

# CHAPTER 36

## ANOTHER DAY IN THE WASTELAND

The next day when we went back to the wasteland, I stopped by the Wells Clan settlement while my workers continued to the outpost for the salvage operations.

In my car were Jane, Vin, and one security guard to watch the vehicle.

When we approached, a small convoy met us just like the previous time, but there was a lot less tension, as we were known quantities to each other, and Jane was with us.

They immediately led us to their clan leader, Eugene. Jane saw him first alone while we waited. After fifteen minutes, we were allowed in.

"Rollo, I've heard you've succeeded in our request. On behalf of Clan Wells, I would like to thank you." He bowed.

"I'm happy everything worked out."

*Being thanked is great and whatnot, but I wonder if there'll be an actual reward.*

"While there are some complications, that is another matter."

I had heard from Jane on the way here about how the girl, Perry, had lost the valuables they entrusted her with through gambling. She got lucky and met some friends who bailed her out and took care of her, but she wanted to get the money back twice over before returning home.

"Our clan owes you for your assistance, and we don't like owing any favors. Is there anything you would like as a reward?"

*This is it, what I've been waiting for!*

"In that case, I would like to request permission for free passage and protection for my business' operations in the wasteland."

"We can promise you that, but we won't be able to guarantee any protection against other corporations."

"Yes, I understand, but you can provide information on their movement and routes for us to avoid them."

"Very well. Speak with Jane later for the details. Our clan shall officially allow you to operate in our territory and provide you with information."

Perfect! One of the major costs of working in the wasteland was the cost of security against wastelander raids, and the information he provided would be a good bonus as well.

After we discussed how we would communicate in the future, the meeting disbanded. Waiting outside were Sarah and Caleb.

"I heard you helped us again. Thank you!" Sarah stepped up and gave me a hug.

"Thank you!" Caleb mimicked her with a slight delay.

"No need to thank me. Your dad has already done so. We'll be keeping in touch."

"Still, at least let us treat you to lunch."

We still had some time from what we allotted to this detour. "Sure."

* * *

Once we left the wastelander camp, we returned to our outpost, leaving Jane behind. The rest of the salvage team had already made two trips from the nearby ruins.

After lunch, we followed along for the next trip into the ruins. I had enough common metals stocked up by now, so the focus was on high-tech parts with rare, extractable metals in them.

When the ruins came into view this time, I spotted the trail of another group nearby.

"Steer us away from them." Vin's voice sounded throughout the convoy.

We made a slight change to our course, headed further into what used to be a downtown area. The high density of buildings around us made it especially dangerous.

Each extra nook and cranny was another possible hiding spot for mutant nests, which meant there could be more mutants in the area than we bargained for. That was why the atmosphere became tense as we entered the downtown area.

Vin had plotted out areas to potentially search, but being here in person gave us a better idea of which buildings were more intact. We found an alleyway clear of rubble to park our Vanguards and set up a defensive position.

As this was a more dangerous area, we only split off into two teams, one to defend our rides and the other to explore.

"Sir, this entrance is blocked too."

"I see. Look for any sublevel entrances in the area instead," Vin replied to his second-in-command.

We continued moving cautiously and found an old subway entrance that led us down. The leading security members turned on the flashlight attachments on their guns as we all activated the night-vision modes on our optics.

*I should really standardize our equipment so we don't look like the ragtag bunch that we are...*

There were several flights of stairs until we passed through a tunnel, when we finally made it to a spacious corridor with storefronts on both sides. This was an underground mall in the past, as I could still see some of the signage intact.

Before we settled on a direction to walk in, a noise rang out from one of the commercial units. We all trained our guns towards it, but found nothing except a cafe in disrepair.

"Fuck!" One of our team members screamed from behind, followed by the sound of something hitting the floor.

I turned around in time to see him knocked over. Standing on top of him was a rat the size of a large dog, and behind it, several of its friends scurried towards us.

"Rudents! Open fire, be sure to keep it low," Vin cried out.

*+1 EXP*

*+1 EXP*

*+1 EXP*

The sound of gunfire instantly filled the tunnels. The giant mutant rats died easily compared to the sandcrawlers, but new ones kept crawling out from the shadows behind them to replace their fallen brethren.

These little shits only gave one experience point each, and my pistol railgun wasn't well-suited for so many targets.

As I reloaded while complaining to myself, I suddenly felt a sharp pain in my calf. I looked down to find one of the rats biting into me, which earned him a quick shot to the face.

"Sir, they're coming from behind us as well!"

"Everyone fighting retreat, go into the department store over there!" Vin decided.

He'd selected a large grocery store. Judging from the elevators, it was in another building's basement, so inside, there must be a way up from these tunnels.

Vin came up to me and lent me his shoulder. We continued to shoot into the crowd of rudents while we retreated.

As we moved into the store and up the staircase, an explosion sounded out behind us as someone lobbed a grenade outside.

The next floor was still part of the same grocery store. There were numerous shelves, all picked clean, some of them toppled near old bloodstains that said it all.

We were able to throw the empty shelves to block the stairway. Then we stood guard, staring at those shelves for a few minutes before we collectively let out a sigh of relief.

"Tend to the wounded and then take ten."

Right after Vin gave out his orders, he came up to me and inspected the leg that had been bitten.

"Doesn't look too bad, just need to inject something to prevent any diseases and patch it up." He opened his pack and fished out a first aid kit.

"I'll leave it up to you. Sorry for letting my guard down... I need more training in a straight-on fight."

"Ha, I'm the one who's supposed to apologize to you. You're paying me for security, right?" He grinned as he dressed my wound.

After a ten-minute breather, we started moving up again. I could still move, though I wouldn't be doing any running. Not fast, at least.

We came to the ground level and found the barricaded entrances that had blocked our way previously. The barricades consisted of piles of metal cabinets with some traces of melding. Whoever did these had some time to reinforce their defenses, but it didn't seem like it worked out for them.

Now we could definitely remove them from inside, so given some time, we could leave without having to go back down into the tunnels.

This floor's various counters had once been filled with cosmetics. Beside the elevator, there were still intact metal signs that displayed what each floor sold.

"Floor seven is for electronics. Let's go there," I said, looking towards Vin.

"Roger that."

Walking through the expired cosmetics sprawled all over the ground, we made our way to the staircase. It was literally a pain to walk up, but it wasn't painful enough for me to want to use the combat stims as painkillers.

The way up was thankfully peaceful. We managed to arrive on the seventh floor, and upon opening the doors, we were met with an entire level of untouched electronics.

"Haha, jackpot!" said Vin. "Seems like no one looted this place when shit went down or anytime after. Empty your packs of any nonessentials. We're going to clear this entire place out."

It took me a second to realize that "when shit went down" meant the nuclear wars. It made sense that people back then would be more worried about stocking up on food and water than anything else.

We threw every electronic device that we could carry into our packs. We would leave the heavier stuff for later when we weren't worn out and injured. Before we left, we locked every entrance into the floor in case some other team took the opportunity while we were away to take our prize.

On our way down, I spotted a giant cockroach crawling along the walls of the stairwell, but fortunately, it scurried away. I wasn't in the mood to deal with them after the rats.

We got back to the ground floor, where the healthy team members started digging through the rubble to clear out the exit. As part of the injured team, I'd be guarding our bags nearby.

I'd taken Vin's bag and was making my way towards where the injured lay when the ground started to shake. It wasn't enough to throw me to the ground, but a disturbing noise came from the concrete underneath me: it croaked.

My fears came true as a loud crack boomed and the floor beneath me gave way, dropping me down as I fell to the clutches of gravity.

The fall didn't last long. I landed, the impact of the fall knocking the wind out of my lungs. I got up as soon as I could and saw that the hole I fell through was now blocked by some rubble above.

I swiftly called out through the comms.

"Anyone there?" I nervously swallowed, trying my hardest to keep away the thought of being alone down here, cut off from the rest of the world.

A short few seconds that felt like an eternity passed.

"—ollo, can you hear me?" To my relief, Vin's voice rang out on the other side of the communication line.

"Yes, are you guys okay?"

"Somewhat. We had a casualty from the debris falling, but the rest of us are fine. The stairway down to you is blocked off. How are you doing down there?"

"I don't have any new injuries besides a bruised butt. I'll find a way back up. You guys get back to the cars first and send the wounded back to camp."

"Roger that, but we're coming right back down to get you after."

"Don't. We don't need anyone else to get hurt with all the rats down there. Not to talk about the potential tunnel collapses from that earthquake just now, it'll delay everything."

"No, we're finding a way to you. You put me in charge of security, so I'm taking charge no matter what you say."

"Fine, but I'll try to find my own way out. Make sure you're ready to pick me up once I make it back to the surface. I'll keep in touch. Go send the wounded back first."

"I will, and you better not take any risks alone, you hear me?"

"I'll make it back out before you get back. Don't worry."

"That's exactly what I'm worried about."

Ignoring his words, I started looking around.

*Now then, let's get out of here before Vin returns.*

# CHAPTER 27

## GETTING OUT

Surveying my surroundings, I found the fall had only brought me one floor below the ground level. It was on the top floor of the supermarket we used to escape from the rudents, the mutant rats. I spotted the bottom of the stairway that led back up, and it was completely blocked off by debris.

My comms couldn't reach Vin anymore, as we were too far apart because he went back with the injured.

*Now then, let's get out of here before Vin returns. I'd rather not have them try to come down only to sustain more injuries.* While it was common practice not to pay if employees couldn't work, one selling point of the contracts I offered was the adequate worker's compensation agreement.

With the way up blocked off, the only remaining exit was back down, where all the mutant rats were.

Once I collected myself, I moved down the stairs and tried to be as quiet as possible. There was a bunch of junk we'd thrown down the staircase when we retreated that I had to move out of the way. I just had to be careful where I stepped, or else the noise might alert the nearby rats.

When I finally made it to the bottom floor of the grocery store, I found it eerily quiet. I made my way out and back onto the main pathway of the underground shopping street, and it was just as silent as it was in the store.

*It hasn't even been that long since we dumped bullets into a horde of mutant rats, and there are no longer any traces of it...*

Not wanting to stay to find out what had wiped the place clean, I headed back to the tunnel we descended from, but as Vin had mentioned, the tunnel had collapsed as well.

The sound of something kicking a bottle suddenly echoed beside me, and I reflexively turned on my active camouflage. Snapping towards the sound, I saw the night vision from my optics clearly outline a rat on its two rear legs sniffing at the air.

*Give me a break...* While I wasn't visible, I did not doubt it could detect the blood from my wound even though it had dried. I really needed to upgrade my personal stealth implant.

I drew my Suri and shot at the rat before it could track my smell.

Maybe it was just dead silent down here, but my gun produced a much louder sound than I had expected. From all around, I started to hear scuttling around in the darkness.

I picked a direction and started running. I needed to get out of here before my camouflage gave out. On the way, I started seeing more mutant rats sniffing around, but when they turned towards me, they stayed confused, as they couldn't see anything there.

In my rush, I accidentally kicked a glass jar in my path. Even though my boots killed any sound, that didn't help when the glass smashed into the nearby debris.

Instantly, lots of movement surged behind me. I refused to look back and picked up my pace.

I continued to run even when my stealth went offline, only slowing when I felt the fatigue in my legs. I had augmented my cardiovascular system, so I wasn't easily winded, but my muscles were another story. Feeling myself slow down, I stole a glance behind me and found nothing there.

*Now that I think about it, I couldn't hear them chasing after me for a while now.*

The surrounding area looked no different from before, with stores flanking both sides. This place must be huge, because I was pretty confident I'd run pretty far away.

An entrance to the basement of an office building came into view, along with a worn-out coffee shop next door. The stairway up was blocked off, but the escalators right beside it were mostly intact.

Pushing down my excitement, I cautiously climbed up to a small lobby with fancy turnstile gates and marble support pillars.

The smell of blood was thick in the area, and I could see dried blood every few meters on the floor. There were even some damaged guns and terminals that lay scattered around. From the emblems on the gear, it was obvious it all belonged to some corporation.

Not wanting to outstay my welcome, I climbed over a turnstile to find the area behind littered with light-colored ovals the size of bowling balls. The stairway at the end of the hall brought sunlight shining down from the floor above. It also illuminated the weird things I saw on the ground.

*Those are eggs... of what?*

A sharp hiss sounded out from a corner behind me, and I swiftly turned towards it. Curled around one of the pillars supporting the building was a giant snake as thick as my body. It could definitely swallow me whole.

It was staring straight at me as it let out another hiss.

*It would really help if I could use my camouflage right now to avoid confronting it, but it needs more time to cool down and recharge.*

*Damn it.*

We stared at each other a short moment before we both moved at the same time. It lunged at me while I drew my pistol railgun and shot at it.

The only good thing about such an enormous snake was the massive target it provided, and with it charging towards me, it was hard to miss. The shot broke off one of its fangs, and the snake recoiled with a loud hiss.

Right when it shrank back, I turned and ran behind the pillar on the opposite side of the room. With solid cover in between us now, I peeked out to catch sight of it crawling between pillars.

I fired several shots into the snake. It hissed out in pain again, but otherwise seemed to be moving unhindered by the damage.

*First the swarm of rats and now this. I need to add firearm shopping to my to-do list.*

I changed my focus to escaping upstairs. Every time I stepped into the open, it made a charge at me. It feinted and dodged a shot, but I reloaded whenever I had the chance, so my next shots kept it at bay.

Then I made my way to the final pillar that was closest to the stairs. It was more than twice as far from me than the pillars were from each other. I took a second to reload and gauge the situation.

While I took my time, the giant snake crossed over to my side and approached by weaving in and out of the cover of the pillars. When it came to the pillar behind mine, I took that as a signal. I ran for the stairs, taking potshots.

I climbed the stairs as fast as I could, but my injured leg was slowing me down. Going up at this rate, I wouldn't make it before the snake caught up.

As I went, I made sure to keep my eyes on the snake. Just as it reached the staircase and was about to lunge, I forced on my camouflage—it had just a few seconds—and dove out of the way.

The snake rammed into the handrail where I had just been and came to a standstill. It swiftly let out its tongue to taste the air and locate me, and it did. But it wasn't fast enough as I unloaded the rest of my clip into the mouth of the stationary target.

*+50 EXP*

I couldn't have been more relieved to see the experience notification. I allowed my legs to give out and plopped myself on the stairs.

Then I opened the status screen to confirm the new experience points I gained.

**Status**
**Level:** 11
**EXP:** 960/1100
**Musculoskeletal:** 76
**Neural Reflex:** 15
**Visuomotor Coordination:** 27
**Endurance:** 24
**Sensory Perception:** 52
**Upgrade Points:** 0
**Upgrades:**
    Stealth +7
    Hacking +3
    Cybernetic Engineering +6
    Stealth Technology +6
    Software Engineering +4
**Enhancements:**
    SAID: Zenitech Hoth Mk.3
    Optics: Nova Tech Stars Mk.4

Cyberarm (Left): Nova Tech Mudra Mk.6
Cyberarm (Right): Nova Tech Shiva Mk.5
Auditory: Amazing Corp FieldTac Gen 2
Cardiovascular: BioGen Labs Marathon 4
Miscellaneous: HSU Custom Shade

I expected Vin to return soon, so I forced myself up after a short break and surveyed the area to reorientate myself. I should still be in range for the comms, but it didn't hurt to be closer.

Upon reaching the ground level, I found all the doors and windows in the lobby were welded shut with metal plates. The lobby had high ceilings towards the doorway, as another floor above shared the same roof.

The windows higher up on the mezzanine had light coming through the glass, so I made my way up another set of stairs. The windows at the front were too far to reach, but a quick survey of the floor allowed me to find one by the elevators towards the back of the building.

I backtracked to grab a chair and threw it towards the glass pane. It cracked, with the chair rebounding back onto the ground. I picked it up and continued to throw it at the window. On the sixth throw, the glass gave way, and part of the chair stuck through the other side.

Thankfully, my arms were prosthetics and didn't tire. I pried the chair out of the window and smashed it a few more times until it had an opening that I could comfortably fit through.

Carefully clinging onto the edge, I lowered myself slowly before making the one-story-high jump down. I tried to do a roll to disperse the force as I landed, but I clumsily fell to my side as my injured leg gave out.

With new scrapes on my knees, I made my way back onto the main street.

The streets felt desolate without any life in sight, but I spotted some movement from within the nearby buildings.

*I really do not want to encounter any more mutants or anything.*

On the side of the street near the building that I came out of, there was a flipped-over vehicle that looked like a more advanced version of our Vanguards. It was heavily damaged, so I couldn't make out its affiliation, but it didn't take a genius to realize its value. The only issue was how to transport the precious salvage back.

Static suddenly rang out from my comms, with a familiar voice that could be made out on the final word. "—there?"

*Well, that solves the issue of transportation.*

I promptly replied, "Hey, I'm still alive and kicking over here. Can you read where I am from the signal? I have something over here we should drag back with us."

* * *

"You really should expand our team and invest in our equipment more if you're complaining about the hazard pay you set."

"Yeah yeah, I know, that's why I'm going back now. You're running a tight ship here without me. Time to make some sales once the products are shipped back."

"You don't plan on opening any clinics here yet?" Vin raised an eyebrow.

"Not right now. We'll have to wait for things to settle back in Elevate City before I even have the resources and money to expand that far." I shrugged.

"I see. Well, have a safe flight. I still want my paychecks, so try not to get killed." Vin grinned and gave me a quick hug.

"You too. I'll be back soon. We'll stay in touch."

I arrived at the boarding gate just as the final call started. The flight was pleasant, as I slept through its entirety. The fatigue from my recent escapades must have been catching up to me.

The view of Elevate City as we landed was breathtaking, as before. It was hard to imagine the sheer amount of people that lived in this concrete jungle.

When I exited the airport, I found the familiar faces of Thorne and Claire waiting by my car. As I walked up, Claire leaped at me while Thorne followed slightly behind her.

"Welcome back!" she said as she hugged me.

"Hey. Hope everything was okay while I was gone?" I smiled at the two of them. We kept in touch while I was in NLA, but almost all of their updates were the same, stating that they had everything under control.

Thorne gazed downwards and scratched his cheeks. "Mostly, yeah, but we just got ourselves a competitor within the last eight hours. Yesterday, some small-time corp launched a similar chrome to ours... they beat us to the punch."

# CHAPTER 32

## BEATEN TO THE PUNCH

The view of Elevate City sprawling with life filled my eyes from the front passenger seat of the car.

"So, tell me about this new competitor of ours." I looked over to Thorne in the driver's seat.

His eyes took on a glow before he replied, "The Hathway Corporation, led by James Hathway, has been a declining corporation since the time of his father. They specialize in projection technology for various large terminals used in presentations and conferences."

"So it wouldn't be hard for them to use that technology to produce working active camouflage."

"Yes, but I've seen their product, and it's just that, a smart projector. It isn't nearly as optimized as ours for use in the field, with much worse reliability and uptime."

"That means their threat is minimal. They only have the first mover's advantage right now?"

"Right... but from my investigation this morning, they have a pretty bad reputation in their industry. They're infamous for corporate espionage and stealing their competitors' tech."

"Well, that fits their image of a declining business that's desperate to stay afloat. We need to stay alert for thieves..."

"Yes, but me and Claire have been more worried about other corporations taking the opportunity to enter the market. If

Hathway can butt their heads into our industry, so can any other corps. We need to launch our product first and snatch up some market share."

"Hmmm, that's what we were going to do anyway. There isn't much else we can do but keep improving our products. Don't worry too much about it. The bigger corporations are more interested in defending their more lucrative markets, so it wouldn't make sense to leak some of their corporate espionage tech to their competitors to earn some chump change. We'll just need to beat out the smaller players."

"Right."

"So... How's it going with you, Claire? Gotten any better with cy-sec and cybernetics?" I turned to look at the girl sitting at the back.

"You betcha. I've been practicing chrome installation virtually, too. I should be ready to get that cyber surgeon license in a few more months, but I'll need to save up for the bribe to get all my credentials like you did."

"I'll foot the bill for it if you keep up the good work."

"Really?! Yes, please! Allow your faithful underling to give you a massage, boss!" She grabbed my shoulder from behind and started kneading.

*As much as she is joking around, she isn't half bad at giving massages.*

"So tell us, how was your trip to NLA? You said you got hurt in the wasteland. Is it really that dangerous out there?" Claire asked.

The massage paused while she awaited my answer. I wasn't sure if she was really interested or just wanted to distract me so she could stop the massage, but I might as well oblige.

"Yeah, the sandstorm that rages in the wasteland was insane. It was a breathtaking scene when I first saw it. I also met Sarah and Caleb with their clan. There were lots of mutant animals, too..."

* * *

"Make sure you adjust the connection here based on the scans for each patient, especially on the first installation. The difference between a good job and a poor job will significantly affect the chances of rejection, infections, swelling, pain, and the entire bag of complications." I held up the cybernetic to be installed for Claire to see.

She had been studying with the surgeons at the clinic, but decided to observe my first installation since coming back. I implanted a health monitor that offered the client details on their condition in real time. It was an entry model that went for a few thousand credits. The more expensive models had nanomachines to help repair any sustained trauma.

The installation was completed without a hitch, and I let Claire do the calibrations with the patient under my supervision.

"So, doc," the patient started. "Do you think it's okay for me to keep chroming up? I've heard a lot of horror stories about people getting corrupted, becoming those emotionless drones when they get too much chrome too fast..."

"You'll be fine for quite a few more augmentations unless you have some faulty SAID. That's why it's important to regularly come in for checkups." I opted not to elaborate further, as it would get too technical.

The calibrations were soon complete, and Claire quickly returned after she walked the client out.

She reviewed the notes she took on her terminal. "What was that talk about people getting corrupted?"

"It's slang for a topic you'll learn soon, if you haven't already, regarding anhedonia as a result of cybernetics."

"Ah, the one that makes you emotionless like a robot."

"Right. It's not that common, or else cybernetics wouldn't be that common, but that doesn't stop people from fearing it because of all the horror stories about how some corporations purposefully inflict the corruption on people to make them their mindless minions." I collected my belongings and stood up. "Follow me if you want to continue our chat. I'm going to work on something in my workshop."

"Nah, I'm okay. I'm going to order lunch. Anything you want?"

I opened the door and turned back to reply, "Nope, just get me whatever."

Just as I cleared the door, I heard Claire's voice catch up with me. "With a milkshake?"

"Yep, thank you!"

Entering my workshop, I continued working on the project I started last night when I heard about Hathway Corp. There was a high chance they knew about our stealth implant and might send infiltrators to steal our tech and dominate the market.

The market for stealth tech wasn't that large. The ratio of mercenaries to the general population was barely a drop in the bucket and expressed as a decimal. The market for stealth implants was even smaller, being only a fraction of all mercenaries.

That was why I was working on a countermeasure. Conveniently, knowing a lot about stealth tech also made you privy to their weakness and detection methods. Based on the stealth tech they were selling, they only did optical camouflage, so we had infrared cameras installed. Still, I wanted more options for me and my personnel because the thermal vision on optics makes you pretty much blind to everything else.

With speed and practicality being the main focus, I rushed the job a little in order to create enough infrared visors for the entire security team.

"Did you need something?" Thorne opened the door to my workshop.

"Here, take these to replace the visors on the headgear we gave to security." I threw a case over to him.

He took one out and flipped it back and forth, studying the dull gray visor. "You sure these are combat-rated? Any instructions on how to use them?"

"No, but it should do its job. It's already calibrated to use our encrypted channels that are only accessible to our employees with the company software, so just slot it on. It'll automatically do the rest."

"Okay."

With Thorne gone, I cleaned up the workshop and headed to the break room, where I found the food and drinks Claire had gotten for me.

*After a quick lunch break, it's back to work time. Why do I feel it hasn't changed much from my part-time job days...?*

The day went by slowly as I continued carrying out my scheduled installations and chatting with Thorne and Claire during the downtime. The clinic closed and most workers went home, except for security. They worked in four shifts, which wasn't that terrible, but that also meant there were only three of them on duty at a time, not counting Thorne.

"They're ordering food, you want anything, Rollo?" Thorne came in to ask, just as I was getting ready to go out for some good ol' community cleanup that paid in experience points.

"No thanks, I'm heading out soon."

"Right."

Thorne would hang back to guard the place, so I would be heading out alone for now.

I finished cleaning my two pistols and collected ammo from my stockpile before I put on a black armored suit. By the time I finished, the deliveryman had already arrived and was at the door of the lobby, where two of the security team members were waiting.

One good thing about delivery here was definitely its speed. It was way faster than what I was used to in my old world. I wasn't sure if that was because the people here were impatient, jobs were competitive, or the food they made here was complete trash and required no prep time at all. Leaning closer to that last one.

I waited for the deliveryman to leave before I did, as I didn't want to startle him with all the gear I was wearing. After all, he was rightfully strapped while he worked in this dangerous world.

Just as the door closed behind him, the conversation between my two employees abruptly ceased. An awkward second passed by in complete silence as they shared looks. The silence was then broken by the sound of weapons being drawn, pointing towards the doorway.

They reacted well to a situation they weren't familiar with, but it was still too slow. I had already pulled the trigger of my railgun, filling the lobby with the noise of the projectile breaking the sound barrier.

Small pieces of metal debris scattered around the area I shot. The space around the entrance flickered before a person decked out in a black suit similar to mine suddenly materialized and slumped to the ground.

*+10 EXP*

Footsteps started up behind me, and Thorne rushed out.

"What's—" He came to a full stop and glanced at the new body by the entrance. "Bring the body inside and clean up the entrance," he ordered one of the two guards. "I'll call someone to repair the door."

I looked up at where the glass window part of the door had cracked and now sported a small hole.

*Okay, another good thing about this world is how fast they build and repair shit.*

"What was that?" Thorne's voice broke me out of my musing.

"What was what?" I looked back at him.

"You know. Suddenly I could see the highlight of someone through the walls."

"Didn't I explain? The visors I gave you are linked to our channels, including the new infrared cameras. They spotted the guy creeping up and shared the view with us in real time. That way, we don't all have to always have thermal on."

"I thought they only had a thermal optic add-on. You only said they allowed us to spot active camouflage. This is entirely different. We'll have to train on how to properly take advantage of the possibilities this allows for."

"Yeah, you should be able to find some references online regarding the training. This stuff is pretty bread-and-butter amongst all corporation securities."

It would be more common among mercenaries too, if it didn't require an expensive main server to process the data, and the know-how to keep the connection encrypted. Otherwise, enemies would just spy on the channel and you would be letting enemies see everything you saw.

We followed the guard, who carried the body into one of the unoccupied operating rooms. The body was placed on the table, where I started performing an autopsy. The equipment I used to scan patients' bodies in preparation for cybernetic installations took care of the majority of the work, but even then, it took a whole hour.

When I finished, Claire helpfully handed me a smoothie to refresh myself, though Thorne didn't let me enjoy my drink as he stepped forward and pressed me for the results. "So, did you find out anything useful?"

"Just some data we can use to look further into things, not much other than—"

Without warning, an explosion shook the building.

I briskly re-equipped my headgear and looked around. My visor highlighted a dozen figures and vehicles through the walls.

"Thorne, you might have to order more than just a door."

# CHAPTER 29

## FIGHTING BACK

The visor I attached to my headgear highlighted the various figures and vehicles just outside the clinic. Just as I finished counting them, they vanished from view. They must have destroyed the cameras outside.

"They failed the quiet approach and quickly switched it up to the loud approach. These guys really are your typical bullies."

"Rollo, we have no time to analyze them!" Thorne cried. "I'll go out and flank them with Peter. You head to the control room."

"I'll go with—"

Thorne interrupted, "No, Claire, it's our job to keep you safe. Besides, you haven't trained with us yet, so you aren't as coordinated as we are."

*Well, I can't argue with that.*

"Okay," I said, "let's try to get this done fast and clean, yeah? I'm really tired of having my clinic be a battleground."

He nodded and jogged out of the room with the security guard, Peter, who had carried the body into the operating room for us earlier.

I headed straight to the control room, unlocked the door using the biometric scan, and found one of the other security guards, whom I hadn't seen yet tonight, sitting inside. He gave me a brief nod before the glow in his eyes returned and his gaze unfocused.

The screens on the walls showed the current situation: the attackers breaking into the lobby through the hole they blew open earlier. They were having trouble pushing in as the turrets in the ceiling deployed and rained hellfire at them.

After our last rodeo at the clinic, I'd had the sense to upgrade our defense, but it seemed I hadn't gone far enough.

I saw the only other guard on shift tonight defending the lobby, working perfectly in sync with one of the turrets. Seeing how that particular turret reacted, I could tell the man beside me had manual control of it and the two guards had practiced their coordination regularly.

*Good job, Thorne.*

Another explosion rocked the building once more as the bastards blasted another hole open through the windows of the lobby, creating a new entry point.

A moment later, the door behind me swung open.

"Are they trying to blow up the entire building?" Claire said as she speed-walked towards an open seat.

"Shouldn't be if their goal was to steal tech," I said, hooking up to the control system.

I gained access to the system and took manual control of a turret in the lobby. This felt like a video game, to be honest, especially with my virtual connection.

"I got the new entry point," I told my nearby partner, who nodded in response.

From the virtual view, I saw a man dashing in through the new hole, holding an LMG. The automated system might need some time to identify him and ensure he was a threat before shooting, but I didn't.

I pulled the trigger, and the turret instantly opened fire. Streams of large-caliber rounds soon ripped the confident man apart.

*+10 EXP*

*+10 EXP*

An extra notification popped up behind him, informing me that I had managed to pick off another one of them.

A few guns then stuck out around the corner and shot the turrets, but the armor plating simply deflected the small-caliber rounds, leaving only shallow dents behind. They refused to leave cover, so the situation devolved into a stalemate.

Just as I checked the ammo count on the turret, I looked up to find the outlines of all the attackers outside the building highlighted in red, with two friendlies in blue beside them. Then the sound of gunfire from their side intensified for a second before it halted entirely.

The red outlines disappeared, leaving only the two blue ones remaining. A voice soon rang out from our comms.

"We've cleared all the attackers out front. We're going to take a look around as well, just in case. Keep the turrets ready until we're done." Thorne's voice reverberated in my head.

* * *

An hour later, I sat in one of the break rooms along with Thorne and Claire, who both looked exhausted. I couldn't fault them, either, as I'd left the aftermath to them entirely, handling the police and the cleanup.

"It's obvious who organized the attack," said Thorne. "They barely even tried to hide it. They used their own employees, for God's sake."

Claire let out a sigh. "Calm down, Thorne. Even if we knew who it was, it doesn't mean we have to rush in to retaliate. Let's talk and plan things out first."

"She's right. Focus on reinforcing our defense for tonight and send out a few teams to dig up some more info about Hathway tomorrow. I want to know where everything they own is. Their production facilities, offices, everything we can find." I stood up and made my way to the door.

"You're going out still?"

"Yes, there are some preparations I need to get done before we strike back."

If Hathway was blatantly attacking us, I saw no reason not to retaliate, but unlike them, we would stick to our specialty of stealth. Our equipment was due for an upgrade, and I just happened to be close to leveling up, so I had some community cleaning to do tonight.

* * *

## Yuki—Security Guard of Rollo Halls' Company

"I heard the CEO sent a team out to retrieve some vital info to improve our project. How come we haven't heard anything back yet?" a man dressed in a typical corpo suit asked. Beside him stood a woman, leaning against his desk.

"I don't know. Everyone I asked has either been tight-lipped or clueless as well."

"You know what that means: it's time to start searching and applying to other companies. You'll come with me, right?" He reached out and grabbed the woman's hand.

"Yes, of course." She rose to her full height and grasped the man's hand with both of hers. "Excuse me for a moment. I'll be right back." She exited the office, and Yuki followed.

She gave a pleasant smile to the few other employees on her way to the washroom, but the moment she was alone, her facade vanished. "Fucking horny bastard, as if I have any more use for him if he can't get me a promotion. I hope he enjoys himself starting out again as the new guy in another company," she vented to herself, vigorously washing her hands.

While the woman was busy with that, Yuki was waiting behind her, stealth active. She brought up her terminal and connected it to the security card that was hanging from the woman's waist.

*Peter, you're green to go, you got about twenty seconds.* She sent the message through her company's network.

There was only a five-second pause before she got a reply.

*I'm in, thanks Yuki.*

As soon as she saw the message, she disconnected the card and waited for the woman so they could exit the washroom together, as it would arouse suspicion if the door opened by itself.

Once she was out, she slipped into the stairwell and deactivated her stealth augment. She gave a quick glance at the camera above, thanking their cy-sec specialist for looping the feed for her.

The newly upgraded cybernetic they had installed had much better uptime than before, but it was still limited. It did have more functions and was invisible to infrared sensors, so she wasn't complaining too much.

In fact, there wasn't much to complain about with her new employer at all. The pay wasn't anything special, but it didn't work them to the bone with long hours and even gave them a few days of paid holiday a year. And she hadn't even brought up the hazard pay for work-related injuries, which she had never seen in any employment contract before.

*I'm done here. Get out within five minutes.* A text alert broke her from her musings.

As instructed, she rushed out of the building by making use of the active camouflage and returned to the car parked a street away. Sitting in the car was Peter, who somehow returned faster than her. He gave her a curt nod and pressed some buttons on his handheld terminal.

In less than a minute, a fire alarm was heard from the building they had just exited, and people soon rushed out. The firefighters arrived within five minutes and started hosing, but they faltered when an explosion threw shards of broken glass down from the twenty-third floor of the building. The smoke coming out the window showcased to all that the raging fire was still going strong.

Having confirmed their mission was complete, Peter started up the car, and they drove away in silence.

Yuki stared at the rearview mirror as they left the scene and felt slightly bad for the corpos gazing blankly at their workplace. The ones who worked at her rival company, Hathway, were going to be out of a job very soon.

*I've really started becoming one of them if I can empathize with them...*

*At least my idea was accepted, and we started a fire to force the evacuation first and prevent unnecessary casualties. Only their decision-makers were at fault, after all.*

Their drive back to the clinic was uneventful. They parked and headed back into the security room, where their boss, Thorne, sat along with another one of their colleagues.

"We're back," Peter reported. "We can confirm the office we went to is destroyed. I made sure to blow up their server rooms."

Thorne looked at the projected map in the middle of the room for a second before he responded, "Good job. You guys can go take a break first. We're moving out together later tonight." He drew an *X* on the map where they had just been.

"Understood."

She saluted in unison with Peter, and they walked out of the room together.

*It's time to enjoy a nice break in the middle of work. How nice, maybe I should take a nap. They did say we were going out tonight.*

* * *

"Rollo, all the attacks were successful. We have either disabled or destroyed all the important assets they own across the city. Though we can't reach the ones located in other cities, they can't operate properly in Elevate City anymore," Thorne reported, his eyes glowing.

I was glad to hear the good news. It was unfortunate we weren't able to touch their production facilities located in the Asia Union, but we'd crippled them enough. We just had to deal the final blow.

"Good, have the team prepare to set out soon. Let's give our friend James an evening visit."

As planned, we headed out once the sun had set. We brought half a dozen men with us, bolstering our numbers up to eight, including me and Thorne.

Leaving two men behind to watch our vehicles, the six of us made our way inside a megabuilding, all dressed casually with the exception of the sunglasses we wore. Those helped scramble our faces on camera and had the technology to sync our vision like the visors we used.

We got into the elevator together, and when the door closed, Thorne plugged into the panel and signaled for Claire to begin her remote takeover.

Automatically, the button to the topmost floor lit up, and the elevator ascended. It brought us to the roof access floor that was normally only open to the maintenance crews. From there, we spotted the penthouse below.

We ensured everyone was ready before we collectively turned on our active camouflage and descended to secure the area.

My vision was soon filled with various outlines of the guards on the floor, as if I was wall hacking in a video game.

*Now then, what kind of welcome gift should I give to my friend James? After all, how can I show up empty-handed?*

# CHAPTER 40

## SENDING A MESSAGE

I stayed back on the rooftop and glanced down at the floor, watching as the red-highlighted enemies slowly slumped down one by one before disappearing. Only the guards in front of the master bedroom were spared.

"They're about done. We should head down lest they notice anything," Thorne stated from beside me.

"Okay, let's go." With that, we leaped down onto the balcony. My boots canceled out any noise of the impact, which saved me the hassle of rolling on the ground to disperse it.

One of our men stood watch by the balcony door as we headed into the living room. Bodies lay sprawled on the ground, reaching every corner.

"Sitrep?" Thorne quietly asked from behind.

"Twenty targets subdued except for the three by the master bedroom, as instructed."

Inspecting the bodies, I found that they were still breathing, as that was the protocol Thorne and I set when ambushing our foes. More often than not, people were more useful alive. It allowed us time to identify them before deciding on an appropriate follow-up.

We headed further into the penthouse, towards the owner's bedroom. We soon rounded a corner, where we heard a conversation nearby.

"—our shift, want to go to the Neon District?"

"Ehh, why not? We've been racking up overtime these past few days. I could blow some credits."

"Now we're talking. Alfred has been down our throats with the protocols and infrared cameras. It's high time you come blow some steam off with me."

"Yeah... When is that bastard Ed coming back from his hush-hush mission? He should come as well."

"No clue. I tried asking Alfred in a roundabout way, but he didn't reveal anything."

"He's always been a tight-a—" I didn't let the man finish his sentence, as I put him in a rear naked choke.

His fellow guard turned in surprise, but before he could scream, Thorne took care of him.

With the guards out of the way, the only obstacle that remained was the door to the master bedroom. It seemed like James had some sense of self-preservation. His room was more like a large safe, locked behind a biometric scanner.

Thorne moved up and connected a terminal to the back panel of the scanner. A moment later, Claire's voice rang out in my head.

"Thanks for the wait, guys! This security is worse than expected. That impressive-looking lock still used the default software it came with, which is something accessible to the public. It's open now. Tell our friend I said hi."

The door clicked open. The light from the hallway leaked into the dark room.

"Alfred? What's going on?" our friend, James, nervously said from his bed. Despite the lack of light, my implants helped me make out the swallowing movement of his throat.

We made our way into the room and closed the door behind us, to James' panic. He jumped up from his bed, reached for the drawer of the nightstand beside him, and held up what resembled a collector's revolver. From its markings, I could tell it was from Premier Arms, just like my weapons, which meant it was probably an electromagnetically propelled weapon.

He grew more nervous and confused as he realized there was no one by the door. Frantically looking around the room, he found only himself.

"Jasper, Gran, are you there?" he screamed out.

When he found no response, he quickly drew another item from the drawer, a pair of glasses, and put it on before scanning his room.

Having seen enough, I lunged towards him, slapped his gun out of his hand, and shoved him into his bed face-first.

"Hey there, James, guess which of your friends came for a surprise visit?" His struggling intensified. "Now, now. Calm down, James, we're all friends here."

"Get off me. Do you have any idea who I am?! You're so dead! You and all your loved ones."

"Oh, are you convincing me to tie up loose ends right now?" I gestured to Thorne for his gun, which I then racked right next to his ear and pressed against the back of his head.

*My fancier guns are cool and all, but too bad I can't rack them to make this iconic sound.*

"Stop, stop! I'll give you way more than what you're getting paid right now. Just let me go."

"Sure, transfer me some credits from your account to this one," I immediately replied.

*Who in their right mind would pass up free money?*

The temporary account I set up soon received a transfer of fifty thousand credits.

"So you think fifty thousand is way more than what I'm getting paid? You're pretty cheap for a CEO, don't you think?"

"That's all I can move right now, trust me! Let me go and I'll wire more to you later."

"Don't worry about that. I didn't come here for the credits."

"What?" He tried to turn back towards me, but I shoved his face harder back into the bed.

"You tried to attack the wrong people. This isn't an issue you can buy your way out of, understand?"

Once he heard my words, his struggling reignited, stronger than before.

"Calm down, James, we're not unreasonable people. We talk reason. That's why you're alive and chatting with us right now."

"What do you want?"

"Nothing."

"Nothing? You sneaked into my home and pinned me to my bed for nothing?"

"We came here today to just warn you, James. Leave the camouflage cybernetic business and stay in your own lane, making projectors or whatever, before anything unfortunate happens."

"Is that a threat?!"

"Yes, it is. Think carefully, now. We can always find you again and have another chat next time, though I doubt we'd be as friendly. It's your choice."

He fell silent.

I brought out the bracelet restraints and put them on James before whispering to him one final time, "We'll always be watching."

On my way out of the room, I threw a milkshake from my pack down on a nearby desk. It may have melted by now, but he'd have to make do with what he got.

*I hope he enjoys my handpicked gift as much as I would.*

* * *

After our visit, we returned to the clinic and disbanded, leaving only one security team on the premises, along with me, Thorne, and Claire. We'd set up a few hidden cameras at James' place just in case of immediate retaliation. The cameras probably wouldn't last once he made a clean sweep of the house, but they allowed us to see what he'd do next from our break room.

"Are you really sure we should let them go?" Claire asked as she munched on some peanuts.

"Yeah, it'll be hard to root them out when their family is scattered around the world. We don't have that kind of reach. Rather than fight a war with them, it'll do us more good if James listens and backs off. Besides, who knows if they have some insurance with a revenge clause or something. Can't be too careful with these corpos."

"But you had to let all his men go too. He's got the manpower to retaliate at any moment now, you know?"

"He always can. We just have to keep our eyes open. There's no point killing all his employees, he'll just hire new ones. Also, I'd rather not murder some poor worker doing their job. There's enough garbage around for me to clean up that I can't get to yet."

"Fine, but we should prepare for the worst-case scenarios."

"That was the plan. We'll need to earn more first to upgrade our security and hire more people. In the meantime, we'll be more careful." I looked to Thorne, who nodded back.

With our conversation finished and nothing unusual spotted with James, I returned to my workshop now that I had some time.

I wanted to study the active camouflage the Hathway Corporation had put together, as from the outside, I could only tell that the tech base for it took an entirely different approach to mine, even though it performed similarly.

Their version had many small, synchronized wide-view lenses installed around the body. These projected images of the surroundings to create the effect, as opposed to my nanomachine-based method. If I could adapt some of their tech for my nanomachines, I could increase their efficiency, allowing for the same result with fewer nanomachines, which in turn would lower the costs.

After a detailed breakdown, it turned out I could replicate their lenses and the software used alongside the implant to keep multiple lenses in sync, though it would take some trial and error.

Without the original blueprint, it took a full week until I could reproduce lenses that performed at ninety percent of the original's capacity. It then took another week before I got a consistent enough production method.

The most fortuitous thing about this new method was that I could use my old stealth products as materials with minimal losses, which further kept my costs down.

I planned to reduce the price slightly, but the people in my target market weren't ones to cheap out on equipment that their lives depended on. That would increase my margins per unit.

Claire entered the workshop with news. "Our existing stock has been changed to the updated version, and the next shipment is on schedule. You have a meeting with Delnar Medical's representative scheduled in thirty minutes and one with State Care Clinics at 4:00 p.m. today," she faithfully recited from her terminal.

"Got it. I'll leave things here to you, then," I said as I started packing away samples of our product into a briefcase.

"Are you sure you don't want to sell our better model, or at least a watered-down version of it?"

I inspected a sample one last time before packing it away. "Claire, our latest model contains some tech that we will want to keep to ourselves, indefinitely."

"Why can't we just patent it and sell a downgraded version? It'll be hard to keep it a secret forever."

"Ha, a patent won't solve anything. It's not a monetary concern but a security one. You can see just from the recent incident with Hathway. Leaking their tech allowed us to prepare countermeasures. A watered-down version will still have the same operating principle that others can extrapolate. We're only going to sell the basic version, where it doesn't matter to us if everyone gets a hold of it."

"Okay, okay—just a suggestion. I got things to do. See you later," she said, and quickly exited my workshop.

She was right in that it was hard to keep our tech a secret, but everyone had that same issue. I already installed a self-destruct sequence in the new cybernetic we gave out to our security team. It had several trigger conditions, such as disassembly, death of the user, or manual activation. Even then, it wouldn't be perfect. I'd just have to keep updating the anti-theft measures and monitor closely.

I arrived at the first meeting place, one of Delnar Medical's nearby cybernetic clinics, with fifteen minutes to spare.

The receptionist guided me towards a meeting room on the floor above, where a middle-aged woman was already waiting.

She was dressed neatly in formal business wear with subdued colors, like a typical corpo, and sat relaxed as she watched me enter. Standing beside her was a younger woman bent over, whispering something into her ear.

"Welcome, Mr. Halls. I am Ida Mereth. I know it's a little early, but why don't we jump straight into it, since you are here already? I believe you have a product you would like us to carry in our clinics?"

"That's right. Our company has recently launched a new cybernetic, the HSU-003 Shade."

# CHAPTER 41

## *SHADE*

"Our company has recently launched a new cybernetic, the HSU-003 Shade," I said as I sat down opposite Ida Mereth and her assistant.

"Yes," she said, "I've read about it but haven't had the chance to see one in person yet. Stealth cybernetics are rare for a reason. It will be a risk for us to carry this product if there isn't a market for it."

*As expected of a corpo. Of course she would probe for any faults possible to push down the price. Good thing I came prepared.*

I brought out my terminal and placed it on the table between us. "You do not have to worry about that. Here is some data from my business regarding the market for stealth implants. As you can see, demand for our product has been exponentially growing, and that is with minimal marketing. There is still a large untapped market with all the mercenaries in Elevate City."

"I see... These are attractive numbers, if true. Let us see a sample, if you will."

Opening the briefcase, I fished out the sample of stealth cybernetic, now known as Shade. It was unimpressive-looking, a small device with the sole purpose of housing nanomachines within the human body.

"Rebecca, if you will."

The assistant then took a full minute to input commands in her handheld terminal before the doors opened and a humanoid robot clumsily walked in.

"Mr. Halls, we wanted to test your product on our G-Pig, if you don't mind."

"Of course, go ahead." I'd seen them before when getting my medical license. They not only were used to test cybernetics, but also served as dummies for practical exercises in med school, though they weren't used in my exam.

It didn't take long for the assistant, Rebecca, to install Shade on the robot.

"Connected with the G-Pig's SAID, activating the cybernetic." She cleanly enunciated with a voice that carried across the entire room, despite it only being the three of us. "Shade, now!"

The robot swiftly blurred out of our vision, and I caught both Ida and Rebecca looking left and right around the room. Ida quickly composed herself when she noticed my gaze.

She took a moment to clear her throat. "I see... I can definitely tell it is up to par, but marketing stealth tech so openly may put us on the wrong foot with other corpora—"

"Please, let's be honest here, Ms. Mereth," I said. "If that were the case, you wouldn't even be sitting here talking to me. We're willing to give you a wholesale price of seventy-five percent of what we retail it for."

The middle-aged woman took a deep breath and replied, "Fifty percent and we have a deal."

All the corpos I'd seen had a habit of negotiating until they felt like they won something. It made it a pain in the ass to negotiate with them most of the time, but predictable, which made it manageable.

After some back-and-forth, we settled on sixty percent of the retail price before we messaged our lawyers to draft up the legal documents. They were on standby, so it was only thirty minutes before we had both read over the written terms and electronically signed the contract.

*Okay, finally. One down and two more to go—for today, at least...*

* * *

### Mia—Mercenary

"Where is Henry? We have to meet our client soon!" the team leader, Magnus, yelled as he paced around one of Haven's private rooms.

He may have appeared menacing with his bulky frame that probably consisted more of chrome than meat, but someone had to be the one to answer him. He wasn't all that bad once you got to know him.

"He said he was going to the clinic earlier, but I wouldn't worry too much about him. I don't think he's ever been late... for work-related things."

"You trust him too much, Mia. He's the type that you have to constantly hassle or he'll instantly slack off. Give him an inch and he'll take a fucking thousand miles."

"I didn't say to stop calling him, but we can relax while doing so."

Magnus took a deep breath before he sat back down on the sofa and chugged the rest of his drink down. He looked like he wanted to say something but decided against it, as no one else in the room seemed to be on his side.

Stealing a glance at the rest of the team, Mia saw them all doing their own thing without a care in the world. Some of them were obviously on their optics while others were caring for their weapons.

*Who was it that said mercenaries all had a screw loose? Because they are so right.*

When there were only two minutes left until the meeting, Henry's lanky figure nonchalantly strode into the private room.

"Where the fuck have you been?" Magnus immediately snapped at him.

His aggression seemed to bounce off Henry, who just shrugged and said in a laid-back tone, "Who cares? I'm on time, aren't I?"

"You... let me have a word with you after this. Everyone, it's time. Let's go."

The five-man team then got up and made the short trip to Haven's much noisier common area. They crossed directly to the stairs to the second floor, which was quieter, reserved for private rooms only.

In a new room, three unkempt men were waiting at a table. It was the team's policy to let Magnus do all the talking in these negotiations, though recently, Mia had started to think maybe that was just because everyone else let Magnus deal with the stuff that was a pain in the ass.

"You the guys Oli sent?" the smallest of the trio asked as soon as they were seated.

"Right. You asked for discretion, so just tell us the details and we'll be on our way."

One of the other men stood up and glared at Magnus. It amused Mia a little, seeing someone try that on the behemoth of a man. She held back her laughter and applauded herself for her restraint. "Show some respect, co. You're working for us now, right?"

Magnus stared right back while the entire room went quiet. It would have been a lot more tense if she weren't only an inch away from bursting out into laughter.

The silence didn't last long before the previous speaker gestured for his friend to back off. "Excuse us, he's not the best communicator. I agree with you, this is no more than a transaction of money and services. Everything you need to know is in this terminal here. Do not download the file, just read it from here."

The other mercenaries sat with glows in their eyes that made it clear that they weren't paying any attention while Magnus read over the details of the job.

To no one's surprise, Mia was the only one who even bothered to go over it after he was done.

Once she finished, the five-man mercenary team exited Haven and began their drive to the location provided. The gig wasn't anything new to them, a simple "kill these guys from the other gang and take over the location." The only thing to note was that the location was a small grocery store, so there would be random civilians in the way and the employer wanted to keep the damages to a minimum.

The team checked their weapons as Magnus briefed the idiots who hadn't paid any attention earlier. This time, it was Mia's turn to zone out as she caressed her beloved Zappy.

*Who's the best submachine gun in the world? Zappy is!*

It wasn't until she finished cleaning every single nook and cranny of Zappy that Magnus finished.

"—any questions or ideas?"

"Me, me, me!" Henry raised his hand like a schoolkid. "I just got a new toy installed. I can go in to pop the fire alarm to get those uninvolved out of the way."

"New toy?" Mia reflexively asked.

"Yeah, active camouflage. Stuff that I always wanted and the corpos hogged for themselves."

"I thought the corpos installed self-destruct mechanisms in all of them or something. How did you get your hands on one?"

"I think a few corps are selling 'em now. Luckily I waited, and a new model just released that was within my budget and had better performance than the old one, so I got it installed earlier. Here, look."

As soon as Henry said that, his body began to vanish, starting from his torso and spreading to the rest of his body. For once, the other team members turned to look as well. A second passed as everyone stared dumbly at the space Henry had previously occupied before he suddenly came back into existence.

"Absolute zero, right?"

A rare sight occurred as the team showed genuine interest in Henry. They started to ask him various questions about the capabilities of his new implant and where he got it, but Magnus silenced the budding discussion in a clap of the hands.

"All right, everyone, we're almost there. We can chat later. We'll go with Henry's plan for now. Mia, if Henry gets you into their network, can you stop the fire alarm's signal from getting out? I'd rather not have the fire department show up to get in our way."

"Sure thing. He just needs to plug this in." She pulled out a small chip from her pack and held it out for all to see.

"Okay, let's finish this job up, quick and easy."

She finished the calibrations, ensured the chip had a connection to her terminal, and handed it off to Henry as everyone but her got out of the car, leaving her to enjoy the extra space by stretching around.

It wasn't long before she gained a connection to the grocery store's network. It was easy to breach, allowing her full access to their cameras and other systems. After she gave the okay to Henry, the team executed their plan and triggered the fire alarms while she kept the signal from leaving the network.

Mia watched from the cameras as the shoppers all trudged out of the store, pissed at the disruption. She spotted a few obvious gang members in the back scrambling to find the source while others exited along with the customers.

"We have a few stragglers," she said into the comms.

She continued monitoring the show as the shootout started. Her team wasn't known for its stealth, after all. The gang members who exited the building soon heard the shooting and headed back to the front doors, where they suddenly fell down one by one, all with their throat slit.

It didn't take a genius to tell who had done that, especially when she spotted the man himself coming out of that active camouflage and joining the fight.

*I guess it didn't last as long as he bragged it would, but still...*

* * *

A few weeks after we started selling our products across clinics all over the city, orders accelerated. Word had gotten around, and with our prices comparable to Hathway's but with better performance, it was only natural the pragmatic mercenary market shifted towards my product.

This allowed us to start a round of expansion with our new credits, hiring additional professionals in areas such as finance and management.

These new hires used analyses of our records to implement structural changes we had sorely needed. And today, yet another one came into my workshop, which was more like my office now, with a recommendation.

"Sir, based on our projected income, we believe the best course of action right now is to incorporate with the Elevate City Consortium. It requires an annual fee, but the lower taxes of becoming a corporation mean it will pay for itself with our projected profits."

I paused my workbench tinkering for a second as I took in what my employee had said. If I'd listened correctly, he meant it was time to officially upgrade the business into a proper corporation.

# CHAPTER 43

## ELEVATE CITY CONSORTIUM

I stared blankly at my status while I organized my thoughts. The topic of incorporation had consumed my research since one of my employees brought it up.

My goal was always to strike it rich so that I had full control of my life and could afford better security. I always knew the only viable way was to create my own corporation. I couldn't change how society worked here, so I could only join them. Maybe when I became one of the top dogs, I could implement some changes to make this place friendlier and more peaceful. After all, I couldn't enjoy my riches without a peaceful world.

Elevate City was an independent city-state controlled by the Elevate City Consortium, a group of corporations that came together to stand on their own feet, away from the influence of governments. Like all corporations in this society, they had immense influence across the planet and even the colonies in space. While all members shared an interest in the consortium, they were in no way friendly to each other, constantly infighting for their own profits.

Still, they allowed new businesses to join their ranks to replenish the ones that dissolved after the cutthroat fighting. This also allowed for new ideas and inventions to sprout up.

Although they allowed it, it wasn't easy to join the exclusive club. They set a simple and effective barrier to entry: a large annual fee in the name of contributing to the city's budget. The fees paid were divided into ten different levels. The more you paid, the more privileges you got. These ranged from lower tax rates to priority with infrastructure, including use of the ports.

The one we were looking into was the lowest, G-tier, and required an annual fee of a million credits. I'd read many horror stories of businesses overreaching themselves by joining the consortium to be recognized as legitimate corporations. Corporations that had no more cash flow to grow, meaning they stagnated and soon could no longer afford the fees.

My accounting department had outlined a detailed proposal on the feasibility of incorporating. They expected that joining the consortium would mean higher profits even if our sales stayed the same as they were now, since we would be taking advantage of the lower taxes for corporations.

The only thing left to discuss was when to incorporate the business, whether now or a bit further down the line. Whether to spend our money on expanding the company and purchasing better equipment now, against more income from a lower corporate tax rate.

I was tired of seeing the security team wearing mismatched gear and definitely wanted to standardize it. Did I really want to put it off even longer? I was also considering expanding into NLA to better make use of our existing facilities there.

A sudden knock broke me out of my musing. "Hey Rollo, you busy?" The door opened and Claire's head peeked into my workshop.

"No, was just taking a break. Need me for something?"

"Nothing important, just that we were planning to buy a VR capsule to play together and wanted to see if you wanted to join us."

"Well, I did tell you guys to spend that money to reward yourselves. No use letting it sit in our account. Why not?"

"Cool! I'll send you the one we're getting. Give me a second."

I watched as she quickly brought out her terminal and searched.

*I've been deliberating by myself for too long. Maybe I need a fresh perspective.*

"Hey, Claire..."

"Hmm? I'm almost done, just one more second... and done. What's up?"

"I wanted to get your opinion on when we should incorporate."

"So you really plan to go through and make this company an official corp, huh?"

"Yeah, or else we won't be able to continue growing. Businesses we want to work with won't take us seriously until then."

"I see... I'm not sure how I feel about that. Or how Thorne would feel, considering what happened with his mom."

*Right, I should talk with Thorne as well about this before we go through with it. He may have a bias against all corporations. A perfectly understandable one, too, since they took his mom away from him.*

"Let's call him here to talk it through," I said as I sent a message to the person in question through my SAID.

He entered the room within a minute, as the clinic wasn't that large to begin with, and Claire gave him a quick summary of our discussion.

"I don't see a problem with incorporating. I know you and it's not like you're going to suddenly become like most of the corpos because of what some documents say."

"That's right."

"Though I do want to ask what your end goal is. How big did you want to grow the company?"

"To be honest, my main reason for starting one in the first place was to get rich and use the wealth to secure my safety and freedom, but it seems like that isn't going to happen until I become such a top player that we become immovable. So I've recently been planning to bring some change to the corporate world while on the way to the top, starting with better working conditions."

"I see," Thorne stated, deep in thought.

Claire smugly added. "Well, that's predictable, seeing how generous you already treat your employees."

Thorne chuckled. "She's right, but you're not in any hurry to incorporate, right?"

"No, but I don't want to take it too slow either, with the threat of the harvesters and Rust Scrappers always hanging nearby."

"Then I still think we should take our time and hire more people first. A new corp, no matter how small, will draw some attention from the hyenas, so we should be prepared."

He was right. I was rushing it a bit in the face of profits. What was more important than making more money faster was keeping the ability to defend my wealth up at the same pace.

"Right. We'll focus on expanding, then. I'll leave it up to you two on that end."

* * *

"I think you'll love what we have next at 1345 SocialCorp Road. It may be an older building, but it's at a prime stop within this district. The plot of land is half an acre in total, though the current building doesn't make full use of the land, and you can freely rebuild it after your purchase," the young man proudly introduced as our ride pulled up to a slightly worn-looking office building.

I exited the car, looked up, and counted five floors. "How high are we allowed to build here?"

"It is currently set to the same height as your current building, so around five stories, six if you stretch it, though it is possible to negotiate with city hall."

*Right, what zoning law could stand up to the might of a bribe in this city?*

Surveying the surrounding area, I found a few small businesses, mainly groceries and coffee shops, spread out between the similar-sized office buildings that likely belonged to corporations.

Apparently, it wasn't popular to share an office building in this world, as it posed a serious security risk with all the corporate espionage happening daily. That meant each corp had its own buildings, which meant the smaller players had mini office buildings on individual plots of land.

The ones in the downtown area were sold only to established corporations, but there were still plenty throughout Elevate City. Fitting for a corporate-controlled city-state to have available offices while the average workers were stuffed into megabuildings. It was also no surprise that the rent for the office buildings actually seemed fair compared to what they charged for residential units.

Still, this old five-story office building and the surrounding land would cost one hundred thousand credits per month, more per year than the annual fee for becoming a corporation. They only managed to convince me of the move due to a recent attack on the clinic by some small-time gang looking for some quick money.

I needed a more secure place to live in and more room for the new employees we'd been hiring. We also planned to turn the ground floor into another clinic.

"There are thirty-six underground parking spots spread across two basement levels. An independent power generator and water filter are included in the rent." The man continued to babble on as I walked into the lobby.

So far, this seemed to be the best one, as it fit the size we were looking for, with ample space to expand into.

"We'll go with this one. Please contact the owner and start drafting up the documents. I also wanted to take a look at the floors above."

"Of course, sir. I'll be here getting it ready. Please feel free to head up at your leisure. There is no one else here today."

The one elevator in the building brought me straight up to the top floor. It wasn't really high up, being only five floors, but the view from all the huge glass pane windows was still a sight to behold. I stared downwards at hundreds of ant-sized people going about their day.

Before I could take a seat and relax, my SAID alerted me to an incoming call request.

"Rollo, this is important, go watch the Elevate City news right now!" Leo's voice rang out.

Leo and Lana had started working for me recently. They had always wanted to return to being corpos, so they took Claire's offer without hesitation. The only catch was that they were the ones who created the software that monitored my employees. That meant they would be under the surveillance of their own program, meaning they could easily hack into my security system, if they wanted to. I didn't think they would, but at their insistence, I put my upgraded software engineering skills to the test and changed the program up a little, just to be safe.

With Leo being my new head of cybersecurity, there was no reason for me to doubt him. My optics booted up the news and a new screen took up half my peripheral vision.

"—are only forty-eight hours left until the time limit. Then I believe most colonies will declare martial law and restrict all travel as the war begins." As I listened to the newscaster, my eyes flew to the bolded headline towards the bottom that read, "*War Declared by Europa Station against Enceladus Station!*"

I found out which consortium was against which, learned more about the notable corporations involved, and heard some expert commentary. Once the program was finished, it looped back to the beginning that I hadn't seen yet.

"For those of you just tuning in, the government of the space colony on Europa Station has just declared war on Enceladus Station for reasons unknown. There is a forty-eight-hour grace period for all those who do not want to get involved to leave as soon as possible. Travel will then be restricted. I repeat, there are only forty-eight hours left until—"

I closed the window and brought the call with Leo back into focus. "That seems serious. Stock up on as many materials and medical supplies as possible before the price rises."

"I've already told Claire to get on that, but you need to be worried about other things. War in space means a lot of resources will be directed off-planet, logistics will be screwed up for a while, and it won't be easy to find someone to ship your products from your factory in NLA to Elevate City anymore!"

"Shit... It's too late to find someone to sign a deal, isn't it?"

# CHAPTER 43

## LOGISTICAL NIGHTMARE

"Rollo!" Claire rushed towards me as soon as I stepped back into the clinic. "We tried contacting our usual shipping company, but they declined all our orders. We're getting the same answer from all the other shipping companies we contact."

"How much stock do we have left?"

"We have enough for a little over a month for the clinic, but we have pending orders to State Care Clinics coming up next week and another one the week after."

*Shit, we're not just looking at the penalties for breaking the contract. Our credibility with our partners will go down the drain before it even begins.*

"Reserve our stock for the orders. We'll temporarily stop selling Shades."

"Okay, I'm on it." She ran off to the back.

This would only stop the bleeding for now. We needed to find an alternative fast.

I headed into the camera room, where I found Leo.

"Got any ideas for our situation?" I stood over his shoulder.

"No... I've tried everything I know. I called up Fitel and some other QGs too, but every corporation out there is looking for more shipping capacity to make a tidy profit."

"I guess that means buying a boat or plane is out of the question too?"

Leo downed his cup and turned to me. "Nothing. The entire city is sold out, from luxury yachts to old scrap buckets that can barely stay afloat. First large-scale space war in thirty years, and everyone is overreacting."

"I'm going to NLA, then. If there's nothing we can do here, then might as well try elsewhere."

"I'll come too. I'm not having the company I just joined go down so soon."

"Book the next flight for us."

* * *

The flights to NLA this time were five times the price, and with carry-on only. Vin was waiting for us when we arrived in the same old car he drove.

"Sorry, boys, I had everyone reach out to see if there was any luck on this side, but we've been getting nothing so far. This may have been a fruitless trip for you guys. Nevertheless, feel free to give it a try yourselves if you want."

"I could try looking for ships to steal from a small company or something," Leo cautiously said. "A smaller yacht would suffice for the quantity we're moving."

"You think a small business will be able to keep their boat in this current landscape? Only corporations with decent security teams will have anything we could use by now." Vin turned to Leo in the backseat to reply, much to my dismay, as he was manually driving the car.

We shared a moment of silence, each deep in thought. Before we knew it, we arrived at our NLA office, which doubled as a production facility.

There were unfamiliar faces on the security team, but they seemed to know who I was, as they respectfully saluted while we walked by. This was true for all the other new employees we passed as well, while the veterans knew I liked to keep it casual.

I briefly inspected our production process and the storage for our Shade stealth cybernetics. There was still quite a bit of room in our warehouse, though if we stopped shipping them out, sooner or later it would fill up.

My office upstairs appeared unchanged from the last time I was here. It was apparent someone had cleaned and maintained the room, though. I had sat down in my chair and spun around to get a view of the streets down below when I heard the door opening.

"I put everything on the shopping list you gave me in your room. Got any plans for the rest of the day?" Vin's voice rang out from behind.

"Where's Leo?" I asked.

"He's just unpacking a few things. He'll be here in a second."

"I see. By the way, thank you for driving through traffic to make the errand run."

"You're the boss. If you want to thank me, then give me a bonus." From his voice alone, I could practically see the wide smirk on his face. I fought the urge to look back and took in the view of the city, where cars moved at a snail's pace in all the traffic.

The door then opened again, and I turned around as Leo joined us and took a seat next to Vin.

"Anyway, how's the ground transportation looking around here?" I asked.

"About the same as everything related to logistics since the war declaration," Vin said. "Though not as intense, since cars are way more plentiful and don't require trained personnel to handle. The main bottleneck is security for transports through the wasteland.

Any large convoy with weak security is just a prime target to be raided."

"Have the wastelanders become more active recently?" Leo asked with interest.

"Yep. They don't like all the new convoys running through their territory, so I guess it's a reactionary response. Armored vehicles and security are in high demand right about now and are hard to find, just like our shipping situation."

"That's it!" I exclaimed. They both urged me to elaborate with their eyes. "You think we can barter ground transport for shipping?"

* * *

"Woah, so that is the wasteland." Leo's expression easily betrayed his amazement. "It's like a wall of sand, but it's so weird that there's a clear border where one side is a raging sandstorm while the other is so tranquil."

"That's what I thought too when I first saw it. You'll get used to it, but don't forget how dangerous it can be once inside."

"Yeah, you don't say."

Our Vanguards soon entered the wasteland, where the sound of the sand hitting the car overpowered any of our conversations until our ears got used to it.

Vin switched from looking out the windshield as he drove to looking at the recorded map and sensor information of the car. The drive went on for a while until our sensors picked up several approaching vehicles.

"We're here, boys. Leo, you better stay respectful and let Rollo do the talking."

Leo nodded in response before we exited the car together.

This time, instead of just the Wells Clan security team coming to escort us, Sarah was here as well. She lightly skipped over and was about to leap at me, only to be stopped by the woman behind her grabbing the hem of her shirt.

Sarah calmed down to straighten her shirt before greeting me. "Welcome back, Rollo! It's been a while. How are you?"

"I'd like to say great, but some issues have come up. I'm hoping to find a solution here today, with the help of your clan."

"So the spacers' wars are affecting you too, huh?"

"You guys sure are well-informed."

"Well, yeah, we have some people who regularly go out into the cities. It's their job to bring back news as well. Anyway, follow me. Dad already knows you're here and will see you right away."

Leo and Vin silently walked behind me as I followed Sarah and her entourage towards the familiar building where their chief resided. On the way, I continued to make small talk about how we were doing, and I learned that Caleb was busy studying. Their school was focused on practical skills for survival in the wasteland.

When we arrived, we were ushered into the room where Chief Eugene resided.

"Welcome, Rollo. I hope you have been doing well in these turbulent times."

"Thank you for your warm welcome, Gene. I actually came here to see if you could help me solve a problem that arose exactly because of these 'turbulent times.'"

He stroked his beard as he stared blankly into the air. "Speak freely and we'll see if we can be of assistance."

"Then I'll get straight to the point. I would like to request that your clan allow us to operate a transportation business through your territory."

"Transportation, you say? I take it you won't only be transporting your own company's cargo?" He stared me straight in the eyes.

"Correct."

He closed his eyes while he lit his pipe, and only spoke again when he exhaled the fumes. "We cannot allow you to help our foes circumvent us so you may make profits, especially not after they tried to kidnap our children and use them to force us to do their bidding."

"We'll be sure to not do any business with the corporations that wronged you. You must understand that corporations are divided and are competitors amongst themselves."

"I fully understand. Exploiting that understanding is how we've managed to survive with minimal interference from any corporation for so long. But what will my people or the other clans say when they see us cozying up to you city folks after the incident with the children?"

*Shit... The wasteland political situation isn't as simple as I thought.*

The room stilled. Our conversation came to a halt while I tried to think of ways to make it work. The silence was only broken when Gene finished smoking his pipe and laid it down.

"The only way we would approve your request is if you assist us with destroying the evildoers who were behind Sarah and Caleb's kidnapping."

"As much as I'd like to help, I don't think I can help with that." Picking a fight with a corporation when I wasn't even a newcomer yet would do me more harm than good.

"Let me tell you about them first, before you decline."

I nodded at his request. There was nothing to lose from it.

"They are a new corporation called Qwklink Logistics. We've investigated quite a bit about them and have already been targeting all of their convoys and their partners for quite a while. Although we are doing a lot of damage on that front, we cannot touch them in the cities. Otherwise, the other corporations would band together to remove us."

"I see. So you want us to take them out for you."

"That's right. If you attacked them, it would just be another day's squabble between corporations. If we attacked them, we would prove to be a threat and a target for elimination. We want you to remove their presence from around our territory. Here is the information we have on them." He went to the corner of the room and found a folder to give me.

I opened it to find real paper, something I had rarely seen since coming to this world. I couldn't help but lose myself in nostalgia for a second, feeling the texture of the paper before reading its contents.

"They may be a new corp," I said as I looked through, "but they have branches not just in NLA and Firebird, but in Miles High, and Can Sauce City." I raised an eyebrow.

"We only want you to cripple their ability to do business in NLA and Firebird, to destroy their route that crosses into our territory. Their headquarters is in Miles High, so it should still be doable."

*"Only" and "doable," he says.* It might be doable in NLA, but going to a new city to attack a corp wasn't to be taken lightly. Plus, this could easily earn us a powerful enemy, if not done right.

"Give me some time to consider it first."

"Very well. There is nothing we can do without your help, so we are not in a position to hurry."

I held back a sigh at his words.

*Right, I'm not the only one that's in a hurry here. I'm going to have to discuss this with Vin and Leo, and maybe convince Claire that attacking a corporation isn't a stupid idea. Well, at least it'll be interesting to pitch to them.*

# CHAPTER 44

## FIREBIRD

"You guys want to do *what* over there?!" Claire's image in my optics video call leaned forward as she chastised us like children.

"We plan to attack Qwklink Logistics' facilities in NLA and Firebird to destroy their route. They're a corp that's only been around for a year or so, and it's just their branches and not headquarters."

"That doesn't change the fact that they're a legitimate corporation. You're going to antagonize them big-time! Think clearly, Rollo, is this really worth it?"

"Yes, I've thought about it all night. This recent shipping issue has highlighted a real weakness for us. We're at the mercy of those we outsource our logistics to. If we go through with this, we'll be able to establish our own transportation network we can profit from."

"You want to go into the logistics business?"

"Yes. Our advantages will allow us to operate at much lower costs than others." I was careful not to mention our relationship with wastelanders over the call. God knows who could be listening.

"And what do you think about this, Vin? Are you sure they're people we can mess with?"

Before he could answer, Leo cleared his throat and jumped in. "I spent all of yesterday and this morning looking into them. While they are definitely bigger than us, they are also very spread out across four different cities."

"Yeah, but what if they have some elite hit squad that will retaliate against us?"

"They're a relatively new corporation that had to spend heavily on security for their transportation routes, so they shouldn't have enough money accumulated to form anything elite. They have also been deep in the red for the past while with their Firebird-to-NLA route because of all the attacks from wastelanders. They shouldn't be willing to invest much into their nearby branches, at least not anything we can't handle."

"So there's still a chance—"

From the video, I could see Thorne pulling at Claire's shirt hem. "Calm down, you know Leo knows what he's talking about."

They argued in whispers for a short while before Claire's attention turned back to the call. "Fine," she said, "do what you think is best. You're the boss, after all. Just don't get killed."

"Don't worry, I'm not eager to pick fights I can't win either."

The call soon ended, and I met Vin and Leo in my office for further discussion in a more secure setting. The people who weren't physically here had no need to hear the details of our plans.

Before we jumped straight into it, I questioned Vin. "So, you think we have what it takes to do this?"

"Yes, but not alone. We'll be able to handle their facilities in NLA if the objective is to just cripple their route. We'll just have to make it too expensive for them to continue running it by attacking their valuable assets. Though in the case of Firebird, we'd have to hire mercenaries to do the job so we can hit them in both cities at the same time. I don't know any reliable QGs there, so I'll have to go to the city myself."

"No, I'll be the one to go to Firebird, then. You take care of things here. You're better at commanding the people you've trained."

"Is that really wise? There are a lot of things that can go wrong in an unfamiliar city. There'll be some serious risks."

"Not much different from anywhere else. I did come to NLA alone at first, too."

"But you knew me already. This time you'll be going in completely alone with no connections."

"I'll go with him," Leo chimed in. He gave me a nod that I reciprocated.

"Fine, I'll send a team to escort you guys over. Then you'll have to be careful."

We then fleshed out the details of the plan, how we would coordinate, and some contingencies.

*On paper, it's a quick sabotage mission. Hopefully, it'll be as simple as it appears.*

* * *

The next day, we rode into the wasteland with two Vanguards. The sandstorm continued to rage on as always, allowing for no visibility once we entered.

This entire trip would take an estimated two full days if we didn't encounter any issues. It was going to suck not having the everyday conveniences I was used to during that time, especially a shower, but there simply wasn't a better way to travel across the wasteland. We had three people in each car, so we had a rotation going where one person rested in the back.

*I should consider hiring a team there once everything settles because it will be hell to make the trip back with just me and Leo.*

It was my turn in the driver's seat, but I wasn't really driving, just ensuring we didn't crash into anything the sensors picked up and keeping us heading straight.

To kill the boredom, Leo and I were currently playing a game of chess through our optics. It was simply too much of a hassle to use a terminal when the car was on the move. Even though it took up some space in our vision, we could still watch videos and keep an eye on the sensors while we played.

"So, how's it going between you and Lana recently?" I started a conversation, as I was stumped on how to get out of the bad position I was in.

"Nothing special, same as always."

"What, really? It's obvious she's into you. Just move in together or something already."

"We agreed to focus on our careers for now. Can we talk about something else?" He turned to stare straight into my eyes.

"Okay, okay, sure. So why did you guys decide to join my company? I thought you wanted to be back with one of the bigger corps, not a tiny business that isn't even an official corporation yet."

"You know both me and Lana have a black mark with our old corporation. We're not likely to get hired back by them, and all the other corps won't either, since they prefer to raise their own cybersecurity personnel for obvious reasons."

That wasn't a surprise. I too would be hesitant to hire someone I didn't know and let them manage sensitive parts of the business. They could easily be a spy.

"Besides, I know you. I'd rather work for someone who I know is a good guy, especially with all the shit we've seen in our time as mercenaries."

*He's definitely mistaken about me being a good guy. I'm a greedy person who simply uses whoever can help me turn a profit.* I wasn't going to refute a compliment, though.

We continued our trip with idle chat and took turns sleeping in the back. They let me sleep during the night while the other employee took over the night shift. It wasn't a fancy bed or anything, but cars always had a way of luring me to sleep.

Just as I felt my consciousness fade, the vehicle swerved to the left. I immediately sat up to assess the situation.

"What is going…" I couldn't finish my sentence as I spotted a giant shadow rapidly stretching upward through the side window. It was visible through the gaps of the sandstorm thanks to flares someone had launched. The cylindrical monster was at least thirty feet in diameter. I couldn't hear it at all, as the sound of the sandstorm was overwhelming.

"What the hell is that?"

"Hell if I know," Leo yelled back from the driver's seat. "Some giant mutant, but who cares? I'm not going to stay around to find out."

I glanced back at the monster. It was still growing. "It's chasing us. Step on it!"

"I already am! Get on the turret and try to slow it down or something! Aaron, go back there to assist him."

While the security guard sitting beside Leo climbed into the backseat, I popped open the hatch into the gunner's cockpit, which was fully shielded from the elements. Getting behind the turret, I aimed towards the monstrosity within the twister.

It was keeping up with us despite our Vanguard going as fast as it safely could, given we were driving in the sand while minding obstacles. I couldn't even spot any limbs or body to shoot at, so I aimed low and pulled the trigger. The night vision provided by my optics made it easy to spot the bright tracer rounds I fired every few bullets, which helped correct my aim.

A low growl rang out in response to my bullets, and the creature sped up.

I kept holding the trigger down as I yelled, "I think we pissed it off!"

"So you got its attention, then, good. Aaron, tell team two to shoot it from another direction. Let's see if we can take turns drawing him between us."

"Roger," said the man reloading my turret below.

Not long after, I spotted tracer rounds firing at the creature from a different direction, and I took the cue to cease fire. The colossal creature appeared to entirely ignore the new threat until well over a hundred bullets had been fired. Much to our relief, it seemed to be fed up with the constant gunfire pelting it and changed targets to the other car.

"Good, it's working," Leo celebrated.

"Sir, at this rate, we'll run out of ammo before long!" Aaron said as he finished loading a new belt of ammo.

I heard Leo hiss just before I started firing again. The two cars continued to take turns drawing its attention, ping-ponging it between us.

After the fifth belt of ammo was expended, Leo's voice rang out again. "I detected some ruins up ahead with some big buildings still intact. Hold on."

I was focused on the target, so I didn't bother trying to spot what he was talking about and continued shooting. Before long, the ground below changed from sand and dirt to concrete, and then buildings started to appear and pass by.

The creature came to a halt near the edge of the buildings. It then let out another growl before shrinking down, burrowing back into the ground.

"It stopped chasing us," I said as I threw myself back onto the backseat. "Let's regroup and spend the night here, and hope it goes away."

"Agreed," Leo said. "Whatever that was, I don't want to see it again."

* * *

After we regrouped, we spent the night in some derelict building. It was always impressive to me how these structures weren't just filled entirely with sand, and could provide shelter despite their shoddy appearance.

In the morning, we resumed our trip, and thankfully, there weren't any giant mutants chasing us down this time. From there, we enjoyed an uneventful trip until we could make out the skyline of the city two days after our encounter.

"It looks pretty much the same as any other metropolis..." I couldn't help but mutter.

"What were you expecting? Some fiery buildings?" Leo replied as he popped up from the backseat.

"Nothing in particular, really. It's a little comforting to see, actually. I can't wait to take a shower and get some food."

It wasn't long until we got close enough to see traffic, both on the ground and in the skies above, where flying vehicles zipped by.

Having gotten used to sitting in the car for such a long time, driving a bit longer to reach the hotel was no big deal for me. Even with the traffic, it felt like an instant passed before we arrived and our escorts started their return trip.

*Good luck to them. Hopefully, they won't encounter that thing again. The last thing I want to do is pay hefty compensation if anything happens to them.*

After I got cleaned up, I immediately began my search for any information on the colossal creature we encountered. Unfortunately, information wasn't freely posted on the web in this world, and I only came across dubious anecdotes. Not even paid libraries had much on the wasteland, as it wasn't in the corporations' best interest to spread that info around.

Having given up, I tried out the milkshakes here and went with Leo to an establishment he found where we could get into contact with a Quest Giver. Unlike in NLA and Elevate City, where the places we went to were bars, this was an underground casino.

Though it was operating openly on the streets rather than sneakily in the back alleys, I knew it was underground because every single corporation supported gambling bans.

It only made sense, as having your employees addicted to gambling was a serious security risk and made them unproductive, so I was surprised to see people operating a casino here out here so blatantly.

I couldn't even make it to the crowded entrance of the place before I felt someone grab onto my legs.

"Sir! Please help me."

# CHAPTER 45

## FRIGHTENED

I glanced down to find a man in a business suit lying on the ground, grabbing onto me, pleading for help.

"Get off him! What are you doing?" Leo stepped forward and tried to push him away. I also spotted the security nearby walking briskly past the casino's crowd and towards us.

"Sir, please, they have my daughter. They won't give me her until I pay them. Please lend me some credits," the man begged, holding my legs tightly and continuing to resist Leo's attempts at removing him.

While it would probably have been a lot easier for me to push him off myself, seeing as I was the one with cybernetic arms, I decided to see this one through.

"Why don't you tell us your story inside, over a drink?" I gestured for Leo to let go of him.

"But Rollo! There's no—"

I sent a quick text over to him. *As much as I trust your information-gathering abilities, might as well get some information from a local like him.*

The security reached us before he could respond. "Sir, is everything okay?" The bulky man looked at me as if waiting for my permission to inflict violence upon the man.

"Yes, everything is fine. He's just a little drunk."

The security guard sighed with a look of disappointment and turned back.

I was grateful we didn't make a scene like I had expected, and we could casually enter the casino without drawing any attention. We passed through a security scanner, where more guards stood by. They didn't comment on our firearms and let us proceed unobstructed.

The first things that came into view were lines of vending machines that dispensed game chips. Card game tables could be seen further in, with crowds of dangerous-looking people gambling. In the middle of the room was a bar with a seating area on a slightly elevated platform.

We headed straight towards the middle, where we found a small table that sat four. A server immediately came to us and took our order before leaving the three of us in an awkward silence.

"Leo, can you go get us some chips? It would be weird coming here without at least getting those."

Taking the hint, he nodded and backtracked towards the vending machines.

"So, umm..."

"Garland, my name is Garland."

"Garland, I'll listen to your story, but in exchange, you'll answer some of our questions. Sound fair?"

"Right, of course. Please, lend me some credits. I got ahead of myself and took a chance, but now my daughter has to pay for it. Please, it should be me who faces the consequences."

He continued rambling nonstop about his life story, even when the server delivered our drinks. Basically, he was having a hard time due to the passing of his wife, but was forced to continue working. And to no one's surprise, he soon made a mistake that resulted in him being fired from his corporation.

The corp made him pay them to compensate for the damages this firing caused, which didn't leave him enough to pay for his daughter's schooling. Unwilling to put her in the public schools, he tried his hand at the casino that he now had the free time to visit.

"I can pay you for useful information," I said. "How much do you know about the QGs around here, the corporations, and the local situation?"

I listened to him, slowly drinking. From the corner of my eye, I spotted Leo strolling by, dropping off some chips and ditching us.

The man finished shortly after I was done with my drink, providing me a basic overview from a corpo's perspective. It wasn't anything exciting, but it was nice to know.

In the end, I decided to pay him his requested amount of five thousand credits, provided he promise to leave this city with his daughter. Mostly because I didn't want to leave any easy trails to track me down if anything went wrong. Five thousand also wasn't that much to me anymore. Probably not a strikingly large sum for him either, if he didn't rein in his expenses and continued spending like a corpo.

"Are you done with your charity yet?" Leo teased as soon as he sat down, once the man was gone.

"It wasn't charity, it was an additional source of information."

"Find out anything useful, then?"

"Mostly names of QGs that aren't afraid to work against corporations."

"Well, yeah, most that operate here openly will fit that criteria. There's an understanding to let these QGs operate, as they're useful when they need to deal with rival corps."

"Then let's go find one. Shouldn't be too hard, since we're dealing with a small-time corp."

"Way ahead of you. While you had your chat, I set up a meeting already."

We had a few hours until the meeting, so we killed some time making use of the chips I made Leo exchange. Surprisingly, the game we played was like one I knew of from my world, baccarat.

Leo simply watched as I went on a roll. By the time we had to leave, I'd doubled the two thousand credits I started with.

The meeting took place in a normal-looking office on a different floor that contrasted heavily with the casino we were just in. People walked around cubicles, the sound of conversations and the constant ringing of the phones filling the area. However, the moment we stepped into the meeting room, all the noise ceased as soon as the door closed.

Sitting inside was an overweight man in a suit who gestured for us to take a seat in front of him with a smile.

"Welcome, the name's Roger. How can I help you today?"

I glanced around the room to find it very bare, but with my knowledge of stealth technologies, I could spot several hidden spaces big enough for turrets within the ceiling and walls.

"We're looking to hire some people for a job. I heard you are well-acquainted with all the mercenaries in the city."

"I see. Is it for logistic security across the wasteland, if I may ask? I assure you of my confidentiality on anything you share with me, but of course, you can let me know as much or as little as you want. It'll just be harder to find the perfect match for you."

"No, it'll be within the city. We'll need someone with discretion and a tight lip."

"Of course, though you'll find that the prices are a little high at the moment. A lot of people are hiring short-term contractors for the moment due to the spacer war. The remaining operators are of higher quality or looking for lower-risk jobs, and I think that between the two, the former is what you're looking for."

"Yes, we'll need enough to form two teams to sabotage secure locations."

"Very well. I will contact you tomorrow," Roger stood up to declare.

We then paid the deposit he asked for and returned to our hotel. I half expected someone to follow us, but we didn't detect anything.

"Are you sure we can trust this QG? The vibe he gave off was really different from the ones I worked with back in Elevate City." I couldn't help but voice my concern as we stepped into my room.

"Should be fine, just a different culture around here. My corporation used to debrief us about it when we went to new places. And it's not like Qwklink is expecting us to be here and has a trap ready for us."

We then discussed our scouting plan for tomorrow before he returned to his room. True to my habit, I decided to gear up, take a stroll, and see where Firebird needed my community cleaning services.

* * *

**Lucy—Mercenary**

*Shit, this can't be happening to me. It was supposed to be an easy delivery job.*

She caught her breath as she hid in a dark alleyway behind a dumpster. She took stock of her weapons as she tried to ignore the pain from ribs that were likely fractured.

*I can't believe Jo, Bartha, and Angel are all dead. How did those gangbangers know which route we took? Damn it, this isn't the time to think. I have to get out alive, screw the job.*

Her auditory implant picked up the sound of a car door opening nearby, and then several sets of footsteps running in her direction. She held her breath and tried to stay as quiet as possible as one drew close.

"Come on out and play," a man yelled. "I promise we'll be nicer to you than we were to your friends, little lady. That is, if you willingly hand over the package, of course." His words were followed by laughter from the people behind him.

They continued walking down the alley until they stood just in front of Lucy, but they didn't spot her, thanks to all the cardboard and garbage bags in the way. The man at the front repeated his message as he occasionally clanged his rifle into the metal pipes and dumpsters around them.

Now that she could look them over, their outfits and tattoos gave away their affiliation: Gearheads, from one of the larger gangs in Firebird.

Taking the chance once they walked by her, she got up and moved in the opposite direction. Just as she pushed off the ground with her prosthetic arm, it groaned and the joints locked up.

*Damn junk must've taken some damage from the crash.*

"Over here!" a voice rang out, followed by footsteps growing louder.

She made a run for it, throwing anything she could find in the path behind her, hoping to buy some time. Deep down inside, she knew it was futile, since there was a small chance their car had already left. She might've had a chance if she could sneak by, but that was no longer an option.

When she came out of the alley, she had her gun raised, ready to go down fighting. What greeted her instead was a parked van, eerily quiet.

*No way... Did they all get out of the car to chase me? Are they stupid enough to leave their car unattended?*

Approaching the car with her weapon at the ready, she spotted two bodies slumped over in the front seats. Glancing around, she found no one on this side street. She listened for any sounds, but for some reason, it had become completely quiet. Before she knew it, even the footsteps of her pursuers were entirely gone.

For some godforsaken reason, she decided to backtrack down the alley she had just emerged from, only to find her pursuers all sprawled around on the ground.

*Hell no! Whoever is responsible, I want no part of it.*

"Leave me alone, I'm just the deliveryman! You can have it!" She threw down the package her team was supposed to deliver and started running out of the alley as fast as she could.

Her mind was a blur, and before she knew it, she was driving the van down the street.

*I'm done being a mercenary. I don't care anymore even if I have to put up with some corpo asshole boss. As long as it's a stable job, I'm fine even if it's boring.*

She quickly selected her QG from her contact list.

"Lucy? Where's Jo—"

She didn't have time for this anymore. She wanted to go home and be done with all of this. "They're dead, the gig was a shitshow, we lost the package, and I'm done! Goodbye."

* * *

I leaned over to pick up what the woman had left behind. I felt a little sorry for scaring her. She'd suddenly showed up behind me and screamed, but before I had the chance to say anything, she threw something down and hysterically ran away.

Opening the package, I found a small data chip. I knew better than to plug random chips into my network. Good thing I had Leo around.

# CHAPTER 46

## *CLOAK*

The day after I found the chip, I handed it off to Leo to deal with while I sat back and relaxed to check my stats.

**Status**
**Level:** 14
**EXP:** 320/1400
**Musculoskeletal:** 76
**Neural Reflex:** 15
**Visuomotor Coordination:** 27
**Endurance:** 24
**Sensory Perception:** 52
**Upgrade Points:** 0
**Upgrades:**
     Stealth +7
     Hacking +3
     Cybernetic Engineering +7
     Stealth Technology +9
     Software Engineering +6
**Enhancements:**
     SAID: Zenitech Hoth Mk.3
     Optics: Nova Tech Stars Mk.4
     Cyberarm (Left): Nova Tech Mudra Mk.6
     Cyberarm (Right): Nova Tech Shiva Mk.5

Auditory: Amazing Corp FieldTac Gen 2
Cardiovascular: BioGen Labs Marathon 4
Miscellaneous: HSU Custom Shade

I realized I was still quite a ways from leveling up, but seeing the daily progress never failed to motivate me. Well, that and the new knowledge the system offered was also a bit addicting. It scratched the itch of my curiosity, and figuring out how to apply the new theories was always a good challenge.

However, at some point I would need to decide on a new direction to take, as it wasn't a smart move to sell more advanced stealth tech to the general public. It would only draw the ire of other corps and give away information that could jeopardize our security.

The system had a large selection to choose from, but with leveling up getting more and more difficult, it would take a while to start off in a new field, not to talk about the investment and equipment needed along with the know-how.

We currently were looking to dive into the transportation business, mainly to become self-sufficient. Maybe I should search for options that could complement that.

The obvious choice would be to research vehicles, but that encompassed various scientific disciplines that couldn't be covered by only one research option in the system. Maybe if I targeted a specific aspect of vehicles, I could hire the relevant personnel for the rest.

There were other options to explore as well, though I wasn't in a hurry to decide. For now, I didn't even have any spare points. I should focus on our current objective in Firebird, or I would be counting the chickens before they hatch.

"Hey, Roll, that chip you gave me is heavily encrypted," Leo said as he walked into my workshop.

"So we can't find out what's on it?"

"No, we can, but it'll take over a week at the minimum."

"Then just—"

An incoming text covered up the corner of my vision. *This is Roger, we talked yesterday. I've put together a team, I'm sending you the information and where to meet them later today.*

"What's up?" Leo asked.

"Got the message from last night's QG. We got a meeting in an hour and a half."

"Send me the info and let's head out. We can grab some food and check out the meeting place at the same time."

* * *

I walked up to a small group huddled around their car in a secluded alleyway. "Kurt? I'm Cloak."

He looked me over. "Can't say we're glad to have an outsider on the team, but it's the client's request. Try not to get in our way."

I had these mercenaries agree to take along one of my people so I could join incognito. Leo was also with the other team, monitoring them remotely so we could coordinate with Vin's strike team in NLA. There was no need for him to be disguised, as he would be sitting in the back, on his terminal, like a typical client.

In my case, I wanted to join in on the action, so I had to minimize the chances that Qwklink Logistics would recognize me.

With more points in stealth tech now, I'd upgraded my personal cybernetics as well as my security team's, though I kept the best to myself. The uptime my new implants allowed for was way longer, with better energy capacity and lower cooldown time. They also hid me from various forms of detection common to typical corporate high-security systems.

With that said, they weren't perfect. I was still physically there, so any weight-based detection or physical contact could still give me away.

For this outing, I chose to wear a mask and visor to keep my face hidden and clothing that didn't show any skin. I definitely looked like some sketchy person you did not want to get involved with.

The sound of a clap drew my attention. "Okay, it's almost time. Everyone get in the car, and we'll discuss any final details on the way."

There were only three mercs here besides Kurt, their leader. Being the quality outfit the QG had advertised, they all wore standardized tactical equipment. It was a sore spot for me, as my own security still appeared to be a motley crew, sporting different gear and equipment.

The moment the car got moving, Kurt continued, "So Tera will run cy-sec in the car as usual and be in contact with the other team, who will be executing this operation at the same time as us. Our target is a vehicle maintenance facility, so expect a lot of cars. Our focus is sabotaging high-value and hard-to-replace equipment. Any questions?"

"How are we taking care of any witnesses?" A man with short green hair spoke up, his helmet held under his arm.

"They are not a priority. Eliminate any obstacles, but no need to chase after any runners. Our main goal is just sabotage."

The man nodded. "What about him? This will be a quick and chaotic operation. I don't want to trust my back to an unknown." He glared at me.

"You'll have to—"

"I'll move separately from you," I interjected. "We'll stay connected to avoid friendly fire, but otherwise, I'll be a distance away."

"It's up to you," Kurt responded. "I have no authority over you, but to ensure you don't jeopardize our mission, I'll have to ask you to wait for our signal before starting anything."

"Sure, be my guest."

With our plan settled, we parked a distance away. The target facility was located in a suburban area, surrounded by a few buildings. It was a huge warehouse that acted as the storage and maintenance facility for the Firebird branch of Qwklink Logistics.

I trailed Kurt's team along the sidewalk as we drew near, staying a small distance behind them. Once they were near the target warehouse, they took a deep breath and started running straight at the building, right through the front toll gates. The security mainly kept unauthorized cars out, which didn't pose any obstruction when the team of three attacked on foot. They shot the two guards in the booth and rushed into the compound.

Their plan was to go in fast and hard, with explosives to blow apart any obstacles in their way and any machinery they could reach. Then they would leave before a more organized response could be mustered.

The garage doors meant for trucks were all closed, but the thin sheets of metal were quickly blown out of the way.

While they went loud and got the party started, I activated my new and improved active camouflage and moved slightly away from the commotion.

Not long after they went inside the warehouse, I spotted a door slamming open and a squad of five security guards rushing out, decked out in armor. I took out a grenade from the pack on my hip and set the timer to three seconds before activating it and slipping it into the tactical vest a guard was wearing.

I then dashed through the door they came from. Before it could slam shut, the explosion vibrated the ground beneath me. My experience notification indicated only three confirmed kills, though I was sure the other two weren't fit for combat anymore. For this gig, I would rather do maximum damage to the facility and worry about experience points later.

Inside, the guardroom near the entrance was empty. The hallway was filled with the sound of people scrambling about. As I turned the corner, I found people rushing towards the exits, past the commotion.

They were no threat, so I left them be, and made my way through until I spotted a room labeled "Machinery."

Instead of a grenade, I had explosive packs prepared for this, similar to the ones Kurt used to blow his team's way into the maintenance bay. I placed them evenly around the machinery room and activated the switch once I was back in the hallway.

The explosions caused even more panic as the employees double-timed out of the premises. With fewer people in the way, I soon came upon the storage room, and blew the place up.

I heard several other explosions in the distance, which should mean Kurt's team was progressing well.

Up the stairs, I found my last room: the supervisor's office. The door was locked and, since this was a shock-and-awe day, I allowed my cybernetic arms to utilize all their strength and slammed a shoulder into the door. The flimsy thing came off at the hinges and landed boldly in the room, crumpled up.

"What the fuck?" a man yelled out in terror as our eyes met. Coming to a realization, he quickly reached for a drawer at his desk. A gunshot rang out.

*+10 EXP*

He slumped down in his chair while I cleared the room of any other threats.

The nameplate on the desk said he was some supply chain manager. As a business owner, I knew too well how difficult it was to find qualified and experienced people, so hopefully this loss added another incentive for Qwklink to pull out from this city.

I noticed his handheld terminal still had an ongoing connection, so I disconnected it, even though it was likely too late.

With that done, I glanced out his office window, which had a clear view of the large open area where their trucks were serviced and parked. I could spot flaming wrecks where the service bays once were and bodies spread across the asphalt.

I entered the open area and rendezvoused with Kurt, who stood guard as his companions busied themselves rigging the place up with explosives.

I deactivated my camouflage before approaching him. "You guys finished?"

His body tensed as it snapped towards me, but relaxed after he met my eyes. "Yes, we were about to clear the back halls real quick and head out. Our spotter outside picked up some activity, so we don't have long."

"I got that taken care of. Let's head out once you guys are done here."

He nodded slowly and gestured to his team with hand signs that I couldn't decipher.

Not long after, we were all on our way out of the compound. Several firetrucks were parked outside, but they simply ignored us as we ran by. As if on cue, a thunderous explosion rang out behind us the moment we crossed the toll gates.

Ignoring the screaming crowd of employees, we moved into a discreet alleyway, where our ride was waiting.

We drove in silence back to where we had met, and I texted Leo the latest updates. After a few minutes, I could make out the parking lot, but just as we turned in, an incoming call blocked out a corner of my vision. It was Leo.

"R—Cloak! If you guys are done, then get over here ASAP. Our team here is pinned down. They have some serious guys over here."

"You okay?" I instantly asked.

"Yeah, I'm monitoring the situation remotely, but the mercenary team has already taken casualties. It's become a shitshow over there."

"Okay, understood." I inspected the mercenaries around me, who seemed to still be fresh, and told them, "The other team needs our help. Our employer has agreed to give out bonuses as outlined in the contract if you assist. You guys in?"

Their team whistled in unison before Kurt responded, "Let's go. We were thinking the gig was going just a little too smoothly. Something always goes wrong. Glad the fuckup wasn't on our end."

# CHAPTER 47

## REINFORCEMENTS

We pulled up right next to an armored van parked casually on the side of the street. Just as I walked up to it, the windows came down, and Leo's face popped out.

"Took you long enough. Connecting you to the live feeds now—oh, and do you still have those EI rounds?"

I reached into one of the pockets on my tactical vest. "Yeah, loading them up now."

I didn't need to question why, because the next moment, camera footage appeared in the corner of my vision and showed me. I commanded my SAID to center the screen and give me a closer look at two men decked out in cybernetics.

"Those cyborgs are some mercenaries they hired for their convoys, which happen to be refueling in the facility we're hitting tonight. They're a team of five who all share an obsessive interest in cybernetics. Our team took out three already in the opening ambush, with the sacrifice of one of theirs."

As sad as it was to hear someone I hired had died on the job, I couldn't help but be a little relieved I had hired some of Roger's top operators. Otherwise, this could've gone a lot worse.

"The team is pinned down inside the warehouse, and they don't have the firepower anymore to take down the remaining two walking tanks, not to talk about the incoming reinforcements."

"Okay, I'll go hit them with the EI rounds. You go coordinate the team here to draw the reinforcements' attention."

I jogged towards the logistics warehouse that served as a fueling station and parking lot for Qwklink. There were obvious signs of gunshots and explosions around, and I spotted a hole in one of the garage doors.

From the live feed in my optics, I could hear occasional gunshots and see people running across the screen. With my camouflage active, knowing I wouldn't have to be too mindful of being spotted, I rushed in.

I stalked around the warehouse. It was more like an indoor parking lot with only cargo trucks, and the vehicles blocked any visibility. Heading towards the sound of fighting, I soon spotted a figure peeking out from behind a truck, taking potshots at the two approaching cyborgs. They kept retreating, using the trucks as cover, while the two beefy men cautiously took cover every time they shot back.

*They must be wary of any surprises, since their comrades got taken out. The small arms fire they're dishing out will have a hard time penetrating all their chrome and armor.*

Readying the Suri that I had loaded with the electronic intrusion rounds, I took aim at the back of the closest target. The bullet might only travel at subsonic speeds, but when I was this close and, he was caught off guard, it was still too fast for the man to react. I fired.

I trusted Leo to breach the cyborg's systems as fast as he could, even without my signal, and pointed my gun at the next target even before the first started to buckle. But what I saw was only a blur that swooped behind the cyborg I had already shot.

His submachine gun then poked up from the armpit of his slumping friend and started spraying bullets in my direction.

Thankfully, I had already moved behind a truck and begun to reposition myself for a better angle.

Before I could be relieved, the man fished out a few grenades from his pack and threw them all around him, prompting me to dive behind cover.

An electric beep rang out, followed by thunderous explosions—or not. Instead, my SAID alerted me to several errors, and then I witnessed my active camouflage glitching out until it deactivated entirely.

*Shit, those must've been EMP grenades!*

There was a moment of silence all of a sudden as we each waited for the next move. I stole glances at the cyborg and noted he was the only one remaining, as his friend lay motionless on the floor nearby.

He must've spotted me, because a rain of bullets chased me as I returned to cover. I stayed prone and crawled away while I commanded my SAID to text the mercenary team in here with me.

*Thank God my SAID still works.*

I heard the cyborg scramble towards where I was last seen, so I hurried behind another row of trucks.

More gunshots rang out, probably from my allies. I allowed the stealth skills engrained in my body to take over and peeked out when the cyborg was distracted. Then I managed to fire two shots at him before ducking out of the way of his bullets.

This time, he threw caution out to the wind and started sprinting straight towards me, ignoring my allies. I fumbled around my utility belt and threw a grenade in his path. The explosion that followed would've definitely made my ears ring from being so close if it wasn't for my auditory implant.

Standing, I tried to regain my balance, but before I was fully up, the cyborg appeared out of the smoke covered in scratches, yet still functional. He threw his damaged gun away and went into another charge.

I timed my next moves, ready to sidestep and aim my railgun once he passed by, but I didn't need to pull the trigger. The cyborg was lying face-first on the ground with his mechanical limbs frozen in place. He shifted as he tried to move, but to no avail.

Taking no chances, I moved closer to the guaranteed headshot on the side of his head, where the plating was thinner.

*+20 EXP*

I went back to his friend and put him out of his misery too. The last thing I needed was a human tank rampaging around the city, looking for revenge. The experience points were definitely a good incentive as well.

Was the system conditioning me to kill? I should be a little more mindful of that before I became someone who killed as easily as breathing. Still, I'd do what was needed in order to survive and thrive. That hadn't changed since the day I was born.

The three mercenaries I had hired soon popped out from behind a truck, with one of them carrying a body over their shoulder. There were five of them last time we met, so they were all accounted for, including the one outside working the cybersecurity.

Our eyes met, but before we could open our mouths, more gunshots rang out from outside the building.

"How much time do you guys need to finish sabotaging this place?"

"We'll need five more minutes, minimum. We didn't get that much time before we had to deal with these shitbags." Kurt glared behind me at the bodies.

"Okay, try to go as fast as you can. I'll go help the team outside." I ran off and got on a voice call with Leo.

"What's the situation outside? I'm heading back out now."

"Kurt's team blew up the leading vehicle and blocked the road in with the wreck. They're in a stalemate, shooting at each other in cover, so they should hold for a while, assuming no more reinforcements show up."

I checked up on my customized Shade unit to see if it could still turn on the active camouflage, but my SAID indicated a few components were fried.

*I guess I'll have to fight fair and square this time. I'd rather not try to sneak up on over a dozen trained corporate goons without the camouflage, no matter how weak Qwklink Logistics is compared to other corporations.*

"Let Kurt know I'm coming out with him."

"You're not going to flank them?"

"No, some asshole fried my cybernetic with some EMP."

*Now that I think about it, only my Shade unit was completely fried, but the rest of my cybernetics were fine. I really need to upgrade it to be EMP-resistant, but that isn't exactly my forte.*

I soon reached the battle, took cover, and joined the defensive line. It was honestly way more boring than I had expected. We simply blind fired at each other from cover, and no one did anything to break out of the stalemate.

Not long after, we got a signal indicating the sabotage was done and we could begin the retreat.

"Cloak," Leo said, "they're blowing out an exit on the other side of the compound. Get out of there quick."

"You sure they don't have anyone waiting to ambush us outside?" I asked.

"Yeah, I'm monitoring it. They don't have any more forces to spare, since they had to split half their forces to the other maintenance facility you were just at." An explosion shook the ground behind Leo's voice.

No longer wanting to waste ammo, I rallied Kurt's team. We threw the last of our grenades and explosives and faked a push towards our adversaries.

By the time we cut through the building, we spotted the hole in the wall that was our ticket out. Just like Leo said, there were no surprises, and we were picked up by our getaway vehicles.

* * *

**Daniel—Qwklink Logistics**

The tension in the air was so thick Daniel was sure he could cut into it if he held out a knife. Jared's holographic figure projected across from him wasn't helping either, constantly taking sips.

Setting down the cup from his twentieth sip this minute, Jared turned his gaze to him as he cleared his throat. "Daniel, you're related to the boss, right? Please put in a good word for me. I'd be satisfied even if I got demoted."

*This fool...*

He couldn't help but burst out in laughter.

"What's so funny, Daniel? Come on, answer! You're scaring me."

Daniel reached out and took a sip before answering out of petty revenge. "You really think we're just going to get a slap on the wrist? This was our chance to turn the company's wastelander situation around, with the demand for transportation rising through the roof. But now, out of nowhere, our entire operation on the West Coast has come to a halt because of this attack."

"If we could just get some more funding to re—"

"No! We're done, you and I both. Our route has barely been turning a profit with those feral wastelanders getting in the way. There's no way headquarters would approve any more funds to help us get back on our feet."

"Then at the very least, just—"

The projection buzzing to life at the head of the table stopped Jared mid-sentence. The duo stood up at the same time and bowed towards their boss.

The silver-haired CEO relaxed into his chair and crossed his legs. "Tell me, why should I tolerate you two any longer?" He held his gaze on Jared first before moving to Daniel. Despite how laid-back he appeared, his aura of authority pressed them until they felt they couldn't breathe.

"Sir, please give us another chance!" Jared's legs gave way, and he fell to his knees.

"I didn't ask for an apology. I asked for an explanation. Tell me, did you even figure out who attacked our facilities?"

Daniel swallowed hard and gathered up his courage. "No sir, all we know is that they hired some capable mercenaries. If you gave me some time, I could—"

"Enough. Our company is in a bad position because of you two. We need to focus on recuperating first. Jared, halt all business operations in NLA and liquidate everything. You're moving out to consolidate with Daniel so that we can keep the Firebird-to-Mile High City route alive. I'll be sending someone to take charge, you'll both be working hard as assistants as penance. Is that understood?"

The two shouted out yes in unison before their boss nodded, and his projection disappeared.

*I can come back from this. I'll just have to work hard and produce results. Then I swear I'll find out who the mastermind of this incident is and pay them back tenfold.*

# CHAPTER 42

## WORK WORK

"Well, then, I'll leave things here to the both of you." I placed a hand on two shoulders, one on my new head of security and the other on the manager of my Firebird branch, before I entered the car with Leo.

The QG, Roger, had come through with some potential hires who were looking for more stable employment. It was a surprise when one of the mercenaries I interviewed wanted to be hired as office staff instead of security, but her resume met our requirements, so I had no qualms about it. I even let her be the branch manager, since our operations in Firebird would be minimal for now and anyone who was vetted would do.

We planned to simply have a warehouse here for our trucks to drop off and pick up their cargo, and it wasn't hard to find a warehouse, even in the current climate. The main bottleneck right now was finding security in NLA to cut through the wasteland.

Back in NLA was the bulk of our workload, as we needed to procure trucks rated for the wasteland, rent a maintenance facility, hire personnel, and start planning our operations, and marketing, and loads of other things. The only saving grace was that we could get away with lowering our requirements for security personnel because we didn't need to fend off wastelanders, only the mutants.

The drive was duller than before, with only the two of us this time. We planned out our route so we could stop for the night to rest. Luckily we didn't encounter the colossal mutant this time and could safely trek across the wasteland in three days.

When we finally reunited with Vin, the first thing he did was not greet us or congratulate us, but instead complain, "Please, Rollo, hire a manager ASAP. I could handle the bureaucracy before when it was simple, but I just can't anymore."

"Okay, okay. I left a lot on your shoulders, I understand. Thank you, you can take tomorrow off." I comforted him on reflex, as I didn't know what else to do, seeing Vin in such a state.

"Yes! I really need that. I'll transfer you all the documents that I was working on and the scheduled meetings I had booked right away."

His enthusiasm scared me a little, so I had him take the rest of today off too.

Within the information Vin left behind were updates on what Qwklink Logistics had been doing since the attack. It seemed they were completely pulling out of NLA and gathering what they had left into Firebird.

Little was as gratifying as seeing our hard work come to fruition. What was left to do was build up a functional logistics network to profit from the current spike in demand while it lasted. The first step of that was to reaffirm my deal with the Wells Clan.

The next morning, we set out with our convoy into the wasteland again and followed the route displayed on the device from the wastelanders. This time we were headed in a slightly different direction, and further as well.

We knew we were close when the usual team of dune buggies came out to escort us. Neither Sarah nor Caleb was there when we arrived. Instead, an unfamiliar man led us straight to the building where the leader of their clan resided.

It was kind of weird seeing the exact same building as before, despite knowing we were in a different location. I wondered what they used to transport it, or if they rebuilt it to the same specifications.

"Welcome, friend. I have heard good things from our information network. Tell me, have you accomplished the mission?" Eugene said as he stroked his beard.

"Yes, your enemies will no longer operate in your territories. We're still monitoring their movements, so I'll let you know if anything changes."

"That is good news. Tell me all about it."

I talked until I was parched, but I managed to narrate our exploits and answer any questions he had. It wasn't until Sarah and Caleb showed up, drawing Eugene's attention and practically ending the meeting, that I was saved. But there was one last thing.

"So about what you promised me before—"

"Yes," Eugene said, "once we have confirmed the news, you may operate your business across our territories as you like. Keep in mind this is about our territories only. Just like your corporations, we aren't monolithic, so the other clans will not take kindly to you if you intrude into theirs."

"I understand, thank you."

*Now the main issue is to set up our logistics network. We'll need to rent a lot of trucks for the moment until we have enough funds to purchase our own. We'll also need the bare minimum facilities to operate with.*

After spending some time with Sarah and Caleb, I returned to the new pile of problems awaiting me back in the city.

* * *

"Nice to meet you, Mr. Halls. I am Jared Reinhart from Qwklink Logistics." The overweight man across from me shook my hand and gestured for me to take a seat.

"A pleasure to meet you as well, Mr. Reinhart."

"Let us get straight into it, then. Here are the terms for leasing this warehouse. If you are able to sign them today, we are willing to give you a ten percent discount for the first three months."

I glanced over the document on the terminal in front of me and redirected the feed to my lawyers to review.

"That is an attractive offer, but it brings along some problems. You see, I'm a very picky person who likes to shop around first. Maybe if you could extend that discount for the entire first year, I could make a decision right away."

"I understand, but this is the best offer I'm authorized to give. This warehouse may not be new, but the price is already well under the market price. It is located in a secured and convenient area with access to the highways."

"Is that so... I thought there were rumors that the location was recently attacked. I wouldn't call it secure."

He grimaced and sipped from his glass. "There's no such thing as a perfectly secure area in this world. Using the advantageous geographic location, we were able to protect our employees, so it is truly secure in that sense. But I regrettably see that malicious rumors have started to spread despite our successes. I'm willing to acquiesce and give you a discount for the first six months."

*Hold it together, me. Please don't burst out laughing when negotiations are near the finish line.* The irony of trying to rent from the people I attacked was just too hilarious to me, and now he was even giving me a discount.

"Very well. I accept," I declared while tensing every muscle on my face to keep them in place.

I had been swamped with paperwork and meetings to ensure we had the proper licenses and equipment we needed to operate. Having finished this final meeting for the day, I decided to leave acquiring trucks to Vin. He'd had his day off, so I was going to put him back to work.

As for me, I was going to spend the rest of the day relaxing and shopping. The first thing I did was get changed out of my stuffy corpo suit and try out a milkshake at a new place. My to-try list had just been building up, since I was always busy or out in the wastelands.

Then my next stop was the mall, to shop around. I'd been putting off a purchase for a while now, so it was about time I got off my lazy ass.

Arriving at one of the smaller megabuildings I'd seen, I was greeted by fancy displays with brand names plastered all over. All the nearby pedestrians were well-dressed.

While this building had only two hundred floors, it was mind-boggling to think that all of them belonged to a single shopping mall.

Just like in the mall in Elevate City, the floor that sold weapons was located in the basement, where security was visibly stricter than on the other floors. The layout was familiar as well, with each brand taking up some space on the shared floor, like a department store.

I spotted the brand I had been using, Premier Arms, and went straight to them.

There were always some moments in a mission when I was forced into a traditional gunfight. While that wasn't my strong suit, I wanted to be prepared. The pistol railgun I had was great and all, but it just wasn't cutting it against multiple enemies.

A clerk quickly came up to assist me. "Hello, sir. How may we help you?"

"Yes, I was looking for something that could handle multiple targets."

"I see. Are you looking for something for close quarters, or more of a medium range?"

"Close quarters. I wanted it to be compact and lightweight as well."

*All of my engagement has been pretty close-range, thanks to stealth.*

"Of course. Let me bring out some options for you. Would you like to test-fire them?"

"Yes, please."

He quickly brought out a few gun cases and led me away. As usual, right next to the typical changing rooms of a big box store was an entire shooting range.

"I have three selections of personal defense weapons for you. Allow me to introduce you to them here," he explained as he took three boxy submachine guns from the cases.

He went on to explain the main features of each gun, with the first one being a directed energy weapon that shot particle beams. It was configured to shoot rapidly, but the beam intensity could be adjusted in exchange for power. This was probably the coolest thing I'd ever shot.

The next one was some weird plasma spitter that shot bright beams of plasma contained in a magnetic field. This one was not a great fit for me, as it would give my position away the moment I shot out glowing projectiles.

The final option was a coilgun I was familiar with. It was optimized to shoot smart rounds that could lock onto targets. Although it was the most boring option, it was also the one that fit my needs the most.

I didn't like putting myself down, but I was honestly not the best shot, so the smart ammo helped. It was also the only choice that didn't shoot bright beams, which made it more effective for stealth.

"Excellent choice, sir. The ECA-17, also known as the Coil Wrath, is probably the most reliable product from our PDW line. Please be reminded to use our company's ammunition, or our warranty will be voided with this weapon."

I glanced over at the price tag, and it wasn't that bad, until I looked down at the section for the ammo.

*I sure hope my new business gets up and running soon.*

After shopping around a little more without an objective, I returned to my hotel with a full harvest. As soon as I got into my room, I spotted Leo on the couch, working away at his terminal.

"Rollo, about that chip you had me d—"

I dropped my bags before he could finish. "Did you already decrypt it?"

"Not fully, just the first level, but I got a sense of what it contains by reading the titles of each column in a spreadsheet."

"Go on, then. What did you find?"

"It's a ledger of some sort, and it belongs to SocialCorp."

"SocialCorp? As in *the* largest corp around, that SocialCorp?"

"Yeah..."

# CHAPTER 49

## WELCOME BACK

"Rollo, Leo, you're both finally back!" Claire cheerfully welcomed us as we pushed our luggage towards the car.

"Yeah..."

"Don't you have anything more to say? It's been like, what? Over a month?"

"Sure... but we've been talking through the net almost every day. What else is there to say?"

"Men," she sighed. "Let's go, then. I reserved a table for us at this new restaurant. Lana will be joining us as well!" She evilly grinned in Leo's direction.

Leo, Thorne, and I nodded in unison before we finished packing our luggage into the trunk so we could get on our way. The car left the airport and got onto the highway while I enjoyed the view.

It was nice to see the familiar landscape of Elevate City again. The space elevator in the background acted as a permanent landmark that made it impossible to mistake it for any other city.

From the rearview mirror, I could see that Claire was on a call, which explained the silence.

"So how was your time in NLA?" Thorne asked as he merged into the traffic that crossed the bridge into the city.

"For the majority of it, boring. The only fun part was before we managed to strike a deal with a shipping company to transport our stuff in exchange for our transportation service. After that, we spent the last few weeks doing paperwork, going to meetings, and doing interviews."

"How about you, Leo?"

"Not too different from normal. As long as I have a good connection to the net, it's mostly the same for me. If Rollo hadn't kept throwing work on my plate, it would've been a pleasant trip."

I glared at Leo beside me. Mainly for show, as he wasn't wrong, but it still gave Thorne a troubled look. "I see… So you guys got the transportation network thing figured out?"

"Well, mostly. Trucks are running and everything. We'll have to see if any issues arise, though. The main thing I'm worried about is if the fake damage we put on a vehicle will be seen through. I'd really rather not deal with another corp that gets any idea of our wastelander connections."

"Don't worry," Leo said as he played around on his terminal, "the monitoring program I made will watch your men and keep them honest, and I doubt any corp would waste resources analyzing your vehicles often enough to figure out anything."

"Yeah," Thorne said. "It's been going pretty well for us here, but I think we should get a dormitory soon. It'll help prevent any possible leaks together with the added security." He signaled to change lanes.

"Well, that will have to wait until we get some funds. We're stretched thin already with this new transportation endeavor and renovating our new office. We'll also want to save a good chunk of credits to incorporate, too."

Claire glanced back at me, her eyes no longer glowing. "The math boys say it'd be best to incorporate in two months when our cash flow stabilizes."

"We'll listen to the professionals, then. It's not like we're in any rush. In the meantime, we can take the time to relax and enjoy life!"

"Yay, I agree!" Claire clapped as I watched Leo and Thorne, frowns on their faces.

"Lighten up, boys," I said. "Let's go enjoy dinner."

Once we arrived, the two of them tried to put on smiles at the insistence of Claire, but Thorne faltered and tensed up once he saw the prices listed on the menu. It wasn't until he started eating that his expression relaxed.

I watched as Leo and Lana bickered in their married-couple fashion. As former corpos, they ate with refined table manners with ease. In contrast, Thorne, who still looked tense at the shoulders, and Claire, who was enjoying herself a little too much, were far from ready to handle business dealings involving other corpos.

*Let's hope business goes well. That way, I can increase their pay so they can eat out at places like this more often and learn more about corporate culture. I'd much rather have them help me manage the business than hire some scheming corpo, even if they were more experienced.*

* * *

After dinner, we returned home, and I prepared to go out as usual. As it had been a while since I'd been in the city, I called up my old friend, Fitel, to purchase some info on any harvester hideouts. I'd been away long enough for them to infest the areas I had previously cleared. They were seriously like cockroaches.

"Fitel, it's been a long time. Do you have any jobs or info on harvester hideouts?"

"Mr. Halls, it has been a while. I don't have any jobs that fit your criteria right now, but I do have some information on harvester locations."

"Great, how much?"

"It will be the standard information fee of ten thousand credits."

"Sent. I'll be around for a while now, so let me know if any jobs come up."

"It surprises me that you would still be interested in taking jobs from me, but alas, it is none of my business. I will contact you if anything suitable comes up." The call ended before I could reply. Typical of Fitel.

Within a minute, the information I had bought from him arrived too.

I set the car to head for the new location while I went over the file.

Normally, with a small den of half a dozen or so harvesters, I could break even with the information fee unless I was unlucky on the loot. The information this time was on a larger one, with an estimated twelve to fourteen harvesters in the hideout.

They operated out of a small warehouse within an industrial district, where they disguised themselves as some of the many workers going about their day in their compound and van.

Despite the late hours when I reached it, there were still many warehouse workers in sight.

Most corporations I knew had their workers either on two twelve-hour shifts or three eight-hour shifts, depending on whether delicate control was needed on the job. For my logistics warehouse in NLA, I implemented four six-hour shifts instead because of the compensation clause I signed with my employees.

If they were always working too long and getting hurt on the job, I would be out quite a bit of money before I knew it, so I tried to prevent that. After all, the compensation policy wasn't something I planned to go back on, considering how effective it was at motivating them.

The truck drivers would still be on three eight-hour shifts, though. Three was the maximum number of people the trucks we rented could hold. It simply wouldn't make sense to have it any other way if we wanted them to be on the move twenty-four seven.

I stuck to the unlit area as I crept closer to my target warehouse. I only used the active camouflage to cross areas that didn't have any blind spots I could traverse.

The warehouse compounds were separated by thin metal sheets they called walls, and large gates that allowed multiple semitrucks to pass at once.

When I reached the correct lot, it was entirely empty outside without a guard in sight. If I didn't know better, I would have thought it was unoccupied.

Just in case of cameras, I made use of my Shade stealth implant until I breached the locked door and entered the building. My hacking had gotten faster. With my software engineering skills up to par now, I could prepare hacking software to be used beforehand.

Once I was in, I made sure the coast was clear before I detached my new submachine gun, the Coil Wrath, from my lower back. I'd had it fitted to my suit, so it hadn't been in the way while I moved around.

Practicing with the gun recently had given me more experience with it. Maybe I was a little addicted to the ease of landing shots with the automated smart bullets correcting my trajectory.

I had gotten the suppressor attachment, and although it wasn't as quiet as the Suri, it was still enough that I could clear an area without alerting anyone in the neighboring rooms, as long as the walls weren't too thin. With this new gun, my tactics leaned more towards brute force than pure precision.

Once I was prepared, I ventured further into the building, where my auditory implant soon picked up jumbled conversation.

Soon I came into the big open area of the warehouse, which was partitioned with the blinds that many harvesters used for their so-called "surgical areas."

I spotted the overseer's office on the balcony and headed that way immediately for the vantage point. The thugs in here, like many others I'd encountered recently, were really sloppy. They were busy watching videos on their implants, or chatting amongst themselves.

Maybe they only seemed sloppy because I was comparing them with the corporate forces I had gone up against. Even a small corporation was still miles ahead of common criminals out in the streets.

Watching from the second floor, I took some time to mark down everyone in sight, as well as the layout of the entire place. I then went to each warehouse exit and blocked it off with a little hacking.

With the stage set, I relied on my Shade to reach the center of the warehouse, where the majority of the harvesters were. Once I was in position, I checked my new Coil Wrath one more time before I aimed and pulled the trigger.

The automatic fire kicked in as the smart bullets flew to all the targets I had already marked. Screams echoed as others scrambled.

*+10 EXP*

*+10 EXP*

*+10 EXP*

*+10 EXP*

*+10 EXP*

*+10 EXP*

One relatively clever woman lay prone and started shooting towards where she thought the bullets had come from.

Unfortunately for her, the bullets' trajectory wasn't completely straight, but I took the cue and kept on the move as I reloaded.

A few stragglers managed to get behind cover and then run away as fast as they could, only to be stopped by doors that they desperately tried to pry open.

With a fresh mag in my gun, I finished off all the remaining harvesters around me, ending with the last few by the doors.

I then took stock of the inventory they had here. Most of the cybernetics and organs were packed away in crates, with a few that were freshly taken out of some poor souls still by the bloody operating areas.

There were still a few bodies in here, dumped together in a pile that was only covered by plastic sheets. A body on an operating table suddenly coughed.

I ran to him and found that he was missing an arm, his optics, and likely various smaller implants in his head, judging by the incision point that still remained.

*I guess I'll be here a little longer than I thought. I'm going to have to find these implants or find ones that would work with what he has. Why can't they have names on them?*

By the time I got back, the sun had already risen.

I opened up my status as I lay on my bed and pondered the future.

# CHAPTER 50

## ACROSS THE OCEAN

The next morning, I took a hot shower and got dressed before going up to the penthouse on the fifth floor. The elevator doors led me straight to the middle of the office, where several employees were already at their desks, busy with work on their terminals. There was a neat line of open cubicles, similar to the desks found in libraries, but with a wider workspace. Each of them had several projection screens that kept their attention.

At the other end of the room, there were three offices behind glass walls, where I spotted both Thorne and Claire at their respective desks. We shared looks as I approached my own office in the middle. Claire got up as soon as she saw me, and she entered behind me while my door was still open.

"Good morning, Rollo, your appointment to incorporate is set for this afternoon at 2:00 p.m. Thorne already arranged for your transport, so you better be on time."

"Yeah, I know, it's not like this just suddenly came up. We've been waiting for this for two months."

"As long as you understand. I got a lunch meeting starting soon, so I'm heading out. See ya!" Claire came and left like a hurricane. As she went on her way to the elevator, her new assistant scrambled to catch up with her.

I checked my emails on my terminal and made sure my agenda was cleared. There wasn't much for me to do today, so I exited my office and called out to a nearby employee to buy drinks for everyone. I then made my way into Thorne's office.

He was focused on his terminal and only noticed me when I opened the glass door. "Thorne, what are you working on? Need some help?"

"No thanks, Rollo. I'm almost done. I'm just ensuring the training itinerary is correct and the orders for new equipment are accurate."

His words drew my gaze to the armor he was wearing. It was mainly black, with midnight-blue highlights. Its armor plates were enough to stop most rounds, and better than the junk we had our security team bring themselves. At least now they all wore a standardized undersuit design, so they actually looked like a professional crew.

*You know what they say, clothes make the man.*

"Your car is ready to leave anytime. I have a team waiting in the garage," Thorne said, his gaze still fixed on the terminal.

"Got it. I'll head out a little early after I drop by Leo and Lana first."

"Sounds good."

He then went on to ignore me, and I simply returned to my office and waited for the milkshake I'd had one of the employees buy. Ten minutes later, with my drink in hand, I headed down to the third floor, where most of the security personnel stayed.

It had the main monitoring room and a server room Leo and Lana had put together. They stayed cooped up in there like shut-ins most of the time, barely ever going back to their unit on the fourth floor except to shower and sleep.

I stood by the entrance for several moments as the terminal by the door scanned me. Once it was done, I entered the passcode and the doors opened. "Hey, Rollo, Leo's busy right now. Need something?"

"Not really, just checking in to see if you guys got settled in here yet."

"Yeah, the connection here is way better than the residential lines we had to endure. The upgraded hardware we bought with the company funds helps too, of course."

"You think Leo can finally crack that data chip with the new setup, then?"

"Hard to say. With a bit of luck, it could be in a few days, or a few months, if we're unlucky."

"As long as progress is being made, I won't take up any more of your time. I'm heading out now. Have fun."

"Ha, you too. It is your big day, after all."

"It's the company's, and you're part of it too. We'll celebrate once we settle everything today."

I headed to the basement garage next. There were several Vanguards parked. Two of them immediately started up, revved forward, and stopped right next to me.

"Sir." The tinted windshields came down as the people inside saluted me.

I nodded in acknowledgment and entered the vehicle.

I'd given up on telling them to be more casual, as new faces were always showing up and Thorne had convinced me that building a habit of discipline was the better option.

"Let's head there early. I'll leave the route to you guys."

It wasn't the most comfortable, being sandwiched by two fully geared guards, but it was a choice I made. This was more practical than having a luxury vehicle customized with defensive armaments; we didn't have that much money to spare.

Even through the heavily tinted glass, I got to enjoy the view of Elevate City. People went about their lives on the streets, and flying vehicles flew by overhead, likely carrying big shot corpos.

As traffic slowed us down, I opened up the status screen to kill some time.

**Status**
**Level:** 15
**EXP:** 1480/1500
**Musculoskeletal:** 76
**Neural Reflex:** 15
**Visuomotor Coordination:** 27
**Endurance:** 24
**Sensory Perception:** 52
**Upgrade Points:** 1
**Upgrades:**
    Stealth +7
    Hacking +3
    Cybernetic Engineering +7
    Stealth Technology +10
    Software Engineering +6
**Enhancements:**
    SAID: Zenitech Hoth Mk.3
    Optics: Nova Tech Stars Mk.4
    Cyberarm (Left): Nova Tech Mudra Mk.6
    Cyberarm (Right): Nova Tech Shiva Mk.5
    Auditory: Amazing Corp FieldTac Gen 2
    Cardiovascular: BioGen Labs Marathon 4
    Miscellaneous: HSU Custom Shade

Once I put the tenth point into stealth tech, the system said it required two points to upgrade it further. Even if it would give me more knowledge, I didn't believe it would be worth it at the moment. I wasn't going to sell any more stealth tech anytime soon, as it would reveal my trump cards, and ten points were already more than sufficient.

There were other things I wanted to upgrade that could be more useful, but I'd hold off for now until I accumulated more points. I needed to think about it some more.

*It's been a while since I upgraded my cybernetics. They seem sorely outdated by the standards of what I could afford now. I definitely need to put that on the agenda.*

Having approached the topic of finances, I had my optics display the financial spreadsheets I had stored in my SAID.

For the past two months, we'd been selling about two hundred Shade units a month. Those numbers included the ones in our own clinics and the ones we supplied to others. We sold each unit for around ten thousand credits retail and had a profit margin of around five thousand credits.

That meant we made about a million per month, but that wouldn't be sustainable. Once we went through all the mercenaries who would purchase our product, our sales would decline.

We also had our transportation business that only ran two convoys of ten rented trucks. Each truck cost about ten thousand to operate per month and pulled in about twice that amount due to the ongoing demand. So that was another two hundred thousand in profits each month while the war was ongoing.

With a total of about 1.2 million credits in profits per month, we still had to carefully plan our expenses to allocate the one million for incorporation today. The company still had other expenses and salaries to pay to about fifty employees, with an average wage of ten thousand per month. We also needed some funds to expand and a cash reserve, but we were more than ready today. The reduced corporate tax rate we would get would pay for itself in no time.

The view around the car opened up as we left the city and proceeded onto the ocean bridge that connected to the space elevator. As the sight of it slowly came closer and grew larger, it became more and more difficult to contain my excitement. Finally, I had the chance to approach that marvel of human engineering.

The ocean-view scenic route soon ended as we approached the first checkpoint, still quite far from the space elevator. The checkpoint was heavily fortified with advanced armaments, and a small army could be seen guarding the area.

Our car waited in line until we were waved towards a booth, where the guard questioned us and asked for our identification. We were scheduled to meet with a representative at the Elevate City Consortium headquarters here, so we were allowed to enter once they found us in their systems.

We had to pass through one additional vehicle checkpoint, plus one more for foot traffic right at the base of the space elevator that prevented us from carrying firearms inside. I managed to contain the urge to crane my neck up and witness the gray tower reaching higher than I could see, and went inside a building that felt somewhat like an airport.

Following the signs, we soon arrived at the Elevate City Consortium HQ in what I would easily mistake for a large hotel lobby.

The receptionist greeted us with a bright smile. "Good afternoon, sir. How can I help you today?"

"I have an appointment for 2:00 p.m. today under Rollo Halls."

Her eyes flashed before she promptly responded, "Yes, of course, Mr. Halls. We've been expecting you. There is still some time until the meeting, so please feel free to tour the commercial area while you wait. We will contact you immediately once we are ready to receive you."

She gestured to a nearby escalator that led us into a luxurious shopping area.

We did arrive a little early, so we toured what the shops had to offer. There were surprisingly a lot of people, despite the strict security and restrictions on who was allowed in. The prices reflected the exclusivity of this place.

I couldn't resist and bought a three-hundred-credit milkshake as I observed the vanity items rich people bought. It was hard to imagine that just several months ago, I was still working a part-time job here, confused by this world, barely making enough to pay the two-thousand-credit rent.

Another well-dressed woman walked past me, or so I thought, until she stopped right in front of me, her eyes staring straight at me. Guards in suits flanked her sides while directing a cautious gaze at my own security team.

"You're a new face. I see that you are a connoisseur of the finer things in life as well." She pointed to my milkshake with her eyes.

"Yeah, it's a vice of mine," I politely replied, unsure of who I was talking to or how to deal with her.

"Oh, please, sugar is hardly a vice compared to the things most *people* put into their bodies. Would you be free to—"

Before she could finish her sentence, a robot wearing the same uniform as the receptionist from earlier came out of nowhere. "Sir, we are ready to meet you now. Please follow me."

I looked between the robot and the woman before she continued, "Evidently, you're not free. Until we meet again." She gave a polite smile and headed off into the distance with her retinue.

*I wonder what that was about? I have been told not to talk to strangers, but that was when I was a kid. Or is this normal among corpos, and I'm just having culture shock? Either way, now is not the time to dwell on it. I have something more important to attend to.*

The robot wasted no time and started guiding my team.

*Finally, we are officially going to become a corporation.*

# CHAPTER 51

# WITHIN THE HALLS OF THE CONSORTIUM

"Welcome, Mr. Halls," a tall, middle-aged man greeted me as soon as I entered the meeting room. "I am Frank DeSantis, and I'll be walking through your application today."

I reached out to shake his hand. "Thank you, Mr. DeSantis." We then took our seats across from each other.

He pushed a terminal on the table towards me.

"I'm sure you'll want to review the contract once more. Please feel free to do so while I go over a few things."

As planned, I transmitted the footage from my optics back to the lawyers we had on retainer.

"So Mr. Halls, I am required to explain to you our geopolitical situation before you join us. Are you already familiar with it?"

"Just what is known to the public."

He paused for a moment. "I see, then allow me to give you an overview. The Elevate City Consortium is a collection of the world's largest corporations. Together they manage the city, run the space elevator, and trade with the various nations on this planet." He took a sip from his cup. "We enforce trade contracts and work together to create a more hospitable business environment. By becoming a member, you are agreeing to help us enforce these trade contracts."

He directed a meaningful gaze at me, to which I nodded.

"Now, with that said, please do not mistake our consortium for an alliance. It is common for fellow members to have hostile relationships and even come to blows. We do not manage the affairs and relationships as long as they don't go over the line and severely affect the market."

"I understand," I replied, fully aware that he meant as long as it wasn't outright blatant, anything went.

"Perfect, now we just need your signature once you are ready," DeSantis said.

When my lawyer team gave the green light, I looked over the form myself one last time before I signed it.

"Congratulations, Mr. Halls. The Halls Corporation has officially joined our consortium today. You will receive a welcome package soon that will introduce you to your new privileges and distinctions within our consortium."

I still winced a little at the mention of our corporation's name. It was embarrassing to have a business named after yourself, but Claire and Thorne wouldn't have it otherwise.

Neither party lingered once business was done. We shook hands once more and departed. I met up with my guards waiting outside and started our journey back to the company to deliver the good news.

We ordered food for the celebration while we were in traffic, as it would probably take a while to prepare enough food for the entire company.

When we parked in the basement of our office building, a small crowd was waiting right beside the elevators.

"So, how did it go?" Claire asked, latched onto Thorne.

*I'm not sure why she's nervous. It's not common to be rejected this late into the application, but I guess you can never be sure until the deal is done.*

"Starting today, Halls Corporation will be officially recognized as a G-Class member of the Elevate City Consortium."

A boisterous cheer filled the basement as the party began.

* * *

The next day, I brought both Claire and Thorne into my workshop.

"So what did you want, Claire?" I asked.

"To settle on our company logo, of course! Now that we're a corp, just using the same colors won't do. We'll want a logo to brand onto our products, uniforms, cars, everything!"

I stole a glance at Thorne, who simply shrugged back.

"Why can't we just use our company name like most corporations?"

"Boo, that's boring. And I thought you hated the idea of having your name plastered everywhere."

"Knowing you, you're just going to have the name included anyway. It'll be even more noticeable with a logo beside it."

"Hehe, maybe. Let's see what we come up with first."

I listened as Claire bounced logo ideas off of Thorne. They quickly settled on an animal theme for some reason, but couldn't decide on much more than that.

"We should do something cute, like a rabbit!" Claire stated.

"No, we should have something that fits our company's image. With our Shade, we should use something like a chameleon," Thorne retorted.

Their exchange was at a stalemate, and they decided at the same time to turn to me instead. "What do you think, Rollo?"

"If you are dead set on an animal, we have to consider if it'll fit our color scheme as well. We already decided on black and blue, so you guys figure it out from there."

They both paused as they fell deep in thought. A minute or two later, Thorne spoke up. "How about a snowy owl, then? We could have a snow-blue color scheme for it, and it also fits into the camouflage theme."

Claire's eyes started to glow, likely searching for images. "Sure, why not? They're cute! They're like Rollo as well, nocturnal."

"Yeah, sure, let's get this over with."

* * *

"Good morning, Rollo, we have a slight issue that just came in last night," Claire said as she came into my office.

"What's the matter?"

"We got an email from our bank, congratulating us on incorporating last night."

"Okay... What's the problem?"

"Our new status requires additional security measures to be in place before we can continue using our accounts. They want you to send someone to their headquarters in Lion City to register the biometrics of the people who you want to have access to the accounts. They'll be covering the travel expenses."

"Not in Elevate City, but all the way in Southeast Asia?"

"Yes, they're the biggest credit-issuing bank for a reason. They're outside the control of corporations and operated by one of the wealthiest city-states. Otherwise, how could corporations entrust their money with another corp?"

"All right, I'll open up my schedule for a trip, then..."

"You don't have to go in person if you don't want to. You can entrust your biometric data to someone and send them in your stead. I think that's what most corpos do."

"Nah, it's fine. I don't mind doing some sightseeing."

"Okay, then I'm coming too, since I manage the finances normally. I'll see who else wants to come." She exited with a hop in her step.

With a trip on the horizon, I had to hasten my plan to upgrade my cybernetics. I opened my status screen so I could review all the implants I currently had. Most of my cybernetics were quite expensive to me at the time I bought them, but my financial situation had drastically changed and stabilized as well. I was long overdue for an upgrade.

I opened one clinic supplier's procurement list and started browsing models for sale. The high-end models started from tens of thousands and went up into the millions. I was sure there were even more expensive options that were only available with connections, but that wasn't my concern for now.

Brain implants that improved my neural reflexes and visuomotor coordination had always seemed dicey, but if I bought the high-end models, I could probably trust them to be reliable enough.

I could also take a look at the SAID with the hypnopaedia feature again. Now that we were a corporation, I should be able to buy knowledge cassettes to help Claire learn. I could then study it and hopefully reproduce it myself. If that worked, I could provide my people the ability to learn while they slept.

First I selected several high-end models to replace what I already had. Although our corporation was raking in money, we were also expanding and had to purchase equipment and vehicles. That meant I didn't have unlimited money, so I settled for the ones around the hundred-thousand-credit ballpark.

The one implant I had to splurge on was the SAID. As the centerpiece of everything, a secretarial assistant had to be high-quality.

With my order placed, I went to check out a downtown mall I had yet to explore. My new cybernetics wouldn't arrive until tonight. With my impatience, I wanted to examine the real thing in person first.

A team of four security guards followed me around on the orders of Thorne. Apparently they would even follow me when I went out at night. He told me they could just watch if I wanted, but he wouldn't budge on siccing these babysitters on me.

Upon entering the mall, we immediately headed for the cybernetics floor. As the head of a legitimate corporation now, one of my privileges included having armed guards accompany me to most places that normally didn't allow it.

We entered the Zenitech store, where I found the SAID implant I had just ordered projected on one of the showcase cabinets. An employee noticed me and my guards and came to assist me.

"Sir, how may I help you today?" she said, bowing low.

"Please give me an overview of the Sebastien model right here."

"Of course, sir. The Sebastien model is one of our flagship products in the secretarial assistance implant market. It can even host a rudimentary AI to provide you with a secretary in the truest sense." She smiled proudly.

"How does it compare to SAIDs in a similar price range?" While I had my own view on the matter, I wanted to see what a Zenitech salesperson had to say.

"While I'd like to tell you it is better in every possible way, our Sebastien model truly shines in its ability to access the web securely. With our proprietary solutions, there are no worries about giving hackers an avenue to invade your systems. You'll have the convenience of staying connected to the web while fully at ease."

From what I could tell with my cybernetics and software knowledge, the Sebastien model did this by using some air-gapping method in combination with read-only access.

While I did not believe any implant could be truly unhackable, with the proper settings on the Sebastien, you could easily detect any attempt at hacking and disconnect to cut them off.

Curiosity sated, I spent some time shopping for clothes and treated the entire team to lunch.

I frolicked around until I got a message that my order had arrived. That led me to the nostalgic clinic that had been my home for a few months, where I met with the cybernetic surgeon on duty.

I'd gone through plenty of installations before, but it was a bit awkward this time around because I had my security team as the audience. I couldn't imagine how the surgeon felt, either. Probably nervous, which didn't comfort me at all.

Having Claire operate on me would've made me feel a lot more comfortable. She was one of the few people I fully trusted.

*I should really try harder to get her that cassette on cybernetic knowledge. But not just yet.*

*You can do it, Mr. Surgeon. Steady hands, please...*

I inhaled the anesthetic and hoped it would all be over soon.

# CHAPTER 52

## LION CITY

When I woke up, I felt a strange dissonance with my body. It still moved how I wanted it to, but it just felt different.

*Well, I did change out almost every single one of my cybernetics.*

"*Correct.*" A feminine synthetic voice suddenly rang out in my head. "*Host has replaced every cyberware in his body except the unit labeled 'HSU Custom Shade.' Rest is recommended.*"

*That's right, my new SAID came with a smart assistant. I still need to set that thing up.*

A smart assistant might be a few steps down from an AI, but it was sufficient to carry out my commands and help me micromanage things as if I had a personal secretary...

"*The only setup that requires the host's attention is setting my designation, voice, and permission level.*"

*Right, it is my SAID, so it can pick up on my thoughts, kind of like how I used to text. I'll call you Kiri from now on, and you can keep the voice as it is. Only pick up on my thoughts when I allow it. Is that possible?*

"*Yes, I can do so.*"

The surgeon soon came in as I was getting used to talking to the voice in my brain. He helped me calibrate the new implants, which made me feel a bit better. My work had taught me I needed some time to get used to the new hardware. There was just no way around it.

My security team drove us back to our office building, which doubled as my residence. I took the time during the ride to inspect and try out my new chrome.

**Status**
**Level:** 15
**EXP:** 1480/1500
**Musculoskeletal:** 211
**Neural Reflex:** 65
**Visuomotor Coordination:** 87
**Endurance:** 59
**Sensory Perception:** 127
**Upgrade Points:** 1
**Upgrades:**
        Stealth +7
        Hacking +3
        Cybernetic Engineering +7
        Stealth Technology +10
        Software Engineering +6
**Enhancements:**
        SAID: Zenitech Sebastien v2
        Bio-Coprocessor: SocialCorp Lightning II
        Optics: Mirage Tech Clear-Sights Mk.12
        Cyberarm (Left): Nova Tech Heracle Mk.3
        Cyberarm (Right): Nova Tech Heracle Mk.3
        Auditory: SocialCorp Echo IV
        Cardiovascular: BioGen Lifepump 5
        Miscellaneous: HSU Custom Shade

My new optics had several modes that could be used concurrently, and could connect those modes to my SAID, which would alert me to any findings. They could also detect if devices were giving out signals, search for wireless connections, and zoom much closer with crystal-clear clarity.

I also got a bio-coprocessor, which was a chip in my brain that boosted how fast I processed things and how fast my brain signals went out to the rest of my body. It was the first implant that raised my neural reflex stat. While I got the jump on others most of the time, I'd been lagging here, and this would definitely take my survivability to another level.

For cyberarms, I got matching models that balanced strength and utility. They had all the functions of my Shiva, but better, with integrated tools that ranged from old-school lockpicks to a freaking blowtorch.

The other upgrades mainly improved performance and durability. That meant they were more shielded from things like EMP attacks and hacking.

Overall, these were definitely a worthwhile investment, especially since my future adversaries might be more corpos.

*Now that I have some wealth, I need to keep upgrading my defensive measures to retain my fortune. Otherwise, I'll just be a prime target.*

* * *

"Excuse me, madam, please be seated for landing," a flight attendant said.

She wasn't talking to me, though, but to the person in the seat beside me.

"Oh, sorry," Claire responded sheepishly, like a kid being caught stealing candy.

She had been glued to the window since we boarded the plane. I couldn't blame her for it, either, considering it was her first time flying.

On this trip to Lion City, there were two teams of security guards, bringing our party to ten. The Bank of Lion City, the one that summoned us, paid for all the expenses, so it was a no-brainer to have our security join us.

We soon landed, and the metropolis came into view. At the center was a giant dome large enough to house megabuildings. The dome was where the actual citizens of Lion City lived, where outsiders were normally not allowed.

The government of Lion City actually had full control of their city-state. Corporations were subject to its regulations, and despite it being authoritarian, it kept the well-being of its citizens in mind.

They had some resemblance to countries back in my old world. I would've wanted to become a citizen of this place too, if I didn't have the system, but they were highly xenophobic.

The fact they weren't under any corporation's influence was why they were trusted to manage the currency of the world, the credits. They weren't the only party like this, as the spacers had their own organization that worked with them to maintain the economy.

Lion City's airport was glamorous, as expected of a place where the wealth gathered. An employee from the bank was already there, waiting to guide us to our accommodations.

On our way from the airport to our hotel, I observed the people on the streets, but they were all similar to what I'd seen in Elevate City. It made sense, since we hadn't entered the dome, and most people outside of it were foreigners.

The next morning, we were brought to a megabuilding that had the Bank of Lion City's logo plastered all over it. In the meeting room, we met the representative of the bank, a young woman.

"Hi, I'm Emma. A pleasure to meet you, Mr. Halls," she said as we shook hands.

"A pleasure to meet you. Let me thank you ahead of time, as we'll have to rely on you to guide us through this process," I replied.

"Of course. I will do my best to be of service to you. If you would please follow me."

She led us to what looked like a hospital room filled with medical equipment. A nurse there had each device take a detailed scan that recorded our biometrics. It took over two hours, but at least we were done after that.

"Thank you so much for visiting us for this. Your accommodations for the next two days are covered, so please feel free to tour the city until you are ready to leave. Did you have any questions?" said Emma on our way out.

"I think we will take a look around the city. By the way, why are there so many foreigners here? They can't all be here for the bank, right?" I couldn't help but ask.

"There is a healthy population of mercenaries and adventurous people that are here for the nearby dungeon," she replied.

*Dungeon? She isn't going to tell me there's magic next, right? Kiri, what do you know about the dungeons in Lion City?*

*"The dungeon in Lion City is believed to be a series of bunkers the people from the past built before the nuclear war. It is a dangerous place with various mutants inhabiting it, but contains many relics from the past. These relics include technologies and knowledge that are long-lost and can have tremendous value."*

"I see. Thank you for taking care of us. I don't have any more questions," I said. With Kiri's explanation, there was no need for her to clarify.

"Thank you guys again for coming. You may want to check out the auction house if you don't have any plans. They usually have some relics you can get a closer look at, if that interests you."

We were then driven back to our hotel, where bank representatives simply told us to inform them when we wanted to leave so they could acquire the plane tickets for us.

Claire and I decided we would stay until our free accommodations ran out. We weren't in a hurry, so we would take full advantage of the freebies.

In the afternoon, we rented cars to go tour the grocery stores, which had a wide selection of exotic fruits that you couldn't get in Elevate City unless you paid an exorbitant price. The things we saw on the streets and in malls were too similar to what we had back home, so we skipped them and spent time in a nearby spa until dinner.

Next, we listened to Emma's recommendation and visited the auction late that night.

When we entered the auction house, a man in a suit soon came to greet us.

"Welcome, dear guests. The entry fee is five hundred credits per person, or ten thousand if you would like a private room. Which one will it be?" While polite, he got straight to the point.

"The main area is fine. Lead the way," I declared.

"Of course. Your bodyguards may go to our waiting area, if you would like. Your security is guaranteed while you are in our establishment."

I agreed to his offer and got seated with Claire in the auction hall. It wasn't packed, though we would've had issues finding enough seats close together if the guards came along.

The auction soon started on schedule, and items were brought forth. I wasn't sure what I expected, but it was plain boring. Relics sounded exciting until you found out they were just trash from the world before the nuclear wars.

The most common items were pieces of furniture made of wood. It seemed like organic wood was scarce nowadays, with how much the nuclear wars destroyed the planet's ecosystem.

"Look at that desk, Rollo! It's made from authentic wood! You should get it for your office. It'd look cool and stylish," Claire said, latching onto my arm.

"Yeah... No thanks, maybe for yourself?"

She shook her head. "Too gaudy."

*Then why would you recommend it to me...?*

When the auction went into overpriced artwork, we took our leave.

"Where do you want to go next?" I asked Claire.

"Umm, how about we get a snack and drive around to see how the nightlife is around here?"

"Sure, let's go."

The ten of us split off into two rental cars and headed to one of the local fast-food chains that was still open. We got out to view the menu and ordered takeaway so we could relax back in our hotel.

When we returned to the parking lot, Kiri suddenly spoke up.

*"I have detected suspicious individuals via the digital layer of your optics. There are four detected individuals at your nine o'clock that aren't visible to the naked eye headed your way."*

My optics instantly entered the digital mode, which showed me wireless connections. I could see signals on my left that matched what came from a typical SAID.

*We're out in a public area with no one else around. If they're using limited-duration stealth tech near us, then...*

"Hostiles! Claire, stay down!"

I whipped out my pistol railgun and shot towards the invisible foes before turning on my own active camouflage.

A member of our security pushed Claire to the ground while the other shot in the same direction I had.

An arm suddenly came into existence, having been damaged. A moment later, more enemies, still hidden by their stealth devices, opened fire.

My guards and I scattered into cover behind cars and turned on our camouflage. I was likely the only one who could reliably spot the enemies, but our company software allowed us to share targeting information. I peeked out in stealth, without firing, highlighting our foes for my allies to see.

Whenever I marked an enemy, my security team followed up with a hail of bullets. Following this strategy, we soon neutralized all our foes. They were all shot up pretty badly, so I finished them off for some experience points.

*+10 EXP*

*+10 EXP*

*+10 EXP*

*+10 EXP*

"Rollo, are you okay?" Claire ran up to me once the fighting was over.

"Yeah, how about the rest of you?" I directed my question to the leader of my squad.

"Just two lightly injured, sir."

Before we could get out of there and examine our wounds, sirens rang out all around us. In the blink of an eye, the Lion City police had us surrounded.

*Why do you have to make me miss Elevate City PD of all things...?*

# CHAPTER 52

## FRIENDMAIL

"So you admit you were the aggressor?" one of the two detectives across from me asked.

"What? No, they were obviously hostile, sneaking up to us like that. It was obviously self-defense. Anyway, it's been an entire night. Where's my lawyer?"

The duo exchanged glances but didn't answer my question.

"Tell us about the incident from start to finish again. What were you doing there?"

They continued to hound me with repetitive questions until they eventually got tired of it. I was then allowed to make a call, so I contacted Emma, the representative from the Bank of Lion City.

"Apologies for your negative experience. The local police don't have favorable impressions of foreigners, especially ones that get into trouble. I will contact them right away."

It was evident I made the right choice on who to call when, fifteen minutes later, the same two detectives returned and immediately uncuffed me.

They wordlessly guided me out, and I was soon reunited with Claire and the rest of our security team in the lobby of the police station.

"How are you? Did they do anything to you?" I asked the tired-looking Claire.

"No, just mouthed my ears off. Let's get out of here. I can't stand being here a second longer."

I nodded in agreement and called a cab once we got our belongings back. We spent the entire day catching up on sleep, and the next day staying around the hotel as we lost our appetite to explore the city.

Soon, it was time for us to leave, and we boarded our flight back to Elevate City. Although it wasn't the best trip ever, I was starting to get used to these incidents wherever I went. They only encouraged me to build up my company even more so we could beef up our security.

Claire glued herself to the window as soon as we boarded, so I took the time to review my gains from the previous night.

Our four assailants had gifted me the last bit of experience points I needed to level up. Now I had a whole three upgrade points waiting to be used. I wanted to upgrade a completely new skill, so I wasn't in a hurry to use them. Just three points wouldn't provide enough knowledge to be worthwhile.

I spent the rest of the travel time browsing the system for any skills I may have missed.

* * *

"Welcome back, Rollo. I got something for you," Leo said.

He came into my office the afternoon we returned from Lion City. Seeing how he hadn't messaged me and instead had come in person, it must've been a sensitive topic.

*Kiri, turn on the privacy mode for my office.*

The glass walls of my office dimmed until they were opaque, and the low thrum of a jamming field indicated it was up and running.

He placed a familiar data chip in front of me. "The chip you had me decipher, it's done."

"And? Is it some sensitive information about SocialCorp that could jeopardize us?"

"If it was, I would've destroyed it already. This is something a little more benign, some ledgers from one of their smaller businesses. It's mainly evidence of some branch manager embezzling funds from the company. It's something SocialCorp would thank us for if we turned it in instead." He smiled.

"You want us to turn this in to SocialCorp for just a thank-you?"

"Look, it could get us invaluable connections."

"Maybe if an individual turned it in, but we're a corp, Leo. They'd just be cautious about us, thinking we were trying to dig dirt on them."

"Then this isn't really useful to us. Want me to destroy it?"

"Well... If your idea was to build a connection, we could still do that."

"What are you suggesting?"

"You see..."

* * *

"ID, and purpose of visit?" the heavily armed guard asked as our car stopped right beside his booth.

"We have a scheduled meeting in the annex. Here's our confirmation," Leo replied, holding out his terminal for them to see.

The guard's eyes shone, and a few moments later, he let us pass.

We then continued our way across the bridge towards the space elevator. The view was great as always as we drove across the ocean.

It was just me and Leo this time, as our meeting was more sensitive than usual.

After passing a few more checkpoints, we soon arrived. Signs in the parking lot led our car to the annex instead of the spaceport.

When we arrived in the meeting room we booked, we found a lanky man already there. He stood with his back facing us as he stared out the window at the ocean view. He didn't turn around until both Leo and I were seated behind him.

"You people are really brave, trying to blackmail a manager from SocialCorp. Tell me, are you just dumb, or do you people have a death wish?" the middle-aged man calmly said.

"Relax, Mr. Paulsen, no need to posture with us. We're not here to work against you, and you know it. Otherwise, we wouldn't even be meeting here today like this," I retorted.

"This is clearly extortion. How can you say you are not working against me? Cut to the chase. How much do you want?"

"We're not here to take anything from you. We just happened to find your ledgers and wanted to inform you of the leak, as friends, of course. So please don't use such repulsive words as extortion and blackmail. Maybe friendmail would better describe it?"

He paused and gave me a thorough inspection from top to bottom.

"We just wanted to make a connection with you, though I'm sure you'd find this suspicious if we really asked for nothing. So our first request is for you to help us buy some cassettes of cybernetic knowledge. Can you do that?" I asked.

"If that is all you want, I can oblige. But I won't be reduced to a dog at your beck and call. Destroy all the information you have on that ledger, and I'll owe you three favors. The cassette will be the first favor, and I won't do anything against SocialCorp."

"Very well. We got off to a bad start, but I hope we can get along. Would you like to join us for lunch?" I asked, as I offered a handshake.

"No, I'd avoid as much contact as possible if I were you. There's no telling if SocialCorp's counterintelligence will investigate me."

"They do that normally?" I scanned the room.

"Only when I'm working on a sensitive project. We have too many employees to monitor the insignificant small fry like me."

With our business done, he soon left, leaving me and Leo alone.

"Well, that went better than expected," Leo said.

"Yeah, hope he delivers. It would save Claire a lot of time, that cassette. Anyway, want to go grab lunch? They have pretty good food here, I think."

"Yeah... And they charge an arm and a leg for it."

"My treat, for cracking that data chip."

"What are we waiting for, then?" He gestured for me to lead the way.

We found a restaurant that served authentic chicken. There was no way I would miss the opportunity to finally have some real meat.

Our server guided us to the second floor, where we sat by the window that overlooked the shopping street.

The food may have taken longer than all that fast food I was used to, but when I took my first bite of the entrée, the chicken disk, tears welled up and clouded my vision.

"Rollo, are you okay?" Leo asked, looking a little stunned.

"Yeah, just some spices got into my eyes. I'll be right back."

I cleaned up in the washroom and swiftly made my way back to the table to finish my meal. Though I had to bear Leo awkwardly stealing glances at me for the rest of the meal, it was a small sacrifice, in my book.

Once we were done, it was Leo's turn to use the washroom. I browsed the web with my optics while I enjoyed an after-meal milkshake. I only stopped when I heard him pulling his chair back.

"That was fast—"

"We meet again," a young woman with a gleaming smile said from across the table. "Let me introduce myself this time. I'm Margarite. And you are?"

I froze for a second before I recognized her as the woman I had met during my previous visit here, when I incorporated the company.

"I'm Rollo, a pleasure to see you again."

"Likewise. So tell me, Rollo, did everything go well in that meeting last time?"

"Yes, it was just to sign something with the consortium."

She raised an eyebrow. "So you own a new corporation, then? What does your company do?"

"Just sell some cybernetics and transportation, nothing major," I replied, and took a sip.

"Transportation. Through the wasteland, I presume? My company's been looking for someone who knows their way around the wasteland, and you know, with the war and everything, none of the other companies have the time or staff to spare. Whereabouts does your transportation business operate?"

"Just around NLA and Firebird. Like I said, nothing major. What does your company want, specifically?"

"We specialize in auctioning off rare items to the cultured around the world. There's been this new trend of capturing mutants as pets. We just need someone to guide us to the mutants. We'll take care of the fighting. Does that sound like something you can help with?"

She set down a small terminal for me to see. On it were preliminary job details and, more importantly, the pay offered. I counted the digits twice and confirmed it was a five, followed by six zeroes. Five million credits to just guide them around. It was almost too good to be true.

That money could accelerate our expansion and add an entirely new route to our transportation network.

"Yes. We'll have to hash out the details, but I don't see why not."

"Perfect, but I have just one condition."

*Okay, maybe it was too good to be true.*

"Shoot."

"I'd like you to accompany us. I'll be going as well, so it'll be a fun trip between new friends."

I took a moment to think it over and didn't find much of a problem. I needed to go to NLA to deal with some bureaucracy anyway.

"Sure, send me your contact info."

She left shortly after we exchanged contacts, and Leo *happened* to return shortly after that. As he took a seat, he stared at me with a shit-eating grin.

I summarized my discussion with Margarite to get his opinion, but the only things he said in response were "I see" and "you decide."

He finally spoke up when we got in the car as we headed out. "You know I'm going to tell Lana and Claire, right?"

After that, I decided to ignore him the entire way back.

When we got back, he followed me up to the top floor, where Claire and Lana were chatting away in Claire's office. Having accepted the teasing to come, I entered the room with Leo.

"You guys wouldn't believe what—"

Before Leo could continue, Thorne jumped into the office. "Guys, take a look at the news channel."

He speedily turned on the room's projector.

"—at's right, folks, Europa Station has signed a peace treaty with Enceladus Station. The war is over. We expect transportation to revert to normal within two months."

That meant the high demand for transportation would soon revert back to normal as well. This was for sure going to have an impact on our transportation business.

*I guess I'm destined to head back to NLA.*

# CHAPTER 54

## MUTANT CAPTURE TEAM

I placed the small rectangular device into the specialized scanner I had installed in my workshop. I would take a scan of it before and after I disassembled it to study its inner workings.

I'd already copied the software on it, so even if I messed up, it wouldn't be a complete waste, with some material to analyze.

We'd gotten the device from the connections provided by Rob Paulsen, the SocialCorp branch manager we friendmailed. It was the hypnopaedic cassette that worked in tandem with compatible SAIDs to help people learn in their sleep.

SocialCorp had a monopoly on them, turning it into a seller's market. From what I'd researched so far, it didn't seem particularly difficult to replicate the technology. The key was how the knowledge was organized when it was fed into the brain. Different knowledge required a whole new set of trial and error to determine the optimal, most comprehensible way to teach the brain without any side effects.

There was an enormous amount of testing and optimization required, so it was no wonder that the largest corp specialized in it.

I wanted to try creating my own cassette based on the knowledge I learned from the system. The sensation when the cassettes imparted knowledge was shockingly similar to how the system worked, except it was able to dump all that information into my brain in an instant.

Though even if I succeeded, there was no way I would sell the cassettes, as that would antagonize a corp I couldn't afford to set off. This would just be for internal use, for people like Claire and Thorne.

Before I knew it, my alarm rang, reminding me it was time for dinner.

I quickly got dressed and exited my workshop. Just as the elevator opened, I almost bumped into the person rushing out.

"Rollo! You actually kept track of time this once..."

"Come on, Claire, I'm always on time if you let me know about it at least a day before. Let's go. We have a reservation, right?"

She pouted and retreated back into the elevator. I stepped in and pressed the button for the garage.

"So, how's it going with the cassette? Is it working?" I asked.

We had bought a few, one with cybernetic knowledge for Claire to use and a few cheaper ones for me to experiment with.

"I think so. It's a bit too early to tell, as it's still going over the things I've already learned. There's a whole month until I get through all of it."

Unlike the system, a single cassette paired with a hypnopaedic SAID required over a month to get through. You had to go from start to finish, as that was the only safe way.

"I see... Well, keep me updated. It may help with my research."

"Yeah, yeah, sure."

The elevator soon arrived, and we met up with Thorne, Leo, and Lana, who were all already waiting in the parking garage.

After hearing about the scrumptious meal Leo and I had, the others, mostly Claire, pestered me about the unfair treatment. This was why we made an appointment today at a high-class restaurant that served authentic poultry.

We moved out together in one Vanguard while another two accompanied us as security. My gaze couldn't help but be drawn to the company logo that decorated our guards' uniforms and cars. The snow-blue owl was fine, but seeing my own last name flaunted around made me grimace.

The decor alone made it obvious how expensive this place was to dine in, and I was never thrilled about expenses. However, there was one excellent perk I found in these fine dining establishments: the waiting rooms they had for guards.

Once we ordered, Claire eased into her seat and grinned in my direction.

"So Rollo, what's this about going to NLA to do some job for your new girlfriend?"

"She's not my girlfriend, and you saw the details in the contract. We'll be netting five million credits, and catering to their request is the least we could do."

"Oh, I wasn't talking about financially." She smirked.

"I'm still against it," Thorne interjected. "We should negotiate with them. There's no need to put yourself in harm's way. They'll be capturing mutants, not killing them, and there are so many things that could go wrong working with an unknown corp."

While what he said was normally true, it didn't apply to my situation. I still often went out to fight harvesters and other miscreants of society, and the risks of going out into the wastelands would be no different. They all fueled my system with experience points so I could continue to improve.

Leo added, "I've dug around and looked into them. There aren't any nasty rumors about them, so it should be okay in that regard. The dangers of the wasteland still remain, though."

"It's fine. It's not much riskier than what I normally do. Besides, I recently got an upgrade, so I'll be able to handle myself better than ever."

"Then at least let me come along," Thorne replied.

"Then who'll take care of our security team here?"

"That's what you say every time. I've trained up a few replacements who can take care of things while I'm gone. Leo will also be here if anything happens." Thorne turned his gaze to Leo, who nodded in response.

"Okay... Then why not? I don't think you've left this city before, have you? The wasteland will be a good experience for you."

I may also have been feeling slightly guilty, having left Thorne behind every time.

*Our company needs to be able to stand tall even if a person or two is missing.*

"Enough business talk, guys. Let's enjoy tonight," Lana said.

We went on to discuss more mundane matters, such as the VR game they had recently started playing. My VR capsule had arrived as well, but I hadn't had the time to try it out yet.

The food soon arrived and the authentic chicken I ordered was delightful. Experiences like these really reminded me of the wonders money could bring.

I still couldn't believe that crap I had forced into my stomach when I first came to this world, but that served as a powerful motivator. My next goal was to make every single one of my future meals at least as good as what we had tonight.

* * *

By now, traveling was a routine affair for me, but the same couldn't be said for Thorne.

We flew to NLA with just the two of us, as airfare was expensive and we had a security team waiting for us at the airport. Our security department there was even larger than the one at Elevate City, since we needed them to guard our production facility, transportation warehouses, and wasteland scavenging team. We also planned to open a clinic here, but we delayed it due to funding issues.

In Elevate City, we only had a clinic and our office, so it wasn't unreasonable that we had less security protecting fewer areas.

We had contacted Vin about our trip, and he and several guards had been scouting out across the wastelands for suitable mutant-hunting spots.

When we exited the airport, we found Vin waiting in his usual beat-up car, along with two Vanguards parked beside it.

The Vanguards had our logo on them, which meant my name as well. Vin had on the same company security outfit I'd grown so familiar with as well.

"Welcome back. You sure brought along an interesting job this time," Vin said as he opened the trunk.

"Yeah, well, I figured it wouldn't be too hard for us to scout along the routes we're familiar with."

I left the part where we wouldn't have to be worried about wastelanders unsaid, as we were out in public.

"Well, you figured right. We have the latest updates on mutant sightings ready for you. You'll need them in your meeting later, right?"

"Yep. Oh, and before I forget, this is Thorne, the head of security for Elevate City."

Vin nodded and looked Thorne over. "Nice to meetcha, I'm Vin. I guess we're the same rank, or maybe you're my superior, as you work in headquarters?"

"Nice to meet you, too. We'll go with equals. I don't think we're that strict with ranks when we can avoid it," Thorne replied.

We headed back to the office that doubled as a production facility, which remained unchanged.

But we didn't stop for long, as we had to attend the meeting with Margarite and the people from Desire Corp, her corporation. Our conference room was in a business hotel in downtown NLA.

When we arrived, Margarite was already there, along with two guards and a skinny man with glasses. It was rare to wear glasses, so they were likely some kind of device instead.

"We meet again. Just in time, too. Please, take a seat," Margarite offered.

I had Thorne and Vin with me, but Thorne opted to remain standing behind us like Margarite's guards.

"Yes, I'm glad to see you well," I replied.

The scrawny man beside Margarite cleared his throat. "I am Dr. Lut. I will be tagging along and deciding which mutants we will be capturing. Why don't we jump straight into it? If you could provide us with the information as promised, we can quickly plan our trip and be on our way."

"Of course. If you would, Vin."

Vin then began his presentation, giving us an overview of what mutants were available in the area, their characteristics, and their habitats. He even went over the colossal wormlike thing I had previously encountered on my way to Firebird, too.

As expected of corpos, they quickly gave up on that creature, as it was too massive and was nocturnal. I couldn't even imagine the amount of men and resources they would need to capture that thing.

They took an interest in mutant spiders and snakes, which brought back some terrible memories of my own encounters.

I let Vin take charge of the conversation as they discussed how many men they should bring and the route to take. By the time they were done, the sun had already set.

The people from Desire Corp must have had a lot to prepare, as they were visitors here. I was impressed they could even deploy that many troops on short notice. As expected of a medium-sized corp, they had a D-class membership with the consortium, which meant they paid the annual membership fee of twenty-five million credits.

After saying our goodbyes, both parties departed quickly. We'd decided to set out in two days.

* * *

That time went by in the blink of an eye. Our convoy of four Vanguards met up with Margarite's party just outside of the wastelands.

We were only guides this time around, so we didn't bring that many people. I had Vin stay behind to manage the operations, so it was me, Thorne, and the four teams of guards.

The vehicles in Margarite's party seemed much newer than our own, but at least we had them beat in cohesiveness, thanks to our standardized paint jobs.

They had rented out their various vehicles, all nondescript gray. There were a dozen cars in their group, along with one big truck for keeping the mutants. Their men, standing guard around their vehicles, were decked out in high-tech gear and cybernetics that I could recognize at a glance.

They were the type I wouldn't antagonize even if I had the drop on them, unless they were alone. I knew they might have active scanners that could detect me if they were on the lookout.

We drove up slowly to them, and once we were close enough, I got out and approached.

I found Margarite wearing high-tech gear, similar to what the rest of them wore, and Dr. Lut in a suit for some reason. They were both staring at the raging sandstorm of the wasteland, looking determined.

"You guys ready?" I called out to them.

# CHAPTER 55

## HUNT

Our four Vanguards took the lead as we brought our client, Desire Corp, deeper into the wasteland.

The convoy of military vehicles, customized for the wasteland environment, drove for an hour before we came to the first stop on our agenda. We arrived at a ruin that had once been an industrial complex, the entire area littered with low-rise facilities and warehouses.

While there were mutants that only resided on the plains of the wasteland, they were a lot harder to track down than the ones that used the derelict buildings as nests.

One of the targets Desire Corp decided on was a mutant spider that they called the webclaw.

We approached a complex that probably served as a production facility long ago. The area the building spanned had to be more than six soccer fields combined.

It always amazed me how these buildings were still standing after so many years of being battered by sandstorms.

I pointed towards the entrance the scout team had previously found, then watched as Margarite and her team moved in to secure the building. Shortly after, I followed with Thorne and a small squad of my security team, and found Margarite and Dr. Lut at the forefront of three dozen men who stood at attention.

Dr. Lut commanded, "Captain Melchior, you and squad one will be the capture team, while your deputy will lead squad two, the distraction team. Squad three will stay here to defend this location and our vehicles outside. Remember, you're not authorized to use lethal weapons on our targets unless as a last resort."

I wondered what they considered a last resort. Surely a few casualties were well within acceptable losses for most corps. For me, on the other hand, I'd rather not have to pay the worker's compensation and retrain personnel.

Soon, the corporate soldiers received their orders and moved out. Two-thirds of them went further into the building while the remainder, including Margarite and Dr. Lut, stayed in the lobby. They placed a few terminals, set up a couple of chairs for their leaders, and created a mobile security room, where screens displayed the body cam footage of their soldiers.

We unfolded our own smaller, less fancy chairs and had a look. From the footage displayed, we saw them move cautiously through the corridors until they reached an open area with high ceilings. It was filled with dusty, worn machines that looked more useful as scrap metal. This was where the two teams split off, with the bait team continuing onwards.

It didn't take them long to stumble upon an area with spiderwebs everywhere. There were large cocoons spread around as well, and when the team looked up, they finally spotted the prey they wanted to capture. The only issue was that there were over two dozen of them.

As if smiling at the cameras, the webclaws all bared their fangs at the soldiers in unison before they dropped towards their intruders.

It wouldn't have been that bad if they were just spiders the size of car tires, but their legs had sharp claws reminiscent of crabs, powerful offensive and defensive tools.

The soldiers of Desire Corp opened fire with their specialized tranquilizer guns, backing away while they shot. Unfortunately for them, the claws of the spiders simply deflected the darts with their thick chitin.

Although the men were at a disadvantage at first glance, they retreated in an orderly manner at a speed that just barely kept pace with the encroaching mutants. They were backing up towards squad two, which had an ambush ready.

Once the mutants were lured in, the trap was sprung. The two squads worked together and pelted the spiders with tranquilizer darts from two different angles. The claws couldn't protect them from two directions, with occasional shots going past their defense. The ones that were hit swiftly went lethargic, except for the particularly large spider towards the back.

Even when the darts landed on the more vulnerable rear of the webclaw the size of a go-kart, they failed to penetrate the monster's hide. It rushed at the distraction team and cleanly cleaved two men in half.

The soldiers panicked and hurried to get some distance from the monstrosity, allowing it to claim several more victims as they turned their back on the threat.

Just when I thought they would have to resort to stronger firepower, the captain I saw earlier rushed into action. He was a giant of a man, standing easily over six-four, with augmented limbs. He definitely fit the classic description of a cyborg, as only his neck and above seemed to be organic.

When he dove in, his large figure blurred and reappeared right next to the mutant. He swung a backfist at the creature and blew its claw away before he stabbed it with a syringe in his other hand.

The gigantic spider faltered, but mustered another swipe. The man blurred once again, reappeared on the spider's flank, and stabbed once more.

This time, the spider lost balance and fell on its stomach. The surrounding soldiers stared at the downed webclaw for a few seconds before erupting into cheers.

"You sure have a pretty powerful helper on your team," I noted behind Margarite.

"I believe so. He's the captain for a reason."

"With the amount of credits invested into his body, he should be ashamed of himself if he couldn't deal with some mindless beasts," Dr. Lut added.

His words drew my gaze back towards the captain and his hardware. The superhuman speed he displayed was only possible with all the augments he'd had done, from his spine to all four limbs. If any parts had still been organic, they wouldn't have been able to handle the strain or keep up at all.

It was a little too extreme for me, as I doubted I would be able to enjoy food the same way anymore if I didn't even have a stomach.

*Maybe I should consider hiring a few cyborgs like that as my bodyguards. I don't believe I can do anything against an opponent like that without catching them by surprise right now.*

"Rollo, can you augment me to be like that as well?" a voice suddenly whispered into my ear.

I looked over to find Thorne, who was staring at the screen unflinchingly.

"Claire would give you an earful if you tried to become a cyborg like that guy. There are other ways without going that far, and you'd still be able to compete."

"But those methods would cost exorbitantly more, right?"

"It's just not worth it. We can discuss this more when we get back," I said, hoping Claire would talk some sense into him.

Margarite soon commanded a few more of her people to go help with the cleanup while Dr. Lut sat there with a teacup in hand, like the snob he was.

They started packing away all the silk in the room, the cocoons, and the paralyzed webclaws. With the way they bound the spiders, I couldn't help but once again think about crabs in the seafood markets.

*I should really look into where they serve actual crab. I'm starting to salivate just thinking about it.*

Once they packed everything away in their trucks, we drove off.

The next stop was in a nearby ruin filled with skyscrapers instead of industrial buildings. It was a high-traffic area with other scavengers as well, so there were more than just mutant threats around. Though with that captain around, I didn't think anyone would succeed in attacking us even if they set up an ambush.

As we came onto an empty plot of land where we could park all our vehicles within this concrete forest, we heard gunfire ring out nearby.

"Should we relocate? We can come back later," I suggested to their leadership team.

"Su—"

Before Margarite could reply, Dr. Lut interjected. "No, we'll be fine. Time is money and I am not in the habit of wasting any."

I watched as Margarite swallowed her words and nodded in agreement.

Our next target was my old friend, the mutant snake that they called a serpentant. As I'd found out the hard way, they liked to nest underground, including in basements.

We left a team to stand guard by our vehicles while we delved into one of the larger office buildings. Like before, they set up a forward base in the lobby and prepared to head to the floors below.

There was ample furniture left on the mezzanine, so I had my security team set up there for us. I had only eight people here, including me and Thorne, as the rest were by our vehicles. We could set up in a cozy corner near Desire Corp's terminals.

Their team soon headed down. This time they didn't find anything unexpected and completed their mission smoothly.

I watched as they tugged a giant snake out of the basement.

"With this haul, our trucks will be full," Margarite informed Dr. Lut.

"Very well. This was a pleasant bonus. Let's complete our main objective and get out of here, then," the doctor declared.

At his words, the vibe their men gave off changed.

Their surrounding guards suddenly drew their firearms on us and opened fire. I watched as half of my guards were instantly slaughtered.

*What?! But why?*

Faster than I could react, Thorne pulled me into cover behind a pillar.

"Rollo, we're getting out of here. Turn on your active camouflage now!"

We both made a run for it while in stealth, but we didn't get far before a hail of bullets chased after us. Thorne pushed me out of the way and soaked up the bullets. The damage disrupted his Shade; he flickered into view until he was fully out of stealth.

"Go…" he muttered as he collapsed.

I didn't even have a chance to hesitate as a figure abruptly appeared beside me. I stepped back in time to feel a burst of wind pass me by. I'd dodged an attack.

Quickly I pulled out my railgun and shot at my assailant, the cyborg captain, as I desperately backed away. The captain blurred out of existence and reappeared beside me, completely unharmed.

I rolled away and fired more, but this time, he simply batted away the bullets with his hand.

*No way, that's unreal...*

I could not compete at all in a fair fight. I needed to get out of here with Thorne somehow. To do that, I'd need to use explosive rounds. The dust they'd kick up would be a distraction.

Before I could plot further, the wind was knocked out of me. My feet lost contact with the ground. My back slammed into something, and I collapsed on the ground. I found myself on all fours, puking my guts out. When I looked up, I saw the cyborg captain standing over me.

His hand began to glow bright blue, and then he grabbed my head with it.My mind instantly blanked as a surge of electricity ran through me.

*"Excess electricity current detected in the host. Several rib fractures detected. It is recommended the host get immediate medical attention."*

*Stop with the unhelpful alerts. I know I'm hurt.*

"Enough, we want him alive. Secure him already."

The captain backed away. From a doorway beside him, Margarite emerged.

The shock stopped, and I instantly gasped for air. At least I could focus again.

"What... do you... want?" I squeezed out.

"Don't worry, Mr. Halls. We want you alive. You're lucky enough to be headhunted by our company for your excellence in dealing with wastelanders," Margarite replied.

"Wastelanders? You're not... from Desire... are you?"

"We know about your relationship with the wastelanders. You'll find out who we are very soon. As for now, why don't you rest up?"

She snapped her fingers, and the captain stepped towards me.

Just when his hand was about to make contact with me, a gust of wind made me reflexively close my eyes. A piercing sound rang out and hurt my ears, followed by a shockwave that knocked me back.

When I opened my eyes again, I found the cyborg looking down at a huge hole in his chest. He tried to raise his arms towards his injury, only to collapse as if his strings were cut.

*What in the...? There's no time for that now. It's my chance to escape! Don't give out on me, legs...*

# CHAPTER 56

## LIFE AND DEATH

The cyborg captain in front of me collapsed as he stared in disbelief at the hole in his chest.

Everyone around was frozen in shock, as if someone had cast time-freezing magic.

"Sniper!" Margarite yelled. The surrounding people immediately thawed and dove into cover.

I struggled to get up, only to fail as my legs buckled.

Several soldiers received new holes in their bodies. Shots punched through whatever debris they had used as cover, in quick succession.

I crawled towards Thorne, but my pace was pathetically slow.

"Find the sniper and have the turrets on our vehicles decimate the attacker!" Dr. Lut shouted.

With the cover proven to be worthless, they all ran out at the doctor's command. The doctor himself wanted to follow; however, he soon collapsed as the next victim.

The surviving soldiers all evacuated, and apparently so did the sniper. I couldn't see what was going on, though the sound of gunshots from outside told a story in itself.

It didn't take five minutes before an eerie silence overcame the sound of fighting.

I had reached Thorne and found that he still had a pulse, but he was losing a lot of blood. I tore my clothes and bandaged his wounds as best as I could.

When I was halfway done, I heard the door swing open. I readied my firearm and hid it under me as I lay still.

There were three sets of footsteps walking towards me.

I needed to take them all out at once or else I'd just be a sitting duck, lying prone like this.

The footsteps grew closer, and I prepared myself to spring into action. I decided I would make my move once they walked past me.

They were soon right beside me, but they then stopped moving.

"Relax, we're not your enemies," said a distorted voice. "I just wanted to tell you to be more careful from now on. We won't be able to protect you forever or from everything. This is your first and final warning."

Their footsteps resumed, though they headed back for the exit instead.

I turned myself over and spotted a tall figure in an all-black combat suit and a tactical helmet that hid the face.

"Who are you? Why did you help me?"

"You'll find out eventually if you keep growing. Let's just say we have similar goals in mind. Take care, Rollo," the figure said as they continued walking away.

The two other similarly dressed figures held the door open for the one who spoke.

As they left, I turned my focus back on Thorne, who urgently needed my help. I finished dressing his wounds, starting to recover control of my body.

I could stand, allowing me to scavenge for medical supplies. We had prepared plenty for this expedition, so I soon found a med kit. I stabbed Thorne with a cocktail of stims and nanite injections, which seemed to help, as some color was restored to his face.

Now that he was more stable, I surveyed our surroundings. Bodies lay everywhere, and I quickly found those of Margarite and my employees.

*I will aven—no, I will get back at who is responsible. For their transgression and making me pay a fortune in worker's compensation!*

I dragged Thorne out of the building and soon found our vehicles. Some of the ones from Margarite's group had familiar gaping holes in them.

Our vehicles were in good condition, but they were jammed shut with debris. There were also these metal rods that perfectly jammed the door latches, which made it apparent that it was done on purpose. I quickly cleared the obstacles and opened the back door to one of the Vanguards.

Just as I threw Thorne into the car, banging could be heard from the other vehicles. It took me a brief moment to recognize several familiar faces that suddenly popped up in the windows, and I moved to clear the debris from the other cars as well.

"Boss! You're okay!" a man yelled out.

From their blue and black attire and the snowy owl logo on their shoulders, I could tell they were members of my security team.

Then I realized this was one of the guards we had left outside to watch our vehicles.

"You guys are all right? How did you survive?" I asked.

"We're not sure. We were suddenly attacked by a sniper, and even the Desire Corp people dropped like flies. For some reason, the sniper left us alone, but then someone snuck behind us while we were in cover and knocked us out one by one. By the time we came to, we found ourselves trapped in the cars, with debris blocking the doors. What about you, Boss?"

"We'll save that for later. We need to return to the outpost. Thorne needs medical attention ASAP!"

* * *

"Rollo!" A tearful Claire dove into me as soon as she found me. "How is he? Will he survive?"

"I don't know. The doctors are operating on him now. He's strong, and he lasted the entire trip out of the wasteland already, so just believe in him," I replied.

"What the hell happened?" Leo yelled out from behind her, holding Lana in his arms.

"I... It's a long story."

I briefed the three of them while we waited outside the operating room. They had a lot of questions, particularly about my mysterious savior, but we didn't dwell on it, as there was no way to find out the truth right now.

Although I knew my body was tired, I couldn't sleep after what happened. The trio here had just arrived from Elevate City, too, so I was sure they were tired as well, but we all sat together in silence for some time after I summarized the recent events.

"It's my fault... I cleared those guys as safe to work with," Leo suddenly muttered.

"Leo, no," Lana consoled. "Then I'm just as responsible as you. They were prepared and had more resources than us."

I said, "She's right. If anything, it would be my fault. I accepted this job even though it sounded a little too good to be true. I'm responsible for your lack of equipment as well."

"Stop it, all of you! It's no one's fault," Claire interjected. "None of us wanted this to happen or saw it coming. The only thing that matters is Thorne's recovery right now."

We all nodded in unison as we sat there in silence, waiting for the surgery to finish.

I stared at the operation-in-progress sign for an entire hour before the lights of the sign finally dimmed.

The doors soon opened and an automated bed came out, transporting Thorne to a recovery area, followed by the doctor.

"How is he?" Claire rushed up and asked.

"He is stable for now, but his spinal cord and the surrounding nerves were damaged. His limbs were also without blood for too long and had to be amputated. He will need replacements grown or cybernetic alternatives. Until then, he will be paralyzed."

We then proceeded to Thorne's room. He wouldn't wake until half an hour later.

"Thorne!" Claire embraced him.

He weakly muttered something unintelligible. After sipping on some water, he tried again.

"Looks like... we made it. How are you, Rollo?"

"I'm unhurt, thanks to you."

He let out a sigh of relief before his eyes opened wide. "I can't move..."

"We'll just need some time to regrow new parts for you, and then you'll be good as new. All on company expense. Just bear with it for a while."

"Yes, the doctor says your limbs had to be amputated, and your spinal cord and nerves were damaged," Claire added.

"I want to replace them... with cybernetics. Can you... do that for me, Rollo?"

*While that is cheaper than regrowing the organic parts, replacing all his limbs plus the spine is no small decision. He'll lose most sensations that humans are used to and become one of those cyborgs for real...*

"Thorne, no! Just replace your hands if you must, but don't become a brain in a jar," Claire cried out.

"I've made up my mind. I want to be as strong as that captain, Rollo."

Our eyes locked for a while as the tension in the room thickened. "I can have your spine and limbs replaced with cybernetics and still keep the rest of your body organic. I'll just need some time to work out the surgery."

"I trust you."

At his words, I felt everyone's gaze on me.

It was rare for someone to have all augmented limbs but an organic torso. The amount of devices running in the body, all the electronics, would start interfering with your organs. That was why they usually replaced the torso, too, resulting in a full-body replacement.

I would need to invest my remaining points in cybernetics and plan out what parts to use, and I would need to keep the implants' functionality in mind without harming his squishy organs.

Though this might have delayed my plans, it was worth it in the long run and for the sake of Thorne.

* * *

Eight days after Thorne's surgery, I watched as he opened his eyes in his new body.

"How do you feel?"

"Absolute zero! I've missed being about to move on my own two feet so much," Thorne declared.

"You've only been bedridden for a little over a week. Calm down, big guy!" Claire quipped.

"Well, I'm glad you're eager to move. We've got a lot of tests to do. While your cybernetics are all well-tested, we need to see if they're integrated into you properly. The architecture of how your implants are unified is completely untested."

"Will I have to limit myself to prevent damage to my body?"

"No. I made sure you can make use of the chrome the same way most cyborgs can. You'll still have a time limit on how long you can push it, but the same applies to other cyborgs."

"That sounds too good to be true. Do you mean I can move super fast like that captain?"

"Yes. It'll strain your brain, spine, and legs, though. That's why that guy only sped up his movements occasionally to dodge and close distances."

"Understood. I'll be sure to practice it well."

"Hurry up, you two," Claire interjected. "We have a reservation today to celebrate Thorne's full recovery! I'll go finish up some work while you guys do your thing, but you two better not be late."

As she left the room, we shrugged at each other helplessly.

We proceeded smoothly, testing if the implants really wouldn't hurt him when working at full power. We examined energy and heat management, along with various things that could be harmful to the human body.

"Rollo, I've been thinking. I want to resign as the head of security."

"What? Why?" I stopped my work on my terminal and looked up at the speaker.

"Don't misunderstand. I'm not quitting the company. I want to focus on being your bodyguard instead. It won't be the last time we meet someone like that captain. There'll be more corporations that we'll be working with in the future."

"I see... In that case, I decline your resignation as the head of security. Just delegate your work to a few people while you guard me. There's no need for you to give up the post."

"But—"

"Don't worry, delegating is an important skill to have in a leadership role."

"Okay. I'll need some time to go back to Elevate City to set everything up first, though."

"Take your time, then. We're not in a race here. The transportation business can wait." Expanding that would require some new technology to improve our vehicles and help me design EMP-resistant devices.

I added, "We can use this time to train more personnel for the new routes we plan to have."

*And I need some time to level up as well.*

# EPILOGUE

???

Inside one of the high-rise towers of downtown Elevate City, a well-dressed man sat at the only desk within the five-hundred-square-foot office on the penthouse level. He had silver limbs, with one of them laid on the desk and half-disassembled. Using a terminal, he controlled dozens of robotic arms on a surgery bot and examined his own, performing cybernetic maintenance.

While he was focused on controlling the arms, an alert popped up in the corner of his vision. With a quick glance, he approved the request for his secretary to enter.

The gears behind the door to his office began to turn, the mechanisms within the gigantic vault door working to unlock it. The sheer complexity and scale of the door rivaled the largest depositories in the world.

When it finally opened, a lone middle-aged man stepped in. He wore a three-piece suit with a well-groomed silver mustache. He came forward and lowered his head towards the man at the desk.

The man continued to work the robotic arms for another minute before he finally spoke.

"Speak."

"Sir, one of the people you wanted me to monitor requires your attention once again," the old man said as he sent a file to his boss.

His eyes glowed as he reviewed the information. The robotic arms soon stilled as he stood up and faced the window behind him.

He stared off into the distance towards the space elevator and let out a sigh.

"He should be able to handle it. It would be putting the cart before the horse if we intervened every single time."

"Very well, then."

"Is there something else?"

"Yes, sir. We are ready to depart."

The man nodded and followed his assistant to the roof of the office building, where several luxurious flying vehicles waited. They were fixed-wing aircraft painted in midnight black. The menacing armaments were hard to miss.

Once they boarded, they immediately took off and flew towards the most iconic landmark in the city. It didn't take long for them to arrive on a landing pad at the base of the only space elevator in the world.

As soon as the man had exited the vehicle, he took a moment to glance up at the imposing elevator. He thought back to the first time he set eyes on the tower that symbolized the reign of corporations back before a certain someone had changed his life.

He didn't reminisce for long and headed into the spaceport with only his assistant joining him. He never liked traveling in a huge entourage; he preferred to stay low-key. His assistant knew this, which was why they got regular seats for the shuttle up into orbit.

Once they passed through the thorough security, they headed towards the boarding gate. The assistant, leading the way, suddenly noticed his boss had lagged behind and was staring deeply into a miniature model of the space elevator.

This wasn't the first time it had happened. He dutifully waited in silence, as there was ample time left before the shuttle would leave.

The well-dressed man closed his eyes and breathed in deeply.

*Can it really be done?*

# AFTERWORD

Hey there, I'm R.B. Cat, otherwise known as RandomBlueCat. If you're a newcomer to Corpo Age, nice to meet you! If you've read the story on Royal Road, I'm glad to see you again. When I began writing this book in the summer of 2023, I honestly had no idea what to expect. It's all thanks to my readers that I've begun to even dare think about pursuing a career in writing. I almost can't believe my work is now being published.

I chose to write Corpo Age as my first book due to what I was reading at the time. I was in a cyberpunk phase, and I had pretty much read every single story I could find. I couldn't stand to wait for the releases anymore and channeled that urge into creative writing. As I had always been a fan of kingdom / business / faction building of all sorts, you can see that preference has influenced the direction of the story.

I'm happy about how far my writing has come in such a short time, but I also can't avoid wanting to reach the next step. I guess you could say I'm addicted to seeing the numbers go up. I started off writing a thousand words per day and slowly increased the amount I wrote every day, but it never seemed to be enough. Even now, I wish to write more, but then daily distractions and social obligations strike.

Anyway, I hope you've enjoyed the story so far, and stay tuned for more. I like to finish what I start so expect to see more of my work soon.

# READING RESOURCES

My writing journey wouldn't have happened if it wasn't for all the support from my Royal Road readers, Patreon supporters, and fellow authors who guided me. You can find several links below to catch up with the latest releases and avenues to find more books to read.

**Patreon:** patreon.com/TheRandomBlueCat

**LitRPG Books:** facebook.com/groups/LitRPG.books

**GameLitRPG Society:** facebook.com/groups/LitRPGsociety

Thank you for reading a MoonQuill original novel, part of the Royal Road Collection. More exciting stories can be found on our website, www.moonquill.com.

We would greatly appreciate it if you could take a moment to leave a review. Every review helps the author and supports their ability to continue writing fantastic books for everyone to enjoy!

Additionally, we're looking for dedicated ARC reviewers and experienced readers to join our beta reader team. To learn more, drop us an email at info@moonquill.com or stop by our Discord.

This novel got its start on Royal Road. Stop by for a sneak peek at the next volume!